# THE BROKEN SKY

## THE FINAL REMNANT
### BOOK 3

## TERRY JAMES

## HEATHER RENAE

**The Broken Sky**
Paperback Edition
Copyright © 2023 Terry James and Heather Renae

CKN Christian Publishing
An Imprint of Wolfpack Publishing
9850 S. Maryland Parkway. Ste A-5 #323
Las Vegas, NV 89183

cknchristianpublishing.com

Paperback ISBN 978-1-63977-127-1
eBook ISBN 978-1-63977-126-4
LCCN 2023930262

# THE BROKEN SKY

# ONE
## THIRSTY, MAX?

CADEN TOOK his time walking to first base; he didn't want to miss this perfect moment. He felt the sun's warmth as the summer breeze carried the smell of hotdogs and popcorn through the baseball field. The buzz of excited onlookers sent an excited thrill through him. He reached the base and glanced over his shoulder. In the front rows were Mama Lo, Ellie, Trace, and Nate. They all were decked out in green and purple, Caden's team's colors, and cheering their heads off. Mama Lo gave him a thumbs up with a sound nod, and Caden's grin gave way to calm focus.

He faced the pitcher again, staring at the opposing player and the little white ball in his hands. He made his stance and drew back the bat. His fingers adjusted on the grip as the bat's weight felt perfect in his grasp. This was his moment, his happy place, his time to conquer. There was nothing else in Caden's life than the baseball and the bat. The pitcher readied to throw. Caden could hear his heart in his ears. The ball was drawn back. Caden's jaw clenched as his eyes narrowed. The ball rocketed toward him. He swung with force.

Caden blinked. Where was the ball? He glanced at the pitcher and saw he, too was gone. The onlookers were suddenly quiet too. The breeze had stopped, but there was a new sound. It was a moving, rushing sound, like wind, but not as whispery. Caden turned and found he was alone on the baseball field. He straightened, glancing around, and held up his hands. Where's the bat?

"Lost something, Max?" Caden flinched back, finding Grant slowly limping across the field. His white Refiner uniform stood out against the green of the field. Caden's breath quickened, and he stumbled back, only to slam into someone. He lurched away as Buck calmly smiled at him. The rushing sound was growing louder by the moment. "Everyone's gone, Max," Grant called.

"They've left you to our mercy." Caden's skin crawled. He knew that rough, inhuman voice. He didn't even have to look as Doeg strolled across the field, the Demon's half bitten off face twisting into a smile. Its long, white tail lashed as its bald hands flexed their long, curved claws. "Pity," Doeg muttered. "I can't recall; are we capable of mercy?" Buck chuckled.

"No," Grant said evenly with a small, amused smile. "Not in the slightest." Caden's eyes darted across the field for his bat. Where could it have gone? He needed it! And what was that sound? It was like something moving faster and faster, like a river.

"Do calm down, young sir," a new voice said. Cold dread washed over Caden's shoulders as he froze, his breath caught in his throat. "There is nowhere to run to." Caden sucked in a breath and forced himself to turn. Coolly strolling toward him was a Sentinel. He had a full beard, and his dark brown eyes were sad and distant. He stopped a pace from Caden and sighed softly. "Hello, Caden."

Caden said nothing, shoulders hunched and sweat

dripping from his brow, as he stared at Officer Nathaniel. He couldn't turn away as terror held him hostage. Nathaniel gave him a pitied smile and looked down. He withdrew the gun from his hip and pulled back the hammer with a loud click. Caden's eyes fluttered as his face turned white. The sound of rushing water surrounded them now. It was louder than ever. Nathaniel and Caden's eyes met as Nathaniel lifted his chin and raised the gun. "I'll make it quick."

Water exploded from beyond the field, the rushing torrent ripping apart the bleachers and grass. Caden had just enough time to suck in a breath before the flood consumed him. He was swept off his feet, surrounded in icy darkness. The current beat against him, trying to break him.

Caden gasped, the shock of icy water jolting him from sleep. He sputtered and gagged, spitting the water from his mouth. Panting, he lay, eyes half closed, and started to shake. "Rise and shine, princess." Why was he lying down? They had tied him to a chair. Oh, that's right. Buck had kicked him over.

Caden stared at the tiled floor as the chair lay on its side. Water streamed from him and circled the drain a few feet away. His cold, soaked clothes stuck to him, and his hair hung over his eyes. His hands and feet had numbed long ago, the leather straps holding him in place cinched too tightly. He couldn't feel the arm he crushed beneath his weight. His brain was in a weird, sleep-deprived, oxygen-starved state. How many times had he almost drowned? At least three times. Maybe more. He had tried to fight them when the water started falling, filling his nose and mouth and down his throat. Now, it only wasted his strength.

Caden closed his eyes as he sucked in the precious air. He could do nothing else as he shook in the cold and longed for sleep. That's all he needed. He hadn't slept in a long time. Days even. Days? He hadn't been in KUS Headquarters that long. Had he? No, no, it was only two days ago Sentinels had dragged him from his room and hauled him down under HQ. Down where no one was seen again, were Rapham made people talk.

*People like Asher,* Caden thought as his fuzzy mind tried to think. He blinked slowly, too exhausted to feel the guilt and terror for his brother's safety. Shouldn't he feel something? After all, he had put Asher down here. *He was going to be executed though. I saved him. Or sent him to a slower death.* He thought he'd feel the internal screaming like he used to whenever overwhelmed and desperate. There wasn't anything. It was like Caden was nothing but a numb, unresponsive shell. That is, until the water poured down his throat and threatened to fill his lungs.

An empty bucket was hurled across the room. Caden flinched back as it bounced, echoing in the bare room. Heavy footfalls fell, Caden sucked in a breath and held it. He never knew when he'd get another chance to breathe. Out of the corner of his eye, he saw a larger Refiner stalking about. He couldn't see what he was doing, but based on his size and manner, Caden recognized Buck. At least it wasn't Grant. Just with a look, Grant could make Caden already feel like his slave. Caden assumed Grant viewed everyone as his slave, even Luca.

"I feel bad for your girlfriend," Buck muttered as he set a leather bag on a metal table across the room. "You snore like I do."

Caden blinked slowly as he tried to focus. Was Buck far away? No, Caden remembered the room not being *that* big. Girlfriend. He didn't have a girlfriend. Caden's hands fisted as his eyes focused. *Dasha. But she escaped. She got away before they came for me.* A hard lump formed in his throat, making it difficult to breathe.

Buck shook his head as he opened the bag and reached inside. "How you scored someone like her is beyond me."

Caden finally felt something. It was deep and seething. His jaw flexed as his eyes narrowed. "Don't talk about her." Buck glanced at him as he removed things from the bag. "Besides," Caden mumbled. "I'm Alex Whitney. I can get anyone I want."

Buck's brow furrowed as he lifted his chin. "Still sticking with that, Max?" He withdrew a black baton. Caden followed it as Buck passed it from hand to hand. His ribs still ached with each breath from the Sentinel's beating. For the life of him, he didn't understand why his bones were still intact, especially his ankle. Maybe, at last, Grant was sick of waiting. "Gotta hand it to you, kiddo," Buck said as he unscrewed the end of the baton. "You're not the same scaredy-cat I found running from that convenience store back State side. Remember that? Say, how did you not get killed by those Haunts?"

"I run fast."

Buck scoffed as he shook his head. "That you do. Faster than the real Alex. Those Haunts really ripped him up, didn't they?"

Caden fought to keep his face emotionless, but he could easily remember Alex's limp body like red ribbons of a shredded doll. "I," he stammered and snapped his mouth shut.

Without looking up from sliding cylinders into the base of the baton, Buck's brows rose, and he leaned toward Caden. "Hum? What was that?"

Caden cursed as he closed his eyes. He needed to sleep. It was getting harder to think. "I'm the real Alex," was all he managed to say. Buck sighed heavily as he screwed the baton's handle back in place. Footsteps stomped closer. Caden's closed eyes squeezed tighter, as though to shut out the hellish world he found himself trapped in. He tried not to cower as Buck grabbed the backrest of his chair. Caden grunted as Buck heaved his chair upright. He clung to his seat, the arm he'd been lying on tingling painfully as blood rushed back into it.

"I just have one question," Buck said as he circled in front of him. Caden's nothingness shifted to icy fear as he continued to shake. He slowly opened his eyes and stared at the drain. Water still trickled down and out through the grate, out to freedom. To somewhere else. Why could it get away and he couldn't? "And I will get an answer."

Caden's hands fisted as he felt the leather straps hold him in place. He thought of Ellie and Elijah, of Yohanan, Asher, and Ophir. Of his family. His people. *I will not betray them.* Buck faced him, his fingers flexing along the baton's grip. Caden forced himself to look at him. He wouldn't turn away.

"What's freakier? This?" Buck stepped forward and pointed the baton in Caden's face. Caden leaned away as a muscle in his jaw flexed. "Or this?" Buck pressed a button along the baton. White, crackling light leapt between two small prongs at the end of the baton. Caden's breath caught in his throat as he shrank back, sending the chair back onto two legs for a moment.

Buck grinned and moved away, lowering the electric baton. He nodded once and turned back to the bag. "Thanks," he said over his shoulder. "Thought so." Caden sucked air through gritted teeth as every muscle tensed for pain. Buck glanced at him and smiled. "Oh, stop being so self-centered, Max. Not everything's about you! You're not my only playmate down here." Caden cursed as his chin dropped to his chest. He shook his head and squeezed his eyes tight, his heart slamming against him. Buck started humming as he packed the electric baton back into the bag. "Thirsty, Max?"

Caden's fists were white-knuckled, and, to his surprise,

he found himself chuckling. He kept chuckling as he met eyes with Buck, who was staring at him. After a stunned moment, Buck also started laughing. Caden shook his head as he blinked the waterdrops from his eyes. "Good one, right?" Buck grabbed the bag and stepped toward the door. "Well, see you in a few." Caden quieted. "Or tonight. Or maybe tomorrow." Buck shrugged, smiled, and left without another word.

Caden cursed and turned away as the door shut with an echoing boom. *Yahweh, what are You doing to me?* He closed his eyes as his hands slowly loosened. He knew there'd be nail imprints in his palms. *I'm going to die down here. Can You see me?* All he could hear was the water dripping down the drain. *Please,* Caden thought. *Please don't leave me. Send Han here. He'll kill Grant with one sweep of his wings! God! Are You listening?*

Caden didn't understand why he always listened for God after praying. As if He was going to say anything. His Spirit was in only two people right now, and Elijah and Yohanan were far from KUS Headquarters. Caden was alone. He had walked into the den of lions and would face his fate. *At least You can help me shut the mouths of lions,* Caden thought, forcing himself to remember a verse from Hebrews. *And escape the edge of the sword.* He slowly lifted his chin as he refocused on the truth. *And turn my weakness into strength. Well, You've got a lot of strength to make out of me.*

He opened his eyes and faced the door as though Grant stood on the other side with a full water bucket in hand. *You will make me powerful in battle.* The naked bulb overhead flickered. *I'm in a battle now. I will win—*

The room plunged into darkness, then flashed to brilliant bright. Caden blinked as the bulb fought to stay on.

Darkness swallowed him again. Inches from his face was a ghostly white, furry monster. Its icy eyes were wild with bloodlust. A smile, distorted by scars, revealed rows of fangs. Clawed hands raised to strike. Caden recoiled with a scream. He kept shouting and pulling against the leather straps, even after the bulb finally stayed on.

Panting, Caden's wide eyes darted around. He couldn't see Doeg, but that didn't mean anything. The Shade could be anywhere. Through curses and gritted teeth, Caden tried to refocus on the truth he'd memorized. All he could think of was Doeg's smile and what it would be like to drown tied to a chair.

# TWO
## STAND FIRM, THEN

CADEN WAS DYING. Everything was black as his body fought to breathe. No matter what he did, he couldn't. Again. He couldn't even feel the water gushing over his face anymore. All he felt was terror. Pure, raw, reckless terror. The flow abruptly stopped, but he didn't notice. The rag over his mouth and nose still made breathing impossible.

Caden was dying. His thrashing slowed. The terror dragged him further down into darkness. The rag ripped from his face. He was falling. Still tied to the chair, Caden landed on the floor on his side again. He choked up water between gulped breaths which echoed in the room. Caden shook as he lay in the water that streamed to the drain and down to somewhere else. Somewhere far away. His half-opened eyes stared at the current, hating its escape while he stayed.

*Just breathe,* he told himself. *Breathe while you can.*

Buck was humming again. Why did he do that? Was that a self-soothing tactic because he knew hurting people was bad? That was dumb. Buck totally didn't care he was hurting Caden. He probably enjoyed it. Halting steps shifted, and the click of a cane's end made Caden's calm vanish. He hated when Grant was there. He was convinced, at any moment, Grant would raise his weighted cane and shatter whatever bone he wished.

*Just breathe!* Caden thought, feeling his already racing heart somehow pick up the pace. He closed his eyes, spat the water still draining from his mouth and nose, and retreated into himself. He imagined a thick, stone wall between him and Grant. No one could get over it to hurt him. No one could control him through it. Caden had imagined similar things when Dad would ask him about his siblings, as though he was a snitch. He'd answer, giving enough truth to make the lies seem real, also while giving Dad what he wanted. It worked. Most of the time.

Caden blinked slowly, realizing Grant had said something. What was it? Something about cookies? Buck's heavy footfalls drew closer. Caden ducked his head, taking in a deep breath without thinking. Buck heaved the chair upright and had Caden face Grant. Grant stood over him, his fingers fidgeting along the cane's weighted ball. Caden, still catching his breath, stared at the ball. He could see his reflection in the polished metal. He looked like a rat pulled from the sewer.

"Max?" Grant lifted his chin, his fingers tapping again.

"My name," Caden rasped, "is Alex."

The corner of Grant's mouth twitched into a smile as he stared down at Caden. "Answer my question, Max." Caden blinked slowly. How did he get that ball so shiny? Was it gold? No, gold was more yellow. This had an orange tint.

Buck seized Caden's hair and yanked his chin up. Caden couldn't hold back a yell. "What?" he shouted and cursed. "Ask again. I didn't hear you!"

"You need to listen—"

"I can't when I'm *dying*!"

He heard Grant chuckle. "A minute under the water won't kill anyone." Caden's eyes darted about. One minute? One? It felt like ten! "I asked what your favorite cookie is?"

"I—" *Stupid! Don't answer!*

"Max?"

*But then the bucket will come back.* Caden heard the slosh of water. A panicked thrill rushed through him. "I! I like oatmeal raisin!" Buck stepped back, throwing Caden's head forward. Caden sat hunched in his chair, finding himself refocusing on the cane's ball.

"How many siblings do you have?" Grant asked.

*Three.* "Um," *You're Alex!* "One. Sammy's dead."

Grant stepped closer. Reflected in the cane's ball, Caden could see one cheek was puffy and red, and his brow was split. "How often did your mother hug you?"

*Whenever she came back from her cancer treatments.* "I don't know. Whenever she felt like it…"

"Who is your contact in Under Fire?"

Caden forced his head to sway back and forth as panic tightened his throat. "I don't know those people."

"What was your favorite TV show growing up?"

"M—Mikey and Stew."

"How many rooms did your mansion have growing up?"

"Does it look like I counted them!"

"Who is your contact from Under Fire?"

Caden cursed. "I'm not connected with Under Fire."

Grant tilted his head to one side and shuffled a little closer. "How many birds have you owned?"

"Ah…Seven."

"Who ran over my ankle?"

Caden flinched, his internal screaming starting up again. He shook his head, his foggy brain feeling like it sloshed back and forth in his skull. "A guy. Just some guy paid to find me."

"Paid by who?"

"He was a headhunter for all I know!"

"Did you know him?"

Trace's excited laugh haunted Caden's thoughts as he shook his head. "No."

"Do you like bikes or scooters?"

"I don't—"

"Bikes or scooters?"

"Bikes—"

"Yellow or blue?"

"What?"

"Who is your contact in Under Fire?" Caden blinked slowly as he tried to think. Why did Grant have two canes? That seemed overkill. And why were there two Grants? "Max?" Buck's backhand sharply captured Caden's attention. The world spun, and Buck caught Caden's chair before it tipped over again. Grant took a slow, calm breath as Caden moaned, blood dripping from his mouth. "I need a name."

"Jack Mil-dingle-do." Caden felt himself smiling. "There's a name for yah."

"You knew him, didn't you?" Caden fell silent. "He wasn't a simple contract hunter," Grant said as he smiled coolly. Caden tried to hide behind his mental wall, to block out Grant and the terror that surrounded him. He could feel the wall cracking as Grant waited for an answer. "Tell me, Max...who is he?"

Caden closed his eyes and ducked his head. The wall wasn't going to last. He sealed his mouth shut and clenched his jaw. *I won't speak. No more. I can't. But the water. It'll come again and...no. I can't—*

Grant's cold fingers lifted Caden's chin until they looked eye to eye. Somewhere, Caden's internal screaming had become white noise again. The panic and terror ebbed to oblivion as he stared into those amused eyes. "Who is your contact with Under Fire?"

A stone on Caden's inner wall tumbled to the dust. Caden hardly moved as he stared. He kept trying to track Grant as he saw two of them, both waving back and forth. Why were they dancing? Did he have a twin?

*Please,* his foggy mind finally produced a thought. *Please go away.*

With a grunt, Grant stepped back, letting Caden slump in his chair. Caden did nothing as he stared at Grant's cane. He still couldn't place what type of metal that was. Copper maybe? Wait, what did Grant just do? He nodded at Buck. That meant—

Caden's chair tipped back, propping against the table. He gulped, filling his lungs, awaiting the smothering water. Something poked his back. No, it stabbed. Caden's back arched the best he could, the leather strap cinched across his chest, making it near impossible. Buck stepped back, leaving the knife or nail or whatever it was prodding Caden's back. Caden's strained body shook as he tried to maintain the awkward position. He saw Grant watching him out of the corner of his eye. That patient, serene smile still clung to his face.

*He could do this forever,* Caden thought, sweat gathering along his brow. *But I can't. I...God! Why are You abandoning me?*

"You will give me a name," Grant said softly. Caden didn't answer as he gritted his teeth and focused on keeping rigid, the knife catching on his clothes. Grant turned and shuffled toward the door as Buck continued to hum. The door shut with a boom, and Caden was finally left alone. His back muscles were already shaking. Caden gritted his teeth and leaned his head back, sweat trickling from his brow. His mental wall crumbled further, the thick stones toppling like a child's clumsy tower of blocks.

*Can't do this,* Caden thought, his breath quickening. *I'm not strong enough. My fiercest defense is child's play to them. I should yield now, end this suffering, and find rest in the oblivion of death. Under Fire will be martyred, our end in Heaven, therefore why not rescue myself? Yahweh will forgive and understand. He says He loves me. Love covers a multitude of sins, and the truth shall set me free. I must confess the truth of Under Fire. Only then can I finally find freedom and peace.*

Caden's eyes clenched tight as a growl lifted from behind clenched teeth. *Doeg, get away from me!*

"What other choice do you have, boy?" Caden shook his head. He buried deeper into himself, behind his stone wall, determined not to listen to Doeg's lies.

"They are professionals," an inhuman voice whispered in his ear. Hot breath washed over Caden's face, and he clenched his jaw harder with a throaty moan. "As am I." Each inhale felt like a battle. Caden's fingers flexed as he fought to arch his back. "We both have conquered your kind before. The weak, inferior failures who thrive on denial and foolishness." Sweat dripped down Caden's back, and he could've sworn the knife was getting closer. "There will be nothing left if your defiance persists." Caden heard Doeg's claws as the Demon paced to the other side of the chair.

"Preserve your sanity," Doeg whispered, drawing closer again. "Death is your only hope."

Caden shook his head with a whimper. *I can't do this.*

The knife caught his back. He sucked in a breath as tears welled in his closed eyes. "Please," he whispered, a tear streaming down his face. His back muscles were spent already and shaking uncontrollably. *God, do something,* he thought. *Why are You letting this happen? I obeyed You! I told You spying was a bad idea!* Both human and Demon silently listened, the only sound was Caden's desperate gasps and the water steadily dripping down the drain.

"I've received a word from your Yeshua," Doeg said quietly. "I read it in the Book of Job."

"Please, stop."

"It states to stay alert."

"Someone, help. Please."

"God has sent this suffering to keep you from life."

Caden felt his entire being shaking. He slowly shook his head as each breath quivered. "No," he whispered. *When you speak, you lie.*

"I speak of your holy Scriptures. *That* is what they declare." Caden gasped as another tear fell. He tried to pull further into himself, but there was nowhere else to run. "You cannot deny the validity of Scripture. This suffering God Himself has sent upon you."

"No!"

"You find yourself exempt from His righteous justice?" Caden's legs kicked and strained, but the leather strapping both ankles held him firm. "The truth shall set you free."

Caden shook his head. "No," he whispered. "Get away!"

"Confess who you are. Confess the truth of Under Fire."

"Help."

"This is your salvation."

"God, please."

"*I* am the only god there is."

Caden's body trembled as the knife caught his back again. He was unsure of what dripped down his back, sweat or blood. He tried to dig deeper into himself, finding a good memory to focus on and escape to. Wherever he looked, there was Doeg. *"There is no escape from me."* Caden groaned. *"How can you not understand, you foolish, pathetic mortal?"*

Caden's inner stone wall was nearly gone. Rubble lay in reckless heaps. Nothing was working. He wasn't strong enough. He couldn't save himself. Grant was going to get what he wanted, and Doeg's threats would come true; the Demon would be the last thing Caden would ever see.

"Good," Doeg purred. "Now you are beginning to understand your utter helplessness. Your complete weakness."

*I am helpless and weak.*

*"Entirely."*

Caden's strained face relaxed as his eyes slowly opened. Doeg's eyes, like murky ice, stared down at him. The Shade's ears were upright with expectation. *Then why,* Caden thought and stopped. Doeg's eyes narrowed as the white fur around its nape bristled. *Why am I trusting in myself? That's why I can't stand firm. I'm leaning on my own abilities.*

Doeg's lips pulled back, revealing fangs nearly as long as the Leovir's. "You will lean on that God who killed your mother? Who stole your grandmother? Who forced you to watch as both your brothers died? You are a fool!" A muscle in Caden's jaw flexed. "You are a failure who cannot possibly overcome *anything* set before you!" Caden's heart quickened as anger tightened his chest. "You are pathetic!"

Caden growled again, his tied hands becoming tight fists. The growl lifted to a cry. "No!" His voice echoed in the room. "I am Yahweh's! You cannot crush what is His! I can't hear Him or see Him, but He sees me and is with me! His promises are my shield and armor! He is my safe place! I'm terrified, but I will trust in him! What can mortal men do against me? What can *you* do?" Doeg reeled, its ears flicking back with a hiss. "I am covered in Yeshua's blood. I am the final remnant. I am destined for Heaven. You cannot crush what's inside me. You've tortured and killed Yeshua before, but that didn't destroy Him! He died, plundered Hell, and came back!"

Doeg's tail lashed as it flinched back, as though avoiding blows. "He is coming again, wrapped in clouds and thick darkness, with an army of angels armed and ready to kill." Crimson crept across Caden's face as he shifted, unable to turn away from Doeg. "I will stand with Him and live! You can try to destroy Caden Johnson, but you cannot destroy King Yeshua! You cannot conquer me! *That* is who I am! And I will refuse to believe anything else!"

Doeg and Caden stared at one another, the Demon's fur bristling as fire lit Caden's eyes. Without a word, Doeg looked up, its ears upright. Caden followed his gaze and saw, standing against the upper level's railing, was Benaiah. The lion Freak of Nature stared down at Caden, his golden eyes studying his every move. A cold crept over Caden. *I just said my real name,* he thought.

As his face turned white, his jaw flexed, and his eyes narrowed. With a deep breath, Caden kept staring at the Leovir, unwilling to stand down. Benaiah's clipped ear swiveled as his massive head tilted to one side. He stepped from the railing, his claws clicking on the tile, and Caden watched as he walked out of sight. Caden blinked, fear closing in and threatening to choke him.

"Now they know," Doeg whispered from the corner. "Your God hasn't saved you."

"I trust in You, God," Caden hissed through gritted teeth. He closed his eyes and leaned back, forcing himself to not let the knife prick him again. *I trust in You. So, because of You, I can conquer the New Kingdom, bring Your justice, get what You promised, and shut the mouths of any Leovir! Shut Benaiah's mouth, Yahweh! I trust You! I will not be moved. Because You've got my back, what can these puny mortals do against me?* Caden lifted his chin as his back continued to shake and sweat drenched his body. He couldn't afford to hide in himself anymore. That was suicide. He'd hide in God instead, no matter what came.

———

GRANT WAS ACTING DIFFERENTLY. He still had that calm, creepy smile as he watched Buck pour water over Caden's face, but something was off. As Caden slowly recovered, again, from not breathing and coughing up water, he could tell. Grant wasn't fidgeting with his cane. He hardly blinked as his eyes hooked into Caden, studying his every move. Caden stared at the floor between them, watching the water spiral down the drain. His lungs felt on fire, and his throat felt raked with a hot iron, but it always felt like that. His head throbbed from panic and lack of oxygen, but he expected that.

*They stopped*, his foggy mind finally thought. *Thank You, God*. He closed his eyes and forced his breathing to calm. At least they'd removed the knife from behind his chair. That had been horrible. He was sure cuts lined the small of his back, but he could handle some scratches.

Buck set down the empty bucket and turned to Grant. *What's he thinking?* Caden thought, trying to read Grant. He seemed like a creative guy and could concoct far more terrible suffering. Such was what Caden deserved. Someone who flippantly blasphemes God should feel the Creator's wrath. It was coming, suffering from God's own hand, as the Scriptures say: God had sent this suffering to keep you from life. He doesn't want you to have life, Caden. You deserve suffering and death.

*I trust You*, Caden thought, his jaw flexing. *I'm afraid, so I'll trust You. Please, save me. Please.* Caden took in a deep breath and lifted his chin.

He opened his eyes to find Grant shaking his head. "I said not to let him sleep."

Buck stiffened and glanced at Caden. "I didn't." Grant tilted his head to one side, his smile faltering. "He didn't sleep. I swear. How could he? He had a knife to his back." Grant didn't answer as his gaze fell on Caden again.

*I'm trusting You,* Caden thought, blinking the water from his eyes. *Raw Peace. Please, let Your Raw Peace come here. Fill every space with Your fire.*

Buck rubbed the back of his neck. "I can get more water…"

"I'm tired of being nice." Caden's heart leapt into his throat. "Time to break him down for good."

Cold consumed Caden. He did nothing but sit and stare at the wall. He wouldn't struggle, for it was no use. He wouldn't plea, for that would amuse Grant. *I'll just pee myself,* he thought, forcing himself to take another breath. *And pray.*

Buck set down the bucket and stood back, awaiting his orders. Grant did nothing as he continued to study Caden. It was getting harder to breathe. Caden's head throbbed, and he started digging deeper into himself. He had to hide somewhere, behind his wall, in a memory. He couldn't mentally be there when Grant started leaning on him! His eyes gently closed as he breathed out slowly.

*We win,* he thought. *Stand firm in God. We win.*

"Waterboarding is unique in that it is not necessary to harm the body." Caden tried not to react as Grant's fingers rapped along the cane's metal ball. "The illusion of drowning forces the body to panic and struggle, but there is no real danger, especially how short of timeframes you are doing." Caden opened his eyes and shifted in the chair. How long had he been sitting in that chair? Three days? Four? A week?

"Bones, however," Grant said as he shuffled forward,

twirled his cane, and cracked the ball against Caden's shin. Caden screamed. He couldn't think as he tried to turn away. Grant quietly waited as Caden's cry became whimpers. "Bones, however," Grant repeated. "Are not as forgiving. There is always harm with bones. Always."

*He broke my ankle,* Caden thought, gasping, trying to think as the pain made his head spin. He felt like he was going to puke, and he could hardly hear Grant, though he stood a pace away.

"Who is your contact at Under Fire?" Caden hung his head, the fiery pain of his leg was overwhelming. Grant gave a low, inhuman chuckle. No, that wasn't Grant. Out of the corner of his eye, Caden saw something white and furry crawling along the wall, grinning ear to ear.

"Max," Grant said gently. "I grow tired of repeating myself." Caden clenched his teeth and faced Grant.

As sweat dripped from his brow and his leg started to shake, Caden's face became chiseled in stone. "So am I." Grant's smile twitched. Caden refused to turn away. *I trust You,* he thought again. *I trust You, God. Save me!*

Grant limped a step back and handed Buck his cane. He began rolling his shoulders and loosening his neck. "I like to begin by breaking ribs," Grant said. "You will scream as they break, and they will break as you scream. It's a beautiful cycle." Color slowly drained from Caden's face, and he opened his mouth to speak. He quickly shut it; there was nothing to say.

"Last chance, Max," Grant said, taking his weighted cane again. "Who is your contact?"

*Save me, I'm begging You, God.* Caden closed his eyes. *But I'd rather be in Your will and in danger than out of Your will and safe.* He took in a sharp breath and faced Grant again. *You're the Boss, God. Do what You want.*

"I am Alex Whitney," he said. "I have no affiliations with Under Fire."

Grant's smile grew. He stepped forward, taking the cane with both hands. Caden forced himself to not turn away. The door swung open. Heavy footfalls thumped in. Grant turned and lowered the cane. Caden let out a held breath and tried to focus on his rescuer. *Why do You always wait until the last second?* Caden asked God.

As he blinked through the haze of pain, Caden found himself looking up and up. It was a Giant. He wasn't in a Sentinel uniform but a blue foreign one. He had olive skin and dark brown, curly hair. On one hip was a baton, the other a knife the size of a sword. Caden stared up into the face and found the Giant looking directly at him. The Giant scoffed and shook his head, either in disbelief or amusement, Caden didn't know. *I've seen you before,* he thought, his eyes narrowing. The Giant crossed his massive arms and turned to Grant.

"Like I said," he said in English, his voice filling the room. "That's him." At his voice, Caden forgot to breathe. He didn't even feel his throbbing shin for a moment. The Giant looked back at Caden and shook his head again. It was Bobby Rut.

# THREE
# THE TRUTH

CADEN SLOUCHED IN HIS CHAIR, his breath shallow as his eyes stared into nothing. All he could hear was the steady dripping of water and Doeg's claws as the Demon paced back and forth. "You are finally identified, Caden," Doeg said softly. "I'm surprised it has taken them this long, but, then again, they are humans, after all."

Caden didn't answer. He felt cold. That was it. No, maybe a numbness or emptiness. *I'm imploding,* he thought, blinking slowly. His shin throbbed in time with his heartbeats. It was the only thing keeping him rooted in reality. Without it, he'd slip away into the dark oblivion he felt inside, where the internal screaming thrived. He could be lost there forever.

With a sudden inhale, Caden straightened and lifted his chin. Doeg's ears swiveled his way as it frowned. *Raw Peace,* Caden thought, letting out the breath slowly. *I trust in Yahweh with everything I've got and totally ignore everything I think I know. I'll do what He wants, and He'll show me what to do.*

"*He longs for your suffering.*" Caden closed his eyes, his head spinning from the pain in his leg. "*Remember, this suffering is from Him.*" Caden's closed eyes tightened.

"Him," Doeg repeated audibly. "You cannot escape God's judgment. This is the wrath He sends against all who blaspheme."

*I will conquer kingdoms*, Caden thought. *Escape the sword, shut the mouths of lions.*

"You will suffer. God wants to withhold life from you."

"Lies," Caden whispered, his voice cracking.

He heard Doeg click its tongue as its tail swished across the floor. "You still cling to lies?"

"*You* are lies."

"I am literally quoting Scripture."

"Out of context."

"No."

"It doesn't apply to me." Caden's eyes opened as he faced the Demon. "I will get the reward King Yeshua promised."

"Wrong." Doeg stepped closer, its mangled face stretching its lips into a frozen smile. "What you receive is in accordance with what you have done. What have you done, Caden?" Caden's mouth opened to speak. "You have failed," Doeg continued. "You have let your siblings die." Caden flinched. "Permitted hate against your father and Nathaniel to thrive. You've cursed God, blasphemed His will and name. You deserve death, boy." Caden's heart quickened. "*That* is the entire verse. It is you who are taking Scripture out of context."

Caden's head slowly shook as his hands became fists. "No," he whispered. *Raw Peace. Please, God! Save me!*

Caden gasped, trying to lean away as the Demon's hot breath brushed his face. Saliva dripped onto his legs. "Bobby Rut is now here." Caden clenched his jaw. "He will devour you. Limbs first." Whiskers brushed Caden's nose, and he leaned further back. "Then your torso, from the inside out." Caden panted through gritted teeth. "Like a wolf, like how they feasted on Trace's body."

Caden moaned. "I will not turn against God!"

"Why not? He has turned against you. There is no rescue. You will die now. Accept it. You have one choice, to cooperate and die swiftly or live a lie and die agonizingly slowly."

Caden shook his head. "Get away from me!"

"You must decide."

"If I live or die, it is not my responsibility!" Caden's eyes snapped open. He turned, seeing Doeg was nearly on top of him. Sweat dripped down his brow as he swallowed the hard lump in his throat. "I am Yahweh's!"

"You are mine!"

"And I will die when *He* decides, not you!" Doeg's fanged mouth stretched into a frown as its ears whipped back. Its icy eyes willed with hate and bloodlust. Caden's chin trembled, but he refused to turn away. *You would've harmed me already if you could.*

*"I am biding my time."*

*Stop lying to yourself! You are denied access to me! All you Demons are! It is fatal to touch me!* The fur bristled down Doeg's neck as it opened its mouth to speak.

The door opened. Several Sentinels rushed in. Caden faced them, Doeg instantly vanishing from sight. *Finally,* he thought, knowing the Demon was still there, but it was so much easier when he didn't see it. Caden stole himself as the Sentinels neared. He had nothing left of his strength. *You've died once before and came back, God,* Caden thought, lifting his chin. *You can make me survive this too.*

He rigidly sat as they unbound his wrists, ankles, and the strap across his chest. It took a moment for Caden to notice the gurney wheeled in behind them. And Dr. Ricci. Caden blinked and tried to focus as they helped him rise. It was like he broke his leg all over again, like back in America with Ophir taking care of him. *She's a better doctor,* he thought as he heavily leaned on a Sentinel. *Please be alive. I need you too. I need all of you.*

He blinked, finding himself staring at the ceiling. Why was there a second level to the room? He stared at the balcony overlooking his level. How much had Benaiah seen? Wait, why weren't they tying him up again? Ricci was talking. Something about exhaustion and an IV bag. The dripping sound finally faded away as the ceiling moved. No, wait. Caden blinked slowly, realizing he was moving. The gurney's wheels squeaked as Caden left the chair with restraints and the endless suffocating of water.

*What's happening?* He wondered before passing out.

———

THE CEILING WAS DIFFERENT. The lights were softer, and there was a fan circulating cool air throughout the room. Caden didn't feel so stiff anymore. Actually, he felt pretty good. Sure, his face was tight and irritated from Buck's hits, his ribs ached from the Sentinel's beating, and his shin still throbbed. But there wasn't any water. Oh, and he could move his arms and legs.

*My leg,* he thought, realizing he could wiggle his toes. Though still in a lot of pain, he could move his ankle too. Bandages wound about his throbbing shin, but it didn't feel broken. With a sigh, Caden slowly looked around as sneakily as possible. No one else was there. No one but...

Who was that? Some guy slumped in a chair beside Caden's bed, fast asleep. His mouth hung open a bit, and someone had draped a blanket over him. Caden blinked the sleep from his eyes and stared. It was Luca. The king's heavy breathing filled the room. Caden stared at him and, without warning, emotion tightened his chest. Caden's nostrils flared as his lips pressed together.

*I should kill you.* He blinked, startled, and turned away.

*I can't do this.* He swallowed the hard lump in his throat. *I can't see him right now.*

He clearly remembered the long line of 'terrorists' ushered into KUS Headquarters to be executed. They were Christians. His church family. His people. And they were killed. Luca killed them. Caden's breath quickened, remembering Asher's bloodied face as he was dragged through the throng. Caden had tried to save him, but he knew Asher was still stuck in the lower levels of HQ. Rapham could be leaning on him, making him talk, and killing him at the same time.

*Who else had been there that I missed?* Caden's eyes pinched shut. Murderous anger heated his blood as he slowly looked to Luca. *No one's here,* he thought, his hair standing on end. *His guard is down. He himself has taught me how to deal with terrorists. If anyone's a terrorist, it's him.*

Luca smacked his mouth and shifted. Caden flinched and looked away, his hands balled into fists. *Keep it together! You're Alex! Alex doesn't want to kill the king. Don't kill the king! What am I thinking?*

The chair moved as Luca sat up. "Alex?" Caden opened his mouth to speak but couldn't. He wanted to curse Luca, to demand justice for all the blood spilled. "How are you feeling?"

Caden scoffed. He couldn't help it. "You ask *now*?" he asked, his voice a cracked whisper. "After handing me over to the ones who kidnapped me." Luca sighed heavily, and Caden heard the chair scoot back. He turned, finding Luca on his knees. Caden's eyes narrowed as he leaned back, unsure of what to do.

"Alex Whitney," Luca said, staring down at the ground. "I have wronged you. Grievously." Caden lifted his chin. "I beg for your forgiveness and to pardon me. I am not a perfect man and made a hasty decision sending you to Refiner Officer Yarrow."

Fire flashed in Caden's eyes as he cursed. "Is that all he gets? A demotion!"

"He can never become a lieutenant again."

"But he is still a Refiner? Still free!"

"He is, but with strict limitations."

"He will come for me! Can't you see that? Grant wants me dead, bit by bit. And you'll let him get that!"

"He has been deported."

"To where? America?"

"Egypt."

"Oh, much better. Instead of across the ocean, he's just a half a day's drive away!"

"Alex, the New Kingdom needs people like Refiner Grant and Buck."

"Kidnappers? Torturers?"

"Men who will stop at nothing to pave the way for my kingdom to come and my will to be done."

A chill washed over Caden as he turned away. *He's messing up Scripture again.*

"Alex, please." Luca spread his arms. "Forgive me. How can I make this up to you?"

*You can die.* Caden said nothing as he turned away, his heart beating loudly in his ears as his face flushed crimson. With a shake of his head, Caden closed his eyes tight, an idea making him sick. *I'm still a spy,* he told himself. *I still have a job to do.*

"Prove you trust me," he said at last. "I want to know everything that's happened with Under Fire and the terrorist found there, what your next plans are, and all that. I want to know everything."

Luca stared up at Caden. "That is a steep request."

"And you require Whitney Wings to fly out all your humanitarians and Refiners and whoever else you want. Want to conquer the world? Conquer the sky first." Luca's jaw flexed as he thought. Caden didn't turn away. He didn't care what happened to him anymore. He was immortal, apparently; God kept walking him out of situations.

"Very well," Luca said softly as he held out his hand. Caden glanced at it before shaking. There was a loud knock at the door, and it opened before anyone answered. A massive person stepped through, stooping and squeezing their way in. Caden's heart quickened, and his face became impassive as Bobby Rut strolled toward them.

"A Prime Minister shouldn't kneel, your majesty." Luca didn't answer as Caden shot him a quick look. "Even if it is the heir of Whitney Wings."

Caden's heart leapt into his throat as he fought to keep his face impassive. *What's he doing? He couldn't be proving I'm Alex, could he? Wait. What did Bobby just call Luca?* "Prime Minister?" He muttered, turning back to Luca.

"Isaac Lapid was killed during the terrorist attack on headquarters," Luca said.

Caden blinked. "When?"

"When the fanatic firebreathers attacked. Weren't you there?" Caden tried to mask his anger. Elijah and Yohanan? Fanatics? They were prophets of God! Couldn't anyone else feel the *Akal Esh* inside them? "The president requested I help rule until order is reestablished, but we'll cover all this when we speak again. Rest now, my friend," Luca said, laying a hand on Caden's shoulder. "I receive daily reports of your recovery from Roberto. Alex, I hope I can prove myself as a trustworthy ally again."

Caden made himself look up at Luca. It took all his strength not to grab the lamp next to his bed and crack it against Luca's skull. Without another word, Luca dipped his head to both Caden and Bobby before leaving. As the door shut, Caden felt his hair stand on end. He could almost feel Bobby's gaze burning into him, like the hot stare of a Fiend.

"Alex!" Bobby said suddenly, extending a hand. "So glad to see you! Thought we'd never find you!"

Caden didn't answer as he fixed Bobby with a dark glare. The Giant grinned, his teeth flashing, and strolled to Caden's bed. "Stay away from me!"

"But I'm your bodyguard, Alex. I'm here to protect you."

"What do you want?"

Bobby's head tilted to one side as his smile faltered. "Wow...look at you. The little puppy finally learned how to bite back." Caden refused to speak. "I'm here to earn my several thousand tams."

Caden shook his head. "From who?"

"Your      people.      Your     network     is surprisingly...thorough."

*Your people? Does he mean Under Fire?*

"When Mr. Whitney sent me here to eat you," a lump formed in Caden's throat, "I thought this would be an in and out job. How did your people know I was coming?"

*We don't know anything,* Caden thought as he lifted his chin. *But God does.* Caden tried to hide his amusement, knowing God must've told Elijah about Bobby coming. He just shrugged and smiled. "What can I say? You guys are an easy mark."

Bobby's huge brows furrowed as a shadow crossed his eyes. "Who's the mole at House Whitney?"

Caden scoffed. "Grant has been asking the same thing for days. I didn't tell him. Why would I tell you?" Bobby's massive head tilted to one side as he studied Caden. *You don't scare me anymore,* he thought, his gaze darkening. Bobby grunted and stepped back, crossing his arms as he turned away.

*This is crazy!* Caden thought. *Bribing Christians and greedy Giants. Who would've thought!*

"So, what now?" he asked. "You've lied to the king and betrayed Thomas Whitney."

"Collect my tams and stay here."

Ice entered Caden's blood. "*Here?*"

"Israel. The Middle East. Maybe Europe." Bobby grinned down at him with a shrug. "I hear there are Giantesses in Germany."

"Get out of here."

Bobby quieted, his shoulders squaring. "Excuse me?"

"You heard me." Steel entered Caden's voice as he faced Bobby. "Leave this place. If you stay, you will die sooner." Bobby actually laughed, the noise shaking the room. Caden didn't laugh, and Bobby fell silent. "My network goes beyond anything you can face, Mr. Rut. You would be wise to stand down and live the remainder of your days *away* from me."

Bobby smiled again, but Caden could tell it was forced. "I will not be threatened by a human."

"You think this is just me? I'm the messenger. There is a force far greater behind this promise."

Bobby blinked, stepped back, and shook his head. "That Yarrow fellow was right. He said you were a cockroach. You just can't seem to die."

"And I won't," Caden stated. "Until the right time."

Bobby's eyes narrowed as a chuckle rumbled from his throat. He turned and started walking toward the door. "He leaned on you pretty good in the end," he said over his shoulder. "Said he thought you drowned. But you kept breathing."

A muscle in Caden's jaw flexed. "You spoke with him?"

"He's a cool guy."

"No, a psycho."

Bobby chuckled as he put his hand on the door. "Just make sure you're not strapped to his chair again. He said he wouldn't be as gentle."

Caden lifted his chin as the Giant left without a word. He finally lay back down and stared at the fan lazily spinning. *My undercover network,* he thought with amusement. He had more questions, but they didn't matter too much now. *What matters is I'm alive, as Alex. And Grant is far away. I hope.* Caden flexed his toes slowly, feeling where Grant's cane had cracked against his shin. *They didn't break me,* he thought, lightly closing his eyes. *Thank You, God.* He slowly drifted off to sleep.

———

CADEN RECOVERED FASTER than Dr. Ricci thought possible. Physically, he was doing better, but mentally, he had a few hang-ups. He didn't talk about it, but whenever water dripped from a faucet, he sucked in a huge breath and braced himself. The shuffling feet of a limp made him tense and wait for a blow. He would tell himself to calm down, that he was safe again. Well, safer. He was still living with the Antichrist. Luca still expected him to train as a Refiner, despite all the hell he put him through.

He learned later he had been under Grant's 'care' for five days. It had felt like an eternity. Roberto, with classic hand waving, had shared how impressive Caden was for not breaking. "The lack of sleep and less food!" He shook his head, pointing at Caden's leg. "Not to mention physical difficulties. The king has expressed many times you are really Alex, and he was such a fool. Now, when has a king said that hum?"

Caden hadn't answered. *Foolish is an understatement,* he thought. *Anyone fighting against King Yeshua is out of his mind.*

"How'd you do it?" Caden shrugged. "They say you

rested without sleep and gained strength when most people's adrenalin would be gone."

"Lucky, I guess." *You cannot crush what God makes strong.*

Through it all, Caden discreetly looked for Dasha. No one spoke of her, as though she was a fleeting memory not worth their time. He missed her. Desperately. *I'll see her again,* he'd tell himself, but he couldn't ignore the loneliness that closed in around him. He also would check his room's vent a few times, knowing he wouldn't find their hidden Bible, but he still hoped. After days of bedrest, several visits from Dr. Ricci, and Roberto there to help, Caden regained his strength.

He started limping in his room, then pacing the hall, then the grounds. Grant hadn't broken his shin. The bone was only bruised. Caden doubted the diagnosis, finding the pain nearly comparable to when he broke his fibula in America. He was walking sooner this time, so maybe they were right. When approved by the doctor, he started weight training again. Though Refiner training was still out of reach, he knew he had to keep up his strength. That, and he needed somewhere to put all his aggression against Luca and his vile followers.

One evening, Caden had heard distant dogs barking and a faucet dripping somewhere and had enough. He hit the gym and worked his body to the max, ignoring the sweat and burn. He even got to wail on the punching bags for a bit. That always helped. Sweaty and tired, he returned to the showers and was grateful to find he was alone. He was shocked he hadn't gotten sick or an ulcer from parading as Alex for so long. Alone, he could let down his guard, just for a moment, and be Caden. Sighing heavily, Caden opened his locker door and reached for a new change of clothes. Claws clicked on the floor. Caden glanced over his shoulder, his hair standing on end, but he kept doing what he was doing. It was about time Doeg started pestering him again, that Demon disappeared now and then and —

Caden's eyes narrowed as he listened. The steps were heavy. Too heavy for Doeg. The panting of massive breaths huffed behind him. Whoever it was, it stood far taller than he. Caden's heart quickened as his face became impassive. *Don't panic,* he thought, grabbing his clothes. *You're not dead yet. Just see what they want.* He slowly turned around and looked up. Standing an arm's length away was Benaiah.

The Leovir's golden eyes studied him as his brown and russet mane made him look twice as big. Caden turned away, the Freak's musclebound body was far superior to his own. *And he has fangs,* Caden thought. *Claws. He could eat me alive. He knows my real name too. What does he want?* He waited for Benaiah to speak, the tension straining between them. "Um," Caden muttered in English. "Can I help you?"

"You are a reckless cub." Hebrew spoken from such a powerful Freak sent shivers down Caden's spine.

"I," he stammered. "I don't speak that."

"You understand. I see it."

Caden's heart quickened as he shook his head. "I'm sorry. I can get a translator. I just speak English."

Benaiah's furry paws planted on either side of Caden's head. Caden cursed as he recoiled, feeling the cold metal lockers butting against him.

Benaiah stooped, his golden eyes never leaving Caden. "I have watched you, Caden Johnson," he said in Hebrew, his voice a low rumble. "You are different." Caden lifted his chin and stared at the animal. It was like he was cornered by the embodiment of wild power itself. "You can fool others, but you cannot fool me, cub." Caden's eyes narrowed as Benaiah's clipped ear swiveled. "Your King is different." Caden said nothing, his breath quickening. "I want the truth of your King."

Caden blinked slowly as his brows furrowed. *Is he talking about Luca?*

Benaiah stared at him, his tail swishing. "The King who puts fire into warriors' mouths, who keeps little foolish cubs like you alive, and who I cannot cut down. That King."

An excited thrill washed over Caden. What was this? The enemy's creation asking about King Yeshua? No, no, this was a trick. An elaborate scheme to get Caden to talk. He lifted his chin, a muscle in his jaw flexing. "Please, let's get a translator and—"

Benaiah's claws slid from his paws, grading across the locker's metal. Caden held up a hand. "Wait! Wait, I want to talk with you, I only speak English!"

"Tell your King I've proven my loyalty." Caden fell silent. Benaiah's tail swished as he stepped back. "Tell Him. We will talk again." Caden watched him go, the Leovir having to duck as he walked from the room. Caden shook his head and ran fingers through his hair. With a curse, he slammed his locker door shut and went on to the showers, knowing Yahweh was up to something again.

# FOUR
# WORLD DOMINATION

CADEN FOLLOWED Luca through KUS Headquarters. He wasn't limping anymore, though his leg still wasn't fully healed. He was assaulted with the memory of the last time he stood in the huge entry room. It had been filled with smoke and prisoners to be executed. The smell of smoke was gone, and workers were finishing up the final repairs on the singed building. In fact, it looked even better than before Elijah and Yohanan came in, bringing their message of fire and brimstone. As he stared across the room, he blinked in surprise.

*There are fewer and fewer people here,* Caden thought as he followed Luca to the elevator. *There are more Freaks, Giants, and Demons. There can't be more creepy creatures, can there?* Caden's stomach coiled, knowing anything was possible in the New Kingdom. He refused to let his unease show and lifted his chin high, keeping steel in his eyes and his strides strong. The Demons were watching. He ignored all of them. They didn't matter. Even if Doeg was there, it probably was, Caden was protected by a Cherub.

He hadn't seen Han in a long time, but he trusted

Yahweh to keep His word. *We win,* Caden thought, step-ping onto the elevator. *And they know it.* He couldn't with-hold a smile as they rode up.

"It is odd being back?" Luca asked, and Caden nodded. "It's glad to have you again."

Caden forced a smile and glanced at Luca. "Do you remember what I asked for? To gain my trust again, your majesty?"

"Yes, Alex, I remember. We are going to my inner office now to discuss things privately."

Caden nodded, shocked Luca was actually giving him a status report. *Am I his apprentice or something?* It made no sense, someone like Caden couldn't possibly trick this many people so successfully. Caden's eyes narrowed as he remembered reading something in the Bible. Revelation had spoken of the spirit of deception overtaking most people. It had been talking mostly about the Antichrist tricking everyone, but maybe Caden was benefiting from the deceptive spirit too.

He sniffed and watched Luca out of the corner of his eye. *Whatever it is, it's working.* They reached the higher levels, the halls filled with more Demons than ever before. Caden wasn't surprised. As they neared Luca's inner office, a small, bald man walked toward them. He pushed up his glasses and wrung his hands fretfully. Behind him trailed three Fiends. Caden's jaw set as he approached Hugh Wilt-shire, and one of the Fiends formed a smoky snout and spiked head, ember eyes burning wherever it looked. Caden felt his hair stand on end but chose to focus on Hugh.

"Your majesty," Hugh said as he bowed low. "And Ally Alex."

"Ally Hugh," Caden said.

"Your majesty, I have unfortunate news, um…" Hugh fell in step beside Luca as Caden gave them a little space.

He made sure he could still hear them as they continued speaking in Hebrew though. "One of our prisoners escaped the lower levels," Hugh said.

Luca didn't answer a moment as he held his hands behind his back. "No one escapes from there."

"Well, apparently not. Your majesty, it happened last night and—"

"Why was I not informed?"

"We tried to find him. I asked the Heralds, yet they could not either."

"Which one?"

"A terrorist. From Under Fire."

"Which one?" Hugh fell silent, and Luca's hands fisted. "Hugh." Luca's voice was soft and calm. Caden's hair stood on end as he discreetly listened. "Don't tell me it was the young Mizrahi."

It was all Caden could do to not shout for joy. Hugh's answer was a small, hesitant nod. Caden ran a quick hand over his face, trying to scrub the overwhelming relief from his expression. He felt tears threatening to fill his eyes, and he gruffly sniffed, turning away. *My brother's alive? I didn't kill him?* He withheld a smile and straightened his back, relief making his hands shaky. He shoved them in his pockets, hoping no one noticed, and realized Luca and Hugh were still talking.

"Keep looking."

"We are, your majesty."

"How did he escape?"

"He had help."

"Obviously."

"We don't know who."

"Possibly the mole."

"Yes, your majesty."

"What do the Heralds have to say about this mess?"

Hugh fell quiet. "They are...distant on the matter." Luca didn't answer.

Even from behind, Caden noticed his face had turned red. Luca's shoulders bunched, and his fisted hands were white-knuckled. *You won't find Asher,* Caden thought. *He can't be killed either.*

*"Everyone can be slaughtered,"* an unwelcome voice whispered inside Caden's thoughts. His mini celebration evaporated at Deog's words. *"Even your God."*

*And He came back, stronger than before,* Caden thought with a scoff. *That's a stupid example.* Doeg had some quick remark, but Caden wasn't listening as he followed Luca into his office.

"Well, Ally Alex," Luca said, turning to a table of maps and documents. The wall before them was covered with the same. Caden glanced at the map of the Middle East and the plane routes Kingdom's Peace, the KUS humanitarian services, had taken. There were far more than before, some reaching as far as northern Canada. "Are you ready to listen? Much has happened."

"Your majesty," Hugh whispered in Hebrew. "Is this wise? He is a mere child."

"He is the future," Luca answered in English. "I have plans for him, and honestly, I would have revealed this to him eventually." Caden's brows rose as he glanced at Luca. Lifting his chin and stepping closer, Caden listened as Luca began debriefing him.

Luca was right, a lot had happened in just five days. Isaac Lapid was a casualty in the terrorist attack, shot in the chest. Caden hid his rage by burying his nails into his palm; Elijah and Yohanan hadn't been armed. The only ones with guns had been the KUS. *Are people that stupid? Luca probably did it himself!*

The president had asked Luca to help lead while Israel still recovered after Russia's assault. Most of Israel had been attacked, and the people desperately needed a strong, capable leader. Luca spoke of it with such humility it made Caden sick. *You will destroy these people,* Caden thought, and he was completely right. Luca detailed their attack against Under Fire had been hasty, for instead of eradicating the terrorists, they instead sent them running. They were now scattered all across Jerusalem.

"More than that, actually," Luca said with a sharp frown as he pointed to a map. "In Judea and Samaria and, well...the ends of the earth." He swept his arm across the map with a heavy sigh. "We don't know how, and no one is blaming Whitney Wings, but we believe the terrorists have hijacked several of Whitney's planes. That's why Kingdom's Peace had to be canceled, unfortunately. Several, if not most of the humanitarians sent, were instead terrorists in disguise."

Caden cursed and crossed his arms, but inside, he wanted to rip down all the maps and scream at Luca that there was no stopping God. Luca sighed as a muscle in his jaw flexed. "Such were my fears. I'm sorry I didn't take more precautions when recruiting volunteers. I tried. But they still got through."

"What are you saying?" Caden asked. "That they're everywhere?"

Luca rubbed his brow and slowly nodded. "They knew this was coming. They knew from the beginning. There are more terrorist cells than my Sentinels can find. It is—"

"Madness."

"It's all the fanatic's fault."

"Who?"

"Elijah Mizrahi and Yohanan Nuri." Their name on the Antichrist's lips sent shivers down Caden's spine. Luca muttered Italian as he waved at the map. "We can never find them, yet they appear out of nowhere, spewing their lies and fire and destroying the New Kingdom."

Caden nodded slowly, masking his emotions the best he could. "Have you tried to assassinate them?"

Luca scoffed. "Several times. Several. Nothing works. Most of the men believe they cannot be killed, which is foolish; everyone can die." Caden stayed silent. He wanted to scream at Luca, shouting that it was his brother-in-law and Abba he wanted dead. "We have a plan when they resurface though," Luca said, and Caden glanced at him.

"What type of plan?"

"One that involves several casualties, which I do not favor, but the fanatics will slaughter hundreds." Caden didn't realize he raised a skeptical brow until it was too late. "They already have," Luca snapped. "There was a plague in this region," he pointed at the map, "Famine over here. This entire town was destroyed by fire." Luca sighed heavily and drummed a finger on his chin. "Wherever these men go, there is death."

Caden glanced between the several locations Yohanan and Elijah had destroyed. "Were those the locations of the assassination attempts?"

Luca straightened and nodded. "They are. Why?"

"Just curious." *They're not just destroying people for no reason. Those people tried to kill them. You can't kill a Witness! They breathe the Akal Esh! Don't you know anything?* "So, what's the next assassination attempt?"

Luca smiled his charming smile and shook his head. "Some things are for only a select few to know."

Caden nodded and rubbed the back of his neck, his anger making him sick. *Stop trying to kill my family!* Luca fell silent as Caden glowered at the several dots across the map. "Are those all terrorist cells?"

"Yes."

There were so many! They centralized around Jerusalem, but quickly spread everywhere like ripples in a pond. *It worked,* Caden thought. *I can't believe it.*

"Worse yet," Luca said. "They aren't attacking, as far as we know, but are recruiting more and more people to their anti-kingdom ideals. There will be a rebellion. It is inevitable."

Caden shook his head. *No, you're the rebel. This is King Yeshua's land!* He cursed and crossed his arms. "What do you do when you find a cell? Executions?"

Luca held up a finger and shook his head. "There are too many of them. I don't want to be accused of genocide. Refiner Rapham had the brilliant idea of labor camps."

Caden lifted his chin, a cold chill turning his blood to ice. "Um...what?"

"We have resources to harvest. Mines and oil fields to man. Mercy seemed the best option for, as everyone knows, I am not without mercy, even for murdering terrorists. Who knows? Perhaps, someday, they will return to me and call me their king, and they will be my people." Caden swallowed the hard lump in his throat. "See for yourself." Luca laid a photo on the table.

Caden blinked, fighting for calm as panic tightened his chest. At first, he thought he was staring at a restored picture of Auschwitz. There were lines and lines of people, all ages and types. Most were Israeli. All were in survival mode, surrounded by Sentinels and dogs. His heart skipped a beat, seeing a young girl clinging to her mother. *Those are my people,* Caden thought. *My church family.*

He hardly heard Luca detail the several labor camps, most located in Egypt, Iraq, Jordan, and Syria. All he could do was continue staring at the disturbing picture, visualizing his Lil El suffering as she worked for the Antichrist. He scooted the photo back and tried to listen as Luca explained he wanted to expand the New Kingdom even further than before. His army was growing. More Sentinels. Even more Refiners. The public loved the

Leovirs, their faith was restored in the New Kingdom's power.

Caden blinked slowly, his heart beating louder and louder. *You're going to kill us all,* he thought. With enthusiasm and many gestures, Luca spoke of the people. Their loyalty to his kingdom was inspiring, or some type of nonsense like that. They were following his every lead, even those far from the Middle East. China was coming soon to form an alliance. The United Kingdoms too. Russia, though their enemy, was reconsidering their assault.

*That makes no sense,* Caden thought. *Russians don't just reconsider, unless…* He blinked, trying hard to not show the steadily growing rage. *You planned this, didn't you? Russia, the attacks, Isaac's assassination. Just another rise to power. All in the name of your false kingdom.* He forced himself to nod, seeing Luca motion to a Leovir standing guard against the wall. *What did he just say? More things like Freaks?* Caden's heart quickened further as sweat dripped down his back. *More Leovirs? Or…something new?*

Luca smiled and waved a hand. "I see I'm confusing you."

"I…I'd like to hear more."

"In time."

"More new soldiers, my king?"

"A soldier of the air. He is a new friend who can, how shall I say? Wash the land of its filth with a cleansing flood. He is the Prince of Heralds." Luca waved a hand again and came closer. "Another time, though." Caden opened his mouth to speak, but Luca held up a hand. "I do need your opinion on something, my boy." Caden faced him. "Hamburgers or steak and potatoes?"

Caden frowned. "Excuse me?"

"I wanted to welcome you home and give you an American meal."

Caden's mouth fumbled for words. *You've just detailed how you'll slaughter thousands, and now you're talking about what food I like?*

"Um,"

*You must be stopped.*

"Steak and potatoes."

*Someone has to stop you.*

Luca grinned as he clapped Caden on the shoulder. "It shall be done! And, in regards to what you will tell others about your five-day absence, you were away on classified business for me. We'll just keep Refiner Yarrow our secret." Caden turned away, his anger nearly overpowering. He saw a paperweight out of the corner of his eye. It looked heavy enough. It could crush a skull.

"Alex?"

"Sure," Caden said. "That's fine with me."

"I am sorry for what happened to you. Truly." Luca leaned in closer. It was all Caden could do to not inflict lethal techniques Luca himself trained him with. "Do you forgive me, my boy?"

*I am Yeshua's.* Caden faced him and smiled. "Of course, my king. I would've done the same if I was you."

Luca smiled and lay a hand on Caden's shoulder. "Good. It's settled. Tomorrow, I expect to see you back here, ready to continue training."

Caden blinked and bit his tongue. *You can't be serious!*

Luca grinned as he clapped Caden on the shoulder. "I am eager to continue your training."

*Yeshua will destroy you.* "I can't wait." *You cannot defeat His Akal Esh. You will pay for these war crimes against the world. Against God.*

"I have work to attend to now," Luca said, stepping back.

Caden nodded as he moved toward the door. He bowed low, nearly making himself sick. "Thank you, your majesty," he said. "Thank you for trusting me with your plans for the future."

Luca grinned. "It's *our* future, Ally Alex." Caden dipped his head again and walked as calmly as he could out the door. He went straight to the training floor and found boxing gloves. He beat a punching bag until his knuckles felt raw. He didn't care. He kept visualizing the bag was Luca's face.

----

CADEN PUSHED his hummus around his plate. He sat at the bar in a small restaurant that looked very odd now after the Day of Vanishing. Half of it looked normal, booths and a bar, even a TV, but the other half was over-sized. On purpose. Giants sat and ate their meal, the portions the size of five normal human plates put together. Special utensils had been made to fit the larger customers' beefy hands. It was unnerving, and Caden couldn't help but notice the Giants occasionally glanced to the humans, their gaze predatorial and hungry. He could easily see Bobby happily chewing on someone's leg here.

Caden rubbed his eyes with a finger and thumb and reminded himself it was a surprisingly blissful day because Luca had nothing for him. He had, somehow, gained permission to leave Luca's house, but not without his bodyguard, slash babysitter. He wished Luca sent Simon again; it had been too easy losing him in a crowd. Roberto was a different story. The bald Italian sat behind him, sipping an espresso without a word. Caden shifted in his stool and returned his focus to the hummus.

It reminded him of the bland yellowness of the Sinai Desert, of where he found God and his Lil El. *Spiny,* he thought with a shake of his head. *That's still a stupid nick-name.* He wondered what Yohanan was doing. If he believed everything from *The King's Modern Times*, he'd guess up to trouble. Caden thought Christians were supposed to turn the other cheek, never lash back, and never, ever hurt anybody. *It's the End Times*, he thought with a sigh. *The Holy Spirit's not whispering what's right or wrong, and we were all just nonbelievers like four years ago.*

Mama Lo made it sound like everyone was still a baby Christian until they were at least ten years into it. Whatever 'baby Christian' meant. What would Mama Lo think of Yohanan torching people who attacked him? That didn't look like turning the other cheek. Elijah did it too, but he didn't do it grinning like a crazy guy. *But those people weren't listening*, Caden thought. *If somebody doesn't want to hear King Yeshua's coming back, then that's their choice. A little early Hellfire might be good in the long run. Teach the fear of God or something like that.*

Caden sighed as he ran a hand through his hair. It just didn't seem Christianly. The TV ended the stream of commercials and continued the news report. Though in Hebrew, Caden pretended he didn't listen as he took a bite of food. "Jordan is suffering a food shortage," the reporter, an older guy with curled hair in a suit, said. "With Kingdom's Peace corrupted by terrorists."

*We're not terrorists!*

"Our gracious king is working night and day to relieve the people of our New Kingdom."

"That's right, Ally Manaf," a woman beside him said, her black hair pulled back tightly. "He also is working to aid those in his homeland. Italy is on lockdown after a sudden outbreak of a disease, similar to the medieval black plague." Caden's stomach churned. He didn't know why, but he knew his Witness friends were behind the supernatural emergency. "But it is nothing beyond what our king can save," the woman said, a smile brightening her face.

"He truly is the messiah," the man said. A shiver ran down Caden's spine as he glanced up, seeing both reporters nodding. "I feel such security under his Sovereign Lion's Watch. To think, after all these centuries. The messiah has finally come."

*No*, Caden thought. *Not you too!*

The woman held up a hand and shook her head. "I still have my doubts. The rabbis have not verified — "

"Time will tell, time will tell. In the meantime, Ally Hugh Wiltshire has begun an educational series that will air very soon. He longs to train the entire New Kingdom on how to protect themselves and their loved ones with the help of the hollowed Heralds." Caden hissed a curse as he lowered his head, trying to hide his anger. "The series will air this time next week and train anyone, regardless of creed, background, or gender. We are all accepted and secure under the Sovereign Lion's Watch. Join us. Learn of the Heralds. Seek their wisdom and be safe."

*No, no, no*, Caden thought. He blinked, realizing he was gripping his fork too hard, and the metal was biting into his palm. He set it down with a sharp exhale and told himself to keep it together. *Of course, the Demons are doing that*, he thought. *We did it too. We're telling everyone about King Yeshua coming, so they're trying to trick anyone they can. They shouldn't be allowed to do that; something should be done! There are just so many bad guys these days. We're going to get overtaking. Has any of our efforts mattered at all?*

Caden sat back and forced himself to focus on the truth of Under Fire. He thought of the several maps in Luca's inner office and the markers for each terrorist cell. They were like the stars in the sky. It was unthinkable Caden had actually helped ship Christians all over the place. There were even a few cells in America and Mexico.

*And to the ends of the earth*, Caden thought with a small smile. He sniffed and sat back, catching himself in the reflection of a distant framed picture. He frowned and touched his hair roots. *Got to dye this again,* he thought, knowing he was slowly losing his Alex disguise. He hated dying it. It wasn't the stinking dye, how much it cost, or how long it took. It was willingly deciding, every time, to pretend to be Alex Whitney for just a little longer. It was letting go of his desire of tracking down Under Fire, joining them, and bringing Luca to his knees. Every time, he chose to do what God had instructed.

*I think that's called dying to yourself,* Caden thought with a grunt. *Dying's right. Hey, Yahweh. Are there more brownie points if the dying involves almost literally dying now and then? That would be great.* He hadn't found the extra brownie points verse either. He knew it was in there, some small part of him kept demanding it was there, and he just had to look harder. A muscle in Caden's jaw flexed as he lifted his chin. *There are no points. If there were, they'd just go to Yeshua anyways; He's the only one who's really died for everyone. Who snuck into this broken world, lived in our dirt, and died like a criminal.* He had done a little research into crucifixions and had no idea how brutal it was.

*All for me,* he thought, sitting back. It was overwhelming. Unbelievable. How could a perfect God let stupid humans beat Him up, several times, drag Him up a hill, drive nails into His hands and feet, and suspend Him in front of His enemies until He suffocates? *Crazy love,* Caden thought as he crossed his arms. *I'll never deserve it.* He could almost hear Elijah saying he never would deserve it, and God loved him anyways. Caden's eyes narrowed. Come to think of it, he *could* hear Elijah.

Caden stiffened and stared down at his plate, his ears straining to pinpoint where the voice was coming from. He turned slowly, trying not to get his babysitter's attention. Down the bar from him was a large man. His hair was white, and his eyebrows were very bushy. He wore spectacles, and a hat covered the rest of his face. He was giving his order to a waitress before quietly sitting, hands folded neatly and placed before him. Caden's breath quickened with excitement. Though in disguise, Caden could spot his Abba anywhere.

# FIVE
## NO GOODBYES

DON'T LOOK AT HIM. *Just don't look,* Caden thought, refocusing on his hummus. *What's he doing here? Don't look!* His back tingled, knowing Roberto was just a few paces away, watching. So why hadn't he recognized the leader of the most threatening 'terrorist' movement?

Caden blinked, stunned that he didn't realize it before. Elijah's hair was white. His beard. his eyebrows even. His mustache was bigger, and those spectacles did detract from his face. He hunched over his plate, not sitting straight and firm like an immovable boulder. *And that's all it takes to fool the king's men?* Caden wondered. He took another bite of food, not tasting it at all, his mind racing. *I've got to warn him about Luca's plans! And the labor camps.* A hard lump formed in Caden's throat. *He has to know what he's up against.* He took a drink, his other hand restlessly drumming fingers on the table.

*How to get Elijah's attention, and communicate with him, without getting Roberto's attention? Any ideas, Yahweh?* For once, God answered quite quickly. Caden stood, finding himself needing to go to the bathroom. Looking around, he couldn't help but smile, seeing to get to the bathrooms, he'd have to walk right by Elijah. *He'll see me,* Caden thought. He noticed Roberto rising, thinking he was finished, but quickly sat back down. At least there were limits to his babysitting.

Caden went to the bathroom and found two stalls and five urinals, one being occupied. As casually as he could, he did his business, his heart thudding against him. His ears strained, hoping the door would open and heavy, calm footsteps would enter. The door did open as Caden washed his hands. The footsteps thudded in. Caden's heart pounded, and he scrubbed his nose, trying to hide the look of relief on his face. The stranger finally left, and Caden glanced at the door.

A quiet, burly Israeli stood, his hands at his sides as he faced the door. Their eyes met, and Caden straightened. It was Noam. He nodded, and Caden nodded back before turning around. Elijah stood waiting. He was grinning ear to ear. Caden rushed forward and fell into his arms. It was like hugging a bear. Caden let that moment take him away from all the chaos and lies he had to live with. Right now, he was with his Abba, and he was safe.

"Hello, son," Elijah said, drawing him back.

"Hey, Abba. I've got a lot to tell you; we don't have time."

Elijah didn't respond as his smile fell and his gaze darkened. "What have they done to you?"

Caden stepped back and turned away. He realized no one had asked him that in a long time. "They were on to me for a bit. Not anymore."

"What did they do?" Elijah's voice was a low whisper. His breath was hot, too hot.

Caden lifted his chin, seeing protective aggression in Elijah's eyes. "Roughed me up. Some waterboarding. Was going to break bones."

A slow, hushed growl escaped Elijah, nearly a growl. "Both you and Asher."

Caden's chest tightened with emotion as he dared to ask the question he had longed to learn. "Is he alive?"

"Yes, recovered now. Not all Leovirs are evil."

Caden blinked. "Benaiah?"

Elijah nodded. Caden ran fingers through his hair, trying to think. "Bobby Rut saved you?"

Caden frowned, then nodded. "You paid him?"

"Found him once he landed at Tel Aviv. Greedy one."

"I thought so. Did Yahweh tell you about him?"

"Yes, as He says now to hurry."

"Right," Caden said, straightening as his eyes narrowed with focus, and he told him everything. When he reached the part about labor camps, Elijah's shoulders bunched as his eyes flashed with an inner fire. Caden stopped and stared at him. "What?" Elijah hissed a curse, startling Caden. What shook him the most were the embers that floated up from his lips. Caden stepped back further, eyes wide.

With another curse, Elijah ran clawed fingers across his face as he straightened, his hands becoming fists at his sides. He sucked in a sharp breath, and Caden got the impression he was quenching the inferno rising within. Caden's stomach twisted as fear made his skin cold. "What is it?" He said, his voice nearly above a whisper.

Elijah said one word, "Ophir." Caden sucked in a breath, his entire body tensing just as Elijah had done. With another curse, Elijah lifted his chin as his eyes closed tight. "They took her, heading toward Egypt."

"Do they know she's your wife?"

"I do not know. Our network hasn't heard from or seen her in three weeks. She has to be there."

Caden's stomach coiled again as anger struck his chest.

"Go get her," he hissed through gritted teeth. "Burn them down. Kill them!"

"That is not my mission."

Caden stared at Elijah, dumbstruck. "Not your...She's your wife!"

"I am to proclaim King Yeshua's coming, not torch labor camps."

"You should!"

"It is non-negotiable!"

"Abba—"

Elijah lurched forward, seizing Caden's arms above the elbow. "I do not want this," he whispered, soft and lethal. "But I want King Yeshua's Kingdom, the real Kingdom, to come and for His will, not mine, to be done. He gives me for today what I need, and apparently, I no longer need my wife!" Caden shook his head as a muscle in his jaw flexed. Elijah sighed, and his hold loosened. "This is bigger than me. Bigger than you. I accepted this long ago. As should you."

Caden looked down and shook his head. "It can't get any worse than this."

Elijah's eyes darkened, and he leaned closer. "It will." Caden swallowed the hard lump in his throat. "Pray for strength or relief in death." Caden's breath quickened as Elijah finally let go of him.

"Sir," Noam tightly said from the doorway. Caden hissed something foul.

"Anything else?" Elijah asked. He stood calmly once again, but his eyes...Caden could see he wanted to burn the Antichrist's entire New Kingdom to the ground.

"No."

Elijah glanced at the door and moved closer. He grabbed Caden's shirt collar. "We win," he whispered. Caden nodded, but hardly felt encouraged. He hardly felt anything at all but murderous rage. "I am proud of you."

Caden blinked, finally focusing on Elijah. "I am honored to be your Abba."

Caden gritted his teeth as he tried to pull away. "Don't you dare say goodbye to me!"

"And I love you like a son." Caden grimaced as tears welled in his eyes. He tried to speak, but couldn't. Elijah nodded once and marched to the door. "We win," he said again and was gone. Caden stood in the bathroom, staring at the floor. With a gruff sniff, he rubbed his eyes and returned to his seat in the restaurant. Elijah and Noam were nowhere to be found. Caden sat and scarfed down the rest of his food.

"Did you fall in?" Roberto asked as the plump Italian sat down beside him.

Caden glared at him. "You want me to detail my bowel movements to you now too?"

Roberto raised a hand and sat back. "Just thought—"

Caden cursed. "You're disgusting. I'm eating!" Roberto's answer was a mesh of English and Italian with random hand gestures. He finally stopped talking and ordered a coffee as Caden tried to calm down. His internal screaming was there with him. He couldn't stop it, but he didn't want to. Sometimes the best response to life was to scream.

————

CADEN WAS REALLY ENJOYING his spy job. It was the best adrenaline rush he ever had! Probably because he knew the enemy couldn't kill him until God said so. Grant and Buck's torture was always in the back of his mind, which terrified him, but he just gave those fears to God and pressed on. What else could he do? The only direction now was forward.

Caden couldn't hold back a smile as he followed the

Chinese ambassador. Luca wanted to show off his Refiner recruits to all the newly arriving ambassadors, so Caden was around them all the time. South Africa came yesterday, Germany before that, and he heard even America was going to join soon. They saw the city, visited HQ, and took tours of the New Kingdom.

Now, Hugh showed the Chinese ambassador and his staff *The King's Modern Times* studio. Caden had laughed when he heard Hugh's educational episodes on how to connect with Demons were to be aired from that studio. Last Caden knew, Levi, the primary reporter, was on Under Fire's payroll. Obviously, more believers were part of the studio's staff. A plan to disrupt Hugh's TV show, *Hark the Heralds*, was already in the works. All they needed were the access codes to get their hands on the video files.

That's where Caden stepped in. When Hugh or Luca weren't available to accept the codes, which changed every week, they had been given to Caden. *They must really trust me*, he had thought, quickly memorizing the number sequence before passing it off to Hugh. He'd posted onto BiggieFishie right away with a coded message and Under Fire readied their plan.

It had worked. Caden passed the codes off while touring *The King's Modern Times*. It had been so easy. Caden followed Hugh out of the studio to the cars, rubbing his mouth to hide his grin. *Now our people have the codes*, he thought. *And they'll mess up your Demon classes. Take that!*

*"Do not celebrate yet, foolish human,"* an unwanted voice whispered inside his mind. *"This pathetic victory will be obliterated by our triumph today."*

A chill washed over Caden, and his face turned pale. *He was with them and gave them rest. He's with me. Now. He's giving me Raw Peace. Now.*

*"I will rip apart those you love before your eyes."*

Caden's breath caught in his throat as he followed Moshe and the other Refiner recruits. He felt his heart quicken and hardly noticed Hugh guiding the tour to the door. "This morning, we have a special treat," Hugh was saying. Caden sniffed gruffly as he lifted his chin, trying to ignore the tightening panic in his chest. "Our messiah, the king himself, will meet us at the Temple Mount. He wants to show you the Final Temple." The ambassador and his staff nodded and muttered together as they walked to the door.

Caden said not a word on the drive, Doeg's words cycling through his mind. *Don't let that happen, Yahweh*, he thought. *I'm begging You. I don't think I can handle more death. More terror.* Lounging on the Sentinel beside him, a Viper's sickly green eyes fixed on Caden as it opened its fanged mouth and hissed. The Sentinel grinned and glanced at the Viper, scratching the top of its head as though it was a puppy.

Caden's stomach turned as he looked away. *If I don't see anyone I know at the Temple Mount*, he thought. *Then I'll know Doeg's speaking lies again. He always lies. Why am I so worried?*

*"The future,"* the Viper hissed in Caden's thoughts. *"Is revealed to the Heralds."*

*You are not Heralds!* Caden's jaw flexed as his eyes narrowed. *You are Demons. Bound for Hell.*

The Viper hissed on and on, the sound slowly dwindling. It took a moment for Caden to realize it was laughing. *"We shall see, human. Hum...who shall we meet at the Wailing Wall? Lil El? Dasha?"*

A coldness crept across Caden's skin as he stared out the window. Images of Dasha's clear, blue eyes meeting his flashed across his mind's eye. His chest tightened with emotion as homesickness, which was wherever his Church family was, filled him.

He sat in anxious tension as they drove through the

city to the Old City of Jerusalem. They walked through the several gates, people leaping out of their way and bowing low as they passed. There were more Demons there than Caden remembered. Some were now casually talking with people. He even saw a young woman giggling as a Fiend swirled around her, covering her in darkness. Caden's heart slammed against him as they entered Temple Mount.

Beside the Dome of the Rock was another building rising high into the sky. Its flat roof was studded with golden points as the top of golden double-doors could be seen between two golden pillars. The Final Temple. People were gathered all around, some going to the Dome of the Rock, others to the Final Temple, or the Wailing Wall. People lined the far wall, rocking and writing prayers to shove into the cracks along the wall.

Sentinel Giants stood guard, their towering forms now commonplace to the people. A few Leovirs crept in the shadows, keeping to themselves. The people were not completely comfortable with them yet, but Caden saw they were getting more and more familiar. A Leovir knelt before a teen, listening as the young girl talked and gestured. Among them, Fiends drifted, Shades strolled, Withers didn't even bother donning skins, and Vipers slithered. Most seemed to notice them, only to give a respectful bow and continue about their business.

*It's not right,* Caden thought, his stomach twisting. *Not right at all!* As discreetly as he could, Caden's eyes darted from face to face.

He followed Hugh closer to the Wailing Wall, he was detailing its history and what it meant. "And we are proud to have this historical and religious sight on twenty-four-hour display," Hugh explained. "Before the World's Crash, the Wailing Wall was on live stream twenty-four, seven so that any and all could view it. Now, the dream is realized again, and his majesty has fixed cameras all throughout the courtyard. Every zone within the New Kingdom can watch, in real-time, the events as they unfold, drawing us all closer together as allies in his majesty's New Kingdom."

*Or to spy on us,* Caden thought as he noticed the little black domes scattered along the walls and at the corners of buildings. He cursed under his breath and continued searching for anyone he knew. *See?* He told himself, feeling the tension in his shoulders loosening. *No one's here.* He lifted his chin and cast Doeg a sharp glare.

The Demon, who walked along the far wall, swept its tail and grinned. Licking its lips, Doeg turned and pointed a bald, clawed hand. A hard lump formed in Caden's throat as he forced himself to look. Across the courtyard, on the men's side of the Wailing Wall, was a crowd. They were all praying loudly, rocking back and forth, or writing prayers. Two men quietly stood among them. They looked no different than the others, but Caden instantly knew who they were. He could feel it deep in his soul. He felt the hot, unquenchable *Akal Esh* coming off them in waves.

Caden's eyes widened as his heart leapt into his throat. He couldn't stop staring at Elijah and Yohanan. He felt like he was walking straight into his worst nightmare. He casually turned around, seeing how many Sentinels, Giants, Leovirs, and Demons were against the two Witnesses. *It's like, one hundred and sixty to two.* Caden coughed, forcing away the lump in his throat. *They've faced those odds before. They'll be fine.*

"*They will be attacked,*" Doeg's whispered words iced Caden's blood. "*And overpowered. And killed.*"

*Nothing can overpower God's Consuming Fire!*

"*What quenches fire?*" Caden's hands became fists as they neared the Wailing Wall. "*Caden?*"

*I won't play your games!*

*"Water."* Caden's nails dug into his palms. *"We have water, Caden. A water this world has never seen."*

Caden hissed a curse as he looked ahead. *God, do something. Do something!*

*"You're God isn't listening. He's abandoned all of you."*

Caden gritted his teeth as Hugh led them toward a man walking through a crowd of people. Everyone buzzed with excitement as the man smiled and touched those in the crowd, his Refiner bodyguards close behind. It was Luca, his warm smile and gentle touch helping him connect with each person he passed.

*"You will see,"* Doeg whispered. *"Let your God prove His never-ending love and loving-kindness by saving your Abba and brother from us. Let this be the test."*

*Do not test my God,* Caden thought as he strode forward.

He tried to hide his rising rage and hatred for the demonic ranks and the New Kingdom, but Luca noticed anyways. When laying a hand on Caden's shoulder, the king drew nearer with a furrowed brow. "What is it, my friend?" he whispered.

*Someone should kill you,* Caden thought and quickly bit his tongue. "I just..." He glanced at the Wailing Wall. "My king, I've always heard of the Wailing Wall. Do I have your permission to go see it?"

"Of course," Luca said with a smile. "Is that what's wrong? Not an issue. Ally Moshe, do show Ally Alex how to respect the wall and the customs regarding it. Any who want to visit the Wall may do so now. Please. I want all to experience what they wish."

Caden forced himself to smile with a thankful nod as he followed Moshe toward the wall. He heard Moshe talking, but he wasn't listening. His eyes were fixed on Elijah and Yohanan. They stood several paces apart, and both were quietly praying. Neither wore disguises. No one else from Under Fire seemed to be present.

*What is going on?* Caden thought, his hair standing on end.

"Got it?" Moshe asked.

"Hum?"

Moshe grimaced and glanced at him. "Here," he said, handing him a small, black piece of cloth.

"What's this?"

"A yamaka. Put it on your head."

"Why?"

"I just said! Listen! To respect Yahweh and the Jewish people."

Caden took it and frowned. "With this?"

"Yahweh instructed us to cover our heads when we pray. The Wailing Wall is for praying. Just put it on! I don't expect you to understand." Caden glared at him and put on the small head covering. "And this," Moshe said as they neared the wall. It was a pencil and a piece of paper. "Write a prayer on the paper and stick it in a crack in the wall."

Caden took it, keeping one eye on Elijah and Yohanan. "Okay." Moshe kept talking, but Caden wasn't listening again. *I've got to warn them,* he thought. *I don't even know what to tell them, but something's going on. Something big! Why are they even here?* The closest Witness was Yohanan, so Caden veered in his direction. He came to the wall and looked up, seeing the top of the Final Temple and the clouds beyond. He licked his lips and glanced down at the paper in his hands.

"Just pray," Moshe whispered. "Just talk about something on your mind or something important to you. Don't think about it too much."

*Oh, God, help me.* Caden closed his eyes and took a deep breath. *Show me what to do. You're letting me be here for a reason. I don't get it, but You do. Please.* Caden cursed under his breath as his heart kept its too-fast-of-pace. He stood and waited, hoping for a sign or direction or something. Anything!

*"Abandon,"* Doeg hissed in his ear. *"Always abandon."*

Something brushed Caden's shoulder. "Hey, bro." He glanced up and found a taller Israeli muttering prayers and rocking. It was Yohanan. He quickly turned away and tried to look focused on praying too. He saw Moshe was a few paces away, deep in thought as he tried to write a prayer.

"Get out of here," Caden hissed under his breath. "The Demons are excited about something."

"Yeah," Yohanan sighed. "Annoying, isn't it?"

Caden grimaced. "They want to rip you apart."

"We're all immortal."

"Not every time."

"Until the right time."

Though Caden couldn't see it, he knew Yohanan was smiling. He shook his head. "You're crazy."

"Thanks."

"Yohanan, I'm serious."

"Wish we met sooner." Caden stiffened, grief striking his chest. "We would've had so much fun getting out of trouble." Caden blinked, his breath caught in his throat. He looked down and gritted his teeth, his stomach twisting painfully. "Go to the mountains," Yohanan whispered as he started writing on a yellow piece of paper. Caden watched out of the corner of his eye, knowing directions were on the paper instead of a prayer. "We're all holding up there. Dasha too." Longing mixed with Caden's grief, making it difficult to focus. Yohanan rolled up the small parchment and stuffed it into the wall. He sniffed gruffly and turned around, facing the mass of people and the Antichrist. "Tell Spiny I love her."

"Don't do this—"

Caden's words cut short as Yohanan marched to the

left of the Temple Mount. As though on cue, Elijah, too, turned from the wall, gave Caden a brief glance, and walked to the right. Caden stared at the rough wall inches from his face, his breath coming in quick bursts as panic tightened his throat. *They'll get out of here. They walked in and out of HQ unharmed last time!*

Hot breath huffed on the back of his neck as whiskers brushed his hair. "Ripped apart."

With a curse, Caden stepped closer to the hidden message Yohanan had left. The courtyard's reverence was shattered by a high-pitched scream. Caden spun as every Sentinel and Refiner lowered their guns, every Giant drew a sword, and each Leovir crouched, lips drawn back in a snarl. *No!*

Every civilian scattered from the two Witnesses casually walking to opposite ends of the Temple Mount, Luca and his people stuck between. "Do not shoot!" Elijah's booming voice reverberated against the walls and over the people's screams. "You will shoot civilians!" Caden stiffly watched, waiting for Yohanan or Elijah to inhale before engulfing Luca in flames. They did nothing but keep walking.

A Giant drew closer to Yohanan, two Leovirs on either side. The younger Witness' chest rose with a gulp of air. "Yohanan!" Elijah bellowed, and Yohanan stopped, embers drifting above his head.

Caden watched as Luca glanced between the two. He raised his hands and lifted his chin. "Stand firm, my allies!" he cried. "Be at peace! I am with you; their fires will not consume you."

As he fought to breathe, Caden could hear the smile in Luca's voice. He slowly turned and regarded the smug Italian, standing straight and firm as the crowd panicked, disheveled and in confusion. That smile. That smile was still on his perfect face. He was so calm and confident, as though he'd already won. Hot breath brushed Caden's neck again.

"We have," Doeg snarled, saliva dripping down the back of Caden's uniform. Caden didn't move as rage washed his face crimson.

"King Yeshua comes!" Elijah cried. "He will come to avenge His beheaded followers!"

"You will curse the day you were born!" Yohanan shouted from the other end of the courtyard. "And beg the rocks to fall and crush you instead of facing the King of kings!"

Luca stepped forward and pointed at Elijah. "You cannot survive my floods of justice!"

"King Yeshua is the one true King!" Elijah called, ignoring Luca entirely. "Kneel to Him! Beg for forgiveness!"

"He is merciful and compassionate!" Yohanan cried. "He is slow to anger and rich in love. Love for the world. Love for you!"

"King Yeshua takes no pleasure in the death of the wicked!" Elijah stopped and faced the Sentinels and Giants, the Leovirs, and watching Antichrist. "He is pleased when they turn from their ways. Turn! Repent!"

"He will forgive you! He will welcome you into His Kingdom!"

"The true Kingdom!" Elijah shouted. "One that will never end!"

Luca, the ambassadors, and their staff had retreated behind a wall of Refiners and Giants. They drew closer to the Temple Mount's entrance as most civilians sought safety behind the white-uniformed barrier. Caden's eyes widened as a rush of panic shot through him. He was on the opposite side of the courtyard. He'd have to walk through the line of fire to escape.

"Turn!" Yohanan called. "Turn and be saved from the

coming bloodbath. King Yeshua doesn't want anyone to perish, but will not excuse the wicked."

A harsh wind struck the courtyard. Caden shielded his face, suddenly remembering Han. *Thank you!* He thought. *Get Yohanan and Elijah out of here! You can take on everyone! Get here and—*

The sun blotted out. Caden could hear wings. People were screaming and dropping to the ground, arms raised overhead. *Good,* Caden thought, stooping and glancing up. *Kneel before a servant of the Most High God.* His thoughts skidded to a halt. Han was not there.

Something else was flying overhead. Something massive and red. In a blink, it was gone, and the sun beat down again. The wind swirled away, following after the great, flying monster. Caden couldn't move as he tried to understand what he had just seen. Were those things wings? They were huge! Far larger than Han's! And the thing at the front of the monster? It wasn't a head. It couldn't have been. Heads don't move around like a ball of snakes.

"Today is your judgment day!" Luca's voice. It rang out, loud and clear, with the authority of a god. "Today will be your end. Have you heard of the prince of Heralds, Tarek?" The sun blotted out again. Wind struck Caden as he cowered lower. Every human shrank back as each Demon stood forward, snarling and growling with glee.

Caden gritted his teeth as panic tightened his throat. *God, please!* His mind screamed. *Don't let them win! We win! Isn't that what You promised?* He felt mighty wings drawing closer, the swooping whoosh of a tempest blasting across him. *They can't win,* he told himself, his breath hissing through gritted teeth. *Nothing can put out the Akal Esh!* Caden shielded his eyes and forced himself to look up. No Demon, he didn't care how big and scary, was bigger and stronger than Yahweh. Nothing in the entire—

Caden's clenching teeth sank into his tongue. He didn't even notice when the blood filled his mouth. A monster was descending upon them. It had two wings, shaped like a bat's, stretching the length of the Wailing Wall. A serpentine tail lashed behind it as two reptilian clawed legs landed, thudding the ground and knocking onlookers over. A second pair of clawed front legs landed next, forcing everyone to their knees. The monster's skin was rough and irregular, like a crocodile. Every inch of it was a deep, bloody red.

At the forefront, and writhing nonstop, was its heads. Seven coiling, lashing, twisting necks supported seven reptilian heads, each gaping with fanged jaws. Forked tongues flicked from the eager mouths as the seven pairs of eyes hardly blinked, each orb solid black. Each head had one curved horn jutting from the middle of their forehead. The three heads at the center had two, one just over each eye.

As it landed, the monster's bat wings, casting all in deep shadows, tucked in at its sides. Saliva streamed from the seven mouths and pooled beneath the clawed feet. Caden could do nothing but kneel, shoulders hunched, and hands pulled in against his body. He sucked in one breath after another, unable to move or think as he stared at the monstrosity. It was like a hydra or dragon. But those things weren't real! None of this was real!

*"This is very real, Caden,"* Doeg whispered, a hushed voice amid the screams and chaos. *"As real as Yohanan and Elijah's blood that will bathe this very ground."*

*No*, Caden thought, finally blinking. He could feel his entire body shaking. *Nothing can put out God's Consuming Fire!* The several heads coiled and twisted, four facing Elijah while three eyed Yohanan.

*"What puts out fire, Caden?"* Caden didn't answer as his breath came in rapid bursts. *"Caden?"* Caden doubled over,

his lips drawn back in a near-pained snarl. His teeth were reddened by his own blood.

Without warning, the red dragon's seven heads lunged forward as each mouth gaped. The stream of saliva became a solid column of projected water. The flood surged from the mouths, crashing against the ground and slamming into Elijah and Yohanan. In an instant, they were lost under the raging current.

## SIX
# FLOODWATERS

WITHOUT THINKING, Caden gulped, filling his lungs, and held it as the water gushed from the red dragon. He was trapped, the only escape he could see was blocked by the red dragon and its floodwaters. The foaming current crashed against the far wall and swirled toward Caden. He scrambled back, unable to fully rise before the waters struck against him, the current dragging him back. Caden fell, the flood's coldness cutting through his armored uniform. He could only hear his internal screaming as panic seized his throat. He was trapped. Again. The enemy surrounding him. Again. With dangerous waters threatening his very life. Again.

*I can't!* His mind screamed. *I barely survived it last time!* He thrashed to keep his head above the waters as he sat up, sputtering. Spots dotted the perimeter of his vision. His head felt light and weak. *Breathe!*

Caden inhaled in a sudden gulp and panted, nearly hyperventilating as he blinked. He was backed against something hard and firm. The Wailing Wall. The water churned around him, grabbing his clothes and trying to drag him down. With a hissed curse, Caden forced himself to his feet, finding the flood reaching to his knees. No, his midcalf. His ankle? What was happening? He looked up to find the red dragon's assault had paused, and the waters simply dribbled from its several heads again.

A few bodies floated in the subsiding waters, some twisted unnaturally, supposedly from being dashed against the wall and ground. Two bodies surfaced, drawing up heads with coughs and gasps. A barked laugh exploded from Caden as he saw Elijah and Yohanan rise. Though soaked and Elijah's brow was split and streaming blood, both were alive. Still on either side of the courtyard, the two Witnesses turned and faced the red dragon. The dragon lifted its several heads, the black eyes staring without blinking as a low, clicking sound lifted from the seven throats.

From beyond the dragon, a voice shouted. "Behold! Tarek! Prince of Heralds!" Luca.

Caden cursed, hearing the cocky arrogance in the Antichrist's voice. *Not anymore!* He thought, bracing himself as the current continued to stream passed him. Staggering, Yohanan drew closer to Tarek, his eyes alive with fire as his chest heaved. Caden's heart quickened as his eyes darted between the dragon and the Witness. Yohanan removed his jacket, throwing it into the flooded courtyard, and sucked in a lungful of air. Even at a distance, Caden could see his mouth aglow with a hot and angry orange. He couldn't withhold a smile.

"Yohanan!" Caden frowned and turned to Elijah, who stood as firm and calm as he always did, ignoring the water dripping from him. The older Witness quietly shook his head. Caden's smile fell. "It is time." Caden's brow furrowed as he looked back to Yohanan. His brother-in-law's lips pulled back like a dog's snarl, the inner glow burning brighter. Without a word, Yohanan's shoulders slumped as he turned away, shutting his mouth.

"What?" Caden whispered, his heart beating faster. "What are you…fight!"

He stared wide-eyed as the Witnesses gave Tarek one final look before facing the civilians hiding behind the wall of Refiners. "King Yeshua is coming!" Elijah called, acting as though Tarek wasn't even there. "He is far greater than us, so much greater that we are not worthy to even be His slaves or carry His shoes. He will baptize you with His *Akal Esh*. King Yeshua is ready to separate His followers from those who follow the false king!"

"He will gather His people into His eternal rest!" Yohanan shouted, his voice echoing off the buildings. "But those who refuse Him will burn with a never-ending fire."

"Into the blazing furnace. There will be weeping and gnashing of teeth."

A cry lifted from the onlookers, it was deep and deafening, nearly blocking out the Witnesses' words. It was the cry of outrage. A cry for blood. Tarek's wings flexed as claws restlessly scraped the ground, splashing water with each movement. A head lowered, black tongue flicking as water started streaming from its mouth again.

Caden's stomach turned, seeing Elijah and Yohanan still weren't acknowledging Tarek. "Do something," he whispered. "Why aren't you frying him!"

"It's simple!" Yohanan yelled, crossing his arms and not moving an inch as Tarek's heads crept closer. "King Yeshua will respect whatever you decide: if you want Him in your life and to follow Him, you will spend eternity with Him in Heaven. Refuse Him, and He will give you what you want; life without Him. But a life absent of Yahweh is pure Hell. Follow King Yeshua! Choose life—"

A reptilian head surged forward, its jaws clamped around Yohanan's shoulder and arm. Caden flinched back, breath catching in his throat. Yohanan's words cut short as he grabbed the head's muzzle. He didn't make a sound as his feet lifted off the ground. Dangled by an arm, Yohanan clawed at the head's face as his legs kicked. Blood streamed down his arm and side, discoloring the swirling water beneath him.

Yohanan threw back his head and screamed. It wasn't a cry of pain or terror. It was one of rage, demanding justice. Embers shot from his mouth, quickening Caden's heart, for he knew nobody, Demon or human, could survive the *Akal Esh*. Still shouting his rageful cry, Yohanan shut his mouth, gritting his teeth, and snuffing out the rising inferno. Caden gasped, shaking his head. "No!"

A second dragon-head drew closer, coiling like a snake. With unblinking eyes, the dragon-head sank its fangs into Yohanan's thigh. Yohanan's body writhed as his cry shrilled to agony. Caden stumbled back, his legs too weak to hold him. He slammed against the Wailing Wall and stared, unable to look away.

"Turn!" Who was that? "There is still time!" Elijah still hadn't moved! The firm-faced Israeli stood with feet planted and arms crossed, squarely facing Luca and his loyal allies. "Any who follows this Antichrist," Another outraged cry lifted, "or receives his mark, the NIIC, or bows to his ways will drink of Yahweh's unrestrained anger."

Yohanan's scream hushed as he gasped for air, only to release another screech as the dragon-heads kept lifting him into the air. A third dragon-head slithered to him and plunged its single horn into his middle. Yohanan's cry gulped to a gurgled moan as blood dribbled from his lips. Caden gasped, watching his brother's blood turn the dragon a deeper hue of red.

"The Antichrist's allies will be tormented with fire and brimstone!" Elijah shouted above the chaos of Yohanan's butchery. "Whose smoke will never cease to rise. There will be no rest, day or night, for the allies of the King's United Society. Please! We want to save you! Only you can choose!"

With a loud pop and juicy crack, a dragon-head ripped away Yohanan's leg. Caden slid to his knees, hardly breathing. Yohanan's body lurched, but he made no sound. He limply hung in the head's jaws, the second head's horn still digging into his middle. With a lurch, the horn emerged from Yohanan's back.

"Choose this day whom you will serve!" Elijah cried. Though he didn't move, his eyes tracked the four dragon-heads slithering toward him. "As for me and my house..."

The dragon-heads slaying Yohanan threw him against the Wailing Wall. Caden could literally hear his bones shattering on impact before he splashed onto the court-yard. Their fangs sank in again as they ripped and tore. The water around them rippled and foamed while turning a deep red.

"We will serve King Yeshua!" Elijah cried, the dragon-heads surrounding him. "Wherever He leads!" His face was red with rage as his voice rose with defiance. "We win!" Elijah's eyes fell on Caden. Tears welled in Caden's eyes as the dragon lowered it's heads, readying to strike. He raised a hand, his lips parting as he tried to breathe. Elijah sucked in a breath and lifted his chin. "I choose King Yeshua!"

Two horns jutted from his chest. Elijah's back arched as his eyes bulged from his head. The dragon-head impaling him gave a low, clicking growl. Steadily, the head lifted Elijah into the air. Stuck to the it's forehead, Elijah's body shook as his eyes rolled back in his head. Blood dripped from his lips and down his beard. Caden gaped as he watched his Abba, tears rolling down his cheeks. Another head bit into Elijah's arm as a third his hip and leg. Each were making that deep, clicking growl, and Caden slowly realized they were chuckling.

Elijah gave a sputtering cough, splattering blood, as forced concentration overtook his face. He looked into the sky and took a sudden, violent breath. "Come, Lord Yeshua, come!" Caden slumped down on all fours, his strength completely gone. The startled onlookers gasped and muttered. Elijah's chest heaved, and he closed his eyes.

Caden shook his head. *Abba!*

The dragon-heads whiplashed back and forth, like dogs playing with a rag doll. Elijah ripped apart, his limbs popping off with ease and innards uncoiling before his enemies. His blood showered like a demonic rain. Caden's mouth opened as he tried to scream but couldn't. He just knelt there, staring, gasping, as the heads gnawed and tore until shredded tissue remained. Each of the seven heads coiled back together, never ceasing in their slithering, twisting movement. Each mouth and head were redder than before as black tongues ran across reddened fangs.

The floods had subsided, leaving shallow puddles and water dripping off everything. Before the water had streamed away, it managed to scatter Yohanan and Elijah's remains across the entire courtyard. Bloody scraps of flesh, bits of clothing, a hand here, and a leg there littered the ground like trash. Two split torsos spilled their insides, creating bloody puddles. Caden's stomach turned as vomit rose in his throat. He stared down at the puddle he knelt in, watching the water drip from his still wet hair.

Drip.

Drip.

Drip.

Caden sucked in a breath and held it without thinking. He was trapped. Again. Abandoned. Again. Surrounded. Again. A coldness crept across him. It pricked his skin and made his hair stand on end. Caden shivered, realizing it was a literal cold, as though ice was pressed into his skin. He looked up and locked eyes with the unblinking stare of Tarek.

One dragon-head lowered level with Caden. It stared, forked tongue lashing as those haunting black eyes stared on. Caden kept holding his breath, and his eyes widened in pure panic. His chin trembled, and he knew, deep in his soul, Tarek knew who he was. Caden's body shook as he started to curl himself into a ball. He stopped and stared back, a single thought slicing through the panic.

*I'm immortal,* he thought. *Until Yahweh says so.* He permitted himself to breathe, and he straightened, unwilling to turn away from Tarek. The dragon's head tilted to one side as another head lowered to stare at Caden. Ignoring the panicked beats of his heart and the ice on his flesh, Caden held firm and wouldn't turn away. *I'm immortal,* he thought. *I'm —*

*"So am I, worm."*

The voice within Caden's thoughts was unlike any Demon he'd heard before. It was several voices in one, as though a legion. It shouted within him, the sound reverberating in his chest and shaking his bones. Caden panted and reeled, unable to keep himself upright. He drew into a ball and shivered.

*"I am the prince,"* the voice continued, shaking Caden to his very core. *"This kingdom is mine."* Caden moaned and buried his face in his hands. He could feel the seething loathing this monster felt against him. It was a fierce, unrelenting force that demanded his blood. Every. Last. Drop. *"We will become drunk on the blood of the saints."* Caden whimpered, shaking his head. *"And all the earth will know nothing you possess shall vanquish me."*

It was a fight simply to breathe as Caden felt another pair of eyes chilling him to the bone. He crawled back but felt the Wall butting against him. No, that wasn't the wall. It was a leg. Caden gasped, seeing multicolored eyes wherever he looked. Full, feathery wings stretched around him like a shield as a sword, blazing and crackling with a white fire, imbedded the courtyard before him. The hilt was held by two strong hands as a second pair of wings stretched high into the air. Caden swallowed and stared, his heart beating loudly in his ears.

*You're late, Han,* he thought, squinting through the glory emanating from the Cherub's armor and eyes.

"No, Caden," Han's human face said as quietly as he could, which wasn't quiet at all. Caden flinched back, curling into a ball again. "You alone are my ward." With a hissed curse, Caden peeked through Han's feathers and saw Tarek. Three heads were glaring at them as their tongues licked the blood from their face.

*Nothing I possess will vanquish you,* Caden thought, repeating Tarek's claim. *That's totally right. But I'm not the only One fighting you.* The three dragon-heads opened their mouths, lips drawn back in fanged snarls, as water flowed from their throats. Caden's heart quickened as he held his breath without thinking.

Han's wings drew closer together as his fingers adjusted along the sword's hilt. His lion face snarled as the eagle screeched. "Caden," Han said. "Do not speak to this one." Caden drew back, and even with Han's glory warming him and his flaming sword crackling in his ears, he knew how pathetically weak he was. "No one can see us," Han said. "You are safe."

Caden drew in his arms and lowered his head, his hands becoming fists as his teeth clenched. The courtyard smelled of a swamp and raw meat. The puddle he knelt in had turned a diluted red. Out of the corner of his eye, Caden could see a severed hand. He shook his head, the tears of fury and grief dripping into the puddle. Moaning through gritted teeth, Caden's eyes squeezed shut. Without a word, he lurched forward and screamed.

Tarek's wings flexed as it turned, kicking up the wind and splashing through the few puddles. The Temple Mount's flood had washed away, now leaving puddles between the carnage. Even across the courtyard, Caden could hear everyone talking at once, the several languages buzzing with excitement.

Caden shook his head, wanting to do what Yohanan and Elijah should've done. He needed a bat. Somewhere in the back of his brain, he knew an M16 would be far more efficient, but he knew bats. He knew how they swung. He knew how they cracked against baseballs. Against Puppet heads.

*When will the wicked be punished?* Caden thought, murderous rage tightening his chest. He stayed on the ground for what felt like a long time. Han silently stood over him, standing guard, and shielding him from the eyes of the world.

In time, Han shifted, the oxen-head flicking its ears as the human glanced at Caden. "Arise, Caden. I am to draw back. I will shield you, yet they can see you now."

Caden didn't respond as he heard Han step away. The glowing heat of the *Akal Esh* stopped warming Caden's face, and he suddenly felt very alone. A hand grabbed his shoulder. Without thinking, he seized it, sweeping his leg, and knocking the person to the ground. He ignored their shouting, and it took him until his hands were around their throat to recognize Moshe. He blinked the red vision from his eyes and sat back as Moshe scrambled away, cursing.

"I'm your ally!" Moshe shouted. "What's wrong with you?"

Caden didn't answer as he turned away. He flinched; everywhere he looked, he saw his brother and Abba's remains. He squeezed his eyes shut. *What do you mean what's wrong with me? How can you be alright after seeing that?*

Moshe was talking again. Caden didn't really hear him. Something about getting back to Luca? Caden felt himself standing, but his legs wobbled. He leaned on Moshe as the two walked across the battleground and joined the others hiding behind Refiners, Giants, and Leovirs. The few women hid behind their men, the ambassador's bodyguards all had guns at the ready, and a few of the Sentinels lowered their own weapons. Everyone was talking at once. Only Luca seemed at ease.

Caden forced himself to suck in a breath, feeling his head getting fuzzy. His hands became fists, and a muscle in his jaw flexed. *That monster should've been able to kill them,* Caden thought, his eyes narrowing. He hissed a curse. *The Akal Esh isn't just normal, physical fire. It's Spiritual fire too! You can't put out Spiritual fire with physical things!*

"That was Spiritual water." Doeg's whispered words silenced Caden's thoughts.

*Then,* his thoughts stammered. *Then that's still not enough to stop God!*

"That isn't what I saw."

*You cannot conquer us!*

"Caden." A coldness shot through him. "The slaughtering has just begun."

Caden's trembling lips parted as he and Moshe found a spot in the crowd. "No," he whispered, the single word lost in the noise about him. *You can't do anything without God's permission!* Doeg didn't answer, and Caden's stomach painfully twisted like ringing out a wet rag.

"God has sent this suffering."

*Misquoted Scripture is a lie!*

"He will keep you, and all those you love, from life."

*No, He —*

"*And Ellie. And Asher. And your darling wife, Dasha. And, finally, you.*"

Caden put his hands over his ears, as though that would block out Doeg's words. *Yahweh, please. I'm begging You!*

"*He has sent this.*" The anger tightening Caden's chest made it hard to breathe. "You know I speak the truth." Doeg's hot breath brushed the back of Caden's neck. He didn't even bother moving away. What was the point? "*Good,*" Doeg said in his mind once again. "*You're finally seeing the truth as it is.*" Caden dragged in one breath after another. He glanced around at the restless crowd.

Turning to face them, and slowly drawing closer, was Tarek. Around it swarmed Demons, each looking so pathetic and small beside it. At the forefront, calmly standing with a pleasant smile on his face, was Luca. His chest puffed with pride as he held his head high. Caden's nostrils flared, fighting the urge to race forward, seize a gun from a bodyguard, and gun the false king down. *I can't let more of God's people die,* he thought, his heart quickening. *Even at the expense of my own life.*

A dark shadow crossed Caden's eyes as he looked up, his gaze darting between the several non-humans guarding Luca. *My life is worth losing. I must save us. I can't stand idle, even if God has permitted this destruction, I cannot let it be! Even at the expense of my own existence, only a spineless coward would simply be a witness. I must act. Even if it is against the will of God, I have to.*

Caden blinked, fighting through the rage and savagery clouding his mind. *I follow God's will,* he thought slowly. *Not mine. I am His slave. I do as He says. Doeg, why are you constantly trying to get me killed? Stop messing with my thoughts.* Distantly, he heard an inhuman laugh. Cringing, Caden couldn't stand listening to his internal screaming and Doeg's constant lies. He gritted his teeth and looked around, determined to focus on his surroundings.

The crowd was buzzing with excitement. They kept pointing and talking. Even though the Witnesses were obviously dead, the people held back, their faces pinched nervously as their words hissed.

"Ladies and gentlemen," Luca called, quieting them. "Please be at peace. I assure you, you no longer need to fear these fanatics." The crowd buzzed, some shaking their heads, and most refused to put their guns away. "Look with your own eyes, allies!" Luca swept his arm toward the bloody piles. "Their lies have ended, and fires will no longer reach us! We are safe."

*You're wrong,* Caden thought, shaking his head. *There's nothing you can do that can put out the Akal Esh!*

*"And yet,"* Doeg whispered in his mind. *"The facts confirm the contrary."* Caden shook his head again as women stepped out from behind their men, and the men slowly put away their guns.

"Our time of being falsely accused has ended," Luca continued, a smile brightening his eyes. "These men's lies will finally be silenced." The crowd tensed with energy, their voices lifting as one with raised fists. "Yohanan Nuri and Elijah Mizrahi have stood before the eyes of the world, night and day, to accuse the allies of the New Kingdom! Now, they are hurled down to their knees, defeated." The masses shouted again, louder still. Caden rigidly stood, each one of Luca's words like a blow to his guts as Tarek's massive form drew nearer.

"They were a serpent among us, shrewd and cunning, but we crushed them under our foot! Good always conquers evil! There is no hiding from us! We are more than victors! We will wash clean the land of its filth. We have water, a *new* water, a *living* water, that cleanses both the body and the Spirit. The water I have to offer will become in my allies a fountain, springing up to everlasting life."

Caden's nostrils flared; he felt like ice had entered his veins. *Is he quoting Scripture again? But inserting his own truth instead of God's.* He swallowed the hard lump in his throat. *Come back, King Yeshua. Please, come soon.*

Hugh, who had been standing directly to Luca's left, his fingers steepled and an attentive grin on his face, raised a hand as the other pressed onto his chest. "Thanks be to the king, our messiah, who has given us victory. He has gone before us and fought against our enemies, giving us triumph!" Someone shouted their agreement as others stepped closer. Luca grinned softly, the smile kind and humble as he nodded to them. "With our king, our messiah, we will conquer, he will trample down our enemies. With mere men, all these things are impossible. But *this*! This is no man. Our king is a god!"

Caden faced Hugh, eyes wide as the people pressed around him. He stumbled, and Moshe helped him stay upright. Many shouted their own praise, thanking Luca for conquering the fanatics and swearing their loyalty. A few bowed low at the waist, their eyes closed in reverence.

"And the Herald's prince, Tarek!" Luca called, turning to face the red dragon. The monster stopped a few paces away, the wings like a great canopy casting deep shadows as the seven bloodied heads coiled like vipers. "He is our prince as well, who has risen up, attacked our enemies, overpowered them, and slaughtered them! He is worthy to be praised!" Caden fought to breathe as the most powerful people in the modern world turned to the red dragon and bowed. Several called out their praises and thanks, and some started offering it gifts. Tarek stared down with unblinking eyes, each head giving its low, clicking sound of pleasure.

*This has to be stopped,* Caden thought. His gaze fixed on

Luca, and he blinked, thinking through the noise around him and his unending internal screaming. *I can't kill a Demon,* he thought, seeing Tarek's tail flex as its heads lifted high. *But I can kill a man.* A muscle in his jaw flexed as Luca calmly smiled and flies gathered over Elijah and Yohanan's remains.

## SEVEN
# BATTER UP

CADEN FELT like he was in a dream. A very loud, very chaotic dream. People were everywhere as music filled his ears. The smell of food mixed with smoke, of tobacco or something else, Caden had no idea, as glasses of alcohol clinked and people laughed. Flashing lights, balloons, banners, streamers, and all sorts of festive decorations cluttered Luca's mansion as everyone, like *everyone*, was partying.

Caden walked past Moshe dancing with one of the French secretaries, Roberto waving his hands everywhere while talking with the Spanish, and Hugh explaining Heralds to the Indonesians. Even Rapham was there, quietly off in one corner, drinking and staring. People were doing more than just dancing, eating, and talking. Caden had only seen drugs in movies, but he was pretty sure about what was going on in one room. In another room, no one was talking or wearing clothes. Caden quickly left, rubbing his eyes and feeling like he needed a shower. He stumbled across several similar instances, shocked the leaders of the modern world were enjoying themselves so openly. It felt like the ancient world. What was that called? Pagans? Something like that.

Among it all, the Demons were having their own party. Caden stopped and stared, realizing it wasn't two separate parties; everyone was interacting together. A Shade approached some Arabs, who bowed low to it and widened their circle for it to join. Vipers leapt from shoulder to shoulder, each human they touched laughing and stroking them as though they were kittens, playing. Withers amused people by showing them their various skins. Fiends swirled around the younger crowd, covering them in darkness, and making them laugh. Caden's stomach twisted as hatred tightened his chest. These *things* shouldn't be permitted here, let alone welcomed. They were evil! Darkness! They were going to get everyone killed!

"No," a voice whispered close to his ear. "Just you, GJ."

Caden gave Doeg a sideways glance as a muscle in his jaw flexed. *Just ignore it, it has no power over you.*

"Do you know what a blood eagle is?" Caden's eyes narrowed as his skin crawled. "I've mentioned that before." Doeg's tail flicked restlessly, like a cat readying to pounce. "I will educate you. In due time." With a hissed curse, Caden kept walking through the festivities. He had to get out of there.

"Hey!" Caden turned, seeing Moshe walking up to him, grinning ear to ear. "Got you something."

He held out a box, and Caden stared at it, his brow furrowing. "What for?" He took it and opened it carefully. It was a pin of the American flag. At the flag's center was a small, golden lion with a crown on its head. Caden wanted to throw the gift across the room. There were enough Leovirs embodying the Sovereign Lion, did he now have to wear one?

Moshe shrugged. "It's just a good time. Everyone's giving each other gifts and stuff."

Caden frowned at his friend. *They think they've won.* A lump formed in his throat.

*"We have."*

*The war hasn't even started!*

"You should give a gift to our messiah at least," Moshe said.

Caden blinked, realizing slowly he was talking about Luca. "The messiah." Isn't that what they called Yeshua?

"I can't believe he's finally here!" Moshe laughed, making fists. "And in my lifetime too! Now, we can conquer our enemies! The terrorists don't stand a chance against us now! Who can fight against Yahweh's messiah and the prince?"

"Prince?"

"Prince Tarek."

Caden stared back down at the pin and locked eyes with the Sovereign Lion. *You will all bow before the real King.*

"Hey," Moshe whispered, stepping closer. "What's wrong, man?"

Caden straightened and tried to smile. It was a very weak smile. "Nothing, I—" He cut short, seeing the searching look in Moshe's eyes. The two stepped aside as partiers passed by, and Caden turned away. "That was just really bloody."

"I know!" Moshe's smile grew. "I'm so glad it was live-streamed to the entire New Kingdom! Everyone saw it. I mean everyone! I heard Ally Hugh say all of the Middle East, most of Europe, even some of Russia, Mexico, and even all the way to your Alaska saw it."

Caden couldn't bring himself to look at Moshe; he was sure his friend would see the fuming rage in his eyes. All he could do was nod and try not to remember Yohanan's screams. He really started howling when Tarek bit into his leg. And then that one stabbed his middle. He bled so much. Did Tarek eat his leg? Caden didn't remember seeing it lying in the courtyard.

He closed his eyes with a sudden gasp and tried to block out the memories. They haunted him. He knew he wasn't going to sleep that night. Or the next. Or ever again. He just kept seeing Elijah's shocked look as he was lifted into the air before getting ripped to shreds. Tarek was outside, Caden had seen it through the window. The cursed Demon hadn't cleaned their blood from its faces yet. Caden doubted it would.

"I," Caden stammered, realizing he was just standing there. "I didn't think of getting you a gift."

"That's fine," Moshe said, laying a hand on his shoulder. "Want some wine? You look pretty bad."

Caden scoffed and shuffled back. "I'll be fine." His voice was hollow. It was all he could do to not scream at Moshe, telling him he was on the wrong side, and that King Yeshua was coming to avenge. *Steady,* he told himself. *Yahweh's still put me here for a reason. He'll get me out of here.*

*"Or kill you."*

*Yeah, or kill me. That's His choice. And I fully give it to Him. If I am to die, I hope He wants me to take a few of the enemy with me.* Caden took in a breath as his eyes darted from one laughing face to another, seeing the nations of the world rejoicing and giving each other gifts. They all needed to die.

*"Your struggle is not against flesh and blood."* Caden looked down. *"What would your King think if He saw your vile, murderous heart?"*

*I want justice,* Caden thought, straightening his back. *This time, justice just so happens to involve killing.*

*"So says you, weak, foolish human boy."*

*So says King Yeshua. He'll come back. He'll kill them all.*

*Why am I even talking to you?* Caden blinked, realizing Moshe had been talking. "Hum?"

"You keep doing that." Moshe scowled at him. "Snap out of it." Caden made a fist, stepped forward to plant it into Moshe's guts, but turned with a growl and marched away. Moshe waved at him. "You're welcome for the gift!"

Caden didn't answer. He wanted to go to his room but was afraid to find people in there. No, what he really wanted was to be with Under Fire and other believers. People who didn't revel in such wickedness. People who didn't rejoice as unarmed men get ripped limb from limb. He wanted to be with —

A young woman walked past him. Her dark brown hair waved as she stepped, her slim body moved with silent poise. Caden's heart leapt as he stared. *Dasha.* He raced forward, taking her hand. She turned with a start, and he stared into her brown eyes and froze. "Sorry," he said, backing away. "I...I thought you were someone else."

She pulled away, said something crude, and Caden cursed himself as she left. *Dasha's not here. You can't be with her now. I hope she's alright and not dead. Not eaten by a monster or turned inside out.* His eyes closed tight, trying not to imagine her beautiful blue eyes widening as blood streamed from her mouth. *I've got to be with her. With everyone on my side. I need to get away from all this darkness!*

Caden's eyes widened suddenly, and he stared at a group eating dessert. A woman lay on the table, laughing and feeding one of the men. Yohanan had given Caden directions on where to find Under Fire. The bloodbath had distracted him from grabbing the little yellow piece of paper shoved in the Wailing Wall. *I've got to go back,* Caden thought, taking in a slow breath. *I've got to find it. I can't stay here anymore. You hear me, Yahweh? I will do whatever You say, but my vote is I'm done here. What do You say?*

"Ally Alex!" Internally, Caden cursed and screamed,

not wanting to answer the call. Putting on the best smile he could, Caden turned and dipped his head as he entered a large room where Luca stood waiting. The room was filled with people drinking and eating, and all were focused on a massive screen covering one great wall. It displayed the live stream of the Wailing Wall. Caden took one glance, seeing the few puddles between bloodied masses of tissue and innards. His internal screaming began, lifting higher and higher as he drew closer to Luca.

"My king," he said, desperate for focus as hatred clouded his vision.

"Alex," Luca answered, laying a hand on his shoulder. "I want to introduce you to someone." He motioned to the tall man standing beside him.

Brown hair, pale skin, and blue eyes, the man smiled. "Is this Anthony's boy?"

Caden blinked and lifted his chin. "Yes, ally, I sure am. It's nice to see another American."

"Alex," Luca said. "This is Ambassador Jack Baker."

"Pleasure, ambassador."

Jack smiled and motioned to Caden's uniform. "I'm pleased to see more of our boys are becoming Refiners under the Sovereign Lion's Watch."

Caden bit back a foul remark and made himself nod. "Yes, sir. It is an honor."

"Oh, we agree. Because of your example, more and more of our boys are becoming Refiners. It is the beginning of a new age! A new time of peace and celebration, obviously!" He swept his hand across the party and laughed. "My king," Jack said, turning to Luca. "I regret to say our commander will join us in a few weeks."

Luca frowned. "Problems?"

"Oh, no, no. A few more terrorist cells were uncovered. He is the man to deal with them and stomp them out." Caden's jaw clenched as the men grinned.

"Very good," Luca said. "I trust the labor camps in New York and LA are operational?"

"Very, my king. And they are far more efficient and economical than mass executions."

*God, help me not go postal,* Caden thought, feeling his heart race.

"But your commander will come?" Luca asked.

"Yes, my king. And he will join your Refiners in flushing out the terrorists. He will be a great asset to you."

Luca grinned and clapped him on the back. "I have no doubt. For now, we can rejoice! I know many Americans love baseball. Ally Alex does. What of you, Ambassador Jack?"

"Oh, I know my men would enjoy a game. Reminding us of before the World's Crash. It would be a pleasant surprise and welcome."

"It's settled." Luca turned to Caden and motioned to Jack. "I don't even need to ask your opinion, Ally Alex. Baseball is in your blood."

Caden nodded and stepped forward. "Just tell me when and where, my king. I haven't played in ages!" *How can I play when my brother and Abba are still unburied?*

"Wonderful!" Luca cried. "Let us keep uniting, even in sport. Today has been a great victory for the New Kingdom!" Caden felt himself smile and nod, but it was such a distant, detached movement. He was sick with rage.

The live feed of the Wailing Wall flickered and shifted to a studio. Everyone cheered, and Caden turned, recognized *The King's Modern Times.* Hugh walked onto the studio's stage and sat as a very cheery voice-over announced, "presenting *Hark the Heralds!* Giving you practical examples of how to interact with your own personal Herald!" Caden's eyes darkened as a shiver shot through him.

"Oh, I love this show," Jack said. "The whole family

gets together and watches it. Very insightful! We had no idea who the Heralds were until Ally Hugh showed us. His insight and wisdom into the unseen places is so... inspiring! He's like a modern prophet."

Luca nodded. "A prophet. I like that. I have known Ally Hugh for several years, and he has always known the mysterious side of life that most didn't understand. We wanted to shed light on the beauty of the Heralds and their loyalty to our United Society."

*Lies,* Caden thought.

"Oh, yes, yes. In fact, just before leaving DC, we permitted Heralds into the White House." Caden stiffened with a cold thrill.

"You did? That's wonderful!"

"Things are running far more smoothly now."

"Yes! That is the benefit of the Heralds. They are our helpers, our advocates, and our guides. I am honored Prince Tarek chose this time to reveal himself to us."

Jack nodded eagerly. "I'm honored you invited us to come, your majesty. I would've missed the memorable defeat of our enemies. Would've regretted it for the rest of my life!"

From across the room, three Fiends drifted about in a black cloud. Beneath them walked a thin, quiet man with a calm smile. The room lifted with a sudden cheer as Hugh entered. He humbly nodded and waved as he walked to Luca. "Messiah," Hugh said with a bow.

Luca leaned closer to him and smiled. "Ambassador Jack just called you a prophet."

"Oh," Hugh swatted a hand and pushed up his glasses. "Nonsense. I see the world through different eyes, that is all. I cannot keep such secrets to myself."

Jack bowed and shook his head. "I'm honored to meet you, Ally Hugh."

"And you."

"How many Zones are watching with us today?"

"The most recent count was eighty-seven, nearly three-quarters of the earth's population."

Luca clapped his hands and rubbed them together. "I'm so proud of you. Prophet."

"Oh, please," Hugh muttered, but Caden could tell he liked it. "Hello, Ally Alex."

Caden nodded to Hugh and tried not to think of punching him in the throat. He quickly put his hands behind his back and stared at the screen as the show's music died down and the camera zoomed in on Hugh's face. Caden felt like a coiled spring, ready to pounce, but unable to release the tension. Everyone quieted as the episode began.

"Good evening," Hugh's large head said on the screen. "Welcome to the fifth episode of *Hark the Heralds*." The viewers cheered, and Hugh smiled. "This is an episodic discovery of the blessed Heralds, their loyalty to the allies of the New Kingdom, and how to interact with them. Today, we will define and discuss how to become a Zealot." Caden's eyes narrowed as his hair stood on end; that sounded familiar. Most of the humans, Giants, and Leovirs present leaned forward as the Demons settled into their seats, some between humans or even on their laps.

"A Zealot," Hugh continued. "Is the highest, most prestige sign of loyalty a mortal can ever offer to a Herald. Only a few have mastered this symbiosis, yet the mystery is over. The revelation is here. We all can taste and see the Heralds are good." Caden's head tilted to one side as he watched the Demons stirring. They restlessly sat, the Shades' tails swishing and Vipers' tongues flicking. Without knowing what a Zealot was, Caden already knew he'd despise it.

"A Zealot is when a mortal, no matter who they are or their past, for the Heralds have no favorites, kneel before

Heralds. They offer themselves up as a living sacrifice, holy and pleasing to the Heralds. By doing so, the Heralds will fill them, like water fills a vase." Caden's eyes widened as all breath caught in his throat. "They will receive power when the Heralds come upon them. They will dream prophetic dreams, walk in visions, be able to scale a wall, and crush their foes under their feet." Caden's mouth opened slowly, a new wave of panic quickening his heart. "Their strength will be unmatched, they will become the new superhumans, and nothing, no darkness, no terrorist, and no god, can stand in our way."

The viewers cheered, drowning out Hugh's final words, as some leapt up, clapping and dancing. Caden didn't move as realization struck his chest. *This can't be happening,* he thought numbly. *Hugh can't really be teaching everyone how to become Puppets?* Caden swallowed the hard lump in his throat and looked down, his heart hammering in his ears. *First Sentinels, then Giants and Refiners. Freaks hunt us, and now a creepy dragon thing, but this! Puppets! They'll come for us too. They'll rip us apart, just like Tarek did to Elijah.* Caden couldn't feel his hands as he blinked, trying to stay focused. *Why are You letting this happen, Yahweh? We can't fight this. There's too much against us!*

"*God sent this suffering.*"

*Shut up!*

"It is very simple to become a Zealot," Hugh continued from the show. "First, and this step is obvious, you must be an ally to the king, our messiah." Another cheer lifted as people turned to Luca, voicing their praise and homage. "Second, you must—" The screen glitched, flickering, then returned to Hugh in the studio. Luca frowned as Hugh crossed his arms. The Demons all stiffened, alert and uneasy. "—followed by a laying down of self," Hugh on the screen continued. He flickered again, and the studio was replaced by a dark room with two simple chairs seated at its center. The viewers muttered amongst themselves, and everyone looked confused.

"Hugh," Luca muttered.

Hugh shook his head. "No, your majesty. This is not part of the program."

As they watched, two men walked onto the screen and sat. One was Yohanan, and the other was Elijah. A shock of excited adrenaline ran through Caden as the room erupted with curses, shouting, and, a few, drawing weapons. *They uploaded their own episode!* Caden thought, thinking of those loyal to Under Fire who worked at *The King's Modern Times*.

"Hello, everyone," Elijah said. "You all know us. I am Elijah."

"And I'm Yohanan."

"If you're watching this, we've recently been killed."

"Slaughtered, actually." Yohanan scowled as he shifted in his seat. "Ripped apart. Gutted. And you can still see it, can't you? We're just left out like a big mess for everyone to look at." Gasps rippled through the room. Caden glanced at Luca and Hugh. Their faces were pale, and mouths dropped open. Luca's mouth closed, and his jaw flexed. His eyes darted to Rapham across the room. The Refiner stiffened and swiftly left.

Caden's fierce excitement was snuffed out, knowing the violent man would find Caden's contact. *He'll be dead within the hour. Maybe me too.* With a gruff sniff, Caden lifted his chin and held firm.

"You're celebrating," Elijah continued. "And the nations are giving one another gifts." The room's commotion lifted as fear distorted many faces.

"How do we know we've been mutilated?" Yohanan asked.

"Because," Elijah said. "The holy Scriptures foretold of

our deaths thousands of years ago. Just as it told of Yeshua's coming and death long before it took place."

"He's the true Messiah, by the way," Yohanan added. "Not that stupid Italian. Luca Battistelli is just a man. He can bleed. He *will* bleed."

Elijah nodded. "More accurately, he will burn." Out of the corner of his eye, Caden saw Luca's lips pull back into a wolfish smile. "And so will you, if you don't follow King Yeshua."

"He's coming," Yohanan said. "How many times do we have to tell you?"

"It's not complicated to follow Yeshua," Elijah said. "Believe in His name. Believe He's saved you from death and the punishment of Hell by dying on the cross, *and* He came back to life by Yahweh's power. Believe He sees you and loves you, regardless of who you are. Also, verbally declare King Yeshua as Lord."

Hugh shifted restlessly as he shook his head. "How is this still aired?"

"And believe He will return," Yohanan said. "With warhorses, justice, and Consuming Fire that the waters of this world, or the Heralds, cannot quench." Jack cursed as Luca shook his head.

"Shut this down," Luca hissed through gritted teeth.

"The Heralds are Demons, by the way," Yohanan said. "They want to possess you. That's what Puppets are. You're just puppets to them. Tools. Toys. Just disposable. Don't listen to that false teacher, Hugh Wiltshire. King Yeshua will deal with him too. Would rather be ripped to shreds than face whatever Hugh's getting." A cup was hurled at the screen as the viewers leapt up, shouting and shaking fists at the screen. Caden shot the English man a quick glance. His face was red as he rigidly stood, his lips a thin line.

"Believe in King Yeshua," Elijah said. "And you will be saved."

"That's it."

"Not complicated."

"No strings attached."

"And you will find life and have it to the full."

"But, um," Yohanan paused and glanced at his wrist. "Times running out. Seriously. Choose today who you'll serve—"

The screen flickered again, and Elijah and Yohanan gave way to an Israeli standing in *The King's Modern Times*. The camera struggled to focus, and there was screaming in the background. "I'm sorry, allies," the man said. "The terrorists' propaganda has been found and destroyed. As well as their accomplices." In the background, there was a solid thud, and the screaming abruptly ended.

Caden's stomach turned; he wouldn't be surprised if it was the young man he'd handed the codes to. *He was with them and gave them rest. Your will be done.*

*"That will be your darling sister next."*

Caden's nostrils flared as his hands fisted. The man on the screen shifted as he nervously glanced off-screen. "Um, back to the show. Thank you. Long live the king!" The screen flickered again, and *Hark the Heralds* started over from the beginning.

With a string of curses, Jack turned to Luca. "Let me send my Refiners over there. We'll burn the place down!"

"Thank you, but no," Luca said, his voice calm and even.

Caden stared at him, seeing his face was still pale as though he'd seen a ghost. *Well, he just did*, he thought with dark amusement.

"My people will handle it." Caden watched as Luca eyed the anxious people, each one near panic. Luca took in a breath and ran his fingers through his hair. Flashing a wide smile, Luca stepped forward and spread his arms. "And they think that will frighten us!" The room quieted, and Luca laughed. "Those fanatics are dead. Dead! We watched it with our own eyes this morning! Let the celebrations continue! We won't let them control us or have the final word. Come! The Americans are going to teach us baseball. Let's all go outside and play ball!"

*That seriously is not going to work,* Caden thought, but stared in shock as smiles returned, people grabbed their glasses and made their way outside.

Luca motioned to Caden. "Come, Alex! I know you've been wanting this for a long time."

*I want you dead,* Caden thought as he made himself smile and follow.

———

"THAT WAS NOT A FAIR GAME," Moshe grumbled as he and Caden picked up the plates. Both were red-faced and sweaty, with grass stains on their clothes. They also couldn't stop smiling. "Stop sulking," Caden said with a nudge. "It's not my fault you guys lost."

"Yes, it is! No one hits like you!"

"Bats."

"Shut up." Caden chuckled as he tucked the plates under his arm and headed back across the field. "How much baseball have you played?"

Caden shrugged. "Oh...a few games here or there."

"You just hit the ball far."

"That's the point."

"Breaking the king's windows is the point too?"

Caden couldn't hold back a dark smile and glanced at the distant side of Luca's luxurious house. Two dark holes smashed through two separate windows. Servants quickly attended to them. "Yep," Caden sighed. "That's what you get for underestimating me." Moshe muttered some inappropriate Hebrew slang, and Caden pretended not to understand him. "Hum?"

"That's one good thing about being your friend. I can insult you without you knowing."

"Great."

"You know, if you took all that power into your left hook, you could really do some damage."

"We should spar again."

"Any chance to beat a foreigner is a good day to me." Caden glared at him, and Moshe laughed. "I kid! I kid!" Caden shoved him away, and the two kept walking.

It had been the perfect day for a game. The sun was shining, a soft breeze brushed the grass just so, and the people were athletic and competitive. A year ago, Caden would've thought he had died and went to Heaven. Not now. Any joy Caden showed was so forced, he hated himself. He shouldn't be playing with his Abba and brother-in-law's killers. He should be destroying them right back.

"Where's everybody?" Moshe asked as they passed a hot tub and neared Luca's house. Before them was a comfortable porch with several chairs and tables placed beneath umbrellas. Caden glanced around, seeing the crowd of onlookers, and both teams weren't there.

"Everyone went inside to wash up or get more food," Luca called from where he sat, sipping tea beside a table of bats and balls.

"That's a good idea," Moshe said, setting down the plates. "May I, your majesty?" Luca nodded, and Moshe bowed before walking to the door.

Caden started walking after him but stopped. "Where are all the Sentinels and Giants?"

Luca sipped his tea and leaned back with a relaxed sigh. "The watch is changing," he said. "They'll come back any moment now." Caden nodded slowly, the wheels of his mind turning. "Now that we're alone, Alex, I have to ask you," Luca said. Caden turned back to him and grabbed a bat. "You were very skeptical of my unconditional love and readiness to fight for my allies. What do you think now, in light of this morning?" Caden held the bat with two hands along the grip. He took a stance and swung. He could hear the bat cutting through the air with force. Luca's brows rose, and he smiled. "I see now why you like baseball."

Caden took in a slow breath. His heart had started racing. "May I be honest with you, your majesty?"

Luca's smile faded as he straightened. "I always want honesty."

Caden nodded as he stepped closer. "I adore my King." Luca's smile returned as he leaned back. "And I will follow Him wherever He leads." Caden swung the bat again, slicing through the air. "I will be loyal to Him, whatever hell He lets me survive." Luca's brows rose as he sipped more tea. Caden moved closer, his heart beating harder and harder. "I will die for my King." He tightened his grip on the bat, standing a pace away from Luca. "I will kill for my King."

Luca straightened as he saw the intense sincerity in Caden's gaze. He nodded once, as though accepting Caden's loyalty. That did it for him. A muscle in Caden's jaw flexed as he took a stance. "I will always serve King Yeshua."

Luca's eyes widened as his neck muscles tensed. Without hesitating, Caden swung the bat. It whizzed through the air and struck true. Luca collapsed to the ground, knocking the chair over. It took Caden a moment to realize the bat hadn't stopped moving as he swung it again and again. It was another moment, and Caden noticed Luca wasn't moving anymore. Stepping back, chest heaving with each gasp, Caden stared down at the false king. He blinked sweat from his eyes and ran a hand over his face. No, that wasn't sweat; his fingers came back bloody. Caden frowned and looked down. He was splattered head to toe in blood.

With a gruff sniff, Caden stared down at Luca. His cracked head sent a widening pool of blood across the porch. His body twitched a little. Caden lifted his chin as he spun the bat in his hands. "Yep," he muttered with a sigh. "I really do like baseball."

# EIGHT
## SHUT YOUR MOUTH

CADEN'S HANDS WERE SHAKING. So were his legs, and that was a problem. It was hard to sprint with shaky legs. He panted, rounding the mansion's side, and darted through the manicured gardens, ignoring the gardeners and startled birds. He blinked the water that streamed from his hair. Soaked pants made running harder too.

"You're not running fast enough." Out of the corner of his eye, Caden saw a huge dog running on all fours, red tongue trailing saliva behind as its long, white tail lashed. He shook his head and focused, choosing to ignore Doeg. "They'll find you. You anticipate this, foolish human. But that's what you desire, isn't it? You are done being a spy for your supposed King."

*No, I —*

"You long for punishment?"

*What?*

"You know you deserve nothing less than Grant shattering your will to live."

*No!*

"With every fracture —"

*Doeg!*

"And every break."

Caden gritted his teeth until it hurt. He went to the front of Luca's house and nearly collapsed on the driveway, wrapping around a fountain and foliage. Coughing, Caden straightened and glanced at the Sentinels on guard.

"Your lies will fail you," Doeg muttered.

"Hey," Caden said breathlessly, giving them a weak wave, and strolled to the edge of the driveway. He grabbed his shirt and squeezed, leaving a puddle at his feet. "Fell in the hot tub," he said and shrugged. The Sentinels didn't answer as they continued their vigil. Caden coughed again and forced himself to walk around. But not pace. Pacing would look like he was impatient. He had to look calm. Fine. Everything was just fine. Nothing wrong was going on, and blood definitely hadn't drenched him a second ago.

Doeg shook its furry head with a scoff. "Crushed skulls do pop like a grape, don't they?"

Caden closed his eyes with a curse. *How many times did I swing?* He wondered and frowned. He had no idea. It was like that little moment in time was a glitch in the system.

"Seven," Doeg said. "Perhaps eight."

Caden put his hands in his soggy pockets and turned away from the snickering Demon. All Caden remembered was swinging, then dropping the bat, gasping at the mess. Luckily, the hot tub had been there. He had dived in, scrubbing and washing the best he could. When he got out, the water looked like someone dumped cherry Kool-Aid into it. While scanning the windows and grounds for any witnesses, and seeing none, he remembered his smartphone. He was shocked when it still worked and dialed the first number he could think of. Roberto.

"Hey!" Caden had said as he started for the front of the mansion. "Yeah, hi, um...the king needs my help, and you need to drive. He wants me to check on something.

Yeah. I know, but I didn't ask questions. Right. Ok, meet you out front." A taxi would've been better, but who takes a taxi from the king's mansion?

Caden sniffed as he wiped water from his brow again and waited for Roberto. His mind was racing, the shaking of his hands was creeping up into his arms. *If he doesn't get here soon, I'm gonna kill him.*

Doeg beamed. Caden felt his stomach flop. As he stood, waterdrops were falling from his elbow and dropping to the pavement. They formed a little puddle and, as they fell, made a small, splashing, dripping sound. Caden shivered as he gulped in a breath without thinking. With a curse, Caden scrubbed his face and stepped away from the puddle.

A car pulled up. Roberto started to say something, but Caden already jumped in. "The Old City," Caden said, slamming the door shut. "The sooner, the better too."

"What's all the hurry?"

"Drive while I answer."

Roberto studied Caden from the rearview mirror. "You're wet."

"And you're not driving." Roberto's brows rose, and the car slowly rolled from the parking lot. "Fell in the hot tub," Caden said. "The king wants me to check out the Wailing Wall. Roll down the windows. I'll mostly dry off by the time we get there in this heat." Roberto raised a finger, about to speak. "This is from the king, Roberto! I'm just saying what he wants. You're not questioning me, but him. Wanna do that?" Roberto's finger fell, and he grumbled something in Italian, his fingers drumming along the steering wheel. The windows rolled down. Caden kept his face from the windows as the hot hair blew against him. He closed his eyes and sat very still. All he could do was wait. And pray. That was a good thing to do too.

Oh, Caden sure hoped God was okay with what he

just did. He wasn't sure. Killing sinners wasn't quite part of the Great Commission though. Caden glanced down at his hands. They were white-knuckled fists as his adrenaline kept quickening his heart. The bat had felt so good in his hands. The way it cut through the air and wacked Luca's head was the justice Caden had craved. Caden wiped his nose, trying to hide the smile that played at the corners of his mouth. His Abba and brother-in-law were avenged, as well as countless others. A fierce joy heated Caden's blood as he longed for the feel of the bat again.

"Murderer."

Caden's smile fell, and he leaned toward the window. The back of the car was crowded as Doeg leered at him, its long tail flicking gleefully. *They'll track you down and add your head to the mass graves.*

Caden swallowed the hard lump in his throat and began ringing out his clothes the best he could.

"You are so enjoyable to toy with."

*Raw Peace. Yahweh is with me and is giving me rest.*

"You are no better than Nathaniel."

*Shut the lion's mouths. We will shut the lion's —*

"Murderer!"

"Hey, Roberto!" Roberto flinched and glanced back. Caden made himself smile and raise a hand. "Sorry. Um, could you turn on the radio?"

"You alright, Mr. Whitney?"

"Yes, please just turn on the radio."

"Because you don't seem alright."

"I just," Caden took a slow, controlled breath so he wouldn't leap over the seat and throw Roberto out of the moving car. "I just need to focus on what my King has for me. That's all."

Roberto nodded. "Very good. Music? Podcasts?"

"I don't care."

"You're messing up the king's car with the water

everywhere." Roberto waved all over the place, indicating everywhere.

Caden didn't answer; he didn't have a good one to give. Roberto turned on the radio, but Caden couldn't hear it. His heated blood kept roaring in his ears as he replayed the bat swinging.

*"Bloodlust is a powerful thing,"* Doeg said within his thoughts. *"There is strength in it, yet you will be its slave."*

*I am a slave to King Yeshua. He can do with me as He wishes.* Caden bowed his head and began reciting all the Scripture he could think of. He ignored Doeg's whiskers brushing his cheek and the desire for vengeance tightening his chest. It was near impossible, and he was a bit distracted; his thoughts were consumed with Luca's cracked skull.

———

CADEN WAS LOSING HIS MIND. The radio's annoying songs, Doeg's constant lies, and his white-knuckled fists didn't help anything. He had started to shake, coming down from the adrenaline was bad. *Why can't it last longer? I'm not safe yet!*

"Because you're a murderer," Doeg whispered in his ear. "And God has sent this suffering to keep you from life, remember? Remember the Holy Scriptures you so foolishly will die and *kill* for?"

Caden scrubbed his face and turned a shoulder to Doeg, as though that would help him. He fixed his distant gaze out the window. He thought of letting the vengeance desiring more blood consume him. It wouldn't be hard. Roberto would be an easy mark. Caden's boots had laces. He could tell Roberto to park and wrap a lace around his throat. Only one problem: was Roberto so overweight he'd take longer to suffocate?

Dasha.

Caden blinked and lurched to the window, staring at the people walking on the streets. "Stop. Stop the car. Stop!" The brakes squealed as the car skidded to a halt.

"What?" Roberto waved to and fro, eyes wide. "We're not there yet! Hey! Hey! What are you doing? Get back here!"

Caden didn't bother shutting the car's door as he ran onto the streets. He realized, a stride or two in, he was in the middle of traffic. Horns blared, the whiz of passing cars made tiny windstorms, and the smell of burnt tires stung Caden's nose. He didn't care. They had passed her, and she had been walking in the opposite direction. The people turned and stared at him, several shouting as he shoved past. Caden's heart thudded in his ears as he surged on, eyes darting from woman to woman.

*She had a hijab. And blue pants. It was her. I know it was her!*

As he ran, his searching becoming desperate, a small voice whispered deep inside him: *"Was it, though?"*

Caden raced past a tumbled building, destruction from the Russian's attack, and a construction crew at work. A man shouted as Caden leapt over a pile of long rebar, his panic slowly returning. *Where are you?*

There. That walk he knew. Those shoulders and posture. Caden felt himself smiling as he ran. She turned and pulled back the hijab enough for him to see those piercing, blue eyes. Dasha's mouth dropped open. Caden took in a breath, readying to call her name. Her beautiful eyes widened. Her face turned pale.

Caden's heart leapt into his throat. From behind, he heard the fall of Giant's feet. *"No, foolish human,"* Doeg hissed inside his mind. Caden could hear the Demon's smile. *"It's far more delightfully horrific."*

Cold shot through Caden, and he glanced over his shoulder. All he saw was sandy yellow. It was moving. Very. Very fast. It punched him in the face. He didn't know he had fallen until he slammed into a parked car. No, he hadn't fallen. He was thrown. He bounced off the car and collapsed to the pavement, rolling, his head bouncing. All he could see were flashes of light as he tried to stay conscious.

What had he fallen in? His head was covered in something sticky and warm. Then it hit him without warning or mercy. Fiery pain slashed across his face, ripping a scream from his throat. He clutched his face, blood slicking his fingers. The thumping footfalls thundered closer. Another punch lifted Caden off the ground and launched him back, slamming him into the stack of rebar. He groaned, slumping.

Distantly, he heard people screaming. Horns were honking and tires were screeching as people skidded across the road. People were shouting orders as others fled. Amid the chaos, he picked out deep, guttural huffs. It sounded like a Shade panting. Caden forced his left eye open, the right wasn't responding. As he looked, his face's agony ebbed to a dull, vague ache.

A Leovir on all fours slowly turned and faced him. The monster's body flexed with muscle as his tail swept. Ears flicked back, and his mouth opened. The mouth was dark, and the fangs a sickly yellow. A deafening roar erupted from the mouth. Caden didn't move, terror holding him down.

"*From God,*" Doeg whispered in his thoughts, slicing through the noise. "*This suffering is sent from God.*"

The Leovir squarely faced Caden, great mane swaying with each movement. Around him, those who had stayed shrieked and raced away, some even abandoning their cars in traffic. Amid the chaos and pain, Caden's good eye narrowed. *No,* he thought. *I'm immortal.* He heaved himself up to wobbly feet, unaware that his forearm and both knees were skinned and bleeding.

Without turning away from the Leovir, Caden reached behind him and grabbed a rebar. The ten-foot metal bar stretched out before him. Something animal-like burst out laughing. "What are you doing?" Doeg cried before doubling over in hysterical laughter. The Leovir's ears swiveled forward as he blinked in surprise.

*Come here,* Caden thought. *I'll shut your mouth.* The creature's muscle-bound body tensed like a spring, readying to pounce. Caden fell into a fighting stance without thinking; Luca's training was finally coming to use. He gripped the mock spear and bared his teeth in a growl of his own.

Heartbeat.

The Leovir pounced, mane blown back, clawed paws extended. Caden lowered, gripping the bar, raising it up to the Leovir's chest.

Heartbeat.

A paw swatted, the blow ripping the bar from Caden's hands. Without thinking, Caden rolled forward, a shadow swallowing him.

Heartbeat.

Panting, Caden rolled to his feet and spun. The Leovir turned with an enraged snarl and charged. Caden reeled, tripping over an air compressor hose. He landed hard, biting his tongue, and scrambled back, panic stripping him of thought.

Heartbeat.

The Leovir's steps thudded, closing the gap between them in two strides. Caden wildly looked around, frantic for anything sharp or blunt. He found the end of the compressor hose. The Leovir's growl filled his ears. Both paws raised, claws curved and reaching. Caden seized the nail gun at the end of the hose and raised it.

Heartbeat.

He pulled the trigger. The Leovir shuddered, a red spot dotting his jaw. Caden didn't stop pulling the trigger, even after the Leovir slammed against him. Caden yelled, in rage or pain, it didn't matter. He writhed and wiggled out from under the monster. The nail gun kept sending the large nails into the beast. It was as though his finger had a mind of its own and couldn't stop pulling the trigger. It wasn't until Caden was several paces away, out in the middle of the street and when the compressor hose could go no further, did he stop.

Gasping, Caden stared at the unmoving Leovir. He blinked slowly and shifted his weight, his head spinning. *It's dead?* He looked down in shock. *I killed it. God's right, I can shut the mouths of —*

Something dripped from his face. Blood. Lots of it. Caden stumbled back and lightly touched his face. He felt raw meat. There was shouting again. It was getting closer, he thought. Things were hard to make out again. A Shade was walking toward him, holding a stick. No, a few of them were. Caden's good eye narrowed as he stared. The Shades had red markings on their shoulders. They didn't have tails either.

*Refiners.* Caden's mouth opened. He aimed the nail gun and slowly turned. *Come and take me!* He gritted his teeth. *I just killed a Leovir!* He turned, seeing more Refiners behind him. Some on his right and left too. He was surrounded. They were all shouting at him, standing a great length away, each readying to fire. Caden cursed, his hand moving to his mock gun's trigger.

Behind the ring of Refiners, in the shadows, was Dasha. She looked horror-stricken. Caden stared at her, forcing himself to remember the first time he saw them together, beating up Demons with God's spiritual armor. *I can't do that if I'm dead,* he thought. Rage engulfed him. With a savage yell, Caden dropped the nail gun and spread his arms. *Your will be done,* he thought as the Refiners took him to the ground.

———

THERE ARE perks to having bad things happen. When surrounded by enemies and helpless again and again, it becomes not that terrible. Well, it's still *terrible*, but not unbearable. Not devastating. Not a threat to the very existence of one's soul. At least, that's what Caden thought as he calmly stood with a bag over his face. He expected the air to get stale after a while and claustrophobia to settle in, just like the two times before. It wasn't a surprise, and he wasn't too bothered. It sucked, but not as bad as before.

What did suck were the chains. Chains he hadn't known yet. He stood in the center of a cold, vacant room as two chains locked each wrist, spreading his arms on either side. Now that he had a moment to think, he figured he hadn't been mentally or spiritually strong enough to handle chains until now anyways.

*Always looking out for me,* he thought to God. *I guess. I'm still chained here.* He figured he was quite a sight; his clothes a bit damp from the hot tub, now covered in blood and sandy Leovir fur.

After being tackled by Refiners and every limb zip-tied more than once, Caden had expected another beating. He was surprised, and secretly grateful, they just threw him into the back of a van. He was shocked when they inspected his face and attended to it. As one held his hair, another his jaw, an older Refiner stood over him and crudely sowed over his entire face. Well, it felt like all over his face; Caden couldn't withhold his screams.

Actually, the pain ripped up his right cheek, over his cheekbone, hardly missed his right eye, and into his brow. Once he was all stitched up, the bag was put over his head, and he fell in and out of consciousness. Someone mentioned giving him blood, which most seemed very unhappy about. The very small, near indistinguishable discomfort in the bend of Caden's arm showed they had given him the blood anyways.

*And pain meds,* Caden thought as he stood, the chains clinking as he shifted. *I'm thinking coherent thoughts, so they must've given me something good.* His stomach twisted with dread. *So, they want something from me.* Caden lifted his chin, his breath sucking the bag close to his lips and puffing it away, only to draw it back again. *God, save me. I'm begging you.*

"Human boy!" Caden flinched, the sudden voice making his heart leap into his throat. "Remember how I warned my tactics were changing?" Caden didn't answer as he heard Doeg's claws click with each step. "That it is your flesh's turn to suffer?" Caden forced himself to breathe, feeling each intake getting shallow. "What you experienced by water under Grant's hand was a simple prefix. But this. *This.*" The Demon's rasping laugh filled the room. "This is what I was referring to. This is sent from God—"

"Lies!" Caden hissed.

"—to keep you from life."

"No." Caden shook his head. His heart quickened, feeling Doeg's body heat brush against his own.

"I *will be* the last thing you will ever see."

Caden closed his eyes tight, his restrained hands balled into tight fists. *If Yahweh approves.* Doeg's whiskers twitched, flicking Caden's cheek as it snarled.

The door opened. Shuffling footsteps entered. Caden's shallow breathing sucked in sharply, every nerve straining. The bag was pulled from his face, and his eyes were already squeezed tight against the light. "Jiminy-sakes-alive, Max!" Caden turned away, hating himself for believing Luca had been a man of his word and deported Grant. Grant chuckled as he pointed at Caden's face.

"Buck! Do you see this? This is incredible! How's your face still together, Max?"

Buck stepped in and cursed. "That's a beauty."

"Hum, sure is." Caden opened his good eye and glanced between the two.

Grant grinned as though catching a dear friend who tried to slip away without saying goodbye. "What were you thinking, Max?" he whispered. "You can't assassinate someone without a get-away plan."

Buck nodded. "Tell 'em."

"You need the layout, exit points, the enemy's weaknesses, a quick way to disappear. I'm talking about being very premeditative." Caden didn't answer as he stared at the door. It was still open. Grant wouldn't just keep a door open. Grant shook his head as he clicked his tongue. "Could've done a bit better, Max. Oh well. Now I can break you. Finally!" A muscle in Caden's jaw flexed as he kept staring out the door. "How long have I been waiting? Buck? How long?"

"Over a year and a half, sir."

"Over a year and a half!" Grant cursed and rapped his fingers on his cane's ball. "Max, do I look like a patient man?"

Caden said nothing. *Shut the door,* he thought. *Please, shut it before whoever you're waiting for comes through.* Out of the corner of his eye, Caden saw Doeg walk from the wall onto the ceiling and sit, its neck craning back to watch the show.

"I asked you a question," Grant said, his voice low and quiet. An icy thrill washed through Caden as Grant shuffled closer. The squeak of wheels stopped the manic Refiner. Both Buck and Grant stepped back, Buck standing straight and tall and Grant clearing his throat.

Caden stared at the opened door, his resolve threatening to crumble. *Come on!* He internally screamed at himself. *I've done this before! Stand in God, not your own strength, idiot! Stand firm in Him!*

Black smoke curled into the room from beyond. It coiled about the entrance without drifting to the ceiling. Two ember eyes blinked to life from the haze. Caden lifted his chin as the Fiends parted, showing Hugh strolling toward them. Seeing the gash slicing through Caden's face, Hugh's lips parted in a hushed gasp. Somehow, Caden stood taller. After all, Han was going to save him at any moment.

As he stared, he noticed Hugh pushing a wheelchair. One of the wheels squeaked annoyingly. Slumped in the wheelchair, and hooked to an IV, was a very pale, weak person. The near limp body was draped in thick blankets, and an odd hat sat cockeyed on the head. Caden's brow furrowed as their eyes locked. Something purely evil stared back at him, as though the Devil himself had taken flesh.

"More accurate than you know," Doeg whispered from the ceiling as Luca Battistelli was wheeled in.

# NINE
## SUFFERING FROM GOD

CADEN REELED, not feeling the chains biting into his wrists, as he cursed. He muttered something unintelligible, spiced with colorful language, and shook his head as horror filled his eyes. "Dead," he wheezed. "You're dead!" Someone was chuckling a very animal-like cackle. Doeg's wide, red mouth gapped as its cackle became a throaty, howling laugh. Sweat gathered along Caden's brow as he tried to turn away from Luca but couldn't. *This isn't real! They're tricking me! It's not! I killed you! I saw the blood! I —*

He felt cold at the look in Luca's eyes. Though weak and hardly moving, the man looked like a dragon readying to destroy all in his path. "What is your name, traitor?" Luca wheezed. Caden panted and finally turned away. He felt Grant watching his every move, that horrible, amused smile tugging at his mouth. Panic squeezed his throat and tightened his chest. His heart was racing. Sweat dripped down his back. There was no use pretending now. He couldn't spy or even be Alex Whitney; he was now an assassin. A *failed* assassin who was going to die very, very, very slowly.

Caden closed his eyes and forced himself to still. *God. I*

*am Yours. Save me.* "Not Alex Whitney," was all he said as his eyes opened. He stared down at Luca and saw a muscle in his sharp jaw flex.

Grant's smile grew as he glanced at Buck, who cracked his knuckles. "May I, your majesty?" Grant asked, shuffling forward, lifting his cane. Caden's eyes darted between them, his entire body tensing, but Luca held up one finger, his hand still limp on the wheelchair's armrest.

"Patience," Luca wheezed. Grant didn't back down, his small smile remaining as a shadow crossed his gaze. Reluctantly, he shuffled back.

*I'm completely surrounded,* Caden realized. *Every enemy I have, besides Bobby and Nathaniel, are here. I'm completely alone too. No support. No cavalry. No salvation. This isolation is a testament of God's futile promises.*

Caden hissed a curse and ducked his head, knowing Doeg would torment him from the inside as everyone else tormented him from the outside. *I can't win.*

*Doeg! Shut up! Yes, I will! We win!*

*"You die."*

*Whatever! That isn't losing!*

*"You will confess everything, leading to the deaths of the ones you adore."* Caden's throat bobbed. He didn't have an answer for that.

"As I said, your majesty," Grant said. "This boy is a con artist. And how long has he been here? Months? Living right under your nose. I wonder how much information was leaked to the terrorists."

"They're not terrorists." Caden blinked, realizing what he just said. Buck stepped forward, slamming a fist into Caden's stomach. Caden's whole body lurched back, and he collapsed, limply swinging back and forth. He gulped for air, coughing as he fought curling into a ball.

"Please," Luca said. "No more. Not now." Buck glanced at Grant, who gave a curt nod, before he backed away. Caden knew they had kept talking, but he couldn't hear them. He was too worried something was broken again and busy trying to breathe.

It wasn't until something hot and searing brushed his back. Stepping away, Caden gritted his teeth and glanced behind him, expecting to see a hot iron. A Fiend stared back, its spiked, transparent smokey face maintaining shape while coiling and moving at the same time. He could see the liquid fire pooling in its mouth. The two others were circling the room as though they were wolves just waiting to strike.

Hugh, eyes lightly closed and steepled hands tucked under his chin, sighed a long, whispering breath. "Ah... they are angry now. The Heralds demand restitution. And they...they have demanded this child's death once before."

Caden's hair stood on end, not that the Fiends were finally talking to Hugh about him, but that Han had ordered them not to. *Why aren't they obeying still? Isn't Han here somewhere?* A coldness crept across his flesh.

"In America?" Hugh's eyes slid open as he regarded Caden. "He has been a terrorist even before reaching our lands."

Luca shook his head as Grant turned to Hugh. "Tell us his name."

"You will speak to me with humble requests only, Ally Yarrow," Hugh said. His voice was just as mild but, as he spoke, the Fiends came together, forming a black cloud over Hugh and Grant. "Or the Heralds will correct your behavior. Permanently."

Grant's face disappeared in the Fiends' cloud, and he limped back instantly. "Yes, sir," he said and quickly turned away.

"As for his name," Hugh said, his tone never changing. He paused again and took another long, awkward sigh. "They cannot say." The room fell silent.

"Why, Max?" Luca whispered. "After all I've done for you. I saved your life. Took you into my home. Taught you how to defend yourself. How to kill." Their eyes met again, and Caden lifted his chin. "How long have you served the false King?"

Caden's brows shadowed his gaze. "I don't follow you."

Hugh clicked his tongue as Luca sighed heavily. "King Yeshua."

"You think *He's* the false King? What is wrong with you, man!"

"Max—"

"My name's not Max."

Grant groaned as his fingers rapped on the metal ball. "Why again are we waiting to inflict justice?"

"Suffering," Doeg corrected from the ceiling. "Which was sent from God."

"I've always followed Him," Caden said, straightening. "King Yeshua has been my Master before we met." One of Luca's eyes twitched, and Caden's stomach turned. He tried to hold back his terror and only show strength, if he had any left. *No, I have lots,* he thought. *Yahweh's going to keep me strong—*

"How, prey tell?"

*—and He'll help me.*

"*Encouragement cannot save a kitten from being crushed by a dump truck.*"

*I don't need to be afraid.*

"*No, be terrified. Beg for mercy. Stop denying how dire and helpless this is!*"

"I trusted you," Luca whispered. Caden's head cocked to one side. "I wanted to give you the father you never had."

Caden scoffed. He couldn't help it. "Before we reached

your mansion during the aerial attack, I despised the very sight of you."

Luca's brows rose. "I am not the enemy—"

"You are the Antichrist, Son of Perdition, the murderer of God's people!"

"I'm here to save people!"

Caden shook his head. "Thought about whacking you one more time. Should've."

Luca slowly lifted his chin as his weak hands drew onto his lap. "Gentlemen, I require your help solving this little dilemma. I want to make an example out of him." Caden's breath quickened. "He will suffer. On live TV." Caden's hands became fists. "I want the world to see every drop of blood and hear every plea. So...any ideas?"

*God, I am Yours. Save me.* The train of thought continued, digressing into cussing and horrific language. With a sucked inhale, Caden lifted his chin. *Raw Peace. I am where God wants me. Raw Peace!*

"Well," Grant said. "I have yet to break his bones, and you require something, how shall I say? Theatrical and memorable?" Luca nodded.

*He was with them and gave them rest,* Caden thought. *He's with me—*

*"You will suffer alone."*

*And is giving me rest.*

Doeg's laughter filled his ears. "Caden! Caden, please! This is intolerable! You cannot deny reality *this* much!" The Demon clicked its tongue as it crawled from the ceiling and down the wall. "Ah, you should know better than that, Caden, my boy. Consider all the times you've blasphemed God and His Spirit either in thought or action. Doesn't that deserve a violent end?" Caden swallowed the hard lump in his throat. Doeg's claws clicked closer to Caden until he could feel the Demon's body heat. "This is all from God. All an elaborate game to trap you where you are now; surrounded by enemies, incapable of salvation, and destined for agony unlike anything you've known before."

Caden opened his eyes and fixed Doeg with a murderous glare. The Demon grinned back, its scarred face twisting the smile into a snarl. "And I know just the thing, too." Doeg held up a bald hand, motioning for Caden to wait, and walked to Grant's side. Without the human noticing, the Demon leaned in close, its whiskers brushing his face, and whispered in his ear.

Grant blinked as his fingers rapped again. "I've got it," he said suddenly. "I know just the thing!" Everyone turned as Caden's heart stopped. The internal screaming had begun again. "What about a blood eagle? Hum? I get to break bones, and you, your majesty, get something memorable. Everybody wins!" Luca thoughtfully stared at Grant as Buck chuckled and shook his head.

"Hum," Hugh sighed. "That may be too graphic for live TV.-"

"It's perfect," Luca rasped. The four men turned to one another, and one by one, they all smiled. Caden felt he was in a room of Demons as his internal screaming grew louder.

"Max, my boy," Grant said, limping closer and laying a hand on his shoulder. "Do you know what a blood eagle is?" Caden stared straight ahead, unable to speak. "It's when an unlucky someone, such as yourself, is tied face down. From the back, the ribs are exposed and severed from the spine," Caden's eyes widened as his chest heaved with each breath, "the ribs are then broken and butter-flied, forming wings." Caden closed his eyes tight, his hands shaking. "The lungs, untouched and still operable if the victim hasn't died yet, are removed and laid across the broken ribs. Voila! A blood eagle."

A low moan escaped Caden's lips as he ducked his

head and tried to pull away from Grant. He could hardly think as Grant grabbed the back of his neck. "I know, I know," Grant whispered consolingly. "Do not worry. I will enjoy this."

Caden turned to Luca and opened his mouth to beg but stopped himself. He sucked in breath after breath, his eyes watery and wide with terror, and shut his mouth. Amid the internal screaming and the shaking of his body, Caden forced himself to think two words: *We. Win.* Doeg's ears flicked back with irritation. Luca, slumped in the wheelchair with exhaustion, didn't turn away from Caden.

They stared at one another, and Caden shook his head. "Do it," he hissed. "King Yeshua will see. He'll kill you all with twice the amount of gore and agony. He's coming. You won't escape Him." Luca smiled. He started to laugh. Hugh lay a hand over his lips and also snickered. Buck barked a laugh as his shoulders shook, and Grant chuckled to himself. Doeg cackled its gravelly laugh as the Fiends made guttural snickers.

Caden closed his eyes, ignoring them all and the internal screaming of his heart. *We win,* he thought. *We will win. Raw Peace. Oh, God, don't let this happen! But we win. But please do something! I can't...no. We win. We always win with God.* He said nothing as he firmly stood on God's truth, his enemies' laughter echoing in his ears.

———

CADEN COULDN'T SLEEP. Even if he wasn't standing up, his pain meds had nearly worn off and his face was a throbbing mess, he wouldn't sleep. Whenever he closed his eyes, he saw Lil El in a labor camp, Asher torn apart by Rapham, Yohanan hunted by Tarek, and Nathaniel's dogs. And blood. *His* blood, all across live TV. Everyone in the New Kingdom, which was slowly becoming most of the old world before the Crash, would hear his screaming.

This was just too much. He should've swung harder at Luca. He should've ran faster, not stopped when he saw Dasha. Where was she? She hinted at becoming a believer the last they spoke. Would the Refiners deem her a terrorist, too, and execute her? Of course, they would; any Russian in the Middle East was a terrorist these days. They were probably tracking her down after seeing he had run after her. She would die beside him on live TV. It would be their final task together.

Caden closed his bloodshot eyes and lifted his chin with a sharp inhale. *What would Elijah do?* He thought. *He wouldn't be shaking. He probably would figure out how to fall asleep. He's not human.* Caden's chin lowered as he shuffled his feet. They had become numb hours ago. *No, he trusts in God. No matter what. Even when it's impossible.* Caden cursed under his breath and looked up. The room was dark. The only light was from the crack under the door, illuminating his shoes.

What was that Bible story again? The one with the two missionaries who were in prison, all chained up, and Yahweh set them free? *What did they do again?* Caden blinked, trying to remember Mama Lo's stories. *Paul,* he thought, blinking slowly. *And...Simon? Sylas? Whatever, those guys. They sang, and God got them out.*

"Pity you can't sing."

*Wonder what they sang.*

"Buck will beat you for opening your lips."

*Some praise song?*

"You are still a heathen. Still uneducated in such Biblical nonsense."

*Would you shut up?*

"Would you accept God has sent this suffering to keep you from life?"

*God wouldn't send—*

*"You deny the power of His Word? It never returns void. It goes out and achieves whatever He intends. Suffering will come from Him. And destroy you."*

Caden nodded slowly. "You're right." Doeg was quiet a moment. "There's power in His Word." Caden closed his eyes and started to sing the first Bible verses that came to mind. It wasn't a technical song, and he was confident it sounded awful. He didn't think it mattered to Yahweh. If it did, He wasn't as good as He said He was.

"Do not fear," Caden muttered in some sort of rhythm. "For I, the Lord, have freed you. I have called you by name. You are Mine. When you pass through the waters, I will be with you. When you pass through rivers, they will not sweep over you, um...For I am the Lord your God, the Holy One of Israel, your Savior." He knew Doeg was saying something, but he was determined to not listen.

"Do not fear!" Caden snapped, less of a song and more of a command. "For King Yeshua has freed you, Caden! He's called you by your name, Caden! I'm God's! When they stick my head under the water again, God's with me. The enemies rivers won't kill me. For the Lord, my God, the Holy One, is here, and He's saving me. Right now." Caden gritted his teeth with a curse. "Whatever that means. I'm being saved. Right now."

The doorknob turned. It was a different doorknob, it sounded from across the room in the darkness. Caden turned in time to see white, hot light slice through the dark, stinging his eyes. With a cry, Caden reeled back, the chains clinking as they pulled tight. He cowered back, the light heating his skin. He could still see the brilliance even with his eyes closed.

This was brighter than Han's glory, brighter than anything Caden had ever seen. He heard a door shut, but the horrible light remained. Caden felt under attack! He couldn't escape from it! His skin felt like it was burning. His eyes were on fire. He gritted his teeth and tried shielding himself. It was like hiding from the power of a bonfire after being thrown in. Worst of all, the most intense burning roared from Caden's insides. He knew this burning, this violent, unrelenting force that wouldn't let anything survive that wasn't from God. Caden felt consumed in the *Akal Esh*. He'd never felt it so ruthlessly before. It was dangerous. Lethal. How was he still alive?

He heard footsteps. They drew nearer. *Please stop,* Caden thought. *Please! I can't survive this!*

"Oh," a voice said suddenly. "I'm sorry." The light dimmed to a not-so-lethal glow, but Caden refused to open his eyes. "Too bright?" It was a man's voice, speaking Hebrew.

"Yes!" Caden gasped in Hebrew. "Please, angel! Don't kill me! Please stop!"

"Oh. How's that?" The light diminished again but still pricked Caden's skin with heat.

Caden shook his head. "Less. Please."

"Seriously?"

"Unless you want me blind!"

The light dimmed again. "How about now? Come on, open your eyes. You'll be fine with this amount."

"Easy for you to say," Caden grumbled, sweat from the heat dripping down his brow. "Living in Yahweh's presence all the time. Normal people don't do that!" Caden pried his eyes open and squinted. He barely made out the outline of a person. They were as tall as he and very chunky. Oh, no, that was armor. Probably the moving spiritual armor Old Caden wore.

"Still too bright?" the Angel asked. He sounded a bit annoyed.

"Pretend I'm a mortal!" Caden hissed. "Pretend too much *Akal Esh* fries me like a Krispy Cream!"

"What's a Krispy Cream?"

"A donut, now turn it down some more!"

"Is this how you talked to Han when you met?" the angel asked as he, again, lowered the glow cutting through the darkness.

"Han's not as powerful as you. Aren't there levels of Angels?"

"Um," the angel muttered, running fingers through his hair. The light was dimming enough to make out facial features. "I'm not an angel."

Caden blinked as his eyes adjusted to the now softer glow emitting from the stranger. He looked Caden's age. He did wear armor, but it was different than Old Caden's spiritual armor. It looked thinner, yet more durable. The plates were sealed by *Akal Esh*, the glow shining through the joints whenever the stranger moved. The armor's shape stayed the same, but Caden could see movement, like coiling smoke or flickering fire in each plate. The movement was fierce. Wild. Unstoppable. Even the large sword sheathed on the stranger's hip lashed with fire along the blade.

Caden looked to the stranger's face and knew he wasn't an Israeli, in fact, he looked European. He wasn't scarred up like Old Caden was, but his firmly set jaw and intense stare made Caden think of Elijah's quiet, unchanging intensity. His hair was a dark brown, and as their gaze met, Caden saw his eyes were icy blue. It reminded Caden of Dasha.

The man grunted with a smile as he put his hands on his hips. "What's up, *Saba*?"

Caden blinked and lifted his chin. "Gideon?"

The stranger nodded and spread his arms. "In the flesh." Relief flooded over Caden as he smiled. He had forgotten about his throbbing head and aching body. God had proven Himself again. He was getting out of there!

"Quick," Caden said, glancing at the door. "I bet your sword can cut through the chains."

Gideon's brow rose. "What?"

Caden glared at him. "Get your sword out. Cut these chains. Get me out of here!"

Gideon raised a gauntleted hand. "This isn't a rescue mission."

Caden stiffened, his relief short-lived. "What?"

He cursed something foul, and Gideon's eyes widened. "Wow. You really did have a potty mouth, don't you?"

"They're going to torture me. To death!"

"Yeah, yeah," Gideon said, waving his hand. "Can't cut you down. Can't do anything, per His orders."

"*Whose* orders."

"King Yeshua."

Caden fell quiet as he stared at his grandson from the future. With a curse again, Caden looked down, his heart slamming into his chest. If he wasn't chained back, he would've attacked the smug, comfortable brat in his cool armor, all safe and secure while his *Saba* fought for his life.

*God, what game is this?*

# TEN

# NARROW GATE

"JUST CALM DOWN, *SABA!*"

"Don't patronize me!"

"I'm not!" Caden rolled his shoulders as he gripped the chains, testing the link's strength. He locked eyes with Gideon, who took a short step back and raised his hands. "*Saba*—"

"Why are you here?"

"Don't look at me like that."

Caden's nostrils flared. He was sure his face was turning red with rage. When he spoke again, his voice whispered through gritted teeth. "I will be tortured!"

"You don't know." Gideon crossed his arms and stepped further away. "You don't know anything, actually."

"Tell me."

"No."

"Gideon!"

"Seriously, stop! I hate when you use that tone."

"I will remember this."

Gideon scoffed as he nodded. "Yeah. I know. Look, I know this sucks."

"Said the guy protected by fire armor. Unchained."

"I'm here to encourage you."

"You failed."

"And feed you! Hungry?" Gideon held up a bag that had been tied to his waist. With a heaved breath, Gideon pulled out a loaf of bread and a flask of water.

Caden's brows bunched as he grimaced. "That's it?"

"Hum?"

"I'm already in prison, and King Yeshua sends *prison* rations."

"No, He—"

"You think this is funny?"

Muttering something under his breath, Gideon set down the bag and tore off a piece of bread. Before Caden could respond, he shoved it into Caden's mouth. Caden tried to spit it out, but Gideon clamped a hand over his mouth. "Eat it, you big baby."

Caden grumbled something and quickly downed the bread, hoping to bite one of Gideon's fingers. Maybe there was a gap in the armor. He knew there wasn't, but still worth a shot. Caden's struggling slowed as he blinked. He finally tasted the bread. No, it wasn't how it tasted, it's what it did to his body. As he swallowed, he felt himself standing taller. His legs didn't feel as numb.

"Yeah?" Gideon smiled, his pale blue eyes flashing. He stepped back and ripped off another piece of bread.

Caden chewed it quietly, gradually feeling sensation in his legs and arms. "What is that?" he asked between mouthfuls.

"Oh, something the Seraphim cook up sometimes."

"The who?"

"Just a type of angel. They said the last time a human got some of this was Elijah."

"Mizrahi?"

"No, the prophet in the Bible. More?"

Caden nodded, and Gideon obliged. Caden ate in silence, each bite giving him strength and energy. After a big drink of water, Caden nodded slowly and lifted his chin. "It's like I just slept for a week."

"There's a little more still."

"In a bit, if you can stay."

"Sure," Gideon said with a shrug. "Yeshua didn't say when to get back."

Caden's eyes narrowed. "So that means you can do what you want?"

Gideon shrugged again. "He trusts me. I know Him. I know what He wants. Even if He wants me back, I'll just hear Him calling, and I'll come. It's not a big deal."

"You have radios or something?"

Gideon grimaced. "Ah, no? He's God. His Spirit's inside me. He just talks to me from the inside. Oh, right. That's not a thing yet for you, isn't it?" Caden shook his head. "Then, how do you know what to do?"

"I guess."

"That's horrible. Wonder why Yahweh chose to withhold His Spirit right now. He has some wanky ideas."

"Don't let Him hear you say that." Gideon frowned. "He's God. He doesn't want to hear when we don't like what He does."

Gideon frowned. "Why not? He's a big Boy. He can handle raw honesty from His kids. Come on, that's what you yourself taught me. You think you can think or say something that will offend Yeshua so much He won't want to be with you?" Gideon snorted a laugh. "You could *try*. Doesn't work, and besides, I've already told Him His ideas are wanky sometimes. To His face."

"What? To His...wait...You talk to Yeshua to His face?"

"Yeah. We all do. I mean, not all the time, because He's

in His physical form and can only do one conversation at a time, but, you know…"

Caden stared at Gideon dumbfounded. "I, I don't know."

"Yeah, I see that. Look, King Yeshua literally changed my diapers as a kid. He's always been in my life. It's pretty cool."

"Pretty cool? That's unbelievable. That's *God* hanging out with just some kid!"

Gideon shrugged. "That's what He's doing with you too, right now. You don't notice Him, but He talks a lot about being with you trying to survive in America." Caden blinked. "Crying when Great Unc Trace was shot." Caden's mouth dropped open. "How scared you were when the Mizrahis found you, but you didn't know who they were. Don't get me started on how proud of you He is about all that spying around and risking everything."

Caden looked down, too stunned to speak. "But He…" Caden's voice cracked. "God sent this suffering." He shook his head. "He sent it to prevent me from life. That's what the Bible says."

Gideon scratched the back of his neck with a frown. "Where'd you hear that?"

"Just some," he sighed, "a Demon that won't leave me alone."

"Doeg?" Caden just stared at Gideon. "That dog. Hate it."

"You know him?"

"It's not a *him,* and yes, I do. It's trying to quote Scripture."

"That is Scripture."

"But Doeg has it all mixed up, of course. Here, let me think a sec…Ah, I remember. Job 36:21. The *entire* verse is this: Be on guard. Turn back from evil, for God has sent this suffering to keep you from a life of evil. See? Not so bad. Has dear ol' Doeg been saying God wants you to suffer?"

"Well," Caden stammered, and Gideon scoffed.

"Its lies are so dumb. Really? Yeshua wanting you to suffer?" Gideon actually started laughing. "Just remind Doeg he loses, and we are more than conquerors. Don't sweat about it."

*God's trying to save me from a life of evil, not from life itself.* Caden blinked thoughtfully as he glanced down. He hoped he could get his hands on some of that spiritual armor; he really needed to give Doeg a good thrashing. "What's going to happen to me?"

"Sorry. Can't talk about your present." Caden glared at Gideon, who held up a defensive hand. "I would, I swear, but Yeshua said not to. You have some more faith to stretch. His words, not mine."

"I'm sure," Caden grumbled as he sighed. "Any hints?" Gideon's left brow raised up sharply. It was a classic Dasha move. "Fine." Caden shifted from one foot to the other as he glanced toward The Door. It was shut, but he knew Gideon could open it at any moment. "Tell me," he whispered, as though talking about some great secret. "Tell me about life out there. On the other side of The Door."

Gideon grinned as he leaned against the far wall and comfortably folded his arms. "Out there? It's pretty great. Better than here, that's for sure."

"But it's not Heaven."

"Oh, no. That's not done yet. No, that's the Millennial Kingdom." Caden's head tilted to one side, and Gideon nodded. "Okay, so…after King Yeshua comes back, He sets up a physical kingdom on Earth for a thousand years."

"What for?"

"One last chance for everyone to change their minds and turn to Him. He's always doing that; giving chances."

"So, what's that look like?"

"Well, King Yeshua's ruling all of Earth in Jerusalem. The veil is really, really thin."

"The what?"

"Right, Christianese, um...the barrier between the physical and spiritual dimensions. Like, before the Rapture, or, like you call it, the Day of Vanishing, the veil is thick. Most people don't see Angels or Demons, unless you're some random American kid who loves baseball."

"Lucky me."

"Well," Gideon said, his head bobbing. "Kind of. Anyways, in my time during the Millennial Kingdom, everyone sees Angels and Demons. Everyone can talk to them, and we all interact together in one society. I mean, the Demons don't. They're not allowed in the Kingdom."

"So, things like Han are just walking around? And it's normal?" Gideon nodded, and Caden frowned. "I'm not sure I believe you."

"Whatever," Gideon said with a sniff. "Truth's still true whether you think so or not. Anyways, mankind's doing a lot better with King Yeshua in charge."

"Go figure."

"Right. Society's working together better. People live longer."

"That's right! How old are you?"

"Seventy-three."

Caden's mouth dropped open as he slowly shook his head. "That's crazy. We look the same age!"

"Things are different in my time. Um, because the veil is thin, technology is able to blend physical and spiritual elements to make new things. Like the Narrow Gates." He jerked his chin to where The Door had closed. "We can go anywhere with them. Like, in space *and* time. Very steep learning curve, but pretty fun."

"Why are they narrow?"

"I think it had something to do with the original design. We've traveled around a bit, helping others of the Kingdom, in our time and the past. Into the Bible too. Sometimes when an Angel appears to help someone, it's not an Angel, it's us."

"What?" Caden spat. "Is Han one of you guys?"

"No. He has four faces. He's totally a Cherub. And there's other tech, like this, too," Gideon said as he lifted his armored arm with a grin. "This is top of the line."

Caden slowly shook his head as he watched the *Akal Esh* swirling about inside the armor. "I think my brain's overloading."

"Sorry."

"No, it's good. So, what do you do there? Eat grapes on clouds or something?"

Gideon laughed. "What? No! That's ridiculous! We work! There are still jobs, schools, getting married, having kids, and living life, just with King Yeshua and Angels."

"What's your job?"

"Oh, think of me as a Demon police. Something like that."

"Excuse me?"

"I make sure they stay in the outlands and don't come into the Kingdom. Them and, well…their followers."

Caden frowned, unable to hide his bewilderment. "Wait. There are people in your time who follow Demons?"

Gideon sighed and ran his fingers through his hair. "King Yeshua calls us sheep for a reason. We are pretty dumb creatures."

Caden stared at the floor, watching the *Akal Esh* from

Gideon dance across the ground with flickering movement. "So, there are still bad guys."

"Yep."

"So, the war's not over."

"Nope. Almost, though. There's one more battle to go." Caden glanced up, seeing the hardened look in Gideon's eyes. "He's been waiting for it all this time."

"Who?"

"Yeshua. He's been training mankind, getting us ready. He said He started teaching us generations ago. Now, in my time, mankind's almost ready."

Caden stiffened, feeling the severity in Gideon's voice. "What's He teaching us? To just trust His crazy ideas?"

Gideon sniffed as he stepped from the wall and lay a hand on the hilt of his sword. "Do you know the only thing that doesn't die in fire?"

"Um...something wet?"

Gideon grimaced. "Water can't quench the *Akal Esh*, just read about Elijah's alter on Mt. Carmel. No, the only thing that doesn't die in fire is fire." Caden blinked, not following. "This entire time, King Yeshua has been teaching mankind how to be entirely consumed in His *Akal Esh*. The goal is that, someday, there will be nothing left of us. Of me. All that'll be left is a living vessel for the *Akal Esh*. *That* is King Yeshua's final army for the final battle in the history of mankind. Living torches that nothing, no Demon or vile person, can extinguish. This transition takes time. Lots of time. That's another reason why the Millennial Kingdom lasts a thousand years. It's only until my generation that mankind can finally house the *Akal Esh* without dying." Caden nodded slowly, realizing his future grandson was a level of soldier he couldn't even dream to be.

"And we need you, *Saba*." Caden blinked as Gideon

drew closer. "We need you to keep fighting. You still have a lot ahead of you, and King Yeshua is with you."

"So, He's not mad I tried to kill Luca?"

Gideon smiled and shook his head. "The Bible prophesied the Antichrist would sustain a fatal blow to the head." Caden lifted his chin, his eyes widening. "Didn't Han tell you you'd fulfill prophecies?"

"Yeah, but...I didn't think that would be one of them."

Gideon stepped closer and lay a heavy hand on Caden's shoulder. "You're going to make it. Stop listening to Doeg; it's so full of lies it's not worth your time. Look for God's signs. I know He's not talking to you directly, but He is guiding you. Want any more bread?"

Caden nodded and tried to wrap his brain around everything as he munched on the Seraphim-made bread. *This is too much, I can't...*Caden closed his eyes and took in a slow breath. *If it's too much, God wouldn't have given it to me.*

After giving him some water, Gideon stepped back and smiled. "Well, I've got to go now."

Caden stared at him and nodded reluctantly. "Will I live in the Millennial Kingdom?"

"Yeah. You and *Ima* have a house on a hill. We played baseball in the backyard all growing up. Yeshua joined in too." Caden grinned. He tried to imagine him and Yeshua playing baseball. It seemed too good to be true. "Hold fast, *Saba,*" Gideon said as he stepped back. "We win."

Caden squarely faced him and stood tall. "We win." Gideon tapped the hilt of his sword and turned to the Narrow Gate.

As it swung open, light shot through the darkness again, startling Caden. He shrank back, feeling the *Akal Esh's* heat wash across his body and the light still pricking his eyes even with them squeezed shut. Caden gasped, unable to bear it, yet never wanting it to end. When the door shut and the darkness returned, Caden straightened and blinked until his eyes adjusted. "The Millennial King-dom," he muttered and shook his head. Would there be flying cars? Floating islands? All the water in everyone's cups turning to wine if Yeshua got too close? Who knows.

*But I will know,* Caden thought, his chest puffing. *I'm going to live there. I'm going to build a family. I'm going to play baseball with King Yeshua there.* His hands fisted as his body, rejuvenated and strengthened, stood tall. He didn't sleep that night, he had too much to think about. Besides, he didn't need the rest; he had felt the *Akal Esh* again. It would sustain him.

———

CADEN QUIETLY HUMMED TO HIMSELF. His eyes were lightly closed, and his foot tapped with the rhythm. Some-where nearby, water was dripping. It was driving him absolutely crazy, and it took all his focus not to keep taking huge breaths and holding them. *Why do I do that?*

"Water is your foe," a voice hissed, a voice that wouldn't stop hissing and seething and growling. Caden lowered his chin as Doeg's tail swished across the floor. He kept humming. He didn't know what the song was, but it reminded him of one of the songs sung during Shabbat with the Mizrahis. "No," Doeg snapped. "The tune is flat. You disgrace the song."

Caden didn't bother acknowledging him. *No, he is an it. He's not a thing like me. He doesn't have a soul.*

"I do too!" Caden raised a brow but didn't open his eyes.

Though there was no way to see the passing of days, Caden suspected it was morning. They had yet to feed him, so he was very grateful for Gideon's visit. Though that had been last night, Caden still felt he'd slept a week, and hunger didn't wear him down. He felt strong, capable, and complete, lacking nothing.

"Feelings are lies." Caden grinned; Doeg's jabs were becoming pathetic. The Demon huffed a low groan as its heavy tail swished on the floor. "Fortify your soul, boy." Caden lifted his chin, his closed eyes tightening. "It is time to spill more blood of the saints." Caden's humming morphed into a growl as he gritted his teeth. He refused to acknowledge the Demon, whatever it said was lies anyway! "Not every time." Caden's stomach twisted.

The door squealed open and light flooded in. Caden turned away and heard a click as more light flickered on overhead. He blinked as several footfalls thudded in. *What does Grant want now?*

It wasn't Grant. Refiners and two Leovirs streamed in. One was Benaiah. Their eyes met. *He saved Asher,* Caden remembered. *He's on my side! Maybe he's here to —*

The Leovir's lips pulled back into a snarl. Caden flinched back, his heart leaping into his throat, while the chains clinked as he pulled against them. *Oh, God, help. Help me. I'm begging You. Yahweh!*

His pleading stilled as Rapham strolled in. He walked to Caden, hands behind his back and eyes like daggers. Caden couldn't face him. He stared at the floor as his heart was beating like a drum. *No,* he thought, sweat breaking out on his brow. *Not now. Please!* He knew what Gideon had said about him surviving and living in the Millennial Kingdom. But, staring face to face with Rapham, surrounded by Leovirs, it all felt like a lie.

*"They never said when they'd slaughter you."* Caden shuffled his feet as his hands became fists. He could almost feel Rapham's stare burning through him like a Fiends'.

"I warned him," Rapham softly said in Hebrew. "I knew you were trouble, Max."

"I've said that's not my name." Caden snapped his

mouth shut, realizing he answered in Hebrew.

Rapham's head tilted to one side as a nearly indistinguishable smile twitched his mouth. "Ready to spread your wings?"

Caden ducked his head with a hissed curse. "King Yeshua is coming," he heard himself saying. *Stupid! Shut up!* And why was he looking up? Stop staring at Rapham! Turn away! "You'll regret this."

Rapham's smile twitched again as he stepped closer. "No," he whispered. "I won't."

*I'm immortal until God says I'm not,* Caden thought. His hands shook, and his legs felt weak and wobbly. *Please! Please, don't let them do this!*

With an amused grunt, Rapham motioned to the Sentinels behind Caden. "Bag him." Caden glanced back in time to see a black bag come over his face. He closed his eyes, telling himself he's done this before, more than once now. He could do this. He's suffered in front of his enemies before. Granted, it was just water, not knives and bone saws before live TV. And, formerly, it was for the sake of information. Not now. The sole purpose was anguish. Pure, unrestrained anguish as flesh is ripped back, bones are removed, and insides are forced to the outside.

*Doeg!* Caden heaved in breath after breath, the bag sucked over his mouth with each inhale. *I will kill you! I swear to God, I will hunt you down like the dog you are!* The Demon laughed as Caden's wrists were chained behind him. A collar locked around his neck, and with a sudden tug, Caden gasped and stumbled as they led him out of the cell on a leash.

"Who's the dog now?" Doeg hissed. Caden didn't answer as Benaiah's clawed paw kept pushing him forward, and Rapham led him to whatever Hell lay in store.

# ELEVEN
# BLOOD THAT DEFILES

CADEN COULDN'T STOP SHAKING, it was getting really annoying. He wanted to be one of those guys who could strut up to the executioner and say he didn't need a blindfold. *But they're not going to offer me one. And this isn't some simple firing squad.* He was going to get ripped open in front of the entire world. Han had proven himself ineffective and unreliable, inserting himself merely when convenient and not when lives hung in the balance. No one from Under Fire could rescue him; his fire-breathing Abba and brother's rotting stench still disturbed the Temple Mount. Everyone else had abandoned him. Even your beloved Yahweh.

Caden growled through gritted teeth, which was cut short by a sharp tug from his leash. Caden stumbled, nearly falling, but hands looped under his arms and wrenched him upright. He gasped, trying to keep up, trying not to fight the rising terror tightening his throat, making it practically impossible to breathe. He was going to die. Slowly. His enemies would revel in his screams as Tarek licked his blood.

*Raw Peace!* Caden thought, squeezing his eyes shut.

*Please! Yahweh! I give You everything I am, but please don't do this to me!* He didn't know where they were. At least he knew they were outside and not alone. After a car ride and getting dragged through tight streets, they had come to a wide-open place. At least it felt wide and open; the bag still covered his face. The mass of people around him was a cacophony of tension and energy. Caden ducked his head, his heart leaping into his throat. *They've come to watch,* he thought. He thought there'd be a camera crew, a few Sentinels, and Rapham with his knives. Grant, too; he'd want the final laugh. But not this. Not an audience.

Without thinking, Caden detached from himself. He sank away, slipping behind his internal walls and defenses, trying to find a place to hide deep inside himself. When the mob saw him, the shouting began. He heard them, but it was far off. He didn't respond when they cursed him, calling him a murderer, assassin, or traitor. Several languages mixed with the chaos, but Caden could guess their cries.

Something smacked into his shoulder, bouncing off and grazing his ear. Caden recoiled with a grunt, his head suddenly spinning. He felt Sentinels drawing closer to him, shouting orders to protect him. Other objects hurled from the crowd, most bouncing off the armored Sentinels while some found Caden's back or side.

By the time they finally stopped, he was sure his ear was bleeding. His body was drenched in sweat as his breath came in hissed rasps. His chest ached as panic overtook him. It was getting harder to breathe. Was the collar tightening around his throat? Were they going to strip him naked, or just take his shirt off? How long would he last before they'd destroy every trace of Caden Johnson?

*"Not long,"* an unwelcome voice hissed inside his thoughts. *"Look at you, GJ. You are pathetic. A failure. You've*

*always known; you and everyone around you.*" Caden's eyes fluttered as sweat dripped from his brow. *"Why else has everyone, and I refer to literally* everyone, *has forsaken you? Your family. Your friends. Even your God.*"

Caden closed his eyes, hearing the crowd cheers rise again as someone spoke to them through a microphone. *God'll never leave me. Never forsake me. He promised.*

*"God sits back to watch you die."*

*I can't hide in myself again. That's fatal.* Caden lowered his chin, slowly shaking his head. *I've got to stand in Yahweh.*

*"They will break you."*

*Yes, they'll break Caden Johnson. But not God. Come on, Doeg, we've done this before. You can't break God.*

*"You've been played with by a child!"* Doeg seethed. *"Now, Rapham will show you what true —"*

*Raw Peace,* Caden thought, lifting his chin. *I am Yours, my Master and King. Save me. I beg You. I am Yours. To the very end.* He cursed under his breath, the panic still painfully pressing on his chest as he felt his body weaken by the moment. *I'm immortal,* he thought, gritting his teeth. *I. Am. Immortal.*

"Assassin!" The voice cried over the speakers.

The bag was yanked from Caden's head. He blinked in the late morning light and squinted at his surroundings. His eyes quickly widened as he gaped, staring all around. He was in a courtyard. Not very big, but every inch of it was stuffed with people from every nation. They were surrounded by a stone wall so thick, Leovirs paced the top of it. Just beyond the wall, vultures circled and cried to one another. Giants dotted the wall's perimeter, and Sentinels stood throughout the crowd. No, those were Shades. Demons were everywhere.

An upright pillar stood before the mob about twenty feet tall. It was hidden beneath a thick blanket, shielding it from the world. Caden saw the base was cast iron but couldn't make out what it was. He glanced to his right, seeing a huge tub-looking thing made of bronze. Twelve statues of cows supported it. To his right, several stairs led up to a raised platform nearly thirty feet in the air. Though he couldn't see what was on the top, he did make out a box-thing with spikes on its corners, kind of like horns.

Hugh stood halfway up the steps, Leovirs on either side, as his Fiends lazily billowed their black misty selves above him. Behind Caden, and casting a deep shadow, was a building. Stairs led to double doors that looked over-layed in gold. They were detailed with intricate flowers, palm trees, and some sort of fruit. An orange? No. More like a pomegranate. Two golden pillars stood on either side, also decorated with golden pomegranates and golden petals.

Caden's heart quickened, knowing he was somewhere important. Very important. Out of the corner of his eye, he saw another building. Its great, domed roof caught the sun's light. The Dome of the Rock. Caden lifted his chin, blinking with realization. *I'm on the Temple Mount. The Wailing Wall's just over there.* He eyed the circling birds, and his stomach churned. His breath quickened, and he knew the scavengers were feasting on his brother-in-law and Abba. His gaze darted back to the building behind him. *The Final Temple.* He swallowed the hard lump in his throat, knowing something far beyond himself was going on.

"We all knew the terrorists lurked in the shadows!" Hugh called to the crowd. "In our United Society? In the very home of our beloved king and messiah?" Hugh paused, letting the crowd shout their hatred and demands for violence before continuing. Caden pointedly didn't acknowledge them as sweat dripped down his back.

"He was like a son to our king, alone and far from home. Our king took him in. He trained him, gave him food, shelter, a place to call home. To what end? So that he could use said training to slaughter the very man who brought peace to this broken world?" Caden shook his head as anger stirred from the depths of his soul.

"And our king," Hugh's words trailed off, thick with emotion. With a deep breath, Hugh began again with renewed strength. "This traitor, this terrorist, fatally struck our messiah in the head seven times. His skull was fractured in two places, his brain almost laid bare. He was left to die, drowning in his own blood." Hugh stopped again as more things flew at Caden. He shrunk back, shielding himself behind the Sentinels guarding him as others held him fast. He heard Rapham curse, Caden hoped he got hit.

"But!" Hugh cried. "But, can a mere child stop our king? A man whose power brought peace to a fractured world. Civilization! Unity! A unity beyond the corporeal dimensions, for now, Heralds walk among the modern man. And Giant. And Leovirs. A man like that is no man at all. He is a god!" The roar of agreement shook the ground beneath Caden. The sound reverberated in his chest and caught his breath in his throat. "A god that cannot be stopped, even by death!" Hugh's voice had risen to a shrill above the mob's cry. "Death has been swallowed up by victory! Where, oh death, is your victory? Where, oh death, is your sting? Thanks be to our messiah, who gives us victory through his sacrifice! Behold! Our king, our messiah! Luca Battistelli!"

The noise that followed reminded Caden of the ocean crashing against rocky cliffs. He shrank back, wanting to plug his ears as they shook from the force. The roar of excitement continued, overwhelming Caden and drowning out all other senses. He finally looked up to see the Final Temple's double doors opening. Strolling out into the sunlight, dressed in his uniform best with a decorative sword at his side, was Luca. The medals hanging from the chest of his armored white Refiner's uniform caught the light as the golden shoulder tassels swung with each stride. He walked without help from anyone and wasn't even limping. He wasn't connected to an IV, and no bandage wound his head.

Caden stared, mouth dropped open, remembering the man he saw just yesterday who looked like a strong wind could blow him over. *It's impossible!* His stomach turned; he'd hoped he at least slowed Luca down by a year. But a day? Not even a day, just a handful of hours! *They were trying to trick me. They made him look weak.* Caden blinked, knowing that wasn't right. No one had staged the blood that splattered him or the cracking sound of a fractured skull.

*"When will you admit we, too, have authority and power beyond comprehension?"*

Caden lifted his chin, seeing Doeg out of the corner of his eye. *No.*

*"It is true."*

*You have no power!*

Doeg's mangled face pulled into a tight smile. *"Oh, ye of little faith."* Caden's hair stood on end as Doeg's pale, icy eyes bore into him.

Behind Luca writhed a mass of horned dragon heads as Tarek tucked in its wings to squeeze through the Final Temple's opening. The great red dragon lifted its heads, the black, unblinking eyes sweeping across the sea of faces. Its wings spread, the horned tips stretching to the skies. Luca raised his hands and smiled as he climbed the dais several steps to Hugh. As he walked, the mob started chanting a word over and over.

Caden licked his dry lips, trying to make out the word. "Messiah! Messiah! Messiah!" Caden shook his head and stared in bewilderment. What idiots! Only Yeshua was the Messiah, not *this* guy! Not him at all!

Luca went up the several steps to Hugh, who bowed low at the waist, nearly bending himself in half. The Leovirs also bowed, their tails tucked and eyes closed. Luca passed Hugh until he reached the top of the dais. He raised his hands again, and the chanting grew louder. Demons joined in the cry, shaking the ground.

Anger burned in Caden's chest. *King Yeshua sees,* he thought. *He will avenge.* That did not quiet his rage or rid his mind of bats swinging against heads.

Finally, the cheering subsided, and Luca smiled down at the crowd, Demons, and cameras waiting. "Allies!" he called into his ear-set microphone. "I am honored you call me your messiah. I graciously accept this title." Caden scoffed, earning him a solid knee to the guts from Rapham. There were too many chains and hands keeping him standing as he tried to breathe again. They jerked him upright and he gasped, refocusing on Luca spewing more lies.

"I was killed by our enemies. Beyond the reach of any man or beast. But here I stand. I am the living one. I died, and now I am alive forevermore. I hold the keys of death and the grave. I have suffered on your behalf! The terrorists long for the destruction of our New Kingdom! They seek to kill, steal, and destroy, but I have come to give you an abundant life. Their assassination attempt succeeded!" Caden felt a crushing wave of hatred sweep over him as countless eyes turned his way. Fists raised. More rocks flew. He ducked down, unable to hear Luca as he struggled to stand.

"They want to destroy the truth I've placed in your hearts," Luca continued. "But, instead of letting them destroy you, I let them destroy me!"

Caden glared at Luca as he gritted his teeth. "Lies!" he

hissed. Rapham rounded on him again, punching his liver. Caden buckled as the wind knocked out of him. They had to drag him to his feet. He gasped, limp in his enemies' hands, as Luca continued addressing the nations of the world. "But what mortal could destroy a god?" Caden gaped at Luca, the absurdity of the claim was shocking. Not to the crowd. Their cry of approval and praise shook the ground, scaring the vultures from their prey, as the Demons shrieked with joy.

"I suffered," Luca said. "For allies and terrorists alike, that I may bring all into our New Kingdom, being put to death in the flesh but made alive in the Heralds." A low clicking lifted above the restless mob's clamor. Caden glanced at Tarek, seeing every head swayed with approval. "You too may be made new in the Heralds. Let them transform you, renewing your mind. Let them give you life and peace by permitting them access to your very soul." Caden's skin crawled as the Demons quieted. Many drew closer to a human, as though waiting. All were grinning.

"Let the same Heralds who raised me from death live inside you. You also may have real, pure life within your mortal bodies. For, once you are children of the Heralds, you are their heirs. Heirs of a New Kingdom without end, where there will be no more tears, sorrow, or pain. Permit them in. Give them control and inherit eternity!"

The roaring cheer shook Caden to his core. He stared at the Demons as a sickening dread chilled him. He watched as the people raised their hands and shouted praise while some bowed their heads and closed their eyes. Some grew still while others bowed low or laid down. Women pressed their hands against their chests as men quieted, becoming solemn.

*No,* Caden thought, his throat tightening. *No! Don't do it!* He sucked in a breath to shout a warning, but it was too late.

Before his eyes, a Shade drew closer to a kneeling woman. It knelt over her, its clawed hands laying on her back. The woman gasped, her back arching as she slowly rose. As she stood, the Shade disappeared behind her. No, that wasn't right. It melted into her. The woman's eyes were different. Wide. Full of knowledge one human lifetime couldn't give. As the woman stood, her lips pulled back into a wide, tight smile of flashing teeth and slick gums.

Caden's stomach turned as his eyes glistened with tears. *She just became a Puppet,* he thought, the realization paralyzing him. As he watched, a Viper hissed as it slithered into a man through his ear. A Fiend swirled around a Refiner, entering him through his mouth and eyes. Caden gasped, shaken to his core. One after another, the humans became one with the evil Spirits. Their praise and homage to Luca grew louder, more animated, and more aggressive.

People started leaping, shouting all the while, and smiling huge, inhuman grins. Caden flinched back as a Wither slunk toward them. It didn't wear a skin, and its corpse-like body turned his stomach. It marched right up to one of the Refiners and held out a boney hand. The Refiner let go of Caden and took hold of the Wither, drawing it into a hug. The Wither wrapped its thin arms around him and faded, drifting into the Refiner. With a sudden inhale, the Refiner stood, his chest puffed and eyes wide with revelation. He slowly turned and stared down at Caden. The man was gone. Only the immortal monster remained.

"A blood eagle is too good for you," the Puppet hissed as he returned to Caden's side and seized his arm. The force of his hold startled Caden; it was like being grabbed by a Giant. Caden squirmed, but the Refiner didn't budge, his fingers digging into his arm. He gritted his teeth as another Refiner guarding him became a Puppet, their hold of him inhumanly strong.

"Holy!" a voice cried above the Puppets' chaos. "Holy!" Caden craned his neck, seeing Hugh rising the several steps higher above the crowd. He stopped, his hands palm to palm with his eyes closed, as though ready to pray. "Holy is our king and our god! He is worthy to receive all glory, honor, and power, for he created our New Kingdom, and by his will we, his faithful allies, exist." Luca, higher still at the dais' top, stood tall and proud before the eyes of the world.

"We stand before you, oh god!" Hugh called out. The three Fiends swooped and curled about him like boiling, black clouds. "We serve you day and night in your Final Temple; and you who rules will shelter us with your presence. We shall hunger no more, neither thirst; the sun shall not strike us, nor any scorching heat from an accursed fanatics' flames. For our messiah and god is our protector; and he will guide us to springs of living water!"

Tarek's seven mouths opened as the heads moved about, the ten horns catching the rising sun's light. From between the fangs dripped water, quickly making a puddle. Without thinking, Caden sucked in a breath and held it. The dripping quickened to a small stream and sent the waters flowing down the Temple's steps and to the crowd. The Puppets cheered and began splashing in the mini stream and drinking from it. Caden turned away. He didn't even feel the chains biting into his wrists anymore.

"Why?" The whispered word hissed in his ear, and he turned, finding Moshe glaring at him. "Why did you do it? He's our messiah!"

Caden shook his head. "He's the Antichrist and will massacre Yahweh's chosen people. That's you!"

"He is our messiah! Sent by Yahweh!"

Caden's lips pulled back, and he lurched at Moshe.

The collar held him back, choking him as he stumbled away. "Then become a Puppet!" Caden hissed.

"They're called Zealots."

"Let the Heralds in! Let the rot begin from the inside out!"

"You blaspheme Yahweh!" Moshe shouted. "He will curse you!"

"We win this war," Caden seethed as the Sentinels held him back.

Moshe shook his head as he stared at him. "You were my friend."

"As a friend, I tell you, you're on the losing side."

"Blasphemer! This is our messiah. There are prophecies about him before your nation even began! How could a foreigner know of our ways?"

A stench stopped Moshe's rant. Caden grimaced, and the two turned, seeing three young boys dragging six pigs toward the dais. Moshe stepped back as his brows drew low. "No," he whispered. "Wait." The pigs, oinking and jumping about by the sound of the rejoicing Puppets, were hauled up the steps to the dais' flat top. Moshe shook his head as he held out a hand. "That's not...what are you doing?" Caden glanced around, seeing the few remaining Israelis responding the same as Moshe. A look of unabashed horror twisted their faces. "You'll defile it," Moshe said, his voice lifting. "Don't defile Yahweh's Brazen Altar!"

His shout was swallowed up by the Puppet's cheering. The crowd was slowly turning into a frenzied mob. The visible Demons leapt and danced about, splashing in Tarek's waters, and actually singing. Tarek itself kept unfolding its massive wings and lightly swooping them forward, sending a gust of wind over the Puppets and exciting them further. Caden's hair stood on end as unease pressed against his chest. *What's happening?* He looked up to Luca. In his hand was a long knife.

"You have made this alter for me!" Luca called as the pigs were dragged to his side. One nearly fell on the steep drop-off, but the boy held it back. "This sacrifice is to me and will be a burnt offering and peace offering." Someone lifted their fists and shouted, their faces red with rage. They were Israeli. "In every place, I cause my name to be remembered," Luca called, "I will come and bless you!" The Puppets nearly screamed for joy, their bodies dancing about, bumping into one another, and, some, landing on each other.

Moshe cried something again, but a Refiner stepped in his way. "This is our god's wish!"

Moshe shook his head, his eyes wide. "No! No, the pig will defile the temple! It's the law! This...this isn't right!" His horror-filled eyes turned to Caden.

*I told you so,* Caden thought as he held his gaze. *I'm sorry, friend.*

The Refiner seized Moshe's collar and dragged him close. "Do you reject the will of our god?"

"He's *not* god! He can't be! God wouldn't defile His own temple!"

"What did you say?"

Moshe tried to pull away, but another Refiner came behind him. "This isn't right!"

"That's enough!"

"This isn't what the real Messiah would do!" Both Refiners moved without warning, and Caden's eyes narrowed, not sure what was happening. It wasn't until Moshe slumped to his knees, his hand clutching his throat as blood spritzed between his fingers, did Caden understand. He cursed the Refiners and Luca. He hung his head, and Moshe rolled onto his side, his eyes wide and vacant.

Panting, Caden turned to the other Israelis who finally saw through Luca's lies. They were too late. Caden couldn't find them and knew they, too, were dead on the ground. The Puppets who noticed laughed as the Refiners cleaned their blades and stepped away, not even bothering with the body. The shrill squeals from the pigs strained Caden's senses further as he squeezed his eyes shut. The crowd of Puppets roared with praise as each pig was sacrificed on the altar. Caden's heart slammed against him as he tried to breathe. He felt weak, his legs nearly giving out beneath him. He wanted to curl up on the floor and hide from all this! There was too much evil here for him to survive.

*"Yet, the festivities have only begun."* Cold, bald fingers ending in sharp claws slid beneath his chin and jerked his head up. Caden gasped as he stared up at Doeg. The Sentinels around him stiffened, obviously seeing the Demon too. They all bowed in homage as Doeg grinned from ear to ear. Though Caden had seen Doeg countless times, the Demon had never looked like flesh and blood as much as it did in that moment. It was no longer a ghost who could disappear at will. Doeg was a monster, with muscles, ligaments, and bones.

"Come," it whispered. "Watch."

*No, please.*

"Watch!" Doeg forced Caden's head up toward the altar and held it firm. Luca was splattered in pig blood. It dripped down the steps and made a puddle on the ground several feet below.

Hugh stood over the altar, arms spread, as the Fiends swirled overhead. "May you all see!" Hugh cried, splitting through the din. "May you all see the power of our god! For we, too, can summon fire! We, too, have consuming fire, like the fanatics!"

"Lies!" Caden hissed as he struggled but could hardly

move. *Yahweh, do something! You see this? Don't let them talk about You like this!*

Hugh's raised hands pointed straight up as he lifted his chin and closed his eyes. Caden saw his mouth moving but couldn't hear the words. The Fiends swirled faster and faster as Luca expectantly looked into the sky. *You can't get the Akal Esh!* Caden's thoughts cried. *It's impossible! You aren't God!*

"Yes, Caden, we are."

*No! Only God's people have the Akal Esh! He's not giving ANYTHING to you and—*

Then, the sky broke.

# TWELVE

# SWEETER THAN WINE

THE ENTIRE GATHERING cowered with screams. Caden gasped, trying to catch his breath as he realized he was on his knees with a Sentinel on top of him. Had he fallen? What was going on? His chest still ached from the force that sent him to the ground. His ears still rang from the clapping sound of the sky ripping in two. And his face stung. Why was that? That's right, a wave of heat had swept over him. Heat like a bonfire.

*No,* Caden thought, his pulse quickening. *This can't be happening!*

*"We are god."*

Caden gave a strangled yell; he could hear the roar of flames. The fallen Sentinels gathered themselves and wrenched him back onto his feet. Caden watched as the Puppets also stood, each standing still as mouths dropped open in awe. Women started weeping. Men beat their chests, standing taller. Some knelt on the ground, bowing low. Caden turned toward the blazing heat and stared in numbed shock.

The altar was a blazing furnace. Luca backed down the stairs, his arm raised against the heat. The boys who ushered the pigs were fleeing. Hugh alone stood close to the wildfire; arms still raised as the Fiends swirled in the flickering tongues.

"Our god is like a consuming fire!" Hugh called. "He will consume his enemies and condense them to dust and ash!" The Puppets nodded, laying hands on their chests or muttering homage.

Caden stared, unable to turn away from the fire. It had ripped through the sky! He could see the clouds overhead swirled, showing its line of descent! It had forced everyone down, just like with Elijah and Yohanan! And it had come at Hugh's command. Just like Elijah and Yohanan. They had the same fire. Is that how the Spiritual World worked?

There was just one source of power, and both sides could draw from it? That didn't make sense though! How could both sides be equally as powerful? Neither would win; they would come to an impasse. Unless…unless God Himself was behind the power. God gave the Angels and Demons equal power, like an unending battery. Was God behind all of this? Was there no winning or losing, just existing? Was there no right side, just the one that survived?

Caden's tears spilled over as he stared, the heat pricking his face. Was this 'war', unending sacrifices, and unrelenting demands from an unseen, indifferent God useless? All Caden's steadfastness and blind faith was simple blind ignorance. This was not about God or His final remnant or Yeshua's return. This was about power, and Caden, obviously, didn't have it. The chains bit into his wrists as the collar seemed to tighten around his throat. Caden coughed, moaned, and ducked his head.

There was no God. There was no Yeshua. There was only the here and now. Only Luca, the messiah, the god of all there is. Caden closed his eyes, his thoughts crying just as loudly as the Puppets. His internal screaming had become white noise long ago. *The same power*, Caden thought. *They have the same.*

A whisker brushed his brow. Caden's eyes clenched shut as he pulled back. Taking a deep breath, gathering all the strength he could muster, Caden lifted his chin and regarded Doeg. The Demon stared down at him, a knowing smile twitching its mangled mouth. Its murky, gray eyes narrowed as a soft purr lifted from its throat.

Caden gritted his teeth until it hurt. *Lies*, he dared to think.

Doeg scoffed, its tail tip flicking. "You are a delusional fool."

*You will die.*

"Spirits cannot die."

*The second death. In the lake of fire. This is nothing.*

"Nothing? This proves your creed is false!"

"That man is what is false!" Caden's face turned red and shook with rage. "You will have to do more than a fire show to convince me otherwise!"

Doeg's smile grew as it glanced at the covered pillar at the center of the courtyard. "Very well."

Caden's stomach painfully twisted as he closed his eyes. *God, save me. Please. You've got to do something!*

The Puppets suddenly calmed down, and Caden glanced up, finding Luca several steps down the Brazen Alter. "As in the days of old," Luca's voice rang out, "the gods would erect a likeness of themselves to be a visual reminder of who they are. I cannot be everywhere at once, not yet anyway. For now, I have established my likeness here in my Final Temple to stand witness to my sovereignty. Behold! Your messiah and god!" The Puppets took up their cries again, and Caden drew back. He couldn't bear to watch.

"Come on, foolish human boy," Doeg growled, grabbing fistfuls of Caden's hair. "Where is your God now?" Caden gritted his teeth as tears welled in his eyes. "Look!" Doeg yanked Caden's hair, jerking his head back.

The pillar's cover pulled away and drifted slowly to the ground. Beneath was a statue that reflected the morning's light with a brilliant shine. Caden squinted in the sudden glare, and he realized, to his awe, it was entirely overlayed in gold. It was a statue of a man. He was in a Refiner's uniform, a sword at his side. He stood tall, his gaze lifted as though to the horizon, as one hand rested on the sword's hilt and the other fisted on his hip. Caden blinked. Though he could only see some of its face, he knew it was Luca.

The twenty-foot statue cast a long shadow as the Puppets voiced their approval and praise. Many dipped their heads and bowed to it. Caden's stomach turned as his entire body wanted to run. He couldn't be here. Death was here! Wickedness beyond anything the world has ever seen! He moaned through gritted teeth as the Sentinels held him and Doeg forced him to watch.

Hugh turned from the roaring fire and faced the mob. His gaze swept across the sea of faces; his expression calm as usual as pig blood splattered his clothes. "The Heralds have bestowed upon us power and authority. Not only is this consuming fire ours, but the breath of life. He who has ears, let him hear!" Hugh pointed a finger at the statue. Those standing closest to it backed away with muttering voices. All stared up, awaiting with smiling faces. Caden shifted; he could feel his heart pulsing the arteries in his throat.

"Believe in the power of the Heralds!" Hugh shouted. "Believe, and you will witness the glory of our god!" Luca lifted his chin and calmly smiled as the people looked between him and the statue. "Heralds, I thank you all for hearing me." Caden's breath quickened. "I know that you always hear me, and those of the New Kingdom. I say this for the benefit of the people standing here, that they may believe you sent our god to us!" Luca's name rose among the Puppets, but quickly quieted as each stared at the golden statue.

*Save us,* Caden thought, sweat dripping down his back. *Yeshua.*

Hugh took in a deep breath, his chest swelling, as his eyes lightly closed. "Come forth!" Hugh's command echoed in the courtyard and reverberated deep in Caden's chest. It penetrated flesh and tissue, and Caden felt the two words deep down in his inner person. It was a command beyond this world.

Shaking, Caden closed his eyes, a tear spilling down his cheek, as Doeg held him firm. "Look!" Doeg barked, jerking his head further back. Caden gasped and obeyed.

The statue. It was moving. Its chest rose as its mouth opened. The eyes, far up above and overlayed in gold, blinked. It turned, the grinding sound of metal against metal filled the courtyard. Puppets leapt back, laughing and pointing. The statue slowly glanced over his shoulder and turned, the great, metal feet stepping and shaking the ground. It towered over Luca, stared for a long moment, and bowed low, a golden arm sweeping behind it. Caden's vision was getting fuzzy, and he realized he wasn't breathing. Forcing an inhale, Caden didn't know what to think as he watched the twenty-foot mass of metal move like a living thing.

As the statue bowed, its golden hair falling about its face as though individual strands, it reverently closed its eyes. "Our god has come." Caden recoiled as several Puppets skirted back, squealing and laughing. Caden moaned as he stared at the new creature. Its words echoed from within it as the undertone of grinding metal mixed with its deep voice. "He is in the flesh and dwells among us." Luca's smile grew as he gave Hugh a simple nod, who bowed even lower than the statue. The statue stared down at Tarek and bowed again. The red dragon's wings flexed as the heads continued coiling like writhing serpents.

*Impossible!* Caden thought. *Only Yahweh can make life! He's the only one! Not you! You're a fake! You can only bring death!*

"*This* is god!" Doeg hissed. "How long will you deny facts?"

*No,* Caden thought, unable to look away from the statue as it stood upright again. *Yahweh, they're stealing Your power. Your name. Your authority.*

"Must not be that powerful of a God."

Caden didn't answer. He felt his strength leaving him. He needed Yohanan to come in and light everyone up. No, he needed Han! That four-faced, fire-sword-wielding Angel would make short work out of everyone. *Not Han even,* Caden thought. *I need Yeshua. Isn't He supposed to come and kill all the bad guys?* He looked up to the sky, searching between the clouds. Would the sky break again? The real *Akal Esh* would fall, consuming everyone in Yahweh's wrath, and Caden could finally be at peace because they won. Another tear streaked down his cheek as he saw nothing but the swirling clouds where Hugh's counterfeit consuming fire had descended.

"No," Doeg whispered, drawing closer. "That was the true *Akal Esh*. We've conquered and plundered the Enemy's camp." Caden's breath shuddered in his chest as another tear fell.

"Zealots!" Hugh's cry shot above the Puppet's noise. "Zealots, please! Let us worship our god properly! We have his image, and we have him, how can we not bow when standing in his presence?" Tarek's several heads started clicking deep in their throats.

Behind him, the double doors of the Final Temple

swung open, and several musicians stepped out. There were harps, flutes, pipes, horns, lyre, and other instruments. They walked around Tarek, bowing while they traveled, which looked awkward, and went down the temple steps. They stood across from Luca, set down their instruments, and knelt to him with their faces pressed against the ground. He nodded in approval as Caden's stomach twisted again. Doeg finally released his hair and drew back, purring softly to itself.

*Yeshua, do You see this? Why aren't You coming?*

"*Because He died the first-time, thousands of years ago,*" Doeg's unwelcomed voice whispered in Caden's mind. "*He died by our hand.*"

Hugh pressed his hands together as he faced the statue and the sea of restless Puppets. "Zealots! Now is when we show our devotion and homage to our god and messiah. When you hear the instruments play, you must fall down and worship the image of gold. Whoever does not worship will declare they are a terrorist and against the New Kingdom. They will instantly be executed."

Caden shifted as he looked down. *I'm already kneeling. I need to stand.* He tried to put his feet beneath him, but the Puppet Sentinels easily overpowered him. He suspected even one Puppet Sentinel could force him down. Panting, Caden dipped his head and gritted his teeth. *Forgive me, Yeshua,* he thought, a tear dripping off the tip of his nose. *I do not want to kneel to this.*

"*This is the one true god.*"

*Forgive me.*

"*You will die on these steps. Your ribs spread and lungs removed.*" Caden growled and tried to pull away from Doeg. "*While the world watches, just as they watched your beloved Abba get ripped apart.*"

Hugh continued speaking; Caden didn't listen as he knelt, the Sentinel's hands on his shoulders and the back of his neck. His chained hands became fists as he shook his head and slowly lifted his chin. He met eyes with Doeg and wouldn't look away. "You will spend eternity in Hell."

Doeg's ear flicked as its clawed fingers flexed. "I will break you, mortal."

The music began, filling the courtyard. Every Puppet instantly collapsed, lying face down, most on top of one another. The Giants fell face down too, as did the Leovirs. A low muttering lifted of chanted words of praise. The Sentinels who held Caden knelt around him. Hugh, who had descended the steps and stood to Luca's right, lay on his face, the Fiends circling him. Only Luca, the golden image, and Tarek stayed standing, all straight and tall and smiling. No, wait. Who was that?

Caden's eyes narrowed as he looked to the back of the throng. Someone was standing. No, two people were. There's another one! Caden's heart leapt, seeing others who refused to kneel. Caden gave Doeg a fierce smile. *You cannot break what Yahweh's made strong!*

Doeg stared down at him, a small smile tugging at its mouth. With a felon trill, Doeg's head tilted to one side. "The saints' blood is sweeter than wine." Caden's smile flinched to a startled frown. Doeg moaned and licked its jaws. "I thirst."

The great statue turned slowly, the grind of metal rising above the music. It faced those who stood, and its large, golden hands became fists. "Seize them!" It cried, pointing. Refiners yelled and turned to the standing few, their faces twisted by rage. Caden's flesh grew cold as he watched them leap to their feet and charge through the prostrate people. Caden watched as those defiantly standing faced the Refiners. A few tried to run, but Puppets grabbed their ankles and legs, dragging them down. A woman started screaming as Puppets seized her. Refiners and Puppets alike grabbed each defiant person and dragged them to the temple's steps. There were a few teens, a handful of women, and some men who—

Caden blinked, all breath leaving him. One man hunkered low, his arm protectively around a tall woman. *Noam,* Caden thought, his fists loosening as his body sagged. *Oh, Yahweh! Please, not...*

Caden's eyes darted to the woman under his arm. It was Auset. She struggled to keep pace as she wobbled side to side. Was she limping? Caden hissed a curse, another tear falling. His fists became limp as he stared at her full, round belly. *Oh, God. You can't...*

"*He is.*"

*Yahweh!*

"*He's not listening!*" Each breath was a chore as pain tightened Caden's chest. Sweat slicked his brow as tears continued to stream from his eyes.

"Arise!" Luca called. The assembly obeyed as he calmly turned and faced those unwilling to kneel. There were ten in all, and they were forced to their knees at the temple's steps in a line, facing the crowd. The Puppets stood as the golden image turned and stared far down at the line of terrorists. Behind each kneeling person was a Refiner.

Caden kept his eyes on Noam and Auset. She was still under his arm and visibly shaking. Noam drew her close and whispered in her ear. He lay a gentle hand on their unborn child, and she started to weep. Caden's heart twisted with agony as he shook his head. He wanted to attack, to shout curses at Luca, to do something! He could do nothing but watch.

The Refiner behind them barked an order and grabbed Noam. Auset screamed, and Noam lurched toward her, kissing her brow one final time. A second Refiner came, and they dragged him away as another held Auset back. She screamed his name and reached out to him. He was shouting something in return, but Caden couldn't hear. A Refiner kneed his middle, hardly slowing the large Israeli down. A third came and rammed the butt of his gun into the back of his head. His body shook, and he collapsed.

Auset's sobs filled the courtyard as the Puppets laughed and booed. Luca stared down with indifference, just as calmly as he had before. The Refiners hauled Noam to the opposite end of the line from Auset and threw him down. They had to hold his arms as his head swayed and blood dripped from his brow. Caden's tears freely streamed down his cheeks as he knelt, his own Sentinels again standing over him. They didn't bother making him stand, and he doubted he had the strength.

Doeg sighed with contentment as it knelt to Caden's eye-level. Caden shook; Doeg had done the same thing when Trace died. "Now," Doeg whispered, "is when I break you." Caden said nothing.

Luca paced before the line of prisoners, ignoring the plea from a father and his teen son and the weeping of Auset and another woman. "I do not want the wicked to perish," Luca called. "I want all to enter into my rest within the New Kingdom." Noam slowly lifted his head, his body swaying as he struggled. "However," Luca called. "I will not tolerate their evilness among us any longer. I will not be mocked. I am god, the messiah, the morning star, and will not —"

"King Yeshua is God!" Caden flinched and realized, with shock, Noam squarely faced Luca. The fury in the man's expression was beyond this world. It was a righteous anger. Luca slowed to a stop and regarded Noam. "You are a man! And you will not survive the wrath of King Yeshua! He is coming, with our reward and your doom!"

The Puppets shrieked at Noam, their faces turning red as many threw fists at him with teeth bared like animals.

Tarek's clicking grew louder as the seven heads lowered, the ten horns catching in the light. Luca's jaw flexed as his head tilted to one side. Caden's heart quickened; he knew that look. Luca held out his hand, and an executioner's ax was given to him. Noam stiffened and lifted his chin, unwilling to look away. Without a word, Luca strolled to the other end of the line.

Caden's eyes fluttered with dread as he shook his head. "No!"

Luca grabbed a fistful of Auset's hair and threw her down. Noam gave a strangled cry and tried to rise. Three Refiners held him back as Auset sobbed at the Antichrist's feet. Luca stood over her and grabbed her hair again, wrenching her upright. Noam cried out as the Refiners held his face, forcing him to watch. Luca turned to Noam, and the two stared at one another. Caden hardly blinked as the tears dampened his clothes. He was shaking all over. A great weight pressed on his chest, making it nearly impossible to breathe.

Luca took a stance and grabbed the ax with two hands. Auset weakly sat and faced the sea of bloodthirsty Puppets. She looked so tired. She closed her eyes and lay protective hands on her belly. Luca raised the ax, and Noam shouted. He swung, Caden ducked his head, and the Puppets roared with pleasure. Gasping, Caden dared to look. He flinched away with a curse and closed his eyes. He gritted his teeth and moaned.

"How many times must I say it?" Doeg hissed. The Demon's claws pricked beneath Caden's chin, forcing his head up again. "Look!" Auset's body lay in a pool of blood. Caden numbly watched as something was seized by the Puppets and held up with cheers. It had long hair and was dripping.

He cursed again and helplessly knelt there as his fellow believers were beheaded. Noam was the last of all.

He knelt, his chest heaving with effort, as his reddened face shook with rage. He wouldn't turn away from his fallen wife. Caden watched as he finally blinked and turned to the mob. Noam glanced Caden's way and did a double take, turning back to him. They stared at one another.

*I'm so sorry, brother,* Caden thought, his tears streaking down his cheeks. *We win. I swear to you! Yeshua will avenge!*

"He has been dead for thousands of years."

*He will destroy Luca!*

"The dead cannot protect. You are abandoned by your God. Again!"

Caden's eyes narrowed as his jaw flexed. *We win.* Noam lifted his chin and refused to look away as the Refiner behind him drew back the executioner's ax. Caden couldn't help cursing as Noam fell, his blood splattering the ground. He shook his head, seeing the ten dead believer's blood had pooled together and now mingled with Tarek's mini stream.

The Puppets danced in the reddened waters all the more and still drank from it. Caden did nothing as he stared at the blood. He felt nothing but the tears continuing to fall and his mouth opened as he fought to breathe. The Puppets started cheering louder again, and Caden blinked, seeing Luca facing them with a wide smile, his white uniform misted in red.

"It is time!" Luca called. "The New Kingdom has come to earth! Let us celebrate the death of terrorists and fanatics and join as one under me, your god!" The Puppets screamed praise. The Demons danced and cheered. The Leovirs opened their wide, fanged mouths and roared. The Giants beat their chests like drums. Tarek's seven heads drew back, and a high-pitched shriek raked from their throats and into the air.

Caden cowered low, the sound deafening. His entire

body was drenched in sweat. He shook all over but couldn't stand. Doeg stepped back, letting Caden's chin drop against his chest. It knelt to Caden's level and drew close until Caden could smell its rancid breath.

"*We* win!" it hissed.

Caden blinked slowly as a small stream of blood oozed by. *God, please!*

Doeg slammed its claws on the ground as its tail lashed and the fur on its nape bristled. Caden closed his eyes and felt the Sentinels around him drawing back. "We are the victors! We are more than conquerors! We will receive the crown!"

Caden felt like he was in a fog. He couldn't feel the chains around his wrists or neck anymore. He didn't even feel the snot running from his nose or the sun baking his back. The Puppets' cries were becoming white noise, and the growing smell of blood and smoke were a distant fact. Caden blinked slowly as he numbly stared straight ahead. It was all he could do to not slump to the ground. *They will kill me next.* The thought was so factual, with hardly a trace of dread or horror. Caden swallowed and blinked, finding Doeg still kneeling at his eye-level. He could see his reflection in the Demon's icy eyes. Doeg smiled at him. Caden stared back, too weak to do anything.

Vaguely, he realized the music had started up again, this time, the tune was more upbeat. Puppets danced and leapt about as others got out goblets of gold and silver. Others bowed to Luca and the golden image. The image itself stood proud and tall, turning ever so slightly to view all as the gold caught the light. Tarek was on the move. The great dragon slowly walked down the temple steps and began mingling with the Puppets. Several bowed to him with their faces to the ground, weeping and shouting their loyalty.

The Puppets began rejoicing in other ways, their

clothes slipping off as they shamelessly enjoyed the flesh. Caden watched as Demons joined in the party. He could tell each Puppet could see them and were delighted. They carried the severed heads through the mob, tossing them around like playthings and laughing. Luca himself stayed on the temple steps with Hugh, the False Messiah and False Prophet, admiring their handiwork.

Doeg gave a soft purr as it sat next to Caden. It leaned closer, grinning ear to ear. "Where is your God?" Caden blinked slowly but didn't answer. "A good God, a *loving* God, wouldn't permit your enemies to conquer so obviously. What do you think?" Again, Caden did nothing as he blankly stared. Doeg sighed and drew closer still, running its tongue along Caden's cheek, licking blood off his face. Gasping, Caden ducked his head and hunched his shoulders. His split lip stung, and he blinked through the pain as Doeg licked its jowls.

"Yes," it purred. "Sweeter than wine." Caden hissed a curse. "Wouldn't you think so, miss?" A lump formed in Caden's throat as he turned.

A woman faced them from the writhing, cheering mob. She wore a purple and scarlet Arabian gown and, sewn throughout, were pearls, gold, and precious stones. The dress was unbuttoned, and her full bosoms nearly spilled from the fabric. She flashed a beautiful smile as her eyes glittered and her large, golden earrings swayed. Caden's eyes narrowed; her bright red lipstick was smeared a bit.

She held up her golden goblet to Doeg and dipped her head before stumbling a step. She bumped into another Puppet, who steadied her, and the two giggled. The woman staggered through Tarek's stream, now a reddish hue, and to the Final Temple's steps. The closer she drew to the line of bodies, the more Doeg smiled, and the more Caden wanted it all to be over. He watched in horrified shock as the woman approached the beheaded bodies, knelt, and scooped up a cupful of blood. Laughing, she turned back to the crowd and staggered back.

Caden stared at her as he forgot to breathe, his mouth slack. She walked to Tarek, who greeted her with one of its heads. She bowed to it and raised the goblet. The horned head clicked an approving purr as its unblinking black eyes stared. The woman laughed and lay a hand on the scaled head before going to the dragon's body and climbing up between its massive wings. Caden raked in a breath as she lounged back and raised the blood-filled goblet. "To our god!"

The Puppets raised their own goblets as she leaned her head back and drank deeply. Caden's stomach turned as his mouth opened further. The woman laughed and wiped her mouth with the back of her hand, smearing blood on her cheek. Caden heaved breath after breath. He realized he wasn't crying anymore; there was nothing left to cry. He couldn't think, he couldn't pray. He could only kneel as the enemy got drunk on martyred friends' blood while the Antichrist grinned.

Through the chaos and noise, the smell of rot and pungent smoke, a small idea illuminated Caden's darkness. It was two words that were merely whispered and nearly drowned out in the roar of debauchery and wickedness. They were all he had. *Raw Peace.* Caden closed his eyes. *Raw Peace.*

# THIRTEEN
# NOT A SPIDER

CADEN DIDN'T SLEEP. In his cell, he hung from the chains around his wrists, too weak to stand, and he just stared. He didn't cry, he hardly blinked. He barely moved. He simply hung, chin to chest, and eyes half closed. He didn't care about his numb arms tingling painfully or his stomach's tight pinch of hunger. He was desperate for sleep, but whenever he closed his eyes, he saw that drunken woman on Tarek's back, smearing her cheek with Auset's blood.

*"Wasn't that delightful?"*

Caden's head swayed as dizziness overtook him. His internal screaming was at such a pitch he couldn't even hear it. He could feel it. It made everything seem so cold and far away, like he was just watching everything happen from the outside. *Yeshua is coming.*

*"He's dead! I saw Him die with my own eyes!"*

*He's coming.* Caden moaned; he couldn't stop smelling the false *Akal Esh's* smoke. It stung his nose, or was that all the blood? He couldn't remember. Something made him sick, and want to cleanse his eyes and memories. *They didn't stand a chance,* Caden thought, wondering what Auset's unborn child would've been like. Was it a girl?

*God just let them all die just like that. Without a fight. Without a word. Where's the God that said, 'vengeance is Mine'? Isn't that part of His job? He's failing. He failed Noam and Auset. And Ophir.* Caden's throat tightened as he thought of the woman who nursed him back to health and welcomed him into her life. *How can I serve a God who does that to His people?* Caden's eyes fluttered with emotion as a muscle in his jaw flexed. *Stop getting into my head, Doeg.*

"*That wasn't me, foolish human. Your own conclusions are rooted in wisdom. Listen to your deductions. Keep yourself alive*"

*God. Save me. I…I can't…*

"*Sweeter than wine.*"

*Yeshua, when are You coming?* Caden's answer was Doeg's mirthless laughter.

The door unlocked and squeaked open as Buck strolled in. Caden didn't acknowledge him as he slowly closed his eyes. He heard Buck grunt. "You look like death." Caden didn't answer as the heavy man's footfalls stopped right before him. "Hungry?" Steam brushed Caden's face, carrying up the smell of oats. He turned his head away with a groan. "Come on. Beggars can't be choosers." Caden's eyes closed tighter, and Buck cursed, tossing the bowl on the ground. It fell with a clang, splattering food on Caden. "Are you ready for tomorrow, ol' sport?"

A coldness crept over Caden as he opened his mouth, trying to find words. "What's tomorrow?"

"The day you learn to spread your wings."

A hard lump formed in Caden's throat as his eyes opened with a jolt of energy. "You will regret it."

Buck stared at him, calmly smiling. "No," he said with finality. "I won't." Caden cursed under his breath as Doeg's ears stood upright, eagerly waiting.

The door opened further, and heavy clawed paws clicked in. "Refiner Buck." The voice was deep and inhuman.

Caden turned, finding five monsters had walked in, their furry coats sandy as yellow fangs jutted from their jaws. *Leovirs*, he thought, his stomach tightening. The head Leovir was a male, his mane cascading down his broad shoulders and back. His ears flicked lazily; one was clipped.

"The holy god sent us to deal with this cub."

Buck frowned, and Caden pretended not to understand the Hebrew words. "Um...no. What for?" Buck asked slowly, seeing each Leovir, another male and three females, encircling Caden.

Caden's hair stood on end, feeling five pairs of golden, predatorial eyes boring into him. *Yahweh, shut their mouths!* His ridged shoulders became slack as he blinked slowly. *What does it matter?* He let out a slow breath. *I'm dead anyways. We're all dead.*

"Classified," Benaiah said.

"No, now hold on," Buck said, holding up a hand. "This kiddo's not to be moved until tomorrow."

"Does the royal pride god say his every plan to you?"

Buck stepped back. "No."

"Then tuck tail and go." Caden hardly moved as Buck slowly turned, regarding each of the creatures standing a head taller than he. Buck was a big guy, but even the smallest Leovir could kill him in a few seconds. With a curse, Buck gave Caden one quick look before going to the door. Caden's chest tightened with dread, but what else was new?

"Hey," Buck muttered. "Where's the guard?"

"Not needed," Benaiah snarled, his inhuman gaze still fixed on Caden. "Shut the door."

Buck obeyed, the door clanging and clapping Caden's

ears. Benaiah squarely faced Caden and stepped closer. If Caden had ever felt in a lion's den, he truly was now. Caden's eyes ping-ponged from the huge paws to the crushing jaws to Benaiah's firm stare. Caden's heart didn't even quicken as he limply stood. *If they maul me*, he thought. *There'll be nothing left for Rapham and Luca to torture. That's a plus.*

"You killed our Jehu," Benaiah finally said.

*He's talking about the Leovir who attacked me*, Caden realized. His eyes flickered as he shifted his weight. He finally opened his mouth and forced himself to speak. "I've told you," he whispered in English. "I don't speak Hebrew."

"You didn't have to kill him," Benaiah continued in Hebrew.

"I...I don't know what you're saying."

One of the Leovirnesses drew back her lips and snarled. Caden ducked his head as a shiver passed through him. "This cub is a waste," she hissed.

"Peace, Jael." Benaiah gave her a quick look before stepping closer to Caden. His claws slid from his paws, curling like the hands of a Shade.

Caden leaned back, the chains clinking with the movement. "Wait!" he hissed in Hebrew. "You can't —"

"Cub," Benaiah whispered. "Hold still. We will be quick."

Caden tried to breathe as each Leovir stepped closer, their tails lashing, and claws slid out, flashing in the light. *This is it*, Caden thought. *I can finally get some rest.* Caden stared straight ahead. He closed his eyes and let himself relax. He'd done his job. Now it was Yahweh's turn to take him Home.

Something slammed into the chains locked around his wrists. He gasped and stumbled, the force nearly knocking him down. His arms dropped limp to his side, and he swayed, feeling how weak his legs were. A velvety paw lay on his shoulder, and Caden leaned into the support with a moan. He grabbed the paw and looked up, seeing his weary face reflected in Benaiah's eyes. They were wide with concern, and his ears swiveled forward.

"He can't even walk," Jael grumbled in Hebrew.

"He can," Benaiah said.

Caden turned away, wanting to collapse and sleep. *Or die*, he thought. *I'm so tired of all of this.*

"Caden." He flinched; no one should know his real name. He glanced back up at Benaiah and the great lion's head lowered. Caden froze as he lifted a defensive hand, only to find Benaiah rubbing his whiskered cheek against his brow. He gasped and found himself grabbing a fistful of the Leovir's mane. "Walk, human cub," Benaiah whispered. "You do speak Hebrew, yes?"

Caden nodded as he tried to understand what was happening. "Are you," he rasped, then coughed. Clearing his throat, Caden raked in a breath and tried again. "Are you saving me?"

"As we did the other cub."

Caden blinked slowly, his thoughts taking forever to form. *Asher. He's talking about Asher.*

"We've got to move," Jael growled, her ears twisting back. Caden heard chains moving and felt a tug on his wrists.

"Walk," Benaiah whispered.

Caden sniffed and shuffled back as he stared at the floor. *I can't.*

Jael's tail flicked as she sniffed him. "Is he crying now too?"

*Just let me die.*

"Caden Johnson." Caden slowly lifted his chin and stared into those golden eyes. "We need you." Caden didn't answer as he kept staring. "Can't let the fake king win." Caden's eyes narrowed. His shoulders squared as he grabbed the chains still bound around his wrist. Benaiah nodded and motioned to another Leovir. Caden turned in time to see a black bag fall over his face. He didn't even flinch. "Move," Benaiah said, and Caden felt his chains tug. He forced himself to stumble forward. The ground felt so hard, and his body so weak. How was he not falling over?

*They need me.*

"It's a lie."

*Someone needs me. Someone knows my name.*

"It will get you killed."

*I'm already dead.*

"Yes. This is another trap. Another way to torment you."

*Yeshua will—*

"He's been dead for thousands of years!"

*He's coming. He's—*

"No. One. Is. Coming."

Caden closed his eyes as he listened to their footfalls echo around them. If he had been paying attention, he'd say they were in a hallway. But he wasn't paying attention. All he could focus on was putting one foot in front of the other and not blacking out. The sounds around Caden changed. He was too out of it to identify what was happening. Something hot shone on his head. Was he under another bright light? In another interrogation room? Rapham would be waiting for him, Grant grinning with his cane ready to swing. There were voices. He descended steps. He could smell gas and rubber. What was going on?

*Does it matter?*

Caden closed his eyes as he struggled to keep up. A paw lay on his head, forcing him to duck. He felt his foot slam into something, and he stepped up. Darkness closed in, and the light's heat vanished. A paw ushered him backward and into a bench against a cold metal wall. Caden nearly collapsed into his seat. He didn't care where they were; he got a moment to rest. He closed his eyes and leaned back before they tied him down again.

The Leovirs grunted as they seated themselves around him. A door shut with a bang, and the ground shook with a sudden rumble. Caden stiffened, and the bag came off. He blinked in the dim light and glanced around. Benaiah sat across him, each Leovir nearly eating their knees as they hunched in the small, metal room. "Transport van," Benaiah said with a nod. Caden nodded slowly as he felt the van roll out.

Jael grumbled something as her furry tail-tip flicked. "Can't even design suitable transportation for us."

"Not too bad," another Leovirness muttered.

"If *I* were a king!" she hissed. "Or god, whatever Luca is now, I'd make sure my creations were properly attended to!" The Leovirness said nothing as Jael huffed, her ears flicking back in irritation.

Caden found himself staring at Benaiah. His eyes narrowed slightly as he leaned his head back and tried not to sag into the Leovirs seated around him. "Where…" his voice cracked, and he tried to swallow any spit to dampen his throat.

Benaiah nodded, and a Leovir reached forward with a canteen. Before Caden could respond, the Leovir held it to Caden's mouth and started pouring. With a curse, he lunged away and sent a shoulder into the canteen. Gasping, he hissed a string of vile curses at the Leovir, the feel of water dripping down his face sending a shock of panic through him. A paw lay on his shoulder, and Caden flinched back. Benaiah frowned down at him as each Leovir stared in confusion. "He thought—"

"Don't touch me!" Benaiah frowned as Jael's lips pulled back in a snarl. Caden took in a breath and held it as he made fists. His eyes narrowed as power surged through him, sending strength to his weary limbs.

Benaiah held up a hand to Jael as he pulled back from Caden. "We are helping you," he said softly. Caden's narrowed eyes blinked as the tension in his neck loosened. "No one will waterboard you. This is no trap. Helping. That's all we're doing, cub."

Caden didn't turn away from Benaiah as he searched his face. It was kind of hard to tell if he was sincere, he was a lion-Freak after all, and lions weren't known for their expressions. "Untie me then." Benaiah motioned for Caden's hands, and the Leovir carefully pried the chain links apart. "Got a key?" Caden asked, rubbing his wrists where the manacle was still fastened in place.

Benaiah shook his head. "We'll think of something."

Caden drew back and moved his arms, feeling some relief as the weight of chains fell away. At least he felt energy again. Good ol' adrenaline. *It won't last.* Cursing under his breath, he ran his fingers through his hair and glanced at the Leovirs. "Sorry about that, um…" No one answered. Caden shook his head and slumped back. "Where're we going?"

"House Battistelli." Caden frowned, and Benaiah lifted his chin. "It is hard to find prey hiding in your own den."

Caden nodded slowly, then frowned. "No," he said. "No, we've got to join the others. Everyone's gone to the mountains."

"Who?"

"Under Fire."

Jael's head tilted to one side. "The terrorists?"

"We're not terrorists!" Caden glared at her. "That's what Luca calls us because we're against everything he is!"

"So, he's not the king? Not the messiah?"

"He's a man." Caden's eyes darkened as a muscle in his jaw flexed. "A man that will burn."

Jael stared down at him, her amber eyes unwavering. With a grunt, she lifted her chin again and nodded once. "I like this one."

"You said I was a waste." She shrugged.

"Caden," Benaiah said. "Which mountains?"

Caden stared at the Leovir and a hard lump formed in his mouth. This was all too fast and too good to be true. Could this be an elaborate plan for Luca to track down the remnants of Under Fire? *They were created by the Antichrist. They are bred for evilness and to literally hunt down Christians.* Caden's nostrils flared as Auset's weeping echoed in his memories. He couldn't see that again; another believer brutally die.

Benaiah huffed a deep, moaning whine as his clipped ear flicked. "We want to follow your King. The true King."

"Prove it." Caden held Benaiah's gaze and ignored the quickened beats of his heart.

"We could not kill the fanatics."

"They are the Witnesses."

Jael's nose scrunched up. "They're dead."

"We couldn't kill the Witnesses," Benaiah corrected. "Their fire and power could wipe out an entire pride. It almost did. They walked out with wounds, but we? I saw my cubmates burn alive in agony. We could do nothing. *Luca* could do nothing. A pride king who cannot protect is no king. He is weak. Unfit to lead a pride. The stronger, dominant King should lead. It is the natural order of things."

Caden's head tilted to one side. He hadn't heard Under Fire's message presented quite like that, but it was true. He glanced around, seeing the other Leovirs were quietly nodding. He kept quietly sitting as his stomach turned, for he realized he believed Benaiah. His brows furrowed as he cleared his throat. "You were made to hunt us." Many of the Leovirs shifted uncomfortably, some drawing back their lips to show rows of fangs while others stared down at their paws.

Benaiah huffed and shook his mane. "We were given hearts of man," he said. "Men are known to change their minds."

Caden slowly nodded as he scratched under his chin. "You know," he muttered. "Benaiah's in the Bible." Benaiah's ears stood upright as he leaned forward. "He's a mighty warrior for King David. He went into a pit, all by himself, and killed a lion."

Benaiah shifted, his tail-tip flicking, then he nodded. "It is good," he muttered. "Maybe I kill the beast inside me. The warrior, who follows your King, will win. It is good." Caden found himself smiling. He glanced at the canteen, and it was handed back to him. "So," Benaiah asked as food was also given to Caden. "Where do we go?"

"The mountains."

Jael huffed, her tail-tip tapping the floor, as Benaiah's eyes narrowed. "Any specific direction?"

"Nope. But I know where to get it." Caden took a huge bite of salted meat and eased back into his seat. He closed his eyes and sighed heavily. "Head for the Wailing Wall."

———

VULTURES STILL CIRCLED over the Wailing Wall. Caden's stomach turned as he walked into the courtyard. He stopped short and gagged. The stench of rot felt like a tidal wave that crashed into him. *They can't just let them rot!* The several happily gliding Fiends overhead and the smell of hot meat and blood proved otherwise. Drawing his shemagh further over his face, Caden pressed on. He had it wrapped around his head, too, and he wore an Arab robe. If only his skin wasn't so white, he'd blend in better. Not like anyone was paying him any attention though.

The Wailing Wall was filled with people. Filled. They were from everywhere, every Zone, every ambassador party. Dark anger struck Caden in the chest, for it looked like the party at the Final Temple had just spilled out into this courtyard. This was a place of prayer and solemn worship. Reverence. Not anymore. Everyone had a goblet; Caden didn't even want to think about what they were drinking. Everyone was laughing or dancing or partaking in some sort of pleasure. It was disgusting. He was sure every single one of them were Puppets. Refiners stood closer to the Wailing Wall itself, but other than that, Luca's men weren't there. There was no need. Demons had taken over. There wasn't a reason to guard against terrorists when they were all dead.

Caden's stomach twisted again as he remembered Benaiah's offhanded comment in the van. "Everyone started a manhunt."

"For who? Me?" Caden had asked.

"For every terrorist...er, believer. Especially Israeli. They're killed on sight. In the streets most of the time."

Caden had felt like ice water had been dumped over his head. "What about the labor camps?"

Benaiah's clipped ear flicked. "Zealots only want blood."

"They're called Puppets."

"It makes no difference." It was mutually decided they had to leave Jerusalem as soon as possible.

Even if Caden doubted the severity of the situation, he had seen it firsthand while walking to the Wailing Wall. It was all he could do to keep walking as a man and a teen were grabbed by Refiners and a mob of Puppets. Their screams chilled Caden's blood as he gritted his teeth and kept walking. *God forgive me.* What else could he have done, unarmed and weak as he was? The food Benaiah had given him had perked him up enough, but he needed to sleep for a week. Probably an IV and a doctor to look him over too.

*God will give me what I need,* he thought, his gritted teeth pressing harder. *Apparently, I don't need much. Hope He changes His mind soon; I'm not doing so hot.*

He forced himself through the crowd around the Wailing Wall and kept his eyes focused straight ahead. He didn't want to see what the Puppets were up to. There were so many Demons Caden suspected one of them would catch on he wasn't part of their New Kingdom. He'd be ripped to shreds in a minute or two. He didn't have any control over that, so worrying about it just sapped his strength and was a waste of time. *Easier said than done,* Caden thought as he weaved between a Shade laughing with a group of women and a Wither trying on a fresh, still bloodied skin for an ambassador's delight.

His heart started to pound as he drew closer to the wall. The smell of rot was so strong, he could taste it. He felt like he was wading through a battlefield. He forced himself to breathe calmly as his hands became cold and sweat broke out on his brow. He passed a grayed, severed hand. It kind of looked like Elijah's. Coiled innards had shriveled to wrinkly strands between dark, nearly black puddles of blood. It wasn't right. God had to see this, right? He wouldn't stand for this!

*Well, Yeshua did hang on a tree in front of His enemies for a while,* Caden thought. *Great. What's going to happen to me?* He shook his head, ignoring that particular disturbing thought.

He held a hand over his nose and stepped from the crowd. He knew the Refiners were watching him. He could feel it burning into his flesh. Caden felt his heart quicken in the arteries of his throat as he stopped to think. He had to get to the wall itself. He had to find Yohanan's directions. He had written it on a blue piece of paper. No, wait. Was it yellow?

*Yellow, rolled up, shoved at Yohanan's eye level, so a bit above mine.* Caden's eyes skimmed along the wall on the men's side. Papers still were shoved in the cracks and between the stones. The ones that had fallen to the ground were gone, probably washed away with Tarek's waters. Out of the corner of his eye, Caden noticed a Refiner watching him. He looked Russian. Caden ignored him and kept staring at the wall. *Please, God, this is another way I can die. Please don't let it happen.* Though his heart pounded with force and sweat dripped down his brow, he kept going. Fear wasn't a reason to stop doing something, or else Caden would've still been in America.

*There*, he finally thought, his eyes falling on a little yellow scroll. *Now how can I get it?* He continued staring and lifted his chin, knowing there was no way to get by without drawing attention to himself. *Maybe if I'm fast?* That was dumb. This was all dumb. Caden cursed under his breath and squarely faced the wall. *Screw it.* He walked to the wall, away from everyone else, between two Refiners.

"Hey!"

He ignored the Refiner and grabbed the yellow paper. *Please let this be the right one.*

"Get back from the wall!"

Caden pulled, and it came free easily. He unrolled the mini scroll and scanned the scribbled sentence: Petra. Leave, ASAP! He gave a half smile.

A hand grabbed his shoulder as a Refiner yanked him back and spun him around. Caden stumbled and faced the Refiner. With one look, he knew he was a Puppet. He was too strong, and there was something about those eyes.

They were too wide, and they looked at him like a wolf drooling over a slice of meat. "What are you?"

Something moved out of the corner of Caden's eye. At first, he thought it was a large spider, but spiders have more than five legs. Caden and the Refiner turned, and they stared in dumbfounded shock at their feet. Crawling around, moving on its own, was Elijah's severed hand.

# FOURTEEN
# HEAD FOR THE HILLS

CADEN BLINKED a few times as he stared down at the hand. It was like watching a zombie movie, but this wasn't a movie. This was real life. Giants seemed believable, Freaks of Nature were a stretch, and Leovirs he hardly accepted as real, but this? Caden blinked again as both he and the Refiner stared in stunned silence. The pale, shrunken hand crawled its way across the carnage until it bumped into a woman's leg. Her scream finally snapped Caden out of his stupor.

With a curse, he yanked his robe from the Refiner's grasp, made a fist around the yellow paper, and plunged into the crowd. Screaming erupted from across the mass of people, mostly around the Wailing Wall. Caden glanced over his shoulder and nearly fell as he saw a mangled foot's toes fidgeting.

"It's alive!" Someone shouted, and the people pulled back like the tides of the sea.

Caden struggled to stay upright as they pushed against him. He nearly turned and started running but noticed something else unusual. The Demons. They didn't look too happy. Actually, they looked more freaked out than the

Puppets. Many were in defensive stances, but some fled faster than Caden had seen anything travel before.

Bracing himself against the panicked crowd, Caden fought to see what was happening. A wide-open ring spread from the Wailing Wall as the rotting bits of meat and severed limbs mysteriously drew together. The hands rejoined with the broken forearms and the shredded skin knit together, reforming over ribs. Even the clothes, which had been scattered in tatters moments before, were coming together and laying over the remains. Caden blinked in astonishment as the nearly black, dried blood flowed back into the forming bodies, adding color to the gray and pale limbs and features. He put his hands on his head as he barked a laugh, desperately wanting his eyes not to deceive him.

Within moments, Yohanan and Elijah were put back together. They still limply lay, eyes closed, and still on either side of the Wailing Wall. Once they formed, panic truly took hold of the Puppets. People frantically raced away, shouting for the Giants or Leovirs to do something. No one left the courtyard as everyone went to the opposite side, hiding behind one another and demanding safety.

"They'll burn us down!" a man beside Caden wailed. "We can't fight them! They're too powerful!" Caden didn't move as he fought the urge to race to his Abba's side and shake him awake. It was like he was asleep after the *Akal Esh* entered him. He just needed to be woken up at the right time.

A sudden gale struck the courtyard. People cried out as they clung to their clothes and one another. Hats, pebbles, and bits of paper swirled in the sharp wind, the current leading to the Witnesses. As the gale struck Caden, he sucked in a breath, and his eyes widened. This was no ordinary wind. There was something in it. Something alive and active. It rocketed to the Witnesses, and

Caden watched as leaves and paper scraps swirled around both Yohanan and Elijah.

The dead Witnesses' hair tossed about as their clothes struggled to stay on. The mob quieted, as though holding their breath. Caden, his eyes growing wide, couldn't hold back a smile. *Come on,* he thought, as though God needed his encouragement. *Come on. Do something!*

Both Witnesses' chests heaved at the same time. No one made a sound. Not even the Demons were moving. Without warning, and beyond the laws of nature or reality, Elijah rolled on his side and stood. A low muttering lifted from the crowd as Yohanan also moved and rose to his feet. The two Witnesses stood in silence as they looked over their bodies and touched their faces. They glanced at one another, and Yohanan laughed.

That was enough for the Puppets. As though on cue, the Puppets and Demons together became hysterical. Puppets fell on their faces, begging for mercy with sobs and hands pressed against chests. Others started yelling with fists raised and guns drawn, though everyone knew weapons meant nothing to these two. Some fled, but many stayed, too dazed to respond.

Caden kept smiling. His hands fisted as tears blurred his vision. Laughing again, Caden scrubbed the tears from his eyes and took in a great breath. He screamed, his teeth bared, and his eyes alive with fire. He didn't know what he was doing, it was such a natural reaction. This was his people, his martyred family that he loved. Though they were ripped to shreds by a multiheaded dragon, they *still* lived.

Caden cried a maniacal laugh as he stepped toward Yohanan and Elijah. "We are immortal!" He bellowed in Hebrew. "Until Yahweh says we die!"

Yohanan turned, his eyes leaping across the crowd, until he spotted Caden. The two stared at one another, and

Yohanan gave a fierce smile. Caden lifted a fist into the air and turned to Elijah. He stood like a victor watching his enemies beg for their lives. He was loving it. Caden felt himself laugh again, and half of himself knew he looked insane. The other half knew the truth; they were winning, and there was nothing Tarek and its goons could do about it. The light shifted, like a great curtain moving across a window. The Puppet's panicked cries heightened as the clouds parted with a sudden force.

It took several heartbeats to hear the blast. Birds scattered as the repercussions from above struck the ground with an exploding wind. The sound of great boulders crashing into one another cracked overhead. All eyes turned up as another light, a new light, seemed to shine from the space the clouds had been. Caden's brows lifted as his mouth hung open. *Is it Him? Right now?*

The sky spoke. Well, it didn't really, but the voice carried across the vast sky, and the words shook in everyone's chests. The simple phrase was spoken slowly, as though from a massive, unseen entity this world didn't contain. "Come up here."

Everyone dropped to their knees, several putting their hands over their heads as everyone, *everyone*, yelled. Giants screamed in panic. Leovirs caterwauled. Refiners screamed. Puppets howled. Demons shrieked. Caden found his face inches from the courtyard's stone floor. His breath shook as his chest recovered from the force of that voice. Had that been God? It sounded so big! So powerful! The authority was beyond what Caden could even think of! His nerves tingled as he waited for the *Akal Esh's* heat to prick his skin.

*No*, he thought. *This is different. There's no fire this time. But this power! This has to be God!* Caden dared to lift his head. Yohanan and Elijah were staring up, their mouths open in awe, but their faces were peaceful. They knew who this was. There was no reason to fear. Without another word, they both started moving. Caden blinked, and he rubbed his eyes. What was wrong with Elijah's feet? Why was he on his tiptoes?

Caden scoffed a sudden laugh as he grabbed his head. They were moving up without using their feet or climbing. They were floating. Caden cursed under his breath as he stared without blinking, watching his Abba and brother-in-law drift higher and higher into the sky. Their shadows rose above their former gravesite and over the trembling crowd. People scattered from their shadow as though it would harm them, shouting and leaping over one another to get away. Caden knelt and stared, mouth hanging open, as Yohanan and Elijah gained speed. They went faster and faster until they shot into a cloud miles overhead within a few moments. They disappeared in the curling cloud and were gone.

Caden stared up after them, unwilling to move. He felt his eyes burning and realized he still wasn't blinking. Rubbing his eyes, he craned his neck up again as he searched the sky. There was no sign of them. Caden slowly smiled as he relaxed his strained neck. Chuckling, he shook his head and ran his fingers through his hair. "Cheaters," he whispered. "They're going Home first." He smiled.

An African American grabbed his shoulder and yanked him closer. Caden gasped and pulled against him, cursing him. "What did you say?" The man's eyes were wild with terror. "Home? What home?"

"They went Home," Caden said, ripping his arm free. "They were the Witnesses talked about in Revelation."

"What's that?"

"The Bible. Yeshua's called them Home to Heaven early. They deserve it; not everyone's destined to get ripped up by a dragon."

"This Yeshua," the man said as he suddenly searched the sky. "He's done? He's not coming to get more?"

Caden actually laughed. "Haven't you heard anything Yohanan and Elijah have been saying?" The man stared at him. Caden saw others were listening too. "That was nothing," he said, looking each in the eye. He puffed his chest, feeling like he was talking about a great big brother who was coming to whip the bullies into shape. "He's going to come back. Soon. If you're not on His side, He's going to give you what you deserve."

"But, I'm a good person."

"He doesn't care! All He cares about is if you choose Him or not! Good person." Caden cursed under his breath. "Nobody's good next to Yeshua. Like, the best you do is still totally disgusting. The Bible even equates it to pads or tampon, something like that. You're disgusting! That's why you need Yeshua! That's why I need him. He died for me, the least I can do is live for Him."

The man looked down at his hands as the people around them quieted. Caden blinked, realizing what he was doing. *Am I*, his stomach twisted, *am I preaching right now?*

"How do I do that?" The man asked, suddenly looking up. "How do I choose Yeshua?"

"You just decide."

"But, what do I give Him?"

"Yourself."

"How?"

"Just! Just do it! I don't know! You just stop living for yourself! You do what Yahweh says!"

A woman, her hijab slipping from her head, lurched forward and grabbed Caden's hand. "What does he say?"

"He says to stop following Luca. He's the Antichrist for God's sake! He'll get you all killed! You're totally on the losing side! Yeshua says to help others and to worship only Him and, and I think He has a lot more rules, but we're kind of out of time so…so I guess just love Yeshua and love His people."

"And who are his people?" an elderly man asked.

"Everyone who doesn't have a NIIC or bows to Luca or Tarek. Those are Yeshua's people." The woman touched her brow as she dipped her head in shame.

"Do you have a NIIC?" the African American asked.

"No."

"Then how can I love you?"

Caden blinked and stared at the man. "Um…I don't… do you have a plane?"

"I have a bus."

"Okay," Caden muttered as he nodded and glanced around. "How big is it?"

"I have a caravan of buses. I can fit a hundred people."

"Can you take us here?" Caden handed him Yohanan's yellow strip of paper.

The man stared at it and quietly sat, deep in thought. "When?"

"Now."

"What about belongings?"

Caden shook his head. "You read the instructions. It says to leave ASAP."

"Who wrote this?"

"Yohanan." The man stared at Caden, who pointed up into the clouds. "The younger one that just came back to life and flew into the sky?"

The man leapt to his feet. "We go."

Caden grinned to himself as he stood. *Thanks, God. You really do provide all my needs.* He started following the stranger through the still kneeling and begging crowd. Caden even had to step on a few to get by. Glancing over his shoulder, he realized others who had listened to him were following. "Do you own the buses?" Caden asked.

"I'm the transportation manager for the Ambassador Ajamu and everyone who traveled with him from Nigeria."

Caden stared at the stranger. "So, you don't own a thing."

"Not a thing."

Caden nodded once as he kept walking. "There's like twenty Leovirs coming with us." The man nodded. "What's your name?"

"Chuk Nweke."

"I'm...Caden." It felt so weird saying his real name. Chuk nodded again as they made their way from the mass of terrified people.

As they left the Wailing Wall, Caden glanced over his shoulder. There was nothing left of Yohanan and Elijah's remains. It was like giving the enemy the bird. Caden smiled a wide, wild grin as he looked into the cloud where the Witnesses had vanished. *You can't beat us!* He thought, facing the Demons cowering along with the humans. He laughed and continued walking after Chuk as others quickly followed.

———

CADEN STARED in the rearview mirror as Chuk drove their van as fast as they could from Jerusalem. Six vans trekked behind them, each filled with people wanting to go with them. One van was for the Leovirs, no one wanted to travel with them, and the others were people who saw the Witnesses' resurrection. There were a few Refiners even, still in their uniforms. It was a bit unsettling, welcoming the enemy to Under Fire. It was like Caden was just handing them everything they ever wanted.

*Not this time,* Caden thought as he adjusted his collar. Why did it suddenly feel so tight? *They saw the truth and wanted to change. It's as simple as that.* Or it wasn't, and Caden was just like Judice, betraying everything pure and holy with a kiss. No one would be surprised, death always seemed a step behind him, devouring any he cared for.

Caden rolled his eyes as he made a fist. He glanced behind him, looking for Doeg clinging to the top of a van or running in stride beside it. He didn't see the Demon anywhere but knew better. *Or those were my own thoughts messing with me. I don't know anymore.*

He sat back, his knee bouncing with unease, and tried to quietly wait as they made their way out of the city. At first, he didn't sit up front, being an assassin and all, but no one was paying attention. Apparently, two resurrected fanatics were enough to turn Luca's people into chaos. That and the ground was acting funny.

It wouldn't stop moving. Already, Chuk had to slow down twice as the road swayed unnaturally. Caden had gripped the dash and hung on for dear life, his pulse racing. After all the craziness he'd seen, an earthquake was not one of them. Each quake didn't last very long or cause that much damage. Cars would sway, a sandwich sign knocked over, young ones in the streets clung to their mothers. It would pass, and everyone would continue on.

With a hissed curse, Caden ran a hand over his face and glanced at Chuk. "Can't you go faster?"

Chuk frowned. He nearly lay back in his seat, his head against the rest, as a finger and a thumb drove while his other hand rested on his knee. "I am."

Caden's eyes narrowed. "You look ready to fall asleep. Didn't you feel the earthquakes?"

"You want to drive?"

"No! Just," Caden sighed and turned. "Never mind."

"Americans," Chuk muttered. "Always in a hurry."

"The message said to hurry!"

"I saw! Do you know why we're to leave so fast?"

Caden shook his head. "I'd say something dangerous is going down. And if Yohanan thinks it's dangerous, then it's *really* bad."

Chuk arched a brow. "Did you know him?"

Caden sat quietly as he scanned the sparce streets and the tall buildings. A few Giants walked past and a jeep of Refiners roared by, but nothing else. He took in a sharp breath and lifted his chin. "He's my brother-in-law and don't talk about him in past tense. He's still alive."

"Brother-in-law?"

Caden shifted in his seat and tried not to look too uncomfortable. "Yep."

Chuk grunted as he smiled. "Liked him?"

"I *like* him. He's still around."

Chuk huffed a laugh. "Do you see him anywhere?"

"I don't see God, but He's still around. I'll catch up with Yohanan later, probably after I'm dead or something. What does it matter? God's got it all figured out. Life's too nuts to not just let Him have control."

"That's hard to do."

Caden grimaced. "You don't make it look hard. All you know of me is that I like bats and cracking skulls."

"I don't see any bats."

Caden shook his head. "What you're doing is faith."

"No," Chuk said, waving a finger. "I just can't see two utterly dead men start walking around and still say what they preach is wrong. What they talked about is real. I don't want to be on the losing side."

"Good thing, too," Caden said. "I needed a ride."

The road ahead rolled like a wave in the sea. Light posts swayed, and a trashcan on the sidewalk toppled over. Chuk slowed, and the road cracked. Caden cursed as he held on, the unnatural movement twisting his stomach. He started praying a very colorful prayer as the van started bouncing him around in his seat. Chuk had to come to a complete stop this time. From outside, Caden could hear people screaming as metal whined and other roads cracked. He held the dash again and grabbed the edge of his seat.

Gasping, he looked up to make sure they weren't under something that could crush them. *Of course, we are,* he thought. *There are tall buildings everywhere!*

A lamp post crashed through the window of a store. A parked motorcycle fell with a crunch as the road's cracks spread as though it were ice. The ground swayed and bucked, looking like a living thing crawled beneath it, trying to claw its way free. Caden gritted his teeth, feeling his battered, tired body bounce around with each quake.

Gradually, it subsided. Slumping in his seat, Caden tried to catch his breath. He ran his fingers through his hair and motioned down the road. "Go. We've got to get out of here."

"That wasn't too big."

Caden glared at Chuk. "Step on it!"

"Was in a bigger one last spring. Knocked monkeys from trees."

"I mean it!"

"Alright! Alright!" The van started moving again. Caden ran a hand over his face as he stared at the broken road. If they didn't hurry, there wouldn't be a road left. "How much further?"

"Not long now."

"That's not a number."

"Relax."

"Chuk!"

"What's wrong with you? You should be better at this faith walking than me. How long have you been following Yeshua anyways?" Caden turned away, his mouth sealed shut. Chuk shook his head and motioned to the road. "We'll be out in ten minutes. Maybe fifteen."

Chuk grunted as he sat further back and let go of the steering wheel. Caden frowned. "Hey, you're driving, remember?"

"I got it, I got it," Chuk muttered as he reached into his belt. He withdrew a pistol. Caden lifted his chin as Chuk pulled the slide and chambered a round with a click.

Caden raised a brow as Chuk slid the gun into the front of his pants. "That doesn't look like faith."

"You didn't specify how faith really looks. Something about short on time?"

They continued driving in silence, their mini caravan making headway. The buildings started to thin, and Caden saw the highway snaking out into the sandy brown hilled beyond. He sat up straighter and dared, for just a second, to think they'll be alright. *Why am I stressing?* He wondered. *God's saved me from so much. He can totally get me somewhere just fine. I need to knock it off. Just chill and—*

He blinked. There was something in the highway right when it left the city. It crossed it, and there were red lights and men walking around with white uniforms. Chuk hissed something under his breath. "Do you have your papers?"

"Me? Are you joking? I've been wanted by the KUS for years now! Papers."

Chuk grunted and shook his head. "That's a checkpoint."

"I can see that."

"They were just setting them up when we arrived."

"Okay, well...take a road that goes around it."

Chuk raised a brow. "There's no going around the messiah."

"Antichrist." Caden cursed again and rubbed his mouth. "Okay," he muttered. "Okay, so...they won't let us through."

"And they'll identify you. Everyone knows your face. King killer."

Images of Rapham and Grant standing over Caden's writhing body flashed across his mind. The overwhelming smell of blood from the Final Temple assaulted Caden's memories. He flinched back with his eyes squeezed tight. *I'm really dead if they take me back. Luca wouldn't let me escape again. I've slipped through his fingers too many times.*

"What do we do?"

Caden didn't answer. His heart quickened again. He suddenly realized the lives of nearly fifty people were his responsibility. *How did that happen? Do these people even know who I am?* Caden lowered his head, feeling his chest tighten with emotion. He rubbed his eyes with a finger and thumb and thought about hiding in himself. As if that worked out well in the past. With a sharp breath, Caden straightened and made fists on his knees.

"I can't do this," he blurted out. "But Yeshua can. Alright! Yeshua! I know You see this mess, but I just want to remind You, there's a checkpoint right in front of us that will ruin everything and get me killed, so," a muscle in his jaw flexed, "so do something to save us, please." Caden fell silent as he and Chuk looked around expectantly.

Chuk leaned closer, his eyes glued to the sky. "What does He usually do?" He whispered.

"He's got a weird imagination, so probably something unexpected. But whatever He does, it'll be awesome."

Chuk nodded once. "You should get in the back. They'll recognize you."

"Oh, and they won't recognize me in the back?"

"Just do it."

"They'll still catch me."

"I can pull over. You could make a run for it."

"No!"

"Oh, so you want to get everyone else gunned down? We join you terrorists and get executed in the same hour!"

"We're Christians! And this is what faith looks like! Just sitting back, chilling, even when the right thing to do is run."

Chuk muttered something and rubbed the top of his head. "Looks stupid to me."

"Yeah, well, the Bible says what's right to Yahweh is stupid to everyone else."

"What for?"

"Because everyone else is blinded by lies and are idiots."

"It does not say that!"

"That's a rough translation!" Chuk hmphed as he sat up a bit straighter, his eyes locking onto the check point. The two didn't speak as they kept driving.

Caden's stomach started to fold in on itself the closer they drew, but he took a deep breath. *Raw Peace,* he thought. *God's protecting me with His Akal Esh. Han's here too...somewhere.* He wished he saw that Cherub more often to give him a little faith-boost. Whatever. Maybe he didn't need to see the goodness of God as much as he thought. *Well,* he thought with a grimace. *It would be nice, like right now.* As always, God was silent.

They reached the checkpoint. Caden wasn't surprised no one else was trying to get out of Jerusalem. The Refiner stepped in front of them as two Giants and several Leovirs stalked from a small building. Caden hissed a curse and forced himself to look calm even while his heart slammed into his chest. *Raw Peace,* he thought, watching the Refiner walk to Chuk's window.

Chuk gave him a wide smile and turned to Caden. "I can't talk my way out of this."

"Try."

"I can't!" The Refiner's knuckles rapped on Chuk's

window. Chuk rolled it down and, in a very cheery voice, said, "Good afternoon, ally Refiner!"

"We'll need to see the papers from everyone in your caravan," the Refiner said. "And search each vehicle."

"Of course," Chuk said. "Whatever you wish."

Caden looked straight ahead. He could feel his heart in his throat. One of the Giants was giving him a funny look. *Anytime now, God.* The Giant frowned and pointed a huge finger at Caden. He started shouting. Chuk flinched back with a startled gasp. *God?* The other Refiners and Leovirs turned to stare at Caden. *Are You listening!* They moved in, weapons raised and claws sliding out from feline fingers.

Caden didn't move as he stared at the enemy closing in. He would've heard the rumbling sound sooner if he wasn't in survival mode. It wasn't until the enemy around them froze and stared, their gaze looking beyond their line of vans, did he finally hear it. He imagined a running crowd of Giants would sound similar. Looking in the rearview mirror, Caden saw the skyscrapers of Jerusalem. They were swaying back and forth as wildly as the light post from before. The highway leading from Jerusalem rippled like a huge tidal wave the asphalt fracturing loudly as the wave of road rushed towards them. Caden's eyes widened, and the van started to shake.

# FIFTEEN
## INTO THE WILDERNESS

CADEN SUCKED in a violent gasp to scream at Chuk to punch it, but he didn't have to. He was thrown into his seat, the seatbelt nearly choking him, as the wheels squealed. They took off, the engine roaring. Caden hung on with all his might. The people stuffed in the van screamed. They rocketed toward the bar across the road. Caden raised a defensive arm, as though that would do anything, and they crashed through, sending splintered bits of wood.

They didn't have time to look behind them. The wide-open road stretched before them, and Caden half expected to hear gunshots at any moment. He highly doubted the vans were bulletproof. *Here we go again,* he thought, his back tingling with the anticipation of a bullet. *Whatever. Yahweh's got it handled.*

Chuk's white knuckles gripped the steering wheel as he leaned forward, eyes hooded, jaw set. He didn't even blink as they raced down the road. Caden felt the slightest movement of Chuk's steering. It kept making his heart leap into his throat. They were going to crash, even with the smallest mistake.

"Stop jerking us around!" Caden cried.

"That's not me!"

Caden's stomach turned, and he dared to look behind them. The five other vans followed. For the smallest moment, Caden was glad they chose to follow and weren't taken out by the Refiners. The Refiners themselves weren't even a problem. Most had been thrown to the ground. Their little building was swaying like a drunk person. Several Leovirs were running away on all fours, ears back and tails tucked. Caden looked beyond them, and his gladness was snuffed out instantly.

In the distance, half of the swaying skyscrapers weren't there anymore. Great clouds of smoke billowed from the ancient city. And the highway. It was destroyed. There was hardly a road anymore as a massive crack shot through it like fracturing ice. And it was racing toward them. Caden felt a cold numbness tingle his fingers as he licked his lips and looked ahead. There was nothing in their path, but was it enough?

Caden motioned down the road, his breath quickening. "Faster!"

"Stop shouting at me!" Chuk's fingers tightened on the wheel. "You're making me nervous!"

"We've got to—"

Chuk shouted a string of random sounds, and it took Caden a second to realize it was Swahili. He didn't have to know what he was saying to take the hint. The van bucked. Everyone screamed as Caden grabbed the dash, his seatbelt still locked tight across his chest. The van swayed and shook, the axles and wheels whining with protest. Caden cursed and closed his eyes, his breath raking his throat. *Hide in Yahweh, not myself.* He took a slow breath and remembered his internal wall was so weak against the assaults of life. But not Yahweh's. *Raw Peace,* Caden thought, forcing his breathing to slow. *I've been given it. Now. I have it. Now. I can live in it. Now. I have Peace, the Akal Esh, that is so violent and powerful, no one can stand against it!*

Caden's eyes opened as his jaw flexed. The van kept bouncing down the road, and the passengers kept screaming, but not Caden's internal screaming. Either he didn't notice it, or it wasn't there. For the first time, Caden wondered if it really was gone. *Raw Peace,* he thought. *God was with them and gave them rest. He's with me. He's giving me —*

The van leapt. Caden felt his stomach float in his body. He gasped, panic grabbing his throat. It was the longest two seconds of Caden's life. They landed with a crunch, sparks flying from the front of the van, and Caden heard the clang of something falling off. A seated woman started wailing. A man started begging in French. Sweat streamed down Chuk's face, and he roughly swiped it from his eyes.

Caden, his heart pounding from adrenalin and every muscle tensed, started to hum. He didn't know where the song came from, it just bubbled up and buzzed in his throat. It took him a moment to realize what he was doing, and half his brain told him to knock it off and freak out like a normal, proper person. He kept humming and humming, louder and louder to be heard above everyone else losing it. He felt Chuk watching out of the corner of his eye.

*Raw Peace,* Caden thought as he continued to hum and bounce down the road. He focused on the end of the road and refused to let himself think of the earthquake destroying Jerusalem. He was one of the final remnants and immortal until God said it was time to go Home. Fear was such a trifle thing next to God's truth.

———

IT WAS Caden's turn to bat. It was his favorite, everyone knew. That's why it was so serious. Everyone would be watching and judging. Well, everyone just meant Dad. He was watching. Always watching like a hawk, ready to pounce at any sign of weakness. Caden gruffly sniffed as uneasiness twisted his guts into knots. He grabbed the bat and walked from the dugout onto the field. It was a nice day. The sun was shining, and there was a soft wind. He could smell hamburgers and knew one of the other kid's dads was having a BBQ during the game. Somebody's kid was crying, and a dog barked in the excitement. The buzz of spectators made his heart quicken; Dad was sitting with them.

*Don't let him see I'm weak,* Caden thought as he kept his eyes trained on the plate. *Don't even look for him. You don't need him. He'll just make this all worse!*

But he had to look for his dad. What kid wouldn't? At the plate, and while getting into his stance and drawing back the bat, Caden glanced over his shoulder. He hated himself for doing it. He didn't want to need someone who never thought highly of him, but he couldn't help it. His eyes shot right to Dad's seat. Front row to the left of the dugouts. He'd sit forward, hands folded in his lap, and a small smile on his lips to trick everyone he was enjoying himself. But his eyes, they would be like a panther's, dark and predatorial.

As Caden looked, he blinked and frowned. Someone was in his spot. *No one* did that. Like, ever. It was a guy in his thirties, and he looked like someone from the Middle East. Actually, he looked Israeli. He wore a green pullover jacket and a striped ballcap. He was sitting forward, intently staring right at Caden. Caden's brows furrowed. The guy looked at him as though he just came to watch Caden. He was grinning too. It was weird. Caden had never seen this guy before. The Israeli smiled further and waved.

*Do I know you?* Caden glanced at his hand and froze. A

huge scar marked his wrist. It was like something had been shoved into it a long time ago. Maybe even through it, the scar was so big. Caden stared at the man's face. He still hadn't a clue who he was, but he suddenly wanted to—

A hand shook him, and there was an accented voice, a voice of someone a bit irritated. Caden blinked open his eyes and turned his head, finding himself curled up in an awkward position in Chuk's van. "What's wrong with you?" Chuk grumbled. "We almost died! And when do I get to rest; I've been driving all day."

Caden glanced around and squinted, seeing the shadows were long outside. He groaned and sat up, wiping the sleep from his eyes. "Where are we?"

"Leaving Wadi Musa."

"Hum?"

Chuk waved a hand. "We're almost there."

Caden nodded and yawned. Running his fingers through his hair, Caden sat up straighter and sniffed. "Got any food?"

"No," Chuk said.

"I was told to leave without packing anything."

Caden glared at him, and Chuk grinned as he handed him a protein bar. "Thanks." As Caden ate, he kept humming and staring out the window. The sun was setting, casting an orange hue, which made the landscape look on fire. Typically, a place of yellows and sandy browns, it was now an electric orange. There were hardly any plants, and the ones that clung to boulders and rocks were practically dried sticks. Caden's eyes narrowed. "How much water is out here."

Chuk shook his head. "Doesn't your Yahweh provide?"

"You mean *our* Yahweh?"

"Right, right. I heard the older fanatic say He does that."

"Elijah's not a fanatic, he's a Witness."

"Alright, man! Sorry! Sorry. Witness Elijah." Chuk muttered something and shook his head again. "Can't believe he's alive. That was out of this world!"

Caden grunted. "That's the point. It was God." As they drove, Caden saw sandstone hills rising in the distance. "Is that where we're going?" Chuk nodded. "Have you been here before?"

Chuk shrugged. "Heard about it. Saw pictures. Wanted to go, actually. It is a very cool place. Very cool."

Caden sniffed as he sat back and stared. "Is it safe? I mean, are there caves or something?"

Chuk grinned. "If I tell you, you won't believe me."

"Yes, I will. Do you have any idea what I've seen?"

"Ah! Ah! Just wait! You'll see. Patience." Caden shook his head with a curse and sat back. "I didn't think Christians had such potty mouths." Caden didn't answer. "You do swear a lot."

"I'm almost about to die a lot."

"Hum," Chuk grunted. "Thought you wouldn't."

Caden opened his mouth with a curt remark, but snapped his mouth shut. *Maybe he's right. I guess I should work on that.*

They drew closer to the hills, and Caden saw sandstone mountains behind it. Chuk slowed as the hillsides drew closer and closer to either side of the road. The deep, black mouth of a cave caught Caden's eye. "Ha!" he said. "I knew it was just caves!" Chuk shook his head, muttering more Swahili, but said nothing.

As they kept going, they passed more caves. Caden stared at one with a furrowed brow. The opening wasn't a rough, irregular hole. It was a rectangle, like a door. He blinked, trying to wrap his head around it, when he saw one rectangular cave with two protruding columns of rock like doorframes. It was chiseled from the sandstone and looked exactly like a door. Caden sat back and shut his mouth, realizing he had no clue what he was getting himself into.

The further they drove, the more doorways were carved right into the rockface, some surrounded by decorative pillars. Chuk led them further in until the hillsides drew closer still to the road. Caden looked ahead and saw a massive sandstone wall cutting across their path. He sat forward as Chuk parked the van and turned it off.

Caden glanced from the cliff-wall to Chuk, and then back to the wall. "This is it?"

Chuk laughed. "No, you silly goose! Just wait!" Caden frowned as they got out of the van, the other vans parking around them.

Benaiah got out and stretched his feline limbs, his tail flicking behind him. The humans stepped back from the Freaks as the lions walked up to Caden. "Is this our new pride?"

Caden glanced up at Benaiah and noticed his ears kept twitching back. "Ah...I don't think so." Benaiah's eyes widened as Jael, who stood beside him, hmphed loudly and crossed her arms. "What?" Caden asked. "I've never been here."

"Why do we listen to this cub?" Jael demanded, waving a paw.

Caden could've sworn her claws were out. Caden frowned and stepped closer to her. "I never have a clue what's going on. I just trust God to take care of it. You know, faith?" Jael stared down at him, her ears back as her tail flicked. In the back of Caden's mind, he remembered she could take him out with one swing. Benaiah glanced at her, and she turned away, muttering something. Caden ran a hand over his face and cursed, seeing how many people had joined them. There were about forty of them, all newborn baby Christians who hadn't the slightest clue what they signed up fcr.

*Let's show them.* Caden thought as he turned to the cliff. "Where to now, Chuk?" Chuk munched on his own protein bar as he walked across the rocky ground toward the cliff. Caden frowned, knowing maybe the Leovirs could climb the sheer rock face, but that was it. He followed anyways, ignoring the people muttering behind him. *I could be leading them all to their deaths,* Caden realized. His heart started to quicken as his stomach flopped. *Just like Nate and Trace. They didn't stand a chance following me. My track record is a list of slaughtered followers. Has Yahweh guided us here to perish?*

Caden's jaw clenched as he took in a breath and squared his shoulders. Out of the corner of his eye, high on the cliff's top, a white thing slunk by. He didn't even bother looking as he lifted his chin and kept walking. *Just do what Yahweh says,* Caden reminded himself, ignoring Doeg and the unease tightening his chest.

He focused on Chuk and looked beyond him. He barked a sudden laugh. "See? I knew it!" Benaiah shot him a look, as did others, but Caden didn't care. Beyond Chuk and slicing through the cliff wall was a slot canyon. The black opening ripping through the wall was shadowed and dark and stuck out like a sore thumb. How hadn't he seen it before? He laughed again as his strides lengthened. The group followed Chuk in, and Caden stared up as the towering natural walls closed in around them. The slot canyon wasn't very wide, and the walls rose up and up. It was suddenly cool in the canyon's shadow.

*Now this,* Caden thought, walking in step beside Chuk. *This is cool!*

"You really didn't know about this place?"

"No!" Caden stared up, seeing the sky far overhead.

He lay a hand on the sandstone, feeling its sheer face. "I've never seen anything like this."

"This is just a fascinating place! Like a present that keeps unwrapping."

Caden's head tilted to one side. "There's more?"

"You'll see."

"Chuk, you know what I hate with a passion, especially these days? Surprises. Just can't stand them. It's probably because everyone's trying to kill or maim me all the time, you know?"

Chuk's grin grew as he shrugged. "Fair enough."

Loose pebbles bounced down the slot canyon, clitter-clattering all the way. Two ropes landed on the path before them, their ends secured overhead. By the time Caden's brain processed they weren't alone, he heard a loud zipping, and two people whizzed down the ropes. Caden stepped back, seeing shemaghs masked their faces, and they were covered in white armor. His heart leapt as he made fists. The strangers blocked their path and raised M16s. A woman behind him screamed. The Leovirs snarled as someone shouted in alarm.

*We can take two*, Caden thought as he moved forward. He froze suddenly, hairs on the back of his neck standing on end. He finally looked up. Ten strangers stood on either side of the slot canyon high above. Each had a weapon trained on Caden and his people. He turned around, seeing another pair had repelled down behind them. They were trapped. All because they followed Caden.

Tension thickened the air in the tight space as the people restlessly drew together, many crying out and clinging to one another. Caden's fists loosened as he looked across the twenty-four armed strangers. Anger tightened his chest. He didn't have time to deal with all this! He had somewhere to be, his sister to find, and,

Yeshua willing, Dasha too. *How many things are going to get in my way?*

It was ridiculous. Swearing under his breath, Caden lifted his chin and squarely faced the strangers before him. He stepped forward, practically feeling their guns training on his chest. *Alright, Yahweh,* Caden thought. *You said You'd talk through Your people. Please convince these guys not to kill us, alright? That be great.*

# SIXTEEN
## HOME

CADEN WASN'T sure what was more disturbing, the fact that they could get gunned down at any second or the fact that he was more irritated than terrified. Sure, his heart was pounding with force, and his stomach knotted again, but he felt his jaw set as anger narrowed his eyes. He stepped between the guns and those behind him and crossed his arms. "Long live King Yeshua!" he declared above the restless panic behind him.

The armed strangers didn't move as more pebbles clattered to the canyon's dusty floor. Caden muttered under his breath, a stupid idea donning on him. He didn't want to do it. It would either prove they were good guys or get them all slaughtered. *No*, Caden thought. *Just get me slaughtered*. What else was new?

He lifted his chin and took a step closer, his heart really pounding now. "Go tell Ellie Johnson her brother has returned." One of the stranger's heads tilted to one side. "I am Caden Johnson." They still didn't move.

One grunted and straightened, bringing his gun down. It still pointed at Caden, but at least it wasn't trained on him. "Assassin." Caden's eyes narrowed as the second stranger also lowered his guard. The first motioned to Caden and looked to the men above. "Assassin!" Caden frowned. Did *everyone* know who he was? He glanced up, seeing others were lowering their guard and muttering among themselves. One didn't move as he stared fixatedly at Caden.

Their eyes locked as Caden faced him. "Well?" Caden called up to him. "Will you show me to my sister or not?" The people quieted as they listened. Out of the corner of his eye, Caden saw Chuk shake his head and beg Caden to shut his mouth. Caden didn't move as he kept staring up at their leader. His crossed arms tightened as his eyes narrowed; he was sick of this. There were just too many barriers when it came to obeying God! Why did it have to be so difficult?

The stranger motioned to his men. "Stand down!" The armed strangers shuffled their feet and drew back, their guns lowering as they glanced between Caden and their leader.

Caden couldn't hold back a smile as he turned away and ran his fingers through his hair. Sweat had gathered at his brow, and his hands felt clammy. He motioned down the slot canyon. "Shall we?"

"Who are these people?" The leader cried.

"They are servants of King Yeshua."

"Not those ones." He jerked his chin towards the Leovirs. The upright lions met his gaze, and the napes of their necks stood on end. "How dare you bring Freaks of Nature defiled by the false king!" Behind, Jael snarled as others drew low to the ground, their great muscles tensing to pounce. Caden had no doubt they could claw their way up the rocks. The armed men raised their weapons again, many tensing for action.

Caden raised his hands and shot Benaiah a quick glance. The Leovir stayed ready, his tail tip lashing and clipped ear turned back. Caden stepped between the Leovirs and the leader. "They have the hearts of men, just like us!"

"They are nothing like us."

"They were twisted by darkness but chose to reject it and follow the one true King! That is exactly like us!"

The man chopped the air with an arm and shook his head. "Stand back! Only humans are allowed in!" A shadow crossed Caden's eyes as a muscle in his jaw flexed. Without a word, Caden strolled to Benaiah. He stood directly in front of him and faced the stranger head-on. "You will be massacring my rescuers." The leader didn't budge. "As well as Asher Mizrahi's! They risked everything to get us out!"

"They are the Devil's creations!"

"So are you!" Caden jutted a finger as though it were a weapon. "You think you're pure and beyond fault? That these *Freaks* are far beneath you? We all need King Yeshua just as much as these things! Besides, why has Yahweh let them come this far? If Yahweh wants to stop them, He'll do it! He's pretty powerful, He doesn't need *your* help, you puny mortal." The leader didn't move again as his eyes darted between Caden and the Leovirs. Caden's nostrils flared as he cursed. "Let Asher decide."

"Asher is not here." Pain struck Caden's chest, and he gritted his teeth. He closed his eyes, longing for his brother, aching in his heart. Shaking his head, Caden faced the leader again, his face void of emotion. He refused to speak as he shielded Benaiah. The leader shuffled his feet as he looked across the Freaks. He muttered to himself and rubbed the back of his head. Without a word, he motioned down the slot canyon.

Caden smiled as the armed men surrounding them started to move. He nodded to the leader and followed their escort. *No,* Caden reprimanded himself. *They're no escort. We're still surrounded, and they'll gun us down if they feel like it. Such a good welcoming home.* He ran his fingers through his hair and forced himself to stand tall and simply walk.

Feeling slowly returned to his fingers, but he kept looking up at the leader, making sure he still wasn't about to change his mind. They kept walking. Caden blinked, realizing he was humming again. He stopped and glanced down. *Why do I keep doing that?* He thought he knew the song but couldn't quite place it. *Singing is the last thing I should be doing right now.* As he kept walking, he realized he had started humming again. *Knock it off! Who ever heard of a tough guy who hummed a little tune?*

The slot canyon wound this way and that, the walls sometimes narrowing so that a car could hardly drive down it. Besides the armed strangers and threats of being turned into a mass grave, Petra was pretty cool. They occasionally passed gated-off sections which protected carvings, more chiseled doorways, and statues from ancient days.

Caden still didn't understand why this was where God wanted to send His remnant. It didn't take long for him to figure it out. He stopped himself from humming again and nearly stopped in his tracks. Peeking from beyond the slot canyon's narrow walls, he saw a building. "What the…"

It looked like an ancient skyscraper that just appeared in the middle of nowhere. The closer they drew, the more Caden stared in awe. The building was chiseled from the sandstone, and the front of it was flush against the cliff face. It looked kind of Roman, with pillars and decorative edges, but not exactly. Caden wasn't one for architecture, but he knew an insane work of art when he saw one.

*Who made this?* The slot canyon widened until it opened completely and Caden and his people spilled out. Each headed for the towering building. It was about ten stories, and the doorway was a massive, gaping mouth. *That's big enough for a Giant,* Caden thought, his hair slowly standing on end. His eyes darted around, half expecting a Giant to step from the shadows or to see huge footprints across the ground. He saw none.

Their 'escort' repelled from the slot canyon and surrounded them once more without a word. Caden felt Chuk stepping close to him as everyone restlessly pulled tighter together. Benaiah and his Leovirs' only moved their tails as their golden eyes faced each armed stranger. Caden lifted his chin as the leader approached. He was a short guy, but he looked strong enough to throw Caden across the canyon.

Caden's stomach turned, and he fought to not think of Grant and his gang of hungry wolves surrounding him nearly two years ago. They were going to make him a slave, then make him suffer, of course. What would these new masters demand of him? Slavery was always an option. The brutality of survivor-like mentality would always crush the weak and leave Caden alone, covered in the blood of those he loved.

Caden hissed a curse and shook his head, ridding his mind of Doeg's implanted ideas. *"You will regret stepping one foot in this place."*

*Go away.*

*"I will never leave you. Never forsake you."*

*How dare you quote Yeshua!* Somewhere, he could hear Doeg's wheezing laughter.

The leader slowed as he walked to Caden, and several others glanced around. Caden blinked, watching them straighten as the Demon's cackling laugh echoed in the canyon. *The veil, right?* Caden thought. *That's what it's called? It's super thin now. Nearly nonexistent.* The leader's eyes narrowed as they fell on Caden. Caden forced a smile. "I've told you my name," he said.

"The Freaks brought that Demon, didn't they?"

"What's yours?"

"They are not permitted."

"That Demon follows me, not them." Caden crossed his arms. "It's a nasty side effect of being a weapon for King Yeshua."

The man's head tilted to one side, and Caden could easily guess he was frowning under his shemagh. "Weapon," the man scoffed. "We will see. Come." They started out again, and Caden was surprised they weren't going to the chiseled-out building. They turned down a road, still carved from the rocks like the slot canyon, but not as narrow.

In the distance, Caden could see a camel racing toward them. Everyone stopped as the camel approached, and an Israeli slid from its back before it fully stopped. He half limped, half hopped from the camel as the armed leader bowed low. Actually, all the armed strangers dipped their heads in respect. The limping guy ignored them and threw off his shemagh.

Caden swore loud and clear and flinched back, burying his face in his hands. The newcomer laughed and spread his arms wide. "He lives!" Caden hissed under his breath as he turned away, shaking his head. He blinked several times and found his vision blurred. Running a hand over his face, Caden faced the Israeli and dragged in a ragged breath. The Israeli laughed again and moved closer.

"Hey, *achi*," Asher muttered as he clapped Caden on the shoulder. "What happened to your face? That scar is massive!" Caden didn't answer as he rubbed his eyes with a finger and thumb. He could feel the tears falling. It was annoying. He was the fearless leader, guiding them on God's paths to freedom, not a shaken up, sniveling baby who couldn't handle an unexpected change. Granted, this change was a positive thing; he expected to find Asher bedridden, hardly conscious, still recovering from Rapham's brutality.

*I didn't kill you,* he thought.

Asher turned to the armed men. "Commander Jaden, this is Caden Johnson, the only other person able to call my father Abba and the brother-in-law to Yohanan Nuri." Jaden's chin lifted as his eyes darted to Caden. He stepped back, and his men followed suit, their weapons lowering. "You will respect him as though he is my blood brother."

Caden vaguely acknowledged the armed strangers standing down, but he wasn't fully listening. *I didn't kill you,* he thought again, summoning his strength to face Asher.

"I was sure I'd see you in Heaven," Asher was saying. "Man! They had you all tied up! I saw it all on TV, when they announced who you were at the Final Temple. Thought the mob was going to lynch you right then and there..." Asher's smile fell as he saw how white Caden was. He straightened, limped forward, and lay a hand on the back of Caden's neck. "You were protecting me." Caden choked suddenly and closed his eyes. His hands were shaking. "It was terrible but didn't kill me."

Caden shook his head. He glanced down at Asher's left leg. It was bent unnaturally, making his entire body slant to one side. He was missing a few fingers, too, and Caden knew if he kept looking, he'd find more deformities. "I —" He choked.

Asher's grip tightened. "There's nothing to forgive, *achi.*" Caden put his face in his hands and leaned against Asher. "Come on." Asher clapped him on the back. "Your sis will want to see you."

Caden nodded and forced himself to calm down. He

glanced around, remembering he stood before a crowd. *Who cares,* he thought with a gruff sniff.

Asher motioned to the towering building before them and all around to the natural sandstone walls. "Welcome home."

Caden half smiled as he fought another wave of emotion. *Finally,* he thought. *I can be with my people. The people of God.*

————

THE LOST CITY OF PETRA turned out to be epically cool. It was no wonder God picked that place for his final remnant to find a haven. The slot canyon, called the Siq, gradually widened and opened up altogether. Caden kept asking if Asher needed help walking, but Asher refused and grabbed a stick tied to his camel's saddle and started using it as a cane. Caden's stomach turned as he watched his brother limp along, unable to rid Rapham from his mind. *He needs to die too,* he thought, anger tightening his chest.

Asher must've noticed, for he told him to knock it off and don't let the enemy rob him of his joy. He was finally able to live with fellow believers! He didn't have to watch his back or keep living under a fake name. Caden didn't answer that; old habits die hard.

"You'll have to get used to introducing yourselves with your *real* name. People are coming in all the time."

"And this is how you welcome them?"

"This is a safe place. We want to keep it that way."

"Which means, sir," Jaden said, dipping his head. "Those Freaks can't be here." Benaiah's ears flicked back as Jael lifted her chin, her lips drawing back into a quiet snarl.

Caden opened his mouth to speak, but Asher was

already moving to Benaiah. He looked high up to the Leovir and held out a hand. "Benaiah," he said with a smile. "It's good to see you again." The Leovir stared down at Asher's hand, clearly never receiving such a welcoming gesture from a human. Shifting from paw to paw, Benaiah gently wrapped his human-like front paw around Asher's hand, completely enveloping his hand in fur and claws. The other Leovirs watched; they seemed startled.

*No one treats them as though they have a soul,* Caden realized. *I guess they do. They have human hearts, after all.*

"I never properly thanked you for saving my life," Asher said. "Please. Let me welcome you to Petra. You and your pride are welcome to stay as long as you wish." That really surprised the Leovirs.

"Um," Benaiah stammered. "Thank you. We stay."

Asher's smile grew. "I'm glad! You all follow King Yeshua?" Benaiah nodded, as did the other Leovirs. "Then you are one of us." Jaden opened his mouth to speak, but Asher gave him a look that would've silenced anyone.

Caden grinned, turned to the crowd, and addressed them, telling them who Asher was. Chuk's eyes widened as he leaped back and bowed low, muttering in Swahili. Several others drew away and raised hands, as though Asher, too, would engulf them in flames from his mouth. Asher cursed under his breath and grabbed Chuk's arm, yanking him back up. "Don't bow to me!" He yelled. "I am nothing! Bow to King Yeshua!" Chuk nodded but refused to meet Asher's gaze. It took a while to convince everyone there to not treat Asher like a god, and Caden saw the irritation in Asher's eyes.

"Is this normal?" Caden asked. Asher nodded and set his jaw as he turned and quickly limped from the group. Caden hurried after him. He was going to recommend Asher ride the camel to save his leg but thought that would annoy him more.

They walked from the Siq and the great, carved building, called the Treasury. As they continued and the sun set further, Caden could hear a distant murmuring sound. They came around some rocks and the orange glow of countless fires speckled across the cliff face. Caden's eyes narrowed, and he saw the mouths of several carved doorways dotting the cliff. His mouth dropped open the closer they drew.

There were doorways everywhere, chiseled right into the rock. Coming and going were people. Beside the cliff was a tent village. Caden stared in awe at the children running and laughing through the tents. He turned to the carved doorways, most now covered with a rug, as women came to and fro, attending to their earthen households. Men worked throughout, attending to camels or donkeys, getting firewood, and guarding their new homes. A dog started barking, and the murmuring lifted as everyone turned to see the newcomers.

Asher and Caden led the way, Jaden on their right and Benaiah on their left. Everyone clearly didn't know how to handle more strangers, not to mention enough Leovirs to maul the entire mini-city. Asher raised his hands and shouted to them, ordering them to lower their weapons and explaining what was happening.

Caden wasn't listening again. His eyes darted through the growing crowd, his heart quickening. *Where are you?* He thought, his gaze leaping from one woman to the next. *Lil El, where —*

There. His heart leapt in his throat as he froze, all attention on the short, blue-eyed woman in a hijab and desert robes. Without thinking, he started running at her. She looked amazing! She should be wounded or beaten down, but she walked like a queen amid her people, her chin up and her strides confident and graceful. She was alright. He really didn't have to protect her; Yahweh was doing a better job than he ever could.

Their eyes met, and she smiled. The smile was short-lived. "No!" She cried, and Caden felt something snag his arm. Both arms, actually. And something wrapped around his neck.

He grunted, coming to a halt as several men seized him. He twisted, freeing one hand enough to jam an elbow into a rib, loosening the arm around his neck. Pain electrified his guts, and he realized a knee rammed into him. He gasped, and then he was angry. No one was getting in the way of him and his sister again.

He lunged, sending a fist into a man's nose, hearing a crunch as his head shot back. He twisted and struck, freeing his second arm. Without thinking, he kicked a man's thigh, sending him to his knees, and struck another in the kidneys. The third was coming back and Caden made a fist, aiming for his throat. *Wait!* Half his brain screamed. *Don't kill him!*

That pause was enough time for another to join. Caden dodged a blow and sent an elbow into his guts before kicking him to the ground. A hand grabbed his shirt, but he yanked free, giving a right hook that dropped him like a sack of potatoes. Someone was shouting. Caden couldn't really hear as something struck his head, sending white flashes across his vision.

A kick to the back of his knee sent him down. He rolled, springing up again. A scream pierced the chaos, and Caden turned. Ellie was rushing toward them, an arm raised as her eyes bugged from her head. Caden blinked, realizing two men with M16s were closing in, the barrels trained on his chest.

"This is my brother!" Ellie screamed. "Stand down! Now!"

Caden's chest heaved as blood trickled down his brow

and the slice across his face throbbed. He waited for everyone else to back off before rising from his fighting stance. Lifting his chin and straightening his clothes, he realized the eyes of the entire village were on him. He didn't acknowledge them as he strolled straight to Ellie. She stared up at him, her eyes just as wide.

"Your face," she whispered, reaching for Caden's cheek, but she stopped. "What happened?"

Those closest quieted, and Caden felt the weight of countless eyes lay on him. "Leovir." A great muttering rippled through the crowd.

Ellie gave a shocked laugh as she shook her head. "And did you kill it too?"

Caden stared down at her. "Yes." Her mouth dropped open as the crowd started to buzz with excitement. *What's the big deal?* Caden suddenly remembered the Narrow Gate and Old Caden, all scarred and ready to beat up Demons without breaking a sweat. With a jolt, Caden realized he was becoming the scarred, unstoppable warrior he saw in his future. *She hasn't seen me since Under Fire was in its first stages almost a year ago. I'm probably so different now.*

Seeing the look on her face, he knew he was *very* different. Ellie grabbed him, pulling him close and muttering something about how crazy Yahweh's will was and how happy she was to see him. Caden closed his eyes, ignoring his pounding head and his inevitable collapse once the adrenaline wore off. *Thank you, Yahweh. You are too faithful to me. I don't deserve it.* He smiled. *That's the point, I guess. I'm honored to be one of Your remnants.*

"You're hungry," Ellie said, stepping back. "Come. I'll make you some food and—"

"Sammy?" Caden's heart leapt into his throat. He turned away from Ellie, his head on a swivel. Walking through the crowd was a brunette Russian, her eyes as pale and blue as Siberian ice. The people parted, letting Dasha through.

Caden laughed and rushed toward her. She picked up the pace, and the crowd backed further away as the two came together. Caden drew Dasha into his arms, and he felt her fingers grab the clothes on his back. "Sammy," she whispered, tucking her head against his neck. He closed his eyes and breathed in that same fruity, sweaty smell he remembered.

"Hey, crazy Russian." His heart hadn't slowed one bit as his smile grew and grew. *There you are,* he thought. *I'm not going anywhere now. Please, God. Don't drive us apart again.*

Dasha stepped back and pointed a finger at him. "Don't you ever jump out of a car for me again!" He laughed. "You got yourself caught! And that Leovir!" Dasha looked at his sliced cheek and clicked her tongue. "At least you killed it."

Caden kept smiling down at her. He cupped her face in her hand, and she leaned into his touch. "It's so good to see you, Dasha." Her left brow arched as she smiled. "Not going to kill me this time?"

"I don't think I could. You just threw off five men!" Caden didn't answer as he stared into her eyes. He thought he remembered how blue they were, but nothing compared to the genuine article. For once, Dasha didn't pull away as her smile remained. Caden's chest swelled with emotion, for he knew, at last, he was home.

## SEVENTEEN
# HUMMING

CADEN WAS RIGHT ABOUT one thing, once his adrenaline wore off, he nearly collapsed. By the time they walked up the stone steps to Ellie's carved home, he was leaning on Dasha and could hardly keep his eyes open. He was vaguely aware of her cave-like home warding off the desert's heat and the spicy smell of her cooking. He was aware he ate but wasn't really paying attention. He just wanted to lie down and rest.

When she showed him the floor mat and gave him a thick blanket, he didn't feel the hard, stone floor. After all, he hadn't gotten a full night's rest in days. Getting arrested, tied up many times, dragged around, and threatened with the most heinous torture he'd ever heard of, he hadn't been able to get a good sleep in days. But it was more than that.

He could finally strip off his Alex Whitney disguise and simply be himself. He was safe, fed, warm, and surrounded by family. Someone stayed with him the entire time, helping him not pass out on the spot. He assumed it was Ellie but, before falling asleep, realized it was Dasha.

When he slept, there were no dreams at all, only the sweet oblivion of silence and deep, inner rest.

When he awoke, he didn't move, as though any change would fracture the inner peace he felt. *Thank You, God,* he thought. *I made it.* He sighed heavily and stretched, unable to hide the smile on his face. When he opened his eyes, he realized he wasn't alone. Actually, the house was full of people.

"Hey," Dasha said as she drew to his side.

Caden rubbed the sleep from his eyes and stared, wondering why everyone was in his room. He glanced around and realized the home was one large room. There were carved-out cubbies, like shelves, and other carved-out benches straight from the rock. Flashlights pointed at the ceiling helped illuminate the rock home, and the doorway's mat cover was thrown back, letting sunshine spill in. Caden sat up, finally feeling the ache of his body. He groaned and suddenly longed for a pillow or mattress or anything squishy.

Dasha grinned as she knelt and held out a cup of water. "You'll get used to it." He grunted and took the water, drinking deeply. "You still snore. A lot."

"Do not."

"Yes!" Ellie called across the wide room. "Yes, you do!" Someone chuckled. It was Asher, sitting on one of the benches next to Chuk.

"Finally!" Chuk said. "You're awake!" Caden sighed as he closed his eyes again and leaned back.

"Give him a break," Dasha snapped. "He's gone through hell!"

"Alright! Alright!" Chuk said, raising his hands.

"Tell your bulldog we all care about you," Asher said. Dasha straightened and cocked the left brow at him.

"Oh," Caden muttered. "You got the don't-you-dare-eye-brow-raise." Dasha clicked her tongue and whacked his shoulder. "Ouch," Caden whispered with a smile, drawing back. Dasha stood, muttering in Russian, and walked to Ellie. A wooden table stood against the wall, and the women started prepping food.

Caden leaned back and closed his eyes. It took him a moment to realize he was humming. It took another second to notice someone else was humming too. Asher and he stared at one another, equally confused. The strangest part was they were humming the same tune. "I keep doing that," Caden admitted. "Humming. Do you know what song that is?"

"Not a clue," Asher said.

"I do it too sometimes," Dasha said and shook her head. "Can't stand it!"

"How odd," Ellie said. "I wonder what it all means."

Caden yawned and rubbed his eyes. "Weird. How long have I been asleep?" He rubbed the back of his neck and moved his head, feeling the stiffness.

"Like, a day," Asher said.

"What?"

"Ah…" Chuk muttered. "More than that."

"Thirty-six hours," Dasha said, not looking up from chopping meat. Caden groaned and leaned against the wall, running a hand over his face. He motioned to Asher. "Where's Benaiah? Jaden didn't kill the Leovirs?"

Asher's eyes narrowed as his head tilted to one side. "We don't lie here, Caden." Caden looked away. "This isn't the Antichrist's lair." Caden nodded once and slowly rose to his feet. Dasha watched him, setting down her knife to help, but he held up a hand. With a sigh, he stiffly walked to a second bench and sat down. Without asking for it, Dasha handed him a plate of food.

"Hey!" Chuk said. "You said that was mine!"

"Did you try to assassinate the Antichrist?" Caden

couldn't hold back his grin as Chuk grumbled something and sat back.

The room was quiet as Caden ate. More like inhaled his food. As he cleaned his plate, he glanced at Ellie. "Sis," he said quietly. She turned to him, smiling. "How, um... how are you holding up?"

She turned away and kept attending to food prep. "I knew I'd become a widow eventually; the Scriptures say so."

Caden's head tilted to one side. "That's not what I asked."

Ellie's smile became tight and forced. "I have good days and bad." She sighed heavily and glanced at him. "But, Yohanan's alive. I saw him! Well, watched it on the live stream. Rising up and up and," she shook her head. "Of course, he beat me Home."

"Sorry, sis," Caden said. "You didn't, I mean...did you watch him die?"

Ellie shook her head. "We said our goodbyes and guessed that would happen. Asher filled me in."

"Did you see?" Asher asked. A lump formed in Caden's throat, and he ducked his head. He suddenly smelt swampy, bloody mess as limbs were ripped from bodies and innards uncoiled. He nodded without a word. "*Achi*, were you there?"

Caden nodded again. The room fell deathly still. "But," he said hoarsely and cleared his throat. "I was there when they came back to life."

"You were?" Ellie gasped. "Tell me! Tell me what it was like!" Caden forced a smile, banishing the thoughts of gore, and told them. They all leaned closer and listened as Caden retold the look of terror on everyone's face, especially the Demons. They all cheered and whooped, until Chuk asked if that would happen to all those executed at the Final Temple.

A dark heaviness fell across Caden again, thinking of Auset's unborn child. Dasha noticed. "You were there too, weren't you? I saw you on TV." Caden didn't answer; he couldn't.

"Um," Asher stammered, giving Caden a sideways glance. "Those who are martyred during the tribulation come back in the end."

Caden straightened. "When's the end?"

"Well...maybe when we get to Heaven. Or before? I don't know. No one really knows."

*How nice,* Caden thought, the heaviness still pressing on him. Clearing his throat, Caden glanced at Dasha. "May I have more food?"

"No," Chuk snapped.

Caden frowned and lowered his plate. "What's wrong?" Turns out, there was a famine. *Everywhere.*

"Well," Caden stammered. "Where'd all this food come from?"

Ellie grinned as she glanced at Dasha. "You're beautiful lady here is a daring genius."

Dasha grimaced as she shook her head, but Caden could see that small smile tugging at her mouth. Caden shook his head as he leaned forward. "What did you do?"

"I provided supplies."

He waited for her to continue, and he waved a hand when she didn't. "So, you stole supplies." Her smile grew as she hyper-focused on cooking. "Out with it," Caden said. "Tell me."

"When you were playing soldier boy with Luca, I helped Kingdom's Peace."

Caden frowned. "You did that too?"

"Of course. Someone needed to manage the survival kits and food reserves."

Caden's brows rose as he nodded slowly. "And did that someone reroute each transfer to here?"

"Don't be silly!" Dasha scoffed. "Luca's not an idiot! He'd follow the trail! We'd all be caught already and beheaded." Caden waited, knowing there was so much more. "I transferred them around Petra and hired local transports to bring it here. Or at least to Wadi Musa and the close towns."

"That's what you were doing the entire time?"

"That's a lot!" Dasha snapped, her eyes flashing. Caden noticed she held the knife a bit tighter. "Do you know how many bribes were made and people I had to frame for that?"

He scoffed and shook his head. "All for the glory of God."

"He can let things slide."

"He doesn't let things slide."

"Whatever. He'll forgive me later. I'm trying to keep His people alive!"

Caden stared at her quietly, the wheels of his mind turning. "Kingdom's Peace wasn't created until after you joined me. What did you do in the meantime?"

"Got to know this guy." She stuck a thumb at Asher.

"She went back to Under Fire," Asher said.

Caden's brows rose. "You guys just let her waltz right in?" "She said she's working with you. Yahweh brought you two together."

Caden rolled his eyes and glared at her. Dasha pointedly ignored him. "She didn't even know I was a Christian until meeting with you guys! You're so full of smoke and mirrors."

"Said the one who wouldn't tell me his name for months!"

"Anyways!" Asher cried, silencing them. "She met with Abba and told him you don't know what you're doing." Caden shot her another look but chose to keep his mouth shut. "She asked what we needed, and we knew we'd come here eventually."

"How?"

Dasha sighed heavily. "How do you think?"

"The Bible," Asher answered.

Chuk grunted. "That's some book. Does it say if we'll all die or not?"

"Oh," Ellie said, her voice tight. "It doesn't specifically say—"

"Most of us die," Dasha said.

"Dasha!"

"But a good death is better than a bad life." Chuk stared at her, his eyes wide, and he glanced at Caden.

Caden shrugged and nodded. "Sorry, dude," he said. "The world doesn't like us."

"Wants to take us out," Dasha added. "Kill us all."

"I get it!" Chuk yelled, raising a hand. "Please stop, I get it! What did I sign up for?"

"It's okay," Dasha said, slamming down the knife. "King Yeshua will come. He will slaughter all who oppose Him. All. I hope I survive until then."

Caden stared out the door, watching people walk by. He blinked slowly, thinking of Luca and Grant begging under King Yeshua's blade. *And Nathaniel. Wouldn't that be a sight.* He rubbed his eyes, ridding his mind of bloodlust he wasn't sure was godly, but it just felt right. It was justice. Didn't God like justice, even if it was messy? He straightened and turned to Dasha again. "That still doesn't explain why you offered to help me in the first place. And! And why you tried to kill me when I knew your name. Don't you think it's about time to cough that one up?"

Dasha scooped up the diced meat and set it into a pot before wiping her hands. She sighed and sat down, giving Caden her full attention. "Before Russian's aerial strike, I disarmed the Iron Dome."

Caden sat back, seeing the sincerity in her eyes. "Of course you did."

"I was part of a team, a team that was ambushed by Refiners. I alone escaped."

"Is that when I found you?"

"When you fell on top of me? Yes."

"Whatever."

"I had just run for my life, knowing anyone who knew me would tell a Refiner. You would get me killed."

Caden nodded slowly. "Why didn't you track me down to finish the job?"

"I did."

Caden smiled. "Of course."

"But you," Dasha rubbed the back of her neck and turned away, "I couldn't do it."

"Why?" Dasha didn't answer. "Dasha."

"I wanted Rapham's head."

"Don't we all." A hardness entered Asher's eyes as he crossed his arms, his hand with missing fingers fisting.

"It was he who found us," Dasha said. "He tortured my team. He took their heads, so I wanted his."

"Did you get close?"

Dasha muttered Russian and sighed heavily. "No. I should've asked you to help; you sounded like you saw him all the time."

Asher's mouth opened. "Is that true?"

Caden shrugged. "I don't think we had one conversation."

Asher shook his head, his crossed arms tightening across his chest. "You wouldn't want to."

Pain stabbed Caden's chest. "You didn't answer my question," he said to Dasha. "Why couldn't you take me out?"

Dasha didn't answer again. "You shielded me from the Refiners," she said, steel entering her voice. "When they shot at us, you protected me. No one had done that. I didn't understand."

Caden quietly sat, seeing her wrestle with confusion still. And what was that? Her shoulders bunched, and she fidgeted with the cuff of her sleeve, no doubt a blade was hidden there. *She feels threatened,* he realized. *By me?* He blinked, finally understanding. *By someone who cares about her.*

"Why did you?" Dasha whispered. The room was very quiet as both Dasha and Caden stared at one another, not seeing anyone else.

"I, um," Caden stammered. "I sometimes see the future." Dasha's left brow arched. "I guess time travel is possible in the future or something? Whatever, the point is, I see stuff. I saw myself, a much older me, and his, um...his wife." Caden took a breath, hoping Dasha wouldn't think he was out of his mind. "That's how I knew your name." Her eyes widened. "You introduced yourself to me. Your older self." No one spoke as Dasha rigidly sat. *Please don't punch me,* Caden thought, quietly giving her time to think.

"Was I as scarred up as you?"

Caden frowned. "*That's* what you want to know?"

"Was I?"

"Nope."

"Ah!" Dasha frowned and shook her head as Caden laughed.

"Don't you get it?"

"I get it! I get it! We're married in the future!" She faced him, her frown still solidifying her face as she continued thinking.

"Well," Caden said, shifting his weight under that piercing glare. "I hope you at least smile whenever I propose." Dasha's only response was her single brow flicking upward. He couldn't withhold a smile.

———

CADEN FELT MORE and more renewed as the days passed. He shared a home with Ellie, and he had forgotten that little whistling sound she made as she slept. It drove him up the wall while they were camping with Papa and Mama Lo, but he just chose to smile now. His Lil El was with him. And safe. It was such a new and weird thing, it took him a while to believe it. It took him even longer to relax.

Every morning, Dasha and Asher came for breakfast. Every morning, Caden's heart leapt as the door flap flew back and two 'strangers' barged in. He always was ready to fight them, which, as Asher pointed out, would end badly. "You can really cause damage now," he said. "I should spar with you; maybe you're finally at my level." Caden grunted and fell silent.

The two sat outside Ellie's house and watched the camp bustling below. Caden glanced at Asher's leg, seeing he bent it protectively close and didn't put any weight on it. He looked down and shifted his weight with a rough sniff. He couldn't help slumping his shoulders under the weight of regret and shame. "I'm —"

"If you say sorry one more time," Asher snapped, "I swear to Yahweh, I'll punch you right in the throat." Caden huffed a mirthless laugh and glanced down the road. Asher raised a finger and leaned closer. "No pitying either. I can see it in your eyes; you'll make somebody cry."

Caden nodded as his smile grew. "Copy that." Asher muttered under his breath as he rubbed his bad leg. "Right in the throat." The two sat in silence as the sun rose higher, children ran between the tents, and people attended to fires.

"How long will we stay here?" Caden asked.

Asher took in a slow breath and glanced into the sky. "Until He comes back."

Caden snorted. "That could be years!"

"Or tomorrow. You never know with King Yeshua."

"You got that right. Seriously, how will we know when it's time to move."

Asher smiled softly. "We'll know."

"*Achi.*"

"Do you know when a Leovir's angry?"

Caden frowned. "Yes?"

"Obvious, right? King Yeshua went all incognito the last time He was here. Not this time. Everyone, and I mean *everyone* will see Him coming. Luca. Your enemy in America, um...Nathaniel," Caden dipped his head, his ears buzzing with merely the man's name, "Rapham too," Asher continued. "They'll freak out. Everyone will."

"Why?"

"Because King Yeshua's not going to be some nice-looking guy. He's described as a warrior, clothes stained red with the blood of His enemies. Flaming eyes. Sword coming out of His mouth. Not something I'd want to fight." As he spoke, Asher's smile grew and grew. Caden recognized the fierce thirst for justice, that borderline on homicidal; he knew those same ideals demanded attention at the back of his mind.

"I hope I make it," Asher said, his eyes narrowing as his jaw set. "It says in the Bible that the one who is victorious and does Yahweh's will to the end, Yahweh will give authority to them over the nations. We will rule with an iron rod and dash them to pieces like pottery." Caden's brows rose. "He will also give a Morning Star."

"He gives us morning stars?"

"Yeah. Wait..."

"Awesome!" Caden sat straighter, a wolfish smile overtaking his face.

Asher frowned. "By your creepy smile, I don't think we're talking about the same thing."

"A morning star! They're medieval weapons!"

"What? No!"

"They're a mace with spikes on the end, kind of like the points of a star."

"The Morning Star is another name for Yeshua!"

"Ah," Caden sighed as his shoulders sagged and he turned away. "I've always wanted a morning star."

Asher's brow arched as he shook his head. "You know, medieval weapons against automatic weapons and grenades aren't exactly wise."

"Yeah, yeah, whatever."

"What is it with you and bats?"

Caden shrugged as he sat back. "It's what I know, I guess." The two sat quietly, but their thoughts echoed with the screams of God's enemies. *Maybe my desire to destroy is Godly,* Caden thought, feeling his fisted hands straining. *Maybe…*

"So," he whispered. "In Armageddon, we'll fight too?" Asher nodded. A hot thrill rushed through Caden as he squared his shoulders, and the wolfish smile returned. *Is that why I'm constantly training how to fight? For the coming battle?*

"Commander Jaden and I have been preparing the people the best we can. Keeping everyone fit and ready for whatever King Yeshua wants." Caden nodded excitedly as his wide smile remained. "I can't wait," Asher whispered even more quietly. The two sat, both staring ahead, the brutal vengeance of God heating their blood.

———

CADEN COULD NEVER FIND Dasha when he wanted to. When he finally did, she always seemed irritated with him.

That left eyebrow would shoot up, and she'd hardly speak to him. It was insufferable. After lunch, he found her returning to camp with buckets of water. Caden just stared at her, a muscle in his jaw flexing. He saw movement out of the corner of his eye as Ellie giggled, waving him on. Taking a deep breath, Caden rushed forward to meet Dasha.

"I don't need help!" she snapped.

"Good," Caden beamed. "I wasn't offering."

She glared at him and continued walking. Cursing under his breath, Caden grabbed a bucket handle. "Sammy!"

"Stop being stupid!"

"I can do it!"

"I know! I'm here to help."

"I don't need help."

Caden sighed and stepped in front of her. "Look," he said and stopped as she went around him. "Dasha!" She didn't slow. "I know it's scary to let anyone close." She scoffed. "I was there too. Then, some crazy Russian hijacked my taxi, jabbing me with her knife."

"I'm not scared."

"No," Caden said. "You're terrified." She stopped. "You haven't spoken to me since I said we're together in the future." She didn't look at him as he drew to her side. "I get it," he whispered. "You watched your team get executed by Rapham. I watched my brother get shot down by a Sentinel." Caden lifted his chin, anger toward Nathaniel tightening his chest. "It's okay to be afraid." Dasha gave him a sideways glance. "It's not okay to let that emotion control you. I..."

Caden's voice cracked, and he looked down, his heart quickening. "I want to be your teammate again, like how we were in Jerusalem. Besides all that spying and lying and stuff. I just," Caden fell silent as he rubbed the back of his neck. *I'm making a complete fool of myself!* Clenching his teeth, Caden straightened and squarely faced her. "I want to help carry your water. And I want you to let me."

Dasha didn't answer as she stared straight ahead. "How could an American boy like you know the emotional distress of a Russian girl like me?"

Caden smiled and ducked his head. "Ellie clued me in."

"Hum." Dasha shook her head as she passed him one of the buckets.

Caden beamed as he took it, and the two walked back into camp. "What're we doing with this?"

"Watering the camels."

Caden quickly masked his disappointment with a smile, all the while knowing she saw through it. "Great!"

"We'll need ten more buckets."

"Yippy."

Dasha grinned. "Keep trying to woo me. I like it."

"Woo you?"

"Yes. Do more."

"Ah, sure. Coming right up. Once I figure out what that means." Dasha chuckled as Caden smiled, and they walked, side by side, into camp. As though on cue, they started humming. It was the same rhythm of the same song. They both stopped instantly and glanced at one another. Without a word, they started laughing.

EIGHTEEN
# THE DEFENSE OF FAITH

CADEN WAS FURIOUS. He was so furious, he didn't notice the people bowing to him or getting out of his way as he stormed through camp. Someone even started to call out to him, but another grabbed their shoulder, telling them to leave him alone. Even Jael turned away when he charged by. He had to cool off somewhere else.

Caden cursed under his breath, jaw set and eyes flashing. He glared into the sky and shook his head. "You're ridiculous!" he hissed through gritted teeth. "Out of Your mind!" As always, God didn't say a single thing. Caden cursed again as he turned away from the path and followed a narrow trail cutting through the rocks, leading away from Petra.

There had just been a security meeting. It was worse than Caden thought. He had asked Asher for a meeting after scoping out Petra himself. The landscape made it near impossible to attack, the sandstone cliffs making a natural fortress. Nothing was impenetrable though. Caden could easily see Giants forcing their way through the Siq, Leovirs climbing over the walls, and Zealots following with no regard for their own safety. Once Caden told them what Zealots were, everyone's thin strand of ease frayed.

Jaden and Asher outlined all the people going through combative training as a precaution, but Caden quickly pointed out that wasn't enough against Demons. "Well, we're not Spirits," Jaden had snapped.

"We can still fight them!" Caden responded and waited, expecting Asher or Ellie to back him up. Only Dasha nodded. He was shocked to find out that no one really knew how to defend against Demons. It was ridiculous! They had the same bible! Most of them went to Under Fire and knew the right prayers, but they didn't have experience.

"And that's not all of it," Asher said quietly as all eyes fell on him. Very uncomfortably, he explained the relationship between Demons and Giants.

Caden couldn't believe his ears. "So...so Giants' Spirits are Demons?"

Asher nodded. "That's why when you kill a Giant, there's a Demon that randomly appears."

"Where's that in the Bible?" Ellie mumbled.

"It's in the Book of Enoch."

"The what?"

"Another book was written way back then. It's not the Word of Yahweh, but it doesn't contradict Scripture."

"Well," Caden said, crossing his arms. "Even more reason to get Spiritual defenses!"

After he ranted for a bit, Caden calmed down, and Ellie suggested asking his Cherub for help. "He's not *mine*," Caden corrected, but no one seemed to care. Caden explained Han had said not to talk to him directly, but they were desperate.

"Just pray to Yahweh," Asher said. "And...while you're at it, be on the lookout for your four-faced friend."

With a curse, Caden stormed out. It was disturbing

how they let Demons just walk on in. Yohanan sounded like he knew how to drive them away, even before the *Akal Esh* filled him. *Does everyone have weak faith or something?* Caden thought as he climbed further away from camp. He needed to be away from the noises of life and all the people staring at him. He just needed to be with Yahweh. *If He decides to answer me,* he thought. *He might just ignore me like He always does!* Caden shook his head as he rounded a corner, weaving between boulders as big as cars. *I swear, the more people involved, the more faith plummets. And IQs! Retards! It would be easier if there were less of us. Or if I was on my own again.*

Caden sighed as he ran his fingers through his hair. *It was easier alone. No one debated with me or couldn't perform. Maybe that's my mission; solitude appears to be God's will for me. Everyone is always slaughtered in due time.* Caden's eyes narrowed as he glanced before him. *Yeshua's coming would be furthered by my departure. Their lack of faith is inhibiting my own destiny.*

Caden blinked and stopped short, turning his head. Pebbles bounced down the massive boulders and scattered across the ground. He glanced up. Doeg sat perched on the boulder high overhead, its long tail trashing as a smile stretched its mangled mouth. The Demon was in perfect pouncing distance, its muscles tensing for action. Caden's stomach twisted, hoping he could kick the Demon down to Hell someday.

"*No, foolish human,*" the Demon's voice hissed in his mind. "*You cannot touch me, remember?*"

Caden didn't bother answering as he turned around and pressed on. *Han. Where's Han? How do I talk with him? He said to never call for him, but to ask Yahweh. Yahweh's ignoring me though. I've got to accomplish this on my own. I cannot rely on anyone to —*

Caden hissed a curse and shook his head, ridding his

mind of Doeg's implanted thoughts. *Yahweh, please,* Caden thought, his eyes narrowing with concentration. *We need help again. Can You break the sky again? Give us more Akal Esh? That would do the trick. Do You, I don't know, but do You think I'm worthy to have the Akal Esh?*

"No."

*I mean, I've sacrificed a lot, and I'm trying to do everything for You. Doesn't that count as something?* Caden strained as he listened to the silence. His hands became fists at his side as he cursed himself; why did he keep listening for Someone who never spoke? Wasn't that the definition of insanity? Repeating the same action, expecting different results? Yes, this is what insanity felt like. The constant near-death experiences all in the name of Someone who was so lax He couldn't even open His mouth to respond. What kind of God was that?

"Doeg!" Caden hissed as he marched on.

*"And who are you to request such a fierce weapon as the Akal Esh?"* Doeg whispered in Caden's mind. Caden squeezed his eyes shut as anger tightened his chest. *"You've accomplished nothing. The Antichrist lives. Your brother is crippled. Your sister will be beheaded before your eyes."*

"Yahweh! Please! I need You! Kick this dog for me!"

"The only dog is you!" Doeg's voice was close. Too close.

Caden dropped, not feeling the rough ground as he rolled. A shadow passed overhead. Claws graded across the rocky ground as Caden stood. He leapt back, finding himself face-to-face with Doeg. The Shade's lips pulled back in a snarl as its nape bristled like quills. Caterwauling like a dying cat, Doeg's tail whipped as it stalked forward. Caden raised a hand but knew that was useless.

"Han?" He started backing away. Doeg slowly shook its head as it drew nearer. "Han!"

"It's just you and me, boy."

"Han! Yahweh! Please!" Caden's breath quickened as he stared into those icy eyes. He couldn't run, he'd never make it. He couldn't fight, a physical thing like himself couldn't even touch a Spirit like Doeg.

*"I told you,"* Doeg whispered in his mind. *"I will be the last thing you will ever see."* Caden's mouth opened as his heart slammed against him. A cold nothingness spread from his fingertips and down his arms. He was shutting down. He wasn't going to make it.

*No.* Caden's steps halted. Raising his chin, he lowered his arm and squarely faced Doeg. *I can stand firm, be still, and know Yahweh is God.* Doeg's ears whipped back as it snarled, teeth flashing in the light. Caden's stomach turned, but he didn't move. He stared down at Doeg, feet planted like an oak.

*"Foolish human!"*

Wind roared between the rocks and cliffs. Caden cowered, shielding his face with his forearm as dust and grit kicked up. Doeg's snarl rose to a caterwaul again. Caden, his eyes tightly shut, staggered back from the blast as the sound of hundreds of wings descended. He couldn't hold back a smile.

The earth shook as two Angelic feet landed. Doeg's cries ended instantly. Caden felt himself butting against a rock as he struggled to see. Even without sight, Caden could feel where Han was; the Cherub's inner *Akal Esh* shone with a fierce, hot energy. Caden felt it pricking his skin with heat, and it reminded him of Yohanan and Elijah's blaze. The wind calmed, and the sound of wings subsided. Coughing, Caden straightened and blinked the fine layer of dust from his eyes. Wiping his hands and face, Caden turned only to shield his eyes again.

"Oh," an unearthly, loud voice bellowed. Caden shouted and cowered against the rock. "Too bright still?"

That was the ox-face. Caden felt the *Akal Esh* dim and the air's electric heat minimize. "How's that?"

"That should be fine," another voice squawked. "He's seen us before. And Gideon! What's his problem?"

*Thanks, Eagle,* Caden thought as he dared to open his eyes again.

"Peace," a third voice hushed in a voice incapable of making a whisper. "Give him time." Caden turned and found a monster of wings, eyes, and fire. His hands still felt clammy, and his heart didn't slow, but he smiled instead of falling to his knees. He was improving.

"Very much," the human-face said as he turned and regarded Caden with a warm smile. The countless eyes dotting the Cherub creased, as though they, too, were smiling. "The *Akal Esh* revealed through us right now is twice as much as when we first met."

Caden blinked and slid his hands into his pockets. "Doesn't seem like twice as much."

The lion-face flicked an ear. "Isn't it grand when the glory of Yahweh most High becomes as expected as the sun's light?"

Caden's smile grew as he stepped closer. "Han, I need to talk with you." The human-face nodded once as the oxen-face licked its nose.

"Yes, dear," the oxen-face said. "The veil is currently gone, so we may speak."

"And we know what you want," the eagle-face from behind cried. "We were there when you stomped away from Asher's meeting." Caden frowned as the lion-face drew back its lips, making a snarled laugh and the human-face rolled its eyes.

"Honestly, do be quiet," the human-face said.

"What? He did!" A pair of wings flexed as the oxen muttered something.

The human-face straightened and stepped toward Caden. "What do you seek?"

"But," Caden asked, motioning toward the eagle. "I thought you know."

"Make your requests known to Yahweh, and He will provide. He always knows what your requests are, but he also enjoys hearing them."

"That sounds...redundant."

"Haven't you heard it melts a grandfather's heart to hear his granddaughter say 'up, papa?'. It is the same in this instance."

"Oh," Caden said, shoving his hands deeper into his pockets. "So, um...Han, the camp's security is pretty good if only physical stuff attack us, but there are Demons too. And Tarek."

"It's a Demon," the lion-face said.

"Okay. We just, we don't have any firepower to handle a Demon assault. Do you have anything to give us?"

Han stared at Caden, and the human-face kept softly smiling. "Caden, dear," the oxen-face said. "Are you asking us, or Yahweh?"

Caden ground his teeth and turned away. *He never listened.* He cut his train of thought short, knowing Han could read his mind. With a curse, Caden ran his fingers through his hair and closed his eyes. "Yahweh," he said, raising a hand. "May You give us Spiritual weapons? We need them. Um...thanks."

Caden opened his eyes and stood there. Nothing happened. No word was spoken. No light shone. Even Han didn't do a dang thing. Caden's shoulders sagged as he looked down, suddenly feeling like he was at a game while Dad watched him strike out.

"Stretch out your hand."

Caden glanced at Han and frowned. "What?"

"Your hand," the human-face said. "Stretch it out."

Caden continued to stare without moving. Han stared back, unwilling to explain. *Fine,* Caden thought, his eyes flashing. He rolled a shoulder and held out his hand. Nothing happened. What a big surprise.

"The other one."

"Oh, my other left?" Caden asked sarcastically. Han's brow arched, and Caden raised a hand. "Alright, alright." With a sigh, he held out his left hand.

"Make a fist."

*Nothing's going to happen.*

He was holding something. It wasn't there before, but now he clearly felt a warm solid thing in his grasp. Not warm, it was almost hot. He held a strap that synched tightly to his hand. Just as his mind grabbed onto this unexpected and weird concept, a small plate appeared on the other side of his hand against his knuckles. The plates continued appearing, getting continually larger, until they were three feet long at his elbow. The plates grew smaller as they reached his shoulder.

At this point, Caden scurried back and held his arm out as far away from his body as possible. He realized he was shouting, and he quickly snapped his mouth shut. He stared dumbfoundedly at the several plates. They were a whitish, orangish, hottish color whose inner structure moved with swirling light. He could easily see through it and noticed Han's wide smile. Caden glanced between the plates stuck along his arm and Han's own armor. They were the same.

With a sudden laugh, Caden's tensed body relaxed. He straightened and moved his arm, seeing each of the plates adjusted to permit the movement with ease. It was the lightest structure Caden had ever felt, but it was obviously thick and unscratched or tarnished. *Of course, it isn't!* Caden thought. *This is Spiritual armor!*

"The Shield of Faith," Han said.

Caden laughed again as he kept staring through the plates. He rolled his shoulder and bent his elbow, feeling the slight weight of the shield as its individual plates moved with him. "This," Caden whispered breathlessly. "This is awesome! Can this stop bullets too?" Han's brow arched again as the eagle-face scoffed. "Right!" Caden cried, grinning ear to ear. "Stupid question! Stupid! Can it stop a grenade? A missile?"

"It will stop whatever Yahweh wills it to stop."

Caden dropped into a fighting stance and held the shield before him. *Now, if only I had a bat.*

"The shield isn't yours," Han said. "Yahweh is lending it to you, thus, He has authority over it. If He wills it not to come when summoned, it will not come." Caden nodded as he adjusted his stance and peered through the plates. "You must be in Yahweh's perfect will to utilize His Spiritual armor."

"How do I know what His will is?"

"He'll inform you." The eagle squawked as Han's wings fanned. "Buckle up."

Caden frowned as the human-face rolled his eyes. "Yahweh knows what you can withstand. He will not give you more than you can handle. When dangers surround you, He will also provide a way out. He is always with you, Caden, and He is leading you into all truth."

"The truth," the lion-face said, "that you are more than a conqueror."

Caden stared down, his hold adjusting on the shield's grip. "When do I get more armor?"

"Peace, dear," the oxen-face said. "In Yahweh's perfect time."

"Can Demons get through this?" The lion-face's ears flicked back as the human-face cocked a brow.

"What do you think!" The eagle called.

"So," Caden said, smiling as he stepped forward, "could Tarek not even break through?"

"The shield, no." Han shook his head. "Your arm, yes."

"Then give me more armor!"

The lion's golden eyes darted to him. "If you required every piece, Yahweh would've provided."

Caden growled through gritted teeth as he looked through the shield again. "Can more people get Spiritual armor? We all need some. Seriously! We're totally defenseless!" A great shout erupted from Han, and Caden stumbled back, cringing at the noise. It took him a moment to realize Han was laughing. The four faces laughed together, making a rushing-water-type sound.

"Defenseless!" The eagle called. "Did you hear that?"

"Caden! Please," the human-face said, trying to breathe. "You occupy your time searching for Demons, you never notice us Angels!"

Caden frowned. "What?"

"Look, dear," the oxen said. "Look up."

Caden did. He actually peed his pants a little. The sky was on fire. Flickering, flashing, hot fire lashed about, covering the sky like a wildfire. Caden, who had fallen to the ground with a shout, blinked through his shock. The air cracked with power like electricity. He stared and realized the flames had a shape. There were boxes of fire, circle fire-things on either side, and they were pulled by fire with four long legs and a lashing tail. A flame stood in the box, guiding the legged fire and—

*Horses and chariots,* Caden thought as he struggled to breathe. He watched as the chariots rode across the heavens, breaking through clouds, as engulfed Angels peered down below, keeping a close eye. After realizing what they were, Caden could hear the whoosh of the flames and the chariots' wheels turning. The distant Angelic voices, which were too loud and harsh to be considered Angelic, could be heard. The horses snorted and neighed, just like a normal horse, but their manes and tails leaped with fire as their eyes glowed.

*Those are Heaven's Armies! The Heavenly Hosts! Have they been there the entire time?*

"Yes," the lion-face called as Han stared up with him. "We are always near Yahweh's remnant."

Caden drew himself up off the ground and nearly fell, his wobbly legs felt so weak. With a gruff sniff, Caden straightened and continued staring up. It was beautiful. And terrible. And awesome! And freaky! All at the same time. Caden didn't know that could be a thing. *Doeg's crazy coming down here! Did it have to sneak past these guys?*

Caden blinked, realizing Han wasn't answering that question. "Han?"

"Yahweh permits only what is just."

"Letting Doeg down here is just?"

"It got you to pursue Spiritual armor, didn't it?" Eagle shouted. Caden cursed and shifted his weight. He stared at the shield again, his grip firm and unwilling to let go.

"It will always be there," Han said. "When you release it."

"But Yahweh might not let me summon it again."

"He will. At the right time." Caden grumbled but wouldn't let go of it. Han glanced at him, and Caden cursed again. He pried his fingers from the grip, and the shield instantly vanished, the slight weight lifting from his shoulders. Caden set his jaw and stared down at his hand.

"Don't think about it," the oxen said. "Have faith."

Caden heaved a sigh and closed his eyes. He made a fist and felt the firm grip materialize in his grasp. He barked a laugh and stared down. "I did it!"

"You did nothing," Han corrected. "Yahweh did it all." Caden nodded as he looked through the shield. He lifted his chin and his shoulders squared. "Return to camp," Han said. "Begin training with your new armor."

Caden stopped and stared at Han. "You mean others will have this too?"

"You aren't the only one Yahweh has been preparing for such a time as this." Caden nodded slowly as he looked between the hundreds of flaming chariots overhead, the Cherub beside him, and the Shield of Faith in his hands. This was more than he expected. A lot more!

"Go," Han said. "Yahweh is with you."

Caden opened his mouth to speak, but wind struck him like a blow to the face. He lifted the shield and, for once, got to see Han fly away. The Cherub crouched before launching into the heavens, the flapping of wings sounded behind him. Caden stared up after him as he rose. The flaming chariots parted and in a blink, they were all gone.

Caden's smile fell as his eyes darted around. They were nowhere to be found. With a sigh, Caden faced the shield. "I still have you," he whispered, his fingers flexing in the grip. He grunted, and the smile returned. *You always provide*, Caden thought as he drew the shield close and started racing back to camp.

# NINETEEN

# KNOCK, KNOCK

CADEN WALKED between Dasha and Ellie as they wound through the Siq. They squeezed by others, several carrying tools and weapons. Ellie kept looking down as they walked, and her smile grew and grew. Caden couldn't help looking down as well, seeing the glowing, shifting light emanating from her boots. They were translucent shoes, rising almost up to her knees, and the inner glow moved and swirled in constant motion.

Several others who squeezed down the Siq also had some sort of Spiritual armor. Some had helmets, others breastplates, a few had shields like Caden, and many had belts. They were easy to spot; the armor's shifting light glowed even in broad daylight. It had come as quite a shock to everyone when they learned they had Spiritual armor and a fiery army constantly rode overhead in the skies. Everyone searched between the clouds, but no one saw a trace of the warrior Angels guarding them.

One by one, people started seeing if they wore armor. Some were, others weren't. Asher assumed it was a faith thing and only those relying entirely on Yahweh would receive. The ones that didn't were annoyed, many even downright angry, and a handful even packed up their stuff and left. A few tried to stop them, but Caden and Asher didn't bother. If they weren't part of the remnant, then there's the door. It was odd how no one had a complete suit or armor.

"It'll probably come in time," Asher said. Caden hoped he reached that time sooner; it felt really weird just having a shield with no weapon.

Ellie giggled and glanced ahead as they continued down the Siq. "Of course," she whispered. "I get the Shoes of Peace."

"They're like heavy-duty combat boots."

"I know! I've always wanted a pair! Remember that?"

"Hum?"

"In high school. When I wore more earth-tones and skirts."

"You mean your awkward emo phase."

Ellie's nose wrinkled in disgust as Dasha laughed. "Emo?" Dasha asked. "I can't see you doing that!"

"I just was learning my style," Ellie grumbled. "Earth-tones and nature-y themes."

Caden shook his head. "Nature-y isn't a word."

"It was better than your punk phase."

"What?" Dasha bellowed, laughing again.

"Whatever! I rocked that!"

"Your long hair made you look homeless."

"Thanks."

"Remember when Nate wanted tattoos and drew all over his arms, saying they were sleeves?" Caden nodded slowly.

"Who's that?" Dasha asked.

"Our brother. Oh! And when Trace, our other brother, tried to take that one chick to Homecoming. He was so nervous, I kid you not, his pants were on backwards."

Ellie laughed as they rounded a bend and waited as a donkey and cart rolled by.

"Spazzy excited," Caden muttered.

"He forgot how to drive to school too."

Caden snorted. "Figures." Caden shook his head as they fell silent.

Dasha put her hair in a ponytail and glanced between the siblings. "Where are they now?"

Ellie sighed, and her smile fell. Caden looked down and turned away, crossing his arms. Pain struck his chest and made it difficult to breathe. "They didn't make it," Ellie whispered, and Dasha nodded and turned away. Caden didn't speak, all he could think of was Nate, face shrunken and sickly, as he starved to death. And Trace. He closed his eyes. He could smell the sting of gunpowder again and hear the distant bays of dogs.

*They couldn't handle coming here,* Caden thought. *It was Yahweh's mercy to draw them Home early.* His head knew the truth, but his heart felt differently. Caden's jaw clenched as his eyes squeezed tight. Vengeful rage stirred his blood as Nathaniel filled his thoughts. The officer was lucky he was on the opposite side of the world.

A soft hand lay on Caden's shoulder, and he inhaled, as though waking from a dream. Dasha squeezed his shoulder as Ellie shook her head, her eyes drawn low with sadness. "No, dear brother," she whispered. "There is no room in Yahweh's Kingdom for unforgiveness." Caden scoffed and turned away. The cart rolled passed, and they kept walking. "Cade," Ellie said softly. "You have to forgive."

"I don't have to do anything." Dasha glared at him, and Ellie leaned away. Caden cursed and ran a hand over his face. "Sorry. I just..." What could he say? Nathaniel couldn't be forgiven? That wasn't justice? Justice was Caden standing over Nathaniel's quivering body, laughing at any plea and scream of agony. Just like Grant had shown him.

Caden's hands became fists.

"There once was a guy who owed his boss almost three point five billion dollars," Ellie said.

Caden arched a brow. "Who has that kind of money?"

"Hush and listen. The guy couldn't pay it back."

"Shocker."

"Shush! The guy would lose everything, and his family was going to suffer. The guy begged his boss for mercy, and his boss agreed and canceled his debt."

Dasha arched a brow at Ellie. "Did this really happen, or is this some story?"

"Yeah," Caden muttered. "What are you talking about?" Ellie socked him in the shoulder, and Caden recoiled as Dasha grinned. "Shutting up."

"The guy thanked his boss and left the office, only to come across a coworker who owed him like six grand. He shoved the coworker against the wall, grabbed his throat, and demanded payment." Caden frowned sharply. "The other coworkers saw this and reported it to their boss. When the boss called the guy back into his office, he was furious. 'I was merciful to you!' the boss yelled. 'You couldn't be merciful to someone else?' The boss fired the guy, sent him to jail, and told the guards to beat him until he paid up."

"What kind of boss is this?" Dasha asked.

"A merciful one," Ellie said. "This is how our Heavenly Father will treat you, Cade, unless you forgive the people who've harmed you." Caden lifted his chin as he fell quiet. He had a lot of responses, most of them colorful and grossly inappropriate. He just kept walking. "And Cade," Ellie continued. "That forgiveness has to be from the heart."

Caden scoffed and shook his head. "Right. And do I

have to lick their boot too?"

"I just retold a Bible story. That was Scripture; don't mock it."

Caden cursed and rubbed the back of his neck. *Impossible*, he thought. *You're crazy, You know that, God? I can hardly do what You ask, now I really can't!*

"Stop it," Ellie whispered.

"Stop what?"

"Overthinking it."

Dasha nodded. "He does that."

"I'm not! It's a confusing, messed up, ludicrous demand!"

"Just choose to forgive, alright?" Ellie sighed. "It's a choice, not a feeling."

Caden shook his head. "Still not going to happen. Even if I wanted to."

"Then Yahweh won't forgive you." Caden glanced at Ellie, and she shrugged. "That's what He said."

"But, but He always—"

"Nope. Forgive, Cade, so you can be forgiven and pardoned, and you don't get put in Spiritual jail, so Demons beat you up all the time. Yahweh's pardoned your debt, that's mega huge, by the way, and you can't ever pay it back. You can pardon another person's debt they owe you, which is, by the way, pennies compared to your debt to Yahweh."

"Pennies? Pennies! It's not that easy—"

"It's just a choice. And prayer." Ellie nodded. "Lots of that. Ask Yahweh to help you want to forgive, then pray for forgiveness for hating, then pray for the person you hate to be blessed."

Caden grimaced and shook his head. "I don't think-"

"Just do it, alright?" Dasha snapped. "Stop pretending so much is over your head. We're *all* in over our heads, but we're still here! Choose. That's it. I had to choose to

246 TERRY JAMES & HEATHER RENAE

forgive Rapham for killing my team. It sucked, but it had
to be done."

"You think Christianity is all about how you feel and
stuff?" Ellie asked, shaking her head. "Silly guy."

Caden fell silent as he shoved his hands in his pockets.
*Stupid, churchy nonsense!* He continued walking silently. He
felt his blood rushing faster as curses roared in his ears.
Nathaniel deserved anything but forgiveness. He should
die again and again until he felt the same way Caden did
as he watched the life leave Trace's eyes.

Caden ground his teeth and shook his head. *You're nuts,*
he said to God. *Well, if that's what You want me to do, make it
happen. I don't wanna do it, so I guess you have to change my
mind first.* He hissed a curse and ran his fingers through his
hair. He was grateful when they reached the mouth of the
Siq, he had something else to focus on.

All the activity was focused on a narrow section of the
Siq, a few yards from Petra's entrance. Jaden's men stood
on the cliffs high overhead as workers labored and Chuk
oversaw. Turns out, Chuk wasn't just good at navigation
and organizing trips. He could organize a lot of things. He
waved as he saw the three approach and weaved through
the working crowd.

"Just in time!" he called. "The boulders are almost in
place." Their conversation halted as a van and hummer
pulled up, the revving engines reverberating through
the Siq.

"There they are," Ellie said with a smile as she shifted
her backpack. "I'll see yah." Dasha playfully bumped
against Caden's shoulder as the two women walked
toward Petra's entrance.

Caden frowned. "El, D," he called. "I don't think you
guys should greet newcomers at our gate." Ellie swatted a
hand without turning around.

"Don't worry," Dasha called. "We'll be back to make

your dinner!"

"That's not what I mean, D!"

Ellie smiled over her shoulder. "Yahweh's protecting us! He doesn't need your help."

"I'll always be your big brother." He wanted to say who he was to Dasha but stopped. He didn't want to make her mad. Ellie grinned, waved, and the two continued without another word.

"She's a tough one," Chuk said, and workers bowed at Ellie as she passed. She nodded to each in turn with a warm smile. "Let her work. She can't just stay all cooped up all the time."

"The people need her," Caden said, shoving his hands in his pockets. "Don't you see how they look at her, treat her? She's a constant reminder of Yohanan and the *Akal Esh*." Chuk nodded as Caden rubbed the back of his neck. *And I can't lose Dasha.* It would be like losing half the team before the final inning of a game.

With a sigh, Caden looked up high to the sliver of sky overhead. Men worked around a great mound of boulders piled across the Siq. A wooden structure, reinforced by beams and planks, held the boulders up. Secured to the central beam was a long rope nearly reaching the Siq's floor. It was secured to an eyebolt screwed into the sandstone.

"So, how's it going?"

"See that rope?" Chuk asked, jerking his chin. "A child could yank that, and the entire thing would come crashing down. There's enough rock up there to bury this part of the Siq. Nobody's coming through!"

"With one pull?"

"One of the Leovirnesses is pretty handy with engineering."

Caden arched a brow and tried not to scoff. "Really?"

Heavy steps fell behind him and a shadow crossed by.

"Don't sound so surprised, cub," a Leovirness said, a clipboard in one hand and a pen in the other.

Caden held up a hand and glanced away. "Sorry." She huffed, her tail flicking, and continued on, her neck craned back as she watched the progress.

"Good work, Chuk," Caden said, clapping his friend on his shoulder. "Has it been tested?"

Chuk nodded. "We used the design on another slot canyon. After the fifth attempt, we got it down."

Caden raised his brows. "That seems fast."

Chuk smiled with a shrug. "Luck."

Caden nudged him. "Yahweh."

"Ah, Yahweh. Still can't seem to remember I'm following Him now."

"You'll catch on. I hear it was easier back when His Spirit filled people." Chuk grunted. "Such a different time."

A sudden cacophony consumed the slot canyon. It overwhelmed Caden's senses and made everyone drop to the ground on their bellies. Gasping, Caden stared at the Siq's entrance. The sound blasted again, and he caught a glimpse of white fire. An automatic weapon was firing. Caden's eyes widened as his blood iced instantly. *D!* His heart leapt into his throat. *El!*

A shadow swallowed the canyon. It was deep and long, casting everything in darkness. Wind followed the shadow. And screams. Men plummeted from their posts along the Siq's edge. They ping-ponged between the sandstone walls and fell with a crunch. Caden and Chuk raised their hands and tried to breathe as dust and the sharp smell of gunpowder filled the air. There was another smell too. Something like raw meat mixed with a murky swamp.

Caden cursed under his breath and stared up. Through the crack of sky overhead, the deep shadow passed again. In a blink, it was gone, but Caden noticed its color. It was blood red. Caden inhaled instantly, his entire body tensing.

Chuk reached for him. "No!"

Caden leapt to his feet as his left hand made a fist. He felt the Shield of Faith's grip and didn't even bother checking if it formed as he took off at a dead sprint. The shield's plates formed instantly, standing between him and the flying bullets. Caden stared through the translucent shield and felt the *Akal Esh's* heat warming his face.

His breath came in rapid bursts. His right hand longed for a weapon. A bat or crowbar or a club even! *No, stupid!* Caden's thoughts screamed. *Why don't I ever think of guns?* Skidding to a holt, Caden unhooked an M16's strap from a guard's limp arm. He felt random tapping against his left arm. He looked and, seeing through the shield, saw sudden sparks fly this way and that. *Bulletproof*, he thought. He suddenly smiled. It was a wild, fierce smile that darkened his eyes and heated his blood.

He continued charging from the Siq, his heart slamming in his ears and body moving as though on instinct. He burst from the slot canyon, the sun falling across him. He hardly had time to comprehend who was shooting at who. A van and hummer parked close. Both were pelted with bullets. Shades were attacking. No, Refiners. Those were Refiners. *Zealot* Refiners. They shot way too perfectly to be just humans. Leovirs leapt between them. Bodies lay across the rocky ground. So many bodies.

Caden peeled his eyes away from the bloodied faces. He had no time to search for D or El. He had no time for anything but to fight. The M16 started firing. It wasn't until the third Refiner fell over did Caden realize he was the one pulling the trigger. He didn't stop, pressing forward, low to the ground, covered by the shield. The shield exploded with sparks as several bullets rocketed into it. Caden grunted, his shoulder tensing as he struggled to absorb the shock. The back of his mind screamed he shouldn't be able to stay standing, but he just kept moving forward.

A Zealot yowled and charged, her own gun flashing fire down on him. Caden braced for impact, but her body stumbled back, and she fell, blood painting the ground. *About time!* Caden thought as Jaden's men opened fire. The torrent of bullets against Caden's shield lessened. Sweat dripping down his brow, Caden swept the area, his eyes constantly moving. *Where are you two?*

There were so many dead. Why was the van on fire? Movement to his right. Big. Yellow. Roaring. Caden pivoted, aimed, and didn't shoot a single round. A force beyond any human strength slapped the gun from his hands. The gun's sling dug into his arm, and he stumbled. The Leovir snarled and slashed claws, severing the gun entirely. Panting, Caden stepped back, seeing the Leovir was an arm's reach away.

The Freak's mouth and lower mane was stained bloody red. His eyes were wide with the taste of it. The Leovir huffed as he stalked upright, towering over Caden. Caden stumbled back, panic tightening his throat and making it impossible to breathe. *God!* His mind cried. *Help!*

More movement. More yellow. More roaring. The Leovir collapsed, another great Freak pouncing on him. Roaring and snarling, a Leovirness slashed claws across the Leovir's face. Tail whipping, she lunged forward, sinking fangs into his throat. He thrashed, but she whiplashed and gnawed. The Leovir shook and fell still. She straightened, ears flat against her head and bristled, nape to tail. She glanced at Caden, her entire face splattered in blood. It was Jael. Caden straightened, seeing more Leovirs joining the battle. Benaiah led them with a roar.

Belting a mirthless laugh, Caden turned to the enemy.

He saw the terror in their eyes, even the Zealots. Caden's laugh solidified into a wolfish smile as he charged. It took him a heartbeat to realize he was humming. It was that same tune again. It took him another moment to realize he wasn't armed. *I am too!* He told himself. *I have a shield!* Without breaking his pace, Caden slammed the shield into a Refiner, sending him to the ground.

"Dasha!" Caden screamed. His ears were ringing with the cacophony of gunfire, screams of pain, and lion's roars. "El!"

There.

Dasha knelt beside a boulder and wildly fired on the enemy. Her clothes were stained red, her hair was a mess, and she had lost her backpack. Gasping for air, Caden raced toward her. He heard a whistle above the chaos. The Zealots called to one another and backed away. Benaiah and his pride roared as the enemy retreated. Caden didn't acknowledge them; all he focused on was Dasha. That crazy Russian was actually smiling! Her eyes locked with Caden's, and her grin grew.

"Get back!" Caden screamed.

"You think?" Dasha dropped her magazine and jammed another one into place before firing again as she retreated. "I'm fine!"

"Dasha!"

"Get El!"

"I can't!"

Dasha lowered her weapon, drew back a boot, and slammed it against his shield. Caden stepped back, stunned. "Get El!" She pointed, and Caden finally looked.

Ellie raced toward them as she cradled a bloody arm. She was a distance away. Without cover. Caden cursed and hardly noticed Dasha holding out a pistol. He seized it and took off, anger tightening his chest. How dare they wound his sister! How dare they!

A shadow consumed the land. It was vast and cold, sweeping by like a tidal wave. Caden's face turned pale. Ellie looked up, her steps faltering. Her scream wasn't heard over the torrent of wind descending upon her. Great, reptilian hands fell on either side of her as Tarek landed. Its seven heads slithered to and fro, each one clicking as solid black eyes watched the carnage. Water dripped between each fanged mouth as Tarek spread its wings, as though trying to blot out the light.

Benaiah stopped in his attack. Jaden's men cried out. Caden watched as bullets merely passed through the red dragon. He alone didn't slacken his pace. Among the slithering heads, Caden caught a glimpse of Ellie. She was gripped in Tarek's human-like, clawed hands. Growling through gritted teeth, Caden lengthened his strides. He threw aside the pistol, knowing it was worthless. Ellie's screams finally met his ears. That was it. An enraged scream ripped from Caden's throat.

One of Tarek's heads turned, the single horn jutting from its brow pointed right at him. The great mouth drew wider as water began to stream from it. Half of Caden's brain panicked, seeing how huge Tarek really was. He easily stood three stories high, and those horned wings made him look twice as big. That part of Caden's brain, however, was tied up and gagged.

The part of him who wanted justice screamed for the charge. Caden had an idea. *This better work, God!* He thought as he grabbed the shield and turned it sideways. Drawing it back, he threw it like a frisbee. It flew from his grasp and sliced through the air. It cut straight into Tarek's mouth.

With a high-pitched scream, the head lurched back as its severed tongue fell to the ground. Caden made a fist, and the shield vanished, simultaneously appearing on his arm again. Tarek stumbled back as the head continued to screech. Its jaw hung at an angle and Caden saw the shield had given it a Glasgow smile. Fierce joy burst in His chest as dark blood mixed with Tarek's waters. The other heads turned to the wounded one as the wings twitched. The wounded head shook and screamed, writhing about. It took another second for the other heads to notice Caden. It was just enough time.

Caden hyper-focused on the demonic beast before him. He couldn't hear the gunfire or even Ellie's screaming. He didn't feel the flaming pain of his lungs or the agony in his tired legs. He just saw Noam and Auset's heads rolling across the courtyard. Caden screamed, throwing the shield again. It slammed into the base of a neck. The head whipped back as the others advanced. Caden summoned the shield, and it instantly formed. He threw it again. It sliced through the air and gouged into another head's eye. Just as his shield formed again, a head lowered to Caden's level.

He saw its black mouth gaping before him. Cursing, Caden leapt. He heard the water blast from Tarek's head, crashing where he had just stood. Caden rolled and jumped to his feet again. Another head rounded, black eyes fixed on him. Caden grabbed the shield, readying to throw it. He was hit by a train. At least it felt like it.

The moment Caden registered he was flying through the air, he collided with a boulder. His head bounced at least once, the wind knocked out of him, and his entire body shook. He gasped for air as he lay in the dirt, blood filling his mouth. His vision blurred as pain overtook him. Someone was screaming his name. Someone he cared for. He turned, seeing Ellie's pale face as she writhed in Tarek's grasp. *El!*

A cold, scaly hand seized his leg. Caden lurched backwards, his leg feeling ready to dislocate. Yelling through gritted teeth, Caden twisted and faced Tarek. The red dragon drew him closer as a head hovered directly over him. Tarek's hand wrapped around Caden's chest and pinned him down, each clawed finger like iron bars. Caden cried out and thrashed. Nothing budged. His chest heaved as he stared up at the watching head. He could've sworn it was smiling. It was like being strapped to the chair all over again, Grant watching with that horrible smile. But this time, his tormenter wasn't even a person. It was the beast of Demons.

The head lowered, clicking softly to itself, as Ellie's screams clapped Caden's ears. It smelt of old mildew and pond scum. Caden saw his pinned body reflected in its black eyes. Water began to drip from its mouth. Caden cursed between gasps as a shivered chill rushed through him. The drips became a steady trickle, then a stream. Caden, now soaked through, kicked ruts in the muddy ground. Panic choked him. He strained, prepared to rip his own body apart to be free. The flow intensified. Caden gasped, feeling it flow into his mouth and nose. Sputtering and hacking up water, Caden heard a new voice in his thoughts.

*"I said I was prince,"* the voice, like many voices in one, shook Caden's very foundations. It was too big of a voice for his puny body to contain. *"And now you will kneel."* The flow stopped.

Caden dragged in each breath as he stared up, locking eyes with Tarek. His limbs were shaking as his lungs already strained with each breath. He knew what was coming; he had nearly drowned dozens of times before. It was agony. But it was better than kneeling to *this*. Caden gritted his teeth as his eyes flashed with fire. "Never!" The looming dragon head smiled. Its mouth stretched wide. A solid column of water shot out, covering Caden's entire torso and head, the force plastering him to the ground. The water didn't stop surging.

# TWENTY

# MEGIDDO

CADEN'S LUNGS were on fire, but he expected that. Panic tightened his throat, but it always did that when he was drowning. His body tried to thrash without his permission, which was near impossible as the water pressed him to the ground. His internal screaming raged again, completely freaking out and screaming about death and the building agony. But Caden expected all this. He expected his nose and mouth to fill with water. He expected to feel like death was staring him in the face.

*It is,* Caden thought. It was a quiet thought, like a whisper from the back of a room of panicking people. But it was there. More importantly, Yahweh was there with him. *Hide in Yahweh,* the whispered voice said.

Caden's head felt ready to burst. His lung pumped for air, and his throat bobbed, but he refused to open his mouth and gasp. His feeble attempts at thrashing slowed. Pain racked his entire body. He clenched his jaw shut, determined not to answer his body's natural demand to inhale. He felt his mouth loosen. He had stopped kicking. *Yahweh,* the thought was near impossible to formulate. *Yahweh, please. This can't be it. This...*

He inhaled.

Water rushed down his throat, choking him. He coughed and gasped, still under water. He felt the water flood into him. All thoughts ended. There was no more time. They became fuzzy and frayed, like a doll getting unwound bit by bit, the stuffing removed, and the pieces getting scattered. He felt his body, but it was distant and unresponsive. He hardly knew he was rolling. Darkness closed in. Something scraped his back and sides. He didn't really feel the pain anymore. It was kind of nice now. Peaceful and calm.

Caden limply cracked against a boulder and fell on his face. Water rushed about him, but at the ground level. His entire body dry heaved, every muscle tensing as water gushed from his mouth. Caden's body arched again, heaving out more water. He felt like his insides were coming out of his mouth. Coughing and shaking, Caden gulped in air, each intake loud and desperate. His chest burned. His head screamed in pain. His limbs shook uncontrollably.

Caden's eyes opened as he fought for life. He saw the water stream on by, nudging little pebbles in the current. *I'm not dead*, he thought finally. He blinked, completely shocked. He saw movement out of the corner of his eye. *I've got to move.* He couldn't. His body wasn't responding. *How hard did I hit that rock?* Panting, Caden managed to drag his arms under him. He heaved his torso up, his head limply swaying as it lifted. Moaning as water dripped from his nose, Caden forced his body up.

He looked around, seeing a stream cut through the desert on its way to Petra. Bodies bobbed in the current, and the waters were turning red from all the blood. Caden blinked, his foggy brain remembering they were under attack and there was something about Ellie. She wasn't okay, or something. Was that right? Caden slowly turned his head and stared. Oh yeah, that dragon guy was here. This was its water. Rage tightened Caden's chest as he watched the heads slither between one another. It held its arm funny as it stalked closer. There was something in its hand.

*El.* Caden's body tensed as his heart quickened. He could feel it pulsing in his neck. He forced in more air as he stared at his little sister kicking. Tarek didn't even acknowledge her; she looked like a barbie doll in its hands. One of the heads turned, and the black eyes locked onto Caden. The head froze and stared. Caden's lips drew back as rage sent strength into his limbs. *Get out of my world!* Another head faced him, just as stunned.

Caden cursed and staggered to his feet. A Zealot he hadn't noticed, who stood quite close, screamed and shot away from him. Caden hardly gave it much thought as another reptilian head faced him and Tarek stepped closer. Tarek stopped suddenly, a few yards from Petra's entrance. Caden stood closer to the Siq as he locked eyes with Tarek. He blinked, realizing every Refiner, Zealot, and Leovir had retreated. It was just Tarek and the believers.

"Sammy!" A voice screeched.

He could hear the panic in Dasha's voice, but he didn't acknowledge her. He had a dragon to stop. Before a plan could be formed, each of Tarek's heads lowered and faced the slot canyon. Caden's blood iced. *They can't get inside, so they'll flood everyone out. They'll kill us all!* His eyes darted to Ellie. She was screaming and crying in rage. His Lil El. His sis he swore to protect. Hatred smacked him square in the face. *You will suffer.* He looked to Tarek. *You will.*

*"I will conquer all that is."*

The voice struck Caden from the inside out, nearly bringing him to his knees. He watched as Tarek's mouths opened, nearly unhinged, as it looked down the slot canyon. Caden's heart literally constricted painfully. *Love you, El.* He turned his back on Ellie and ran to the Siq without another thought. He heard screaming. Believers around him scattered, each fleeing from Petra's entrance. He sprinted toward it, jaw set and eyes locked. Water roared behind him. He ignored his primal instinct to preserve his life and kept running.

He entered the Siq's shadows, blood roaring in his ears. The surge hit. He gasped, dragging in more precious air. The torrent swallowed him, sending him off his feet. He didn't know what was up or down. The beginning stages of drowning started all over again. *Raw Peace,* he thought, gritting his teeth and fighting through the agony. *Focus!*

He kicked and dug through the water, praying he was headed for the surface. His head broke through and he gasped, drawing water into his mouth. He sputtered, splashing, trying to say above the current. He blinked water from his eyes, watching the sandstone walls rush by. *I'm too late!* Caden forced his head back as he searched overhead. *Come on! Come on!* If he had enough air, he would've been screaming curses. *Come there!*

The rope. Caden's chest quivered with breath as his body fought to face the single strand that could save them all. The rope leading to the mound of rocks overhead drew closer at an unbelievably fast rate. He wasn't going to make it. It was a battle to not let the current drag him under, let alone reach up, grab a rope, *and* pull everything down.

*The strength of a child,* Caden remembered Chuk saying. *That's all I need. And, that's as much faith as I need, too.* Caden coughed and gasped, ignoring the water in his nose and his body screaming for mercy. The rope was close. Too close. With a strangled cry, Caden raised a hand. His fingers felt something, and he seized it. Clinging on for dear life, the surge dragged Caden along. His grip was weak. The rope slipped from his hands. *No!*

Caden kicked to turn around, but his head went under. Everything fell dark as water filled his nose and mouth. He thrashed uncontrollably and tried to find the surface. He wasn't going to die like this! This was stupid! This wasn't God's plan, and if it was, He needed a new plan! *I am Yours,* Caden's mind screamed. *Save me! Do something! I can't do this on my own!*

Something struck his foot, then his other one. It was hard and unmoved by the flood. He struck it again and was dragged against it. Sputtering, Caden realized he wasn't moving anymore. Water rushed around him, but his head was at last free. Shaking and coughing up more water, Caden opened his eyes. He lay on the ground as the water continued around him. It wasn't a destroying flood but had thinned to a rushing river. And it kept thinning.

Chest shuddering with each breath, Caden heaved himself up and rolled on his back. He coughed, and the fuzziness of his mind cleared with each lungful. *Get up.* His body didn't respond. *Get up!* He slowly lifted his head and looked behind him. Petra's entrance was sealed off. A mountain of rock rose nearly to the top of the slot canyon. Trickles of water dribbled through, but Tarek's water lessened more and more. Caden slowly stood, his body screaming for him to not move, but his mind was telling him to get up. He leaned against the canyon's walls and stared. *It worked,* he thought. *We're going to be —*

A shadow filled the canyon. Caden's head snapped back, catching sight of Tarek's red, vast wings. A scream went with it. Caden froze, all breath caught in his throat. Ellie was still alive. Still held in Tarek's grasp. Caden stepped after them but with two wing beats, Tarek was gone. Caden gasped as he stared at the wall, straining to hear Ellie. There was nothing. Caden dipped his head as panic tightened his chest. His hands became fists, and the roar of blood in his ears didn't slow. His jaw set as his eyes darkened. *I will slaughter them all.* Supporting himself with the canyon's wall, Caden limp-hopped down the Siq toward Petra. He needed a hummer and supplies. He had a sister to save.

———

CADEN'S EYES OPENED SLOWLY. His neck hurt. And his chest. Oh, and his head throbbed. And his...

Everything hurt. He was staring at his feet as he sat in an awkward position. The seat was bouncing and humming, and a leather strap crossed his chest. *Grant found me,* he thought, his eyes widening. With a jolt of energy, Caden bolted upright, making fists and wildly looking around.

"Hey! Hey!" someone cried.

The seat wiggled back and forth, and the humming rhythm changed. Caden blinked and stared wide-eyed at Chuk. His friend stared back, arm raised in defense as his other hand gripped a steering wheel. Caden glanced all around, his fists still raised. He was in a hummer in the passenger seat. Chuk drove. Behind him, wedged in like sardines, were Benaiah and Jael. The Leovirs looked exceptionally unhappy, especially Jael. Between them, taking the cake for being miserable, was a guy in a white uniform. A plated, white uniform with three red diamonds on his shoulders.

Caden turned and fully faced the Refiner. The man shrunk back and raised his tied hands. The man was muttering something. Caden couldn't quite make it out.

"Mercy, Assassin. Mercy!"

Caden lifted his chin and glanced at Benaiah. "This isn't what I meant."

Benaiah locked eyes with him, his clipped ear twitching. "I got intel."

"I didn't mean to *bring* him with us!"

Benaiah didn't turn away. "His name's Eitan." Caden shook his head with a curse.

Chuk shot him a look. "Didn't you say you'd work on that potty mouth of yours?"

"Not a good time," Caden snapped as he turned around. Sighing heavily, he scrubbed his face and sat up straighter. He felt terrible, even after falling asleep in the hummer. *Almost drowning twice in a day can do that,* he thought. Hatred heated his blood as his eyes darted ahead. He had to find Ellie. There was no telling what Tarek and its Demons were doing to her. Vivid images of Noam and Auset's beheaded bodies flooded his mind as Puppets got drunk on their blood.

Moaning, Caden lowered his chin and ground his teeth. The helplessness he felt was overwhelming. And his desire for blood. *That's not being a good Christian.* He didn't care. Sometimes justice was bloody. Didn't God think so too?

Caden slowly closed his eyes, realizing his constant aggression wasn't just violent protectiveness for his sister. He had another someone he cared about. Sure, Dasha was capable, but her safety was constantly on his mind. She had asked to join him, but he refused. "I can't have you both taken," he had said.

She opened her mouth to respond but saw the severity in his eyes. She turned away and rubbed her arms. "I," she stammered. "I just don't want to lose my team again."

Caden blinked as she looked down and shifted restlessly. "I'll come back," he whispered. She nodded without a word.

Caden stepped closer and gently lifted her chin. She looked him in the eyes as he drew closer still. They kissed, their arms wrapping around each other and drawing closer. Though they had kissed before, this one was real. They melted into one another, letting themselves show the other how they felt without words.

Chuk cleared his throat, and Caden's eyes slowly opened and rubbed the back of his neck. "We're passing Jerusalem soon," Chuk said.

Caden shifted in his seat and stiffly nodded. "How long have I been out?"

"A few hours. We wanted you to rest." Caden rubbed his brow. "You know, you shouldn't have come." Caden didn't answer. "You almost drowned. Twice."

"I just can hold my breath a long time."

Chuk shot him a quick look and shook his head. "Why can you?"

Caden fell silent as he sighed and leaned back, his eyes lightly closed. "I've been waterboarded a lot." The hummer fell silent.

"Oh," Chuk finally muttered.

Caden shifted in his seat but refused to open his eyes. He didn't want to find Grant stooped over him while Buck hummed and readied another bucket of water. "More of God taking care of me, right?" Caden said with a mirthless laugh. *Seems to be how He takes care of all of us.*

"Well, yeah," Chuk said, and Caden frowned. "I mean...Petra would've been flooded if you didn't know how to drown and stay calm. You pulled the rope just in time. It saved everyone."

A muscle in Caden's jaw flexed and he turned away. He thought of his restraints and the countless times he thought he'd die as water flowed into his mouth and nose. *Were You preparing me all along?* Caden blinked thoughtfully and shook his head. *You do the strangest things.*

With a sigh, he stared down the highway. It was littered with crashed and abandoned cars. Chuk had to swerve now and then and even drive off the road to avoid the pile-ups. Even from inside the car, Caden noticed the stench of bodies. Several of the cars' windshields were pelted with holes, but they weren't near perfect circles like bullet holes. Caden's stomach clenched as he saw a pillar of smoke in the distance. "What's been going on out here?"

Chuk grunted. "We got out when we did. I wasn't so sure about all this Yahweh stuff, but now!" Chuk shook his head. "I'd be toast right now if I didn't go with you."

Caden glared at him. "I'm nothing special."

Chuk shrugged. "You're impossible to kill."

Caden grimaced. He shook his head and turned away. Glancing in the rearview mirror, he eyed Eitan. "Hey. You? What happened out here?"

Eitan flinched back again and tried to hide. Jael snarled as she nudged him, nearly sending him from his seat. Eitan gasped and looked down, visibly shaking. "The locusts, Assassin!"

"Stop calling me that."

"Yes, sir!"

"What happened?"

"The locusts, sir! Horrible bugs! They just...they..." Tears welled in the man's eyes.

Caden's brows rose, and he wondered if Eitan was going to have a breakdown. "Bugs?"

"Yes! They looked like locusts, but...I swear to you! They had armor!" Caden's brows rose higher. "And, and human faces with long hair! They came in swarms! Stinging and—"

"Locusts don't sting," Jael snapped.

"These did, Sovereign Lion and—"

Jael's lips drew back as she lowered into Eitan's face. "I am *not* the Sovereign Lion. You say that again, and you'll be untangling your guts from around your body."

Eitan shivered, and Caden fought back a smile. "These...these ones sting. And they have tails like scorpions."

"Anything else?" Caden asked.

"And fangs like, like," Eitan glanced at Jael. "Like you."

"Hum," Caden grunted. "That sounds like pretty bad Freaks."

"They are evil! They don't kill anyone, just sting and torture! All the time. There's no escape. No help." Eitan shook his head and kept shaking it, drawing his hands over his face. "No help. Even when people try to kill themselves, it doesn't work. You can see." Eitan motioned out the window. "The swarm went through here. Nothing's left. Nothing."

Chuk frowned. "Then why are there so many dead?"

Caden faced the carnage again, the wheels of his mind turning. "Do the bugs harm any Christians?"

Eitan's brows knotted as he blinked. "I'm sure terrorists died too, I mean..." His voice was quiet and hoarse.

Chuk chuckled as Benaiah grinned. "So, no confirmed cases?" Caden asked. Eitan said nothing. "Coincidence?"

"No," Eitan said, his jaw flexing.

"Our god can save us from bugs." Caden shook his head. "So, lots of deaths?" Eitan nodded. "Famine?" Eitan nodded again. "Plagues?" Eitan glanced up, his eyes narrowing. "And wild animals going berserk and eating people?"

Eitan's head tilted to one side as his mouth dropped open. "How did you...yes, sir."

Caden nodded as all eyes fell on him. "We're living Revelation 6. It details all this chaos; that's why there are so many dead." He sighed. "So glad I'm protected by Yahweh."

"Your God is dead." Caden didn't respond as Benaiah

and Jael snarled at Eitan. Cowering in a ball and breathing heavily, Eitan shook his head. "Dead Gods can't defeat my real god."

Caden didn't bother looking back as Benaiah and Jael forcefully silenced him. He shifted and looked out the window. *Thank you for protecting us in Petra,* Caden thought. *But the moment we stepped out, the protection was gone. Thanks.* His eyes darkened. *Why couldn't You have done a better job?*

Caden closed his eyes and gritted his teeth, not wanting to think that way. *I'm sorry, God. I didn't mean that. God, save Ellie. I'm begging You. Even though she has no use anymore and You slaughter Your followers like cattle. Why did I pledge myself to You? You cannot safeguard a single—*

Caden hissed a curse and crossed his arms. He hadn't seen Doeg since he received the Shield of Faith. He knew the Demon was around. He stared out the window again, half expecting to see a Shade keeping pace beside the road. He saw something else. It was a horse and rider. The black horse was so sickly and thin, Caden could see its individual ribs. Its mane and tail were thin, scrappy strands that dragged on the ground.

The rider was even worse. It looked like a Wither, except even thinner. His clothes hardly hung on his boney shoulders. His arm limply hung at his side, and dangling from loose fingers was a pair of scales. Eyes nearly popped from the man's head as his skeletal face turned to Caden. Caden's heart skipped a beat; the eyes were solid white. A sickly chill made Caden shiver as he leaned away from the window.

"What's up?" Chuk asked.

"Did you see that?" Caden asked, glancing at him.

"Hum?"

"There."

"What you talking about?"

"There! Over by the—" He was gone. Caden breathed

out heavily and stared, his pulse racing. With a curse, he sat back. "Never mind." He closed his eyes, his fingertips cold and clammy. *Another horsemen,* he thought. *I saw the one about war and the one that represented Luca I missed, thank God! So this is number three. Famine. That's what he means.* Caden shivered and he rubbed his eyes with a finger and thumb.

Homesickness suddenly struck his chest. He had to save his sister but hated leaving Petra. Leaving Dasha. Things weren't crazy there. People actually lived and didn't get attacked by freaky locusts. *I just want to go home,* Caden thought, closing his eyes. His chin lowered, and he straightened, his eyes suddenly opening. *That's what Heaven's for.* He stared down the highway and tilted his head toward Chuk. "Where are we going?"

"Megiddo."

"Why there?"

"He said that's Tarek's camp." Caden waited for more of an explanation. Chuk stared at him and shrugged. "What?"

"That's it? That's your only reason?"

"Everyone's going there."

"Everyone."

"Yeah."

"Who's everyone?"

"All the Antichrist's allies from across the world."

"And why would they do that?"

"Beats me."

Caden cursed and turned back to Eitan. "Hey. Why are all the world leaders following Luca to Tel Megiddo?"

"They're assembling."

Caden's hair stood on end. "For?"

"Battle."

Caden's chin lifted as his blood turned to ice. "Is there another name for Tel Megiddo? I don't remember hearing that place in the Bible."

Chuk scoffed. "You expect to know every single place?"

"Shush! Eitan. The name."

Eitan stared down at his feet, his eyes glassy and wide. "In the ancient world, it was called Har-Megeddon. Har means hill, Megeddon is the place. They put the words together and dropped the h."

"What is this?" Benaiah grumbled. "You're a Refiner! Not a teacher!"

"I was before becoming an ally to the one true god!"

Caden completely ignored Eitan's outburst as his eyes widened. A slow, sinking feeling consumed him as a lump formed in his throat. "You're telling me," he nearly shouted, silencing the others. "You're telling me we're heading straight for Armageddon?" The hummer was deathly quiet.

"Yes, sir." Caden felt cold all over as he leaned back in his chair.

Chuk turned to each one of them and licked his lips. "That's a real place? Like, an actual, physical place?"

Caden blinked slowly, feeling his heart quickening. He took in a slow breath and stared down the abandoned highway. "Apparently."

# TWENTY-ONE

# THERE WILL BE BLOOD

CADEN STARED straight ahead as they neared Tel Megiddo. He was drenched in sweat, and his heart hadn't stopped pounding with force. He hated wearing the Refiner uniform but tried to ignore the plated armor as he looked through the helmet covering his face. Benaiah had stripped some of the fallen Refiners before they left Petra. Caden held his arm against his side, hoping no one would notice the bullet hole ripping through the uniform. He also prayed no one asked him to take off his helmet. Everyone knew who Caden Johnson was. His massive scars were an easy giveaway. Chuk had suggested he stay behind, but Caden shut that down real quick. His Lil El needed him.

"She needs you alive, too," Chuk had said. "And not ah...what were they going to do to you?"

Caden hadn't answered, and Benaiah flicked his ear. "Blood Eagle."

"Yeah," Chuk had nodded. "Don't want that."

Caden had still stayed quiet. He was going. End of story. At least they were armed. He sat as still as a statue as he hummed. *His wrath will flare up in a moment,* he thought, in tune with the song he was humming. *Blessed are all who take refuge.*

He blinked and fell silent. *Why do I keep doing that?* He wasn't a hummer, and he never cared for singing. And this, of all times, was the worst time to sing. He just wanted to. It felt...right. *Raw Peace,* Caden thought. *Raw Peace.* He cursed, thinking of how insane he was for wanting Peace while willingly driving to Armageddon. Literally! *Raw Peace,* he thought, taking a breath as sweat dripped down his back. *Raw...*

They entered Megiddo's valley. Caden's mouth dropped open as he stared. Chuk gasped. Jael leaned forward, peering out the windows as her nape bristled. Benaiah's claws slid out. The evening light illuminated a vast oasis amid the dry, sandy yellows of Israel. Megiddo was green. Not kind of green, but with grass, trees, and fields. It was a fertile valley of life.

Life that was completely overrun by darkness. Every square inch of the valley was covered with an army. It looked like a mobile city. Caden forgot to breathe as they kept driving, seeing the valley more and more. The army stretched on and on, and he knew it continued beyond the boundaries of the valley. There were sections of obviously different military styles hailing beneath different flags. There was the flag of China, Russia, Germany, South Africa, England, and so many others. Caden's eyes fell on the American flag. His stomach turned, grief for his people striking his chest. Each flag was altered to include the Sovereign Lion at its center.

At the very heart of the army city was a hill overseeing everything. Standing upright at its center, and large enough so that everyone could see, was a massive New Kingdom flag. The white fabric stood out amid all the colors and activity as it lazily waved. Even at a distance, Caden saw the Sovereign Lion, its outline and crown stitched in glittering gold. He felt those unblinking, ever-watching eyes staring straight at him, knowing who he was and why he'd come.

A lump formed in his throat. *We can't defeat this,* he thought, thinking of their army in Petra and any other remnant in hiding. *They completely outnumber us. Does God want a genocide?*

*"Your blood is sweeter than wine."* Caden flinched as his eyes narrowed, longing to shut Doeg out. *"You cannot. Even when you die, I will be with you."*

*That makes no sense.*

*"You will be in Hell."*

*No. I won't.*

*"You've poorly stewarded every single person God has charged you with. They're all dead."*

*Ellie isn't dead.*

Doeg started laughing; it chilled Caden's blood. *"True. Yet, she longs for it."*

Caden lifted his chin, rage heating his blood and forcing a vein to pulse in his throat. *What are you doing to her?*

Doeg chuckled. *"What God permits."*

"Drive," Caden muttered.

Chuk glanced at him. "What?"

"Drive faster! We have to get to her!"

"Caden!"

"Come on!"

"Be quiet," Benaiah said, his voice firm with finality. "That will draw bad attention. Slow. Calm. We are one of them." Caden cursed and looked down. "What is it you say?" Benaiah thought a moment and nodded. "Raw Peace. Do that."

Caden forced himself to be quiet and sit still, but he wanted to draw his gun and encourage Chuk to hurry up. *"That won't save her, human."*

Caden's eyes closed, hating himself for letting her get captured. If only she listened to him! This was all avoidable! God knew this would happen. He did nothing. Again! He would eternally fail Caden! Caden didn't require God. God was a farce, and truth was not found in Him.

*Doeg,* Caden thought. *I will destroy you.*

*"Silly human. You can't destroy me."*

*I can with God.*

*"Where is this God of yours?"*

Caden hissed a curse. *Why do I talk to you?*

He noticed Chuk watching him. "I know," Chuk muttered, nodding. "This is a bad plan." Caden didn't answer.

After ignoring Benaiah for the tenth time, saying their rescue mission was futile and deadly, they had made a plan. Caden knew Luca would enjoy Ellie's captivity and want her near to him. "Find him," he had said, "and we'll find her."

"And," Chuk muttered. "How do we get to her?"

"We just got back from Petra with more intel to report."

"Such as?"

"We know the location of Caden Johnson." They really didn't like that idea. "What? I won't say I'm standing right there."

"That won't work," Jael hissed.

"No," Caden muttered thoughtfully. "Find Tarek. Luca will be with it. Ellie will be with Luca. Eitan here will help us get through."

"What if he doesn't have clearance?" Chuk asked.

"He does," Benaiah said. "I wanted a valuable asset, not a weak one."

Caden nodded. "Good plan."

"No," Jael scoffed. "I'm not agreeing to—"

"Then get out, and don't slow us down." The van fell quiet as Caden started praying, doubting everything he just said.

Chuk shook his head as they entered Megiddo. "We shouldn't do this—"

"Do it." Chuk snapped his mouth shut and kept driving.

"What do we do with him?" Jael asked, prodding Eitan.

"You need me!" Eitan looked to Caden. "I know how to get through security. You need me."

"Tell us how," Jael said.

"We've been over this," Caden said, interrupting Jael. "He has a NIIC. They'll scan it. We need him."

"I don't have one," Jael grumbled. "Why won't they scan me? Any of us?"

Caden didn't answer as he continued looking across the army. "Just trust God."

"That's not comforting."

"That's all I've got!" Jael fell quiet as Caden cursed.

"But that's all we need," Benaiah calmly added.

*I guess,* Caden thought as his stomach twisted on itself more and more.

———

SECURITY WAS TIGHT. Caden's throat felt tighter. He could've sworn they saw the bullet hole in his second-hand armor. They'll ask him to take off his helmet. They'll see his facial scar and know instantly who he is. Wasn't it odd to have two Leovirs crammed in the back? At least Eitan said all the right things.

He sat in the driver's seat now, talking to the Zealot security. They made Caden's skin crawl. There was something about them and how they talked that wasn't right.

They were too excited, too hyped up, too ready to kill. *Like attack dogs choking themselves on a chain.*

"*Exactly!*" Caden gritted his teeth, trying to ignore Doeg. "*Aren't they magnificent?*"

Caden didn't answer as he tried desperately not to lock eyes with them. He felt them watching; it was like the hummer was surrounded by Shades. It nearly was. There were Demons everywhere, and he knew there were far more because each Zealot and Giant hosted one. *Hundreds of thousands*, Caden thought. *More like millions.* A lump formed in his throat; he could never conquer this!

He was shocked when the twitchy Zealots motioned them through. They directed Eitan down a road, and he drove as a Zealot led the way. The man was running in front of the hummer at fifteen miles an hour. Caden watched him as his unease quickly grew. *They're machines! The Demons work them to death!*

It was hard staying focused, there was so much to see in this new, vast camp. Withers donned skins by the dozens. Shades prowled about, some clinging to humans and others exiting and entering humans at will. More Fiends than Caden had seen at once turned the sky dark, their smoke-like forms coiling together into one mass. Vipers hung onto nearly everyone as some slinked up tent poles or across roofs. Through it all, narrow streams rushed. Caden didn't know for sure, but he wouldn't be surprised if the water came from Tarek itself. He felt the very air he breathed defiled him.

Closing his eyes, Caden lifted his chin and squared his shoulders. *He was with them and gave them rest*, he thought. *Please, Yahweh. Please, save us.*

By the time they reached the makeshift garage, their Zealot escort was red-faced and gasping for air, even though he casually looked around and completely ignored his weakened state. "Park here!" He called. Caden knew it was time to get out of the hummer. He didn't move. His pulse hammered against his throat. Cursing under his breath, he ripped open the door and leapt out.

*Time to act,* he thought, turning to his team as they, too, exited. *Find Tarek, and I'll find Ellie. It likes killing the righteous.* His stomach twisted as his hands firmly gripped his automatic gun. *She'll be with it.*

"Where are you going?" the Zealot called.

Caden stopped and turned. "We must report to—"

"You will report to the commander!" A shiver ran up Caden's spine. "Those are his orders, Refiner! Move it!"

*No!* Caden didn't move. The Zealot shifted, holding his automatic gun with two hands.

Eitan wasted no time walking behind the Zealot. "I said that wouldn't work." Zealots stepped from the shadows as the click of loaded guns lifted around them. Caden didn't move as rage washed over him. Chuk spun in a panicked circle, stopping whenever he saw an armed Zealot. Jael and Benaiah crouched low, ready to fight.

Eitan removed his helmet. He was smiling. "Coms," Eitan said. "We got those up and running a few months ago. Remember what those are?"

Caden cursed under his breath as Chuk raised his hands. *Yahweh, what are You doing? This isn't how You rescue people!* He listened, as always, and as always, there was no answer.

*"Little GJ,"* Doeg whispered in his thoughts. *"Rejected is your definition."*

Caden didn't answer as God's silence drove a dagger to his heart. *God is faithful. He said He'll never leave me. Never forsake me.*

*"He has forsaken your Lil El."* Caden blinked as the men closed in around him, screaming orders. *"Her blood is sweeter than wine."*

*I will slaughter you!*

*"And her screams are just music,"* Doeg posed, and Caden caught movement out of the corner of his eye. A Shade with a scar-twisted smile. Caden stiffened as Doeg drew beside him. The Zealots stared up at the Demon and made room. Caden alone did nothing. "Welcome to Camp Lion."

Caden shivered; he hated Doeg's audible voice! *Go to Hell.* Doeg's smile grew. *This isn't right, God. Please! Do something!*

Doeg leaned closer, and Caden could feel its body heat. "No one is listening." Caden didn't answer as he felt a gun prod his back. He rigidly stood and refused to drop his weapon. He heard the gun chamber a round and he shook his head. He dropped the weapon, knowing he had an invisible shield they could never take from him.

His eyes darted to each Zealot as a thrill rushed up his back. His heart quickened. His body tensed for action. He made a fist and dropped into a fighting stance. He focused on the closest Zealot, wondering how many he could cut down by throwing the shield. Tarek's face had sliced like butter.

He froze, his heart leaping into his throat. The Shield of Truth didn't come when summoned. *What have I done?* Ice entered Caden's veins. *I've lost it!*

Doeg's ears flicked as it didn't stir from its relaxed posture. Its mouth twitched wider in a gaping smile as a red tongue ran across its lips. *"The blood of the saints —"*

*Shut up! Shut up! This can't be happening!*

*"You've always been defenseless,"* Doeg whispered. *"Now you finally see."*

Caden sat facing forward again and stared. He was going to die. They all were. And his Lil El. He just prayed they'd be quick.

———

THE CAPTIVES and Zealots drove through the camp as the sun's light slowly slipped into the west. They were stuffed into the back of a transport truck, each bound with hands behind their backs. The Leovirs were forced to run behind with chain leashes keeping them contained. With each passing minute, Caden's stomach coiled like a snake. "Dead," Doeg whispered suddenly as it sat beside him. "She's dead."

*Raw Peace.*

"After screams and pleas—" Caden hissed a curse. "She, as you Christians say, fell asleep." Doeg chuckled, the Demon's rasping laugh grading Caden's nerves.

They drove on, rising in elevation, until Caden realized they had ascended Mount Megiddo, the hill at the valley's center. The tents and barracks were behind them. At the very top, Caden could see a building. No, that was a tent, or lots of tents. It looked so sturdy and comfortable, like a house or building. It was out of place from the armies stretching beneath it. Fluttering overhead and larger than life, was the New Kingdom's flag. Caden could've sworn it was nearly the size of his high school gym. There was no escape from the Sovereign Lion's Watch now.

A hard lump formed in Caden's throat as he curtly shook his head. *Who was I kidding? Why did I come?*

"Prophesy must be fulfilled," Doeg muttered, the Demon's icy eyes half closed as it lounged against the seat. "You shall watch as your beloved little sister is beheaded." Caden said nothing as he blankly stared at the floor. Murderous rage made the blood roar in his ears.

When they entered the lush quarters, everyone recognized Caden instantly. Demons stopped and stared, whispering and pointing, Leovirs drew back their lips and snarled, and Giants crossed their arms, obviously uncomfortable. *They're afraid of me,* Caden realized. *Or at least God working through me, I guess.* He found they looked away when he stared at them. Even though his enemies were uneasy in his presence, it didn't slow his racing heart or ease his numbing terror. *He was with them and gave them rest,* Caden thought, knowing to hide in God's truth instead of himself. He was weak. He was a failure. He was nothing but dust and a worm. He was also more than a conqueror with God. He'd been surrounded by his enemies before and survived. What about this time?

*Do not test the Lord your God,"* Doeg said. *"Isn't that what your beloved Scriptures say?"*

Caden didn't answer. He was too busy softly humming. *The Lord said to me,* Caden sang inside. *'You are my son; today, I have become your Abba. Ask Me, and I will make the nations your inheritance.*

Doeg snarled and motioned to Caden. Instantly, something hard slammed between Caden's shoulders. He flew off his feet and hit the floor hard, rolling. A boot kicked his guts, sending him into a ball. Another his back and thigh. Caden drew his knees against his chest and ducked his head, his gritted teeth holding back cries. In moments, they stepped back, and Doeg's claws scraped across the floor. The Demon knelt down and stared as Caden spat blood and tried to blink through the lights flashing before his eyes.

"Don't," Doeg whispered. "Don't sing."

Panting, Caden stared up at him with a frown. "Why?" He rasped. "Afraid?"

Doeg's ears drew back as a corner of its mouth twitched. "Up!" He barked, standing.

Hands hooked under Caden's arms and yanked him upright. Head spinning with pain, Caden tried not to fall over as they dragged him on. *God, save us, save us. Or. Just let us die and end all this madness. I don't know what's better. Just spare my sister.*

*"Her death is unavoidable."*

*Please! I'm begging You!*

*"They've been waiting for you."* Caden cursed as emotion tightened his chest and his blood ran hot with rage. This wasn't what should happen to God's people! This wasn't right.

They were outside again. The sky was washed with reds and oranges as the sun set. Grays and darkness crept from the east, clashing with the color. The vast army spread across the valley and beyond, their colors waving in the wind. Caden stared, knowing millions of people were down there, and he was only facing one direction. *We can't conquer this. God has intentionally sabotaged us. He desires our gruesome death. How can I stay loyal to such a Tyrant?*

Caden closed his eyes and shook his head, knowing that wasn't his thoughts. He felt whiskers brush his cheek, and he flinched back, only to have Zealots hold him in place. "You thought those things, dear boy," Doeg whispered. "Because we both know it is truth."

*Raw Peace.*

"Your *Akal Esh* isn't coming. The sky will not break for you."

*Raw Peace.*

"There he is!" Caden's blood iced. "The prodigal son returns!"

Caden didn't respond as someone approached. He was in casual clothes and holding a glass of wine. At least, Caden assumed it was wine. He never knew what they were drinking these days. Luca took a sip and slid a hand into his pocket, grinning at Caden. Every trace of his head injury was gone as he smugly stared down at his captive. Caden's face slowly turned crimson as a vein pulsed at his temple.

"I'm pleased you've joined us, *Alex.*"

A muscle in Caden's jaw flexed as his bound hands became fists. Out of the corner of his eye, Caden saw

Chuk cowering back, nearly shrinking away into the arms of his captors. Benaiah's ears were straight back, and Jael's tail thrashed, but neither met his gaze. Taking a breath, Caden lifted his chin and locked eyes with Luca. "Surrender," he heard himself say. "King Yeshua is coming."

Luca's grin broadened and he threw back his head and laughed. "Did you hear that, Yarrow?" Caden blinked, desperate to mask his rising panic as Grant and Buck stirred from their seats. How had he missed them? "This *boy* is telling *me* to surrender."

"I wasn't telling you," Caden snapped. "King Yeshua will throw you into Hell, along with Hugh."

Grant scoffed. "Will He? How terrible. Hell. Isn't that the fake, fiery place to scare us all into repentance?"

"It's real." Buck shook his head as he took a drink of whisky.

"Let me inform you what is real," Grant said as he stood and leaned on his cane. "If I may, my worship?"

A shiver shot through Caden as he looked at Luca. *Is that what people call you now?* Luca nodded and stepped back, taking another sip.

"The reality is, blood will flow this very night." Caden straightened as Grant drew closer. His heart quickened, and he forced his face to stay impassive. Inside, he was screaming for mercy and thrashing for his life.

Doeg's smile grew; it saw the rising panic. *"They swore to give you a Blood Eagle."* Caden's internal screaming rose to still white noise as cold, raw nothingness closed in around him.

"Are we ready, my worship?" Luca lounged back in his chair as though readying to watch a football game and nodded. A camera crew, who had stood off to one side Caden hadn't seen, got into position.

Caden didn't react as dread choked him. His world

dialed down to a narrow, isolated moment. His reality was the present, specifically Luca and Grant giddy with amusement. *Into Your hands, God.* His thoughts flooded with curses towards Yahweh. *No! No! I am His slave! He will do with me as He wills! Like a narcissistic tyrant! Destroying all life and...No. This is His choice. I gave myself to Him years ago.*

*"Renounce it."*

*I...I am His!*

*"He will let me slaughter you."*

*But...He is God. Not me.*

*"You are the one suffering, not Him!"*

*I will not reject my God!*

*"He rejected you long ago. Look at your life! Look at your reality!"*

In full view of Luca and the cameras, chopping blocks were set up. Chuk started shaking and whimpering. He fell to the ground, begging and crying. Jael snarled, receiving a blow from another Leovir. They were on her in moments, thrashing and pinning her down. Benaiah leapt to help, but the Giants yanked the chains around his neck and held him back. More Refiners came into view. They carried an ax and a human-sized doll. They had painted it red, and its clothes were nearly ripped away.

Caden stopped breathing. His eyes widened as he stared at the doll, his chest physically ached with agony. In a sudden rush of adrenaline, he lunged toward Luca. "I'll kill you!" He screamed, his voice shrill and raking his throat. "You animal! I'll kill you; I swear to God!" Zealots struggled to hold him back as he screamed. He had to get free. He had to save them!

The butt of a gun cracked against the back of his head. He collapsed, panting. Caden growled, managing to get a foot beneath him. They struck him again, nearly sending him all the way down. They yanked him upright, and his head hung, swimming in pain. Grabbing his hair, they craned his neck and forced him to watch.

Blinking through tears and sweat, Caden met eyes with the doll. It was Lil El. She was hardly conscious as they tossed her to the ground. Her clothes were hardly there. Blood covered her body; from her puffy and purple face, between her legs, a slash on her side, her hands. All over. But not her feet. The Shoes of Peace still emanated swirling light. Bloody marks outlined where Zealots had tried to remove the boots. Nothing had worked.

Caden moaned as he stared, tears of rage and anguish falling. Doeg sauntered forward and nodded to Luca, who nodded back as though they were old friends. "Thank you for waiting," Doeg said. "I promised this boy he'd watch his sister die."

Luca straightened. "Sister?"

"He must learn," Doeg turned squarely facing Caden, "I always keep my word." Caden's nostrils flared as he looked at Doeg. His brows drew low, and he opened his mouth, but he had no strength. Doeg waited, grinning, and suddenly growled. "Beg!" Caden flinched at its cry. "Beg for her life, human boy!"

Caden turned to Ellie. One blue eye had turned and was staring at him. Tears silently streamed from her eye. *I'm so sorry, El,* Caden thought, each breath a strangled gasp. Her arm slid from her side and flopped onto the ground, pointing at him. She rolled closer, like a half-dead person trying to rise. Ellie scooted her head, facing him more fully. Her lips parted, and she mouthed two words: We win.

Caden's chest shook as he ducked his head. Making fists and dragging in a breath through gritted teeth, he turned to Doeg and Luca. "Precious in the sight of Yahweh is the death of his faithful servants." Doeg's ear whipped back as the Fiends overhead formed into horned, snarling faces.

Luca leapt to his feet and marched to Caden. He seized his throat, arching his back and making him face him. Caden gagged as his eyes rolled back, his arms shaking. "Never!" Luca hissed, spraying saliva. "Never quote Scripture here!" Caden's mouth gaped as he tried to breathe, but nothing entered him. With a curse, Luca let go, and Caden limply hung in the Zealots' arms, coughing and gasping. "Precious, you say?"

*Oh, God.* Caden closed his eyes as another tear fell.

"Let's give your God several precious things to consider."

The Zealots grabbed Chuk. They dragged him to the chopping blocks as he kicked and screamed. Jael snarled as other Leovirs nudged her to a block. The Giants yanked Benaiah, who nearly knocked over Grant in the process. They made Caden look up again. He could hardly see through the tears and sweat. He didn't know what to do as his enemies placed his brothers in arms and his darling sister on the blocks. Chuk was screaming. They had to chain Benaiah down. Jael's torso had been wounded and blood steadily flowed, quickly weakening her.

*God, do something,* Caden thought. He couldn't look away from Ellie. He wanted to, but it didn't feel right. *God! You see this! This isn't right! Where's Your justice?* A Refiner, his uniform more decorated than the others, grabbed the ax. Caden didn't look away from Ellie as the Refiner strolled to Chuk.

"I don't want this!" Chuk screamed. "I'm not a terrorist! I didn't—"

Caden flinched and heard a wet thump. The Refiner moved to Jael before Chuk's headless body slumped to the ground. *I'm sorry*, Caden kept thinking as he stared at Ellie. *Sis. Please, forgive me.*

Jael's groaning snarl ended abruptly, and the ax had to fall twice before her head thumped to the ground. *I just wanted to protect you.* Caden shook uncontrollably. Benaiah roared, his chains clinking with thrashing limbs. One Giant planted a knee on his back while another yanked his mane, holding his head in place. *I wish—*

Caden's thoughts ended as the Refiner's shadow fell on Ellie. She met eyes with him again. Caden shook his head. His body disconnected from his brain. He wasn't thinking. He felt like a third party, watching himself scream and lash out. He rammed a shoulder into someone. Something struck him but didn't slow him down. His throat burned because of his cries. Hands seized him, holding his neck and head. They turned him, making him watch.

Caden screamed as a tear streamed from Ellie's eye. The ax fell. It twonked into the chopping block. Caden fell deathly still. He stared without a sound, frozen and pale. He couldn't move or breathe. After a moment of silence, a vengeful wail ripped from his throat.

# TWENTY-TWO

# CORPSE STILL BREATHING

CADEN DIDN'T KNOW what he was doing. He wasn't thinking. He wasn't feeling. He didn't know he had started fighting again. He didn't realize he hadn't stopped screaming. He was vaguely aware three people stood watching. He was more aware of the smell of blood steadily growing stronger. Others were shouting. A Leovir roared.

"Do we have a tranquilizer available?" Caden's body strained as he felt himself slam into the ground. A knee dug into his back. Each limb was held down.

"Why? This is amusing."

Caden felt something poke the back of his neck. In the back of his brain, he knew it was the barrel of a gun. It didn't stop him. Exhausted, and shaking all over, his screams became strangled cries. Heaving in breath after breath, Caden lay there. Laying on the ground, staring between the Refiners' boots and Leovir paws, he saw a pool of blood. It was slowly spreading.

The clicking of a cane drew closer. Caden didn't care. Grant could do his worst, and Caden would let him. In a sudden rush, Caden envied Trace and Nate. Shouldn't there be a limit to the trauma God inflicts on His follow-ers? *Kill me,* Caden thought. *I can't take this anymore.*

"You're next." Grant said, standing over him. "Refiner, go get that table."

"Lieutenant." Who was that? "A moment, please." The stranger turned, and Caden caught sight of him; he still held the executioner's ax. Blood steadily dripped from its razor edge.

"My worship," the stranger said, turning to Luca. "I have a request."

"Speak."

"I failed the blessed Heralds years ago, bringing great turmoil to our New Kingdom. I wish to redeem myself."

Luca chuckled softly, and Caden's eyes widened as his breath quickened. *I know that voice.* He thought.

"Let me get this straight," Luca said. "You want to perform the blood eagle instead of Lieutenant Yarrow?"

Grant's fingers rapped on the ball of his cane. "That was not what was discussed, my worship."

"Lieutenant Yarrow," Luca said. "I know you have history with his boy and long for vengeance. You may assist Commander Mason."

All breath left Caden in a rush. They kept talking, but he couldn't hear them. Hands grabbed him, pulling him upright. He felt like he'd fought a war as he slumped to his knees. *I'm wrong,* his mind begged. *Please! It can't be him! It can't!*

He locked eyes with Lil El's murderer. It was as though he had gone back in time, but there were no baying dogs or the sting of gun smoke in the air. Caden refused to turn away from Nathaniel Mason.

He looked nearly the same. Tall, thick beard, and brown eyes that still flashed with life. His officer uniform now had golden tassels on the shoulders, and the symbol of a Refiner sat beneath. Looking into those eyes, Caden knew he was a Zealot. A very calm, very lethal Zealot. Caden set his jaw and, somehow, found the strength to sit taller. "You." The whispered word hissed through his teeth. Nathaniel lifted his chin and looked down. "Well?" Caden seethed as his teeth bared. "What are you waiting for!"

Nathaniel's brows furrowed as he glanced down at Caden. "Where is the young sir I found, half-starved and terrified?"

"He died." Caden leaned forward, feeling the Refiner's holding him back. "The day *you* murdered my brother!" Buck threw back his head and laughed as Luca's brows raised.

Nathaniel stroked his jaw. "Trace, correct?"

"Do not speak his name!"

Grant motioned to Nathaniel. "Commander, would you describe this Trace?"

"An adolescent. Tall for his age. Curly blond hair."

A fierce smile stretched Grant's mouth. "You killed him, commander?"

"Did you know him?"

"He was the fool who drove over my ankle."

Nathaniel grunted as Luca chuckled to himself. "This is spectacular," Luca muttered.

Caden ducked his head, his heart beating in his throat. *Why are You doing this, God?*

"And now," Grant said calmly, "you've also killed his sister."

*What am I supposed to do?*

"I've always admired symmetry."

Claws scraped the ground as Doeg drew closer. "You have also brought my prophecy into fruition, Commander Mason. I swore he would watch as his sister is beheaded."

"I'm honored to have served you," Nathaniel said, bowing.

Caden flinched back, his eyes squeezing tight. Hatred struck his chest, physically hurting his heart. He knew without a doubt, if roles were reversed, he would gladly give Nathaniel the blood eagle. He would take his time, letting his enemy's suffering last as long as he was able. But it wouldn't be enough. It would never be.

Caden gritted his teeth as he looked at Ellie's body, remembering their conversation about forgiveness. *I can't do what You've asked, God.* He shook his head as anger stirred in his chest. Anger toward God. Obeying Him was injustice! It wouldn't make anything better!

Taking a slow breath, Caden closed his eyes and lifted his chin. *I am not God.* He turned and looked up at Nathaniel. "I forgive you." Silence struck the group.

Nathaniel's mouth opened to speak, but he snapped it shut. "Ah, I'm sorry?" He stepped closer. "I didn't hear you right."

"No." Caden squared his shoulders. "You did." The two stared at one another in silence.

Grant broke the stillness with a mocking scoff. "Max, you are a fool."

"You're following a false god," Caden said to Nathaniel. "This *man* is death." Luca frowned as he paused in taking a drink. "Follow him, and you will be butchered."

Nathaniel's brows rose. "By you?"

"By King Yeshua."

"Ah!" Grant groaned, waving an arm. "This nonsense again! I thought we'd hear the end of it once the fanatics were put down!"

"He is coming," Caden continued. "And this army you've assembled will all die."

"Max!" Grant shouted. "There is no army on earth who could match us!"

"That's the point!" Caden shot Grant a harsh look.

"King Yeshua is not from earth, idiot! He's going to come down with the armies of Heaven! With flaming chariots and warriors! I've seen them!"

Buck shook his head. "You see a lot of things, Max."

"Change whose side you're on," Caden said, turning back to Nathaniel.

Luca stepped forward, raising a finger. "Caden, are you seriously trying to convert America's most faithful Zealot?"

"It's not too late," Caden said. Nathaniel wouldn't turn away. "But in the Battle of Armageddon, King Yeshua will slaughter you with the sword coming from His mouth."

"Hum," Luca grunted, pointing. "I love that part. It discredits the entire prediction."

"Nathaniel." Caden licked his lips and leaned forward. "I hate your guts and want to watch you die."

Nathaniel's eyes narrowed as Grant barked a laugh. "The truth comes out!"

"But," Caden said, "King Yeshua died for you because He...He loves you. He wants to save you, just like He saved me. Yeshua's mercy is offensive. But. But He's truth, and He says to forgive so...I gotta." Caden shook his head. "So...I forgive you."

The others started laughing and mocking, calling him a fool and cursing him. Nathaniel did nothing as he stared. The ax in his hands slipped, but he grasped it tighter, as though the weapon had grown heavy. *That was stupid,* Caden thought. *He needs a bullet, not forgiveness. Ah, why did I do that? God, did You see that? I'm trying to follow You. Still! Even though it's probably going to literally kill me!*

A Sentinel stooped to his level and stared with a smile. No, that was Doeg. Caden leaned away, feeling the Demon's body heat. "You may do what you wish to his flesh." Ice washed through Caden. "However, when his death comes, I will be the last thing he will see."

*Then I'll shut my eyes. You won't get what you want.*

"*Then I'll remove your eyelids.*" Caden shuddered. "*You have no choice. You see my threats are not empty, as you proclaimed? Your sister's blood is still oozing from her severed head.*" Caden bared his teeth and shouted curses at the Demon. Doeg just knelt just out of reach, pleasantly amused.

"Very well," Luca said. "He will receive the blood eagle, after we obliterate every trace of the terrorists in Petra and abroad."

Caden panted as Refiners held him back. "You can't!"

"I want to prove to you your King Yeshua died thousands of years ago and never rose again."

"You're wrong!"

"No one is coming." Luca drew closer until he stood over Caden. "No man or God can save you from me."

Caden shook his head as he struggled to breathe. "He will avenge us."

"Hum," Luca hummed softly. 'I hope you are right; I grow tired of unworthy opponents."

Caden cringed. "He can hear you."

"Gag him and take him away."

Grant eagerly stepped forward. "Want me to handle him, my worship?"

*Oh God,* Caden thought, looking down and closing his eyes.

Luca raised a hand. "I want him coherent to see the downfall of his people. Be patient, Lieutenant. Your time of blood will come."

Caden didn't respond as they gagged him. He looked up at Nathaniel. The commander still hadn't moved. He seemed stuck somehow. *Please end this, God,* Caden thought. *We're all dying off. Can't You see us?* He wasn't sure God noticed as he was dragged from his sister's corpse.

———

CADEN REMEMBERED ROVER, the family dog, hated getting into his kennel at night. He'd whine and hide under the table, and Nate would have to drag him out. He'd always listen to Nate. Not that Nate had a way with animals, he just didn't mind grabbing his collar and dragging. Now, Caden wished he'd stepped in and helped Rover out.

Kennels sucked. Caden had to kneel and duck his head at the same time to fit in his. His hands were still tied behind his back, and the gag made breathing difficult. It tasted awful too; he wouldn't be surprised if it was someone's used handkerchief. Shifting and trying to get comfortable, Caden knew he wouldn't. He couldn't hold still. The kennel's wire floor kept digging into his knees. The only place to lay his head was against the wire wall, which also dug into his brow. His hands were numb and tingled in pain. At least he didn't have a bag over his face. He hated bags.

The kennel was in the parking lot between Humvees. Two Zealots stood watch, restlessly pacing back and forth and ever-vigilant eyes leaping all around. Caden knew they'd guard, without a break, for days if they had to. They weren't human anymore, but Puppets of the enemy.

Caden stared at his knees and the gravel beneath the wire floor. He was shivering in the night's cold. Sweat, snot, and tears kept dripping off the tip of his nose. He was making a small puddle in the gravel. He sat there, without a sound, crying. He couldn't help it. He wanted to be strong and not show his enemies he was breaking. But he was.

Everything he held dear was slowly getting slaughtered right in front of him. First his Mom, then Mama Lo and Papa. Next was Nate and Trace. Even though Elijah and Yohanan came back to life, Caden would never forget their gutted, mangled corpses lying about. Now Ellie. His

Lil El. The one who always remembered his birthdays and had a way of calming him down and smiling even when life was miserable.

Now, her head was lawn art. What had Luca done with it? Caden closed his eyes as his chin trembled. It wouldn't be farfetched to suggest it was placed on a stake, showcasing Luca's victory. First, the fanatics, now one of their wives. Ophir was long dead, slain in a labor camp. Who is next to fall? Better question, who had survived? Your numbers are thinning. Your ability to overcome is overwhelmingly pathetic. You are defeated. A corpse still breathing.

Caden bit the gag and yelled. He snapped his eyes open and found Doeg, crouched and staring through the kennel. The Zealots had taken a few steps back, letting the Demon have its privacy. *Go away!* Caden's mind screamed. *God! Do something!*

*"Why keep calling on One who refuses to answer?"*

*He will come! He will destroy you! You'll see!*

Doeg's ear twitched. *"But will He come in time?"*

Caden's chest shuddered as he tried to breathe. He turned away. His strength was almost gone, but he fought to keep his guard up. He couldn't grieve! He couldn't lean on anyone, even God. No, *especially* God! He wasn't fulfilling *any* of His promises! Never leave you or forsake you. Fables! Tales from —

*Doeg!*

*"I long to show you truth."*

*All you know are lies!*

*"Caden, lad."*

*Raw Peace.*

*"Your God has abandoned you. Can't you see?"*

*Raw Peace!*

*"You are on the losing side."*

*God, please! Why aren't You answering?*

*"Change, Caden. There is still time. Luca is kind and tender-hearted."*

*Save me or kill me, but stop this in between, God!*

*"Luca doesn't want any of the wicked to perish."*

Caden's head snapped up as his eyes flashed. *Don't you dare misquote Scripture to me! Luca is not god!*

"Final chance." Something moved in the background. It looked like the shadows stirred, or something slithered on the ground. "Without us, you are a corpse still breathing." Caden's eyes locked with Doeg's. His heart pounded with force. His flesh was cold. He felt an empty numbness in his chest. He was all alone. Completely, totally.

He heard the crunch of gravel beneath heavy footfalls. There were two pairs of feet coming his way. Caden's breath quickened as the night grew colder. A figure came into view. It towered over him as it calmly headed in his direction. It was a horse as pale as a ghost. Its mane waved in the wind like frail spider silk, and its muscle-bound body rippled with each stride.

On it rode a thing. It wasn't a man. It couldn't be. It was dressed in a black robe that gradually disintegrated to dark mist. The robe's hood was a black, vacant chasm where nothing but emptiness stared back at Caden. Two swords were strapped to its back, and its gauntleted hand firmly gripped an ax at its side. Following behind the horse were Fiends. Wait, no. Caden blinked, the coldness enveloping him sinking further into his being, chilling him to the bone. Those weren't Fiends. It was a...a...

It was living darkness. Caden cursed and recoiled as far as he could go. He ignored the wire biting into his shoulder and knees. He ignored the gag and his bound hands. He could only pant and groan in terror as the horseman rode by. He felt the unseen eyes falling on him. He felt the living darkness draw closer, threatening to suck the very life from him.

The closer the horseman came, the more terror struck Caden's chest. He found himself shouting through his gag, his eyes squeezed tight, as his body shook uncontrollably. He felt their shadow pass over him. He was pleading for his life between breathless gasps. The horseman didn't respond as it kept riding by. Caden shivered and listened to the horse hooves clomping through the gravel. He didn't stop shaking as they continued around the bend. Gasping and blinking through tears, Caden finally lifted his head. He only saw Doeg.

"Choose," the Demon whispered. "Us? Or your absent God?"

Trembling with his heart pounding in his ears, Caden stared back at Doeg. *I can't do this.*

"Choose!"

Caden flinched back and closed his eyes. He knew his answer; it filled him with terror. *I will die for King Yeshua.*

The Demon grinned. *"Yes, you will."* Caden didn't answer. "Come," the Demon whispered audibly. "Let us play with our new toy."

Caden's blood iced. The shadows took shape. Several Fiends drifted closer. Vipers slithered through the gravel. A Wither or two donned larger, threatening skins. Caden moaned as he drew into a ball and helplessness consumed him. He could only pray. *Save me. Save me. Raw Peace. Save me!* He heard them surround his kennel. He felt the Fiend's ember gazes heat his back. The Vipers hissed as the Withers snickered. The scrapes of claws drew closer, and Caden knew more Shades approached. He heard them all and couldn't face them. He really was a corpse still breathing.

———

THE NEXT MORNING, Zealots dragged Caden from his kennel. He couldn't hold back a cry as his folded-up body painfully straightened out. The Zealots laughed as they jerked him around. "Move it!" One cried, throwing him to the ground. Caden bounced, his body aching, and tried to breathe.

He hadn't slept at all the night before. Though the Demons hadn't touched his body, he felt his deep, inner self was a bloodied, shredded mess. The only way he didn't lose his mind was by visualizing King Yeshua massacring Luca and his armies with the sword coming from His mouth. He didn't know if that was a holy thing to think about, but he was beyond that right now. He was surviving.

The Zealots heaved him upright and dragged him through camp. Caden could hardly keep up; his legs had no strength as adrenaline kept his eyes open. He gnawed on the gag and longed to spit it out. If only Gideon was here with some of that amazing bread and water. That would keep Caden going! *He's not coming,* Caden thought as he struggled to keep up. *I need to focus. If I keep going like this, I'll die from adrenaline.*

They walked along Mount Megiddo's crest, and Caden caught a glimpse of the vast army. They were moving. Every tent had been taken down. Every vehicle lined up to move out. Every weapon was ready. As the morning sun rose higher, bathing all in light, a vast shadow swept across the valley. Tarek's leathery wings stretched across the clear sky as its seven heads coiled and twisted about, staring down with unblinking eyes. Water dribbled from the mouths, raining down on the army. Wherever the water fell, a cheer rose. Caden ducked his head, knowing Jaden and Asher were going to be dead by this time tomorrow. There was nothing Caden could do.

*"And your beloved betrothed."*

Caden closed his eyes and couldn't hold back a moan. *Save Dasha, God. Please! If You won't save me, save her! She's done nothing wrong!* His chest literally ached with the thought of her ravaged and slain as brutally as Ellie. Caden sucked in a breath, his bloodshot eyes narrowing as he made a fist. He summoned the Shield of Faith and waited. And waited. Cursing, he waited longer. Nothing happened.

*"The righteous shall live by faith,"* a voice whispered in his mind. *"You, apparently, are not righteous."*

Caden gasped and tried again, but the shield would not come. *Han! Han, are you here? Please!* Caden looked all around. Where was that Cherub? *Han! I need —*

The tents thinned to a flat section of frenzied activity. Zealots packed and assembled belongings as Nathaniel oversaw. Their eyes met, and the commander's back straightened. Caden simply stared back until Nathaniel shifted and turned away to correct a pair of Giants. Through the constant motion, Luca and Hugh strolled through with the three Fiends lazily swirling over their heads.

"...nearly complete," Hugh was saying. "Within a half-hour we may begin for Petra, my worship." Luca nodded, and the two stopped by Caden. Luca turned and calmly regarded him as Caden sent all his strength into not bowing. Even if he was fully rested, nothing could stop the Zealots from forcing him to his knees. Caden groaned as they grabbed the back of his neck and shoved his head into the gravel.

"Good morning, terrorist," Luca said. Caden panted and didn't answer. "Here," Luca said, scooting his boot beneath Caden's nose. "Lick it." Caden's stomach turned. "Come on, little con boy." The gag was untied and yanked from his mouth. Caden's jaw flexed as he gritted his teeth.

"You're familiar with unquestioned obedience to your god."

*Go to Hell.* A boot rammed into his guts. Caden gasped, buckling, as another kicked his ribs. Caden was thrown to his side, and he curled into a tight ball, ducking his head and praying they'd stop. He cried out, gasping, and the blows ended abruptly. The Zealots yanked Caden to his feet again. His head spun at the sudden motion. He coughed, unable to stand straight, as blood dribbled from his nose. Someone was talking. Someone he knew.

"...men are ready, my worship," Nathaniel was saying.

Caden blinked through the pain and splotchy vision as Hugh and Luca listened to Nathaniel's report. His side throbbed, and he felt ready to puke. Forcing himself to breathe slower, Caden lifted his chin and ignored the blood dripping from his nose and getting into his mouth. *Raw Peace!* He cursed through bloodied teeth. This Christian faith-stuff was impossible!

"...then you will execute the lad?" Caden blinked, realizing Luca was talking about him.

Nathaniel was nodding. "It will be my honor."

"Indeed," Hugh said softly, shooting Caden a quick glance. "If you hadn't failed in executing him years ago, a majority of our New Kingdom would have succeeded."

"And," Caden rasped, "and the Witnesses wouldn't have come together." All three stopped and stared at Caden. He realized he was grinning from ear to ear like a madman. With a hoarse chuckle, Caden shook his head. "But let's not start pointing fingers here. If you hadn't been such a fool, you would've slaughtered all of Under Fire after the Witness' attack, too. I warned them first."

Nathaniel shifted, his teeth clenching. "Who are you addressing?"

Caden jerked his chin at Luca. "The Antichrist."

Caden folded in half around Nathaniel's fist. All breath

left him in one exhale, and he limply hung in the Zealot's arms. Nathaniel stepped back, quietly giving Caden a moment to cough and take in air. "Never," he hissed, "never address him as such. He is our god."

Caden stayed bent in half, his eyes clenched tight. He wondered if something was broken. *You're all going to die.*

*"I'd stop focusing on their demise, boy,"* Doeg's words hissed. *"And focus on your own. Remember, I will be the last thing you will ever see."* Caden's chest tightened with dread. A clawed hand slid under his jaw and gently lifted his chin. He stared up, meeting eyes with Doeg. "My threats are never empty, boy." The Demon grinned, its scared mouth twisting unnaturally. "Your sister's death proves as such."

Caden didn't answer. He had nothing to say. His strength was almost gone. It would be easier to succumb to the lies and hate. He would suffer, but he currently was. Suffering by Nathaniel's hand would promise the sweet release of death, unlike God's hand. God inflicted continual suffering. There was no hope in serving a brutal, uncaring—

*Doeg,* Caden finally managed to think. *Stop.* Doeg chuckled as its claws beneath Caden's jaw tightened around his face. Caden inhaled and froze, knowing the Demon could pop his head like a grape. Without a word, Doeg stepped back. Caden stared at the ground, wondering if he was strong enough to stand.

"...very good," Luca said. "Within the hour?"

"Half hour," Nathaniel said.

"It will be a shame," Hugh muttered, "destroying Petra. It has such historical magnitude."

"It's a den of terrorists," Luca said.

"Hum," Hugh grunted. "If we could preserve the architecture, I wouldn't be displeased."

Luca sighed as Caden shook his head. *Animals.*

A shadow swallowed them, and the ground shook.

Caden didn't even respond as Tarek landed behind them, the great red dragon scattering men like a cat scatters mice. It lumbered toward Luca, the heads clicking together with glee. Luca nodded to it and walked over, Hugh close behind.

Nathaniel cleared his throat and glanced at Caden. "Open your mouth." Caden didn't move as he snapped his mouth shut. "Caden."

"Don't touch me!"

Nathaniel's head tilted to one side. "What do you suspect I'll do, young sir? I am not a monster."

"No, you're just my brother and sister's murderer."

Nathaniel smirked. "I thought you've forgiven me."

Caden hissed a curse and faced Nathaniel. "Forgiveness is a choice. Regardless of how I feel. I *feel* like taking that rock and bashing your brains out." Nathaniel's brows drew low. "But I *choose* not to curse your name and fight against the hate I've been carrying forever! See the difference?"

Nathaniel didn't answer as he withdrew a canteen from his belt and held it out to Caden. Caden turned away, snapping his mouth shut again. "Just water."

"Is it *that thing's* water?" Caden asked, nodding at Tarek. As he looked, he noticed one of the heads faced him, forked tongue lashing. Its mouth was offset from a wound he had inflicted. It wanted to kill him. So badly.

"It came from the valley's spring."

Caden's jaw flexed as he turned away from Tarek, a shiver snaking down his spine. Nathaniel took a swig and held it out to him again. Cursing, Caden leaned forward and opened his mouth. Nathaniel gently poured a generous amount of water. Caden hadn't known how thirsty he was. Nathaniel stepped back, returned the canteen to his belt, and crossed his arms as he looked over the army.

"Thank you," Caden muttered. Nathaniel shot him a look but didn't answer. The two quietly stared at the army readying for war. Nearly every nation of the earth had gathered. *We're dead*, Caden thought. *So very dead.* He suddenly envied Ellie, already resting in death. *Run, Dasha. Please, God, do this last thing for me. Please!*

Luca belted a sudden laugh. He patted a runner on the head and motioned to Nathaniel and Rapham. "Inform the men! Enemy sighted!"

"Enemy, my worship?" Hugh asked.

"The terrorists."

*Oh, God*, Caden thought, his throat suddenly dry.

"Apparently, several cells had managed to assemble into a ragtag army." Caden's stomach twisted painfully. He knew Dasha would be with them. That crazy woman! Couldn't she not be so brave and hide this time? Luca laughed along with several of the Demons. "Let the lambs come to the slaughter instead of hunting them down. Fools!"

Caden stiffened as Doeg's ears perked up like an excited dog. *She's going to die too.*

"Tell the men to move out!" Tarek lifted its several heads and spread its wings as the hilltop cheered.

Caden felt nothing as he impassively stared. *There is no hope. We're all corpses breathing…no, no. Don't think like that. Just…just…Raw Peace. Raw Peace. Raw…*

The rising sun vanished.

Deep blackness swallowed the land. Lightbulbs speckled over the valley flickered on and off until finally falling into darkness too. Caden's eyes bulged as he tried to see. The air quickly felt chilly. No one spoke. The cheering instantly died down, and Tarek's clicking silenced. Across the valley, the sound of movement and voices ended. Caden knew if a pin dropped miles away, he would hear it. Nature itself acted like it was holding its breath. There was no wind. No dog barked. No bird twittered. Everyone stared into the black sky.

Even a moonless night wasn't this dark. It was unnatural and disturbing. The sun didn't just turn off; something was making this happen. Something with enough authority to command nature. Someone who the land, the skies, winds, and the waves obeyed. Caden blinked, taking in a slow breath. A wolfish smile overtook his face.

He whispered two words so softly, but in the strangled silence, everyone heard him: "He's coming."

Then, the sky broke.

## TWENTY-THREE
# SING PRAISES TO YAHWEH

THE SKY RIPPED IN HALF.

The darkness parted, split in two, as a white light erupted from the west. It streamed across the black sky like the points of an arrow, rainbows arching each ray. Everyone flinched with gasps and stared in silence. Caden's guards weren't holding him anymore, but he didn't notice as he stared, mouth gaping, eyes wide with wonderment. Out of the whiteness streamed clouds that looked like light condensed to rolling, boiling shapes. The clouds were on fire too, but the fire didn't move normally. It flickered, but the inner glow was white and brilliant and...and riding something?

Caden blinked, recognizing them. *The Armies of Heaven!* The white brilliance within the fire was shaped like horses. On each was an upright flame the shape of a man. Men with weapons and armor that shimmered like Han and Gideon's ever-moving yet solid Spiritual armor. A shockwave rushed from the ripped skies. It obliterated any normal clouds. It swept across the earth, blasting against the trees and flattening the grass. Caden watched as it swept across the enemy armies filling the valley. His heart leapt in his throat, for he knew he was next.

The wave struck him, a mighty torrent that threatened to sweep him off his feet. The air thickened with electric power, a might that struck Caden in the chest and made him feel as small as an ant. It was hot and flashing and a wild thing. *There You are,* Caden thought, the tears in his eyes spilling over as the shockwave passed. *Welcome, Akal Esh.*

The *Akal Esh* flashed from each individual warrior, like living torches. The Heavenly Hosts charged from the sky's ripped opening, moving faster than a jet. Caden blinked, hardly able to track them. As they streamed across the sky, the land illuminating with brilliant oranges, golds, and whites. He could feel the power making the air warm again. No one moved as the entire sky filled with flaming horses and Heavenly warriors. There were millions! Trillions!

They continued from the west to the east and rounded the edge of the horizon. Caden knew they weren't slowing down. But what were they doing? *Every eye will see Him,* Caden remembered. *Yeshua's showing off. He's making sure EVERYONE get's a chance to see His return.* It was impossible *not* to look at them. They were the only source of light the earth had. Sure, one could curl into a ball and hide, but Caden knew the *Akal Esh* didn't let such childish defenses stop it.

He noticed he was humming again, that same familiar tune all over believers were singing too. For once, Caden didn't stop the singing. *To the one who is victorious,* the song sang inside his heart, *and does My will to the end,* he didn't know what the song was, it just felt right. It felt powerful. *I will give authority over the nations.*

A blood-curdling scream reminded Caden he was surrounded by his enemies. "Kill him!" It was a Shade, its fur trimmed in golden light. Its fur bristled as its lips pulled back into a snarl, revealing every single fang. "Kill him now!"

Wait a sec. Caden's head turned at an angle. *It's pointing at me?* Caden blinked, realizing the Shade was Doeg. The Demon was shaking, and its tail stuck between its legs. It reminded Caden of a trapped raccoon he saw in Papa's traps. Desperate and near death. And very, very lethal.

The thrill of joy evaporated upon seeing the murder in Doeg's icy eyes. He felt Nathaniel watching him. He stepped back and faced his enemies. "I said!" Doeg screamed. "Kill him!" No one moved. "Kill—"

Thunder rolled in the distance. No, it *kept* rolling, getting louder and louder. All stared up at the ever-growing army of flaming horses and warriors. The thunderous sound continued, rising in strength and reverberating through every living thing. Beneath it, and also steadily rising, were voices. They were shouting as one. It wasn't a battle cry, as Caden suspected. It was a command. Several commands. He couldn't quite make out the words yet, but they were ordering something in a rhythmic, patterned sort of way. Not a chant, it was more like a, like a…

*They're singing!* Caden lifted his chin, his own humming growing louder in his throat. *My faithful one will rule them with an iron scepter!* the song inside him shouted. *And will dash them to pieces like pottery—*[1]

A shrill caterwaul sliced through Caden's song. Doeg crept across the ground on all fours. Its claws dug into the gravel as saliva dripped from its fangs. Its eyes were locked onto Caden. Caden froze, knowing the Demon could easily rip him to shreds. *Han?* He couldn't see the Cherub anywhere. *Han! You're fired! I need you!* Someone on fire stepped around a tent. They had huge arms over their head, several fingers curled down to grab and —

"Han!" Caden cried, straightening. "Save me!"

"You are armed with the Shield of Faith."

"I broke it!"

Han's human-like face lowered as he smiled. "Have faith."

"Are you kidding me right now?" Han didn't answer as Doeg glanced over its shoulder.

Every one of the Demon's muscles tensed as it saw the Cherub. With an outraged snarl, Doeg turned and charged at Caden. Caden's heart leapt into his throat. He stumbled back, falling. He didn't even feel him squish his tied hands as he tried to rise, kicking ruts in the gravel. Doeg leapt, claws extending.

Cursing, Caden made a fist. He felt something. A solid, warm grip. The Shield of Faith's plates fell into place, rising up his shoulder. As they formed, the pointed down-ward tips sliced through his bonds. Caden wrenched his arm free and drew the shield over his torso and face. Doeg landed, nearly crushing Caden under the weight. With caterwauls and yowls, Doeg clawed at the shield.

Caden gritted his teeth, his left forearm straining as it held the shield while his other hand gripped the shield's edge, supporting it. The shield swirled and glowed with inner strength from the *Akal Esh,* and Caden could see through it. He saw Doeg's saliva dripping down the shield. The Demon raked along the shield but didn't leave a single mark.

Panting and snarling, Doeg's clawing slowed. It stared down through the shield at Caden. For the first time, Caden saw fear in the Demon's eyes. *I told you!* Caden's mind screamed. *We win!* He drew back his legs and kicked. For once, he didn't pass through Doeg. He felt the Demon's furry body and bones. Doeg heaved, breath caught in its throat, as its body buckled. Caden crawled back, able to sit up, and swung the shield. It cracked against Doeg's skull, sending the Demon to the ground.

Caden scrambled to his feet and stopped. His feet felt funny. He looked down and froze. He now wore thick, glowing boots. *Aren't these Ellie's boots?* The Shoes of Peace. Caden laughed and turned back to Doeg, who was still on the ground, blood smeared down its face. Next to Doeg, Hugh and Nathaniel stared at Caden in shock. Everyone else was still staring at the sky exploding with flaming warriors. Caden raised his shield and planted his feet. "Come on!" He hissed through gritted teeth.

From behind, hot, swampy breath washed over him. Every muscle tensed as Caden whipped around. One of Tarek's heads stared him eye to eye. Its mouth hung awkwardly as it vengefully stared at the shield. Caden cursed, and the dragon's offset mouth swung open. Water gushed out. Caden raised his shield. The force nearly knocked him off his feet. Nearly. *What in the...*

His shoes dug into the ground and permitted him to stand firm. As sweat gathered on his brow and body, straining to stay on his feet, Caden smiled. He was humming again. It just kept happening. *I will proclaim the Lord's degree!* The song inside Caden screamed. *He said to me, 'You are my son; today I have become your Abba.*[2]

"You have no father!" Tarek's multi-voices shrieked within Caden's mind.

*Ask Me, and I will make the nations your inheritance and the ends of the earth your possession.*[3] Even as the water roared in his ears, the Heavenly Hosts roared louder still. Caden blinked, realizing in a jolt of energy his inner song was the same tune as the Heavenly Hosts' cry. *We're all singing the same thing?* He laughed through gritted teeth. *Tarek, you're so going to lose!*

Caden summoned his strength, which he somehow

knew was drawn from the *Akal Esh* in his shield and boots. With an inhale, Caden leapt from the column of water. He lunged forward, ramming the pointed end of the shield's plates right behind the dragon's jaw. Blood sprayed across Caden. The water stopped abruptly as the head lurched back with a scream. As it moved, Caden yanked his shield free. Blood spurted from the wound as the head thrashed, screaming.

The other heads snapped down from looking at the sky. Caden blinked the blood and sweat from his eyes in time to see six mouths opening, water flooding from wide throats. Caden didn't think. He just acted, and it was the last thing he thought he'd do. "Come, behold what Yahweh has done!" The song burst from him. One of the heads reeled, screaming. The wounded head wasn't responding too much anymore. It limply hung, hardly keeping itself off the ground as blood trailed behind it. Luca turned, staring up in shock at the great dragon shrieking in pain.

"How He brought desolations on the earth!" Another head lurched away as Tarek's wings twitched. Caden stepped forward, his eyes widening. What was coming out of his mouth? As he spoke, little, white lines zipped from his mouth into Tarek like little bolts of energy. "Be still and know that He is Yahweh!" Tarek screamed, more bolts flying into it. "He will be exalted among the nations and the earth!" Tarek retreated, nearly trampling the Zealots around him. "The Lord of hosts is with us!" Caden bellowed, stepping closer. "The God of Jacob is our refuge!"[4]

All of Tarek's heads writhed and shuddered. Caden grinned. *Spiritual warfare!* Each of Tarek's mouths snapped open. Caden took in a deep breath to scream more. A flood surged into him. He took in a reflexive gasp and raised his shield before getting blasted off his feet. He was flung back and slammed against the ground. Water rushed around the shield, filling his mouth and nose. His body tensed, but he didn't respond. *Raw Peace,* he thought, too familiar with drowning to panic. The waters sent him back, grading across the ground. Suddenly, there was no ground.

Caden fell.

And fell.

And fell.

The waters gushed around him, thinning to a waterfall, then a heavy rain. Caden sucked in a breath in time to have it heaved out of him. He slammed into something. Hard. Rocky. He rolled and continued falling. He slammed into more rocks and earth, panic finally grabbing him. Where was the ground?

He slammed into solid rock and lay there on his back. His body felt broken in half as he sucked in a ragged breath. His head spun. He could taste blood. He slowly opened his eyes. The sky was on fire. The Heavenly Hosts were *still* streaming from the ripped-open sky. There was no sign their numbers were thinning. They continued charging, each one circling the earth from west to east. He could clearly see the horses and warriors now. They were brilliant!

The white horses' manes and tails flickered with hot, orange fire. Their hooves and eyes were like molten metal. Each warrior's eyes flashed like fire. Their armor glowed like flaming jasper, the light flashing with moving power whose rays sent rainbows this way and that. Each warrior's mouths were wide open as they sang a loud, thunderous chorus. It was beautiful. And terrifying. *They're on my side,* Caden reminded himself. *We're going to win.*

A deep, beast-like cry lifted high above. More beast voices joined, nearly meeting the Heavenly Host's volume.

Caden's blurry eyes focused, and he saw a large hill stood before him. Mount Megiddo. On it, Tarek's great wings spread as each head faced the charging armies. Even at a distance, Caden could hear Luca. "Assemble the men!"

*He's kidding, right?*

"Band together! This is a trick of the enemy! *I* am god, there is no other! Mankind has lived in this false God's captivity for far too long! We will break our chains and throw off our shackles! We will fight! We will be our own gods!" The hilltop roared with Zealots' battle cries. "Tell the other war camps! Prepare to fight!"

*He's serious!* Coughing, Caden realized he had to get up. There was movement around him. Craning his neck, he found he was surrounded by infantry Zealots. Cursing, Caden heaved himself upright. His head spun, but his body wasn't broken. Groaning in pain, Caden stood and tried to knock off whatever clung to his back. It didn't budge. Looking over his shoulder, Caden saw his back was glowing with more Spiritual armor.

"Do you see this?" Caden cried, smiling. "Do you see?"

Many automatic guns clicked, readying to fire. Caden snapped his head around as a dozen Zealots closed in. Caden pointed to the guns and stepped back. "You know, those don't work against this type of armor." His back butted against the rocky slope of Mount Megiddo. Each Zealot raised their weapon. "You need Spiritual weapons to conquer Spiritual armor!" In a blink, he realized his shield would protect his head and torso. His feet were safe, but what about his legs?

Caden's disturbing thoughts were cut short as he ducked behind the shield. Gunfire thundered in his ears. Adrenalin tensed every muscle and his eyes squeezed shut, readying to be thrown against the hill. With several blinks and exhaling sharply, Caden relaxed. It felt like several people were tapping on the other side of the shield. His eyes opened, and through the shield he saw the rage-filled faces around him.

The Zealots' gun barrels blasted orange fire with each volley. The bullets plunked off the shield, sending up sparks as gunpowder filled the air. Caden relaxed entirely and simply held the shield before him. He couldn't hold back a smirk as he continued humming. *This armor rocks!* In a minute, the Zealots' guns started dryfiring, and they lowered their weapons, red-faced and confused. Caden lowered his shield and shifted. He felt hundreds of flat-tened bullets beneath his boots. Better yet, his legs were fine. Better than fine! Spiritual armor now covered them too! Caden laughed as he peered over the shield. "Told ya!" The Zealots quickly reloaded their weapons. "No!" Caden cried. "Stop wasting my time!"

"He's mine!"

Caden flinched and looked up. Doeg was in midair, claws reaching. Caden ducked, gasping, and raised the shield. The Demon slammed into him, bringing him to his knees. Caden reeled and swung the shield, but Doeg lurched back on all fours, avoiding it. The Demon snarled, its twisted face smeared in blood. The Zealots around them scattered instantly. *"This isn't my first battle against that armor!"* Caden didn't answer as he held up the shield.

"No weapon formed against me shall stand!" Caden hissed. Doeg flinched and snarled. "What can mere mortals do against me?"

Doeg stepped back and reared up on its hind legs. It rose a head taller than Caden, tail thrashing and eyes wide with bloodlust. "I am no mortal!" The Demon leapt. Caden swung the shield, but Doeg changed direction. His clawed, human-like hand caught the shield and ripped it from Caden's grasp. It clattered to the ground and vanished. Caden stumbled back, panic seizing his throat.

*"Will the shield obey when summoned?"* Doeg swiped, claws lashing. Caden fell back, hearing the claws slice through the air. He crawled back, breath caught in his throat. "Or has it abandoned you too?" Doeg snarled, hind legs bunching to pounce. Shouting, Caden rolled, hearing Doeg land inches from him, and dragged himself to his feet. He raised his forearm. *"It won't work!"* Doeg screamed in his mind. *"We all know you're a failure, GJ!"* Caden's stomach coiled. *"Especially God!"*

*Please, come back, shield.*

"That doesn't sound like faith, boy!" Doeg walked closer, snarling. "Without faith, your shield won't operate!"

Caden panted as he stepped further away. *God, please.*

"Has begging your unseen God ever resulted in salvation?" Caden retreated further, sweat dripping down his brow. *"No,"* Doeg said with finality in his mind. *"You are a waste. You amount to nothing and will never deserve this armor!"*

Caden blinked and stared up at Doeg. His eyes narrowed. *Lies.* He made a fist. The shield materialized in a blink. Sneering, Doeg's ears whipped back. Its fur bristled, making it look twice its size. Caden's flesh chilled; Doeg was done playing games.

*"I am a Demon of my word,"* Doeg whispered. Caden's jaw set, and he realized he was humming again. *"You will see only me as you breathe your last breath!"* The Demon dropped to all fours and flew forward faster than lightning.

Caden's heart leapt into his throat. He raised the shield, bracing himself. Doeg crashed against it, one hand's claws snagging it and yanking down while the other descended toward Caden's head. Caden lurched forward, slamming a shoulder into the shield. He cracked against Doeg's face, but fire touched his shoulder. Caden screamed, drawing back. Warmth dripped down his arm.

He turned, finding claw marks raking along his right shoulder. *Why isn't there armor there?* Caden's mind screamed as he let out another cry through gritted teeth.

Movement flashed out of the corner of his eye. The Demon jerked, changing direction, lashing with one hand while shoving the shield away with another. Fighting through the pain, Caden raised the shield, aiming its pointed end at Doeg's face. He lunged. The Demon was too fast. It spun, its long tail whipping around and slamming into Caden's back. If not for the Spiritual armor, Caden knew his spine would've been broken.

He stumbled, gasping for air, and he drew up the shield in time to deflect Doeg's claws. He panted, feeling his clothes dampen with blood from his right shoulder. *I need a bat!* Caden's mind screamed. *Some sort of weapon!* He wasn't humming anymore. He was fighting for his life, and Doeg knew it. The Demon grinned ear to ear as it readied to pounce again.

The ground shook. Doeg and Caden froze. It was coming from the south, miles and miles away, close to Jerusalem. Caden didn't know how he knew that, but he just felt it deep in his soul. Something was happening. Something terrifyingly wonderful. Tarek roared. The war camps buzzed with orders as Zealots, Giants, Leovirs, and Demons seized weapons and readied for war.

Caden's heart quickened as the *Akal Esh* pulsing in his armor swirled faster with restless tension. He felt the *Akal Esh's* excitement, and it filled him with the same eagerness to conquer. The sky moved again. A great portion near the ground of it swung out, like two upright rectangles swinging open. *A Narrow Gate!* Caden gasped, his eyes widening. *It looks like double doors!*

The Gate butted against the ground and scraped against any rock and boulder, easily shoving them out of the way. Caden blinked and stared. Beyond the opening, he could see dusty hillsides covered in green, ancient trees. The Mount of Olives. Ophir had pointed it out to him long ago. Streaming from the opening came the Heavenly Hosts, their song nearly deafening. The ground started shaking with the glowing horses' hooves. Glowing comets of light shot from the warrior's mouths, blasting into anyone close.

The Demons screamed, reeling in agony. The Zealots' backs arched, dropping their weapons as Demons ripped out of them. The former Zealots collapsed, stunned and overwhelmed as the Demons scrambled for cover. There was none to find. The Heavenly Hosts kept singing as they raised their swords, Halberts, bows, and arrows and assaulted the Demons. Caden lifted his chin as he focused on the Heavenly Host's melody.

"No!"

Caden spun on his heels, facing Doeg. "May the praises of God be in the mouths of His faithful ones!" he screamed. Doeg flinched back, the zipping light from Caden's mouth shooting at it. "And a double-edged sword in their hands, to inflict vengeance on the nations and punishment on the peoples!"[5] Caden blinked and looked at his right hand. His empty hand. His hand that needed a weapon.

"NO!"

Caden made a fist. Instantly, the hilt of a sword was in his hand. The blade rose up and up, catching the light before bursting into flames. Caden held it away from his body, too stunned to move. "They will rule with an iron scepter," he mumbled the song, staring dumbfoundedly at the sword. It was magnificent! Ornately designed, pulsing with the *Akal Esh's* ferocity with chaotic jolts of light from deep within.

Caden's eyes narrowed; it also didn't feel right. He had no idea how to stab or cut things. "And," Caden stammered, continuing his song. "Will dash them to pieces like pottery." Did you swing it like an ax, or was it more like a poker? "Just as King Yeshua received authority from Yahweh, He will also give His faithful ones the morning star."[6]

Caden stopped short and stiffened, the wheels of his mind turning. *Morning Star?* Doeg's eyes widened, its ears snapping upright. With a rush of fierce excitement, Caden summoned something else. The sword's hilt became a solid shaft as a sling wound around his wrist. The blade telescoped in, condensing into a solid, weighted end, nearly a ball. Several pointed spikes jutted from the ball in every direction. It was a medieval-styled mace. More specifically, a Morning Star. It was a weapon that didn't stab or poke. It was swung. Like a baseball bat.

Caden smiled wolfishly as he faced Doeg. He laughed mirthlessly, which rose to a cry. He gasped and cried again, baring his teeth and readying to fight. With another cry, he slammed the Morning Star against the shield and advanced. *I am immortal,* Caden thought calmly as he continued screaming a battle cry. *Until the moment Yahweh calls me Home.* His Shoes of Peace dug into the ground as he shot forward, drawing back the Morning Star, and Doeg shrank with a scream.

## TWENTY-FOUR
## JUSTICE

DOEG RAN for its life on all fours, and Caden couldn't stop smiling. He was keeping pace with it. He knew Demons couldn't be killed, but pain and suffering weren't beyond them. Caden didn't know what he had in mind, but it sounded like Yeshua was pretty clear. Dashing something to pieces like pottery needed no interpretation from where Caden was standing. His heartbeat was swift and strong, yet not out of control. His breathing was quick, but also not as manic as he'd thought. Especially how he kept humming. He couldn't help it. As the Heavenly Hosts charged, he heard their song surrounding him more clearly. They *were* singing the same song. A song of praise to Yahweh. A song of vengeance and victory!

Doeg leapt through Zealots firing heavy guns at the Heavenly Hosts, the bullets passing through them as though nothing. Caden took in a breath as he plunged into the volley, the shield covering him. The massive bullets ricocheted off the armor, the blows hardly noticeable as sparks and casings flew.

Caden burst from the Zealots, knocking a few over as he shot past. Laughing like a wild man, Caden halfheartedly checked to see if any bullets got through. With no surprise, and not slacking in his pace, he found no wounds. He was gaining on Doeg. He could see the terror gripping the Demon; its ears were back and its tail tucked. *I have you.*

Doeg leapt onto a boulder, turned, and flew at him. Savagery haunted its eyes. Caden raised his shield, drawing back the Morning Star. Doeg spun, whipping its long tail around the shield's defenses. Caden reflexively turned his shoulder, praying the blow would land on his armored back. It did. Sort of.

Caden flew to the ground, gasping. No air entered him. He inhaled with a panicked gulp. He looked up in time to see Doeg's head. The Demon's mouth gaped, aiming at his throat. Caden could see its several yellowed fangs were serrated. He turned, swinging the Morning Star. Doeg yelped, its body snapping to one side. Panting, Caden stood and yanked the weapon free from between Doeg's ribs. The Demon yowled and struggled back as blood discolored its white fur.

"Serve Yahweh with fear," Caden said in time with the songs being shouted around them. Doeg fell back, avoiding a bolt of energy from Caden's mouth. "Celebrate His rule with trembling." Caden advanced; it was time to put this dog down. "Kiss His Son, or He will be angry. You hear that? Kiss Yeshua!" Doeg snarled as claws slashed. Caden cursed, kicking the blow away. "And your way will lead to destruction!"

Doeg crawled away and tried to rise. Caden lunged, swinging the Morning Star down. It crunched into Doeg's middle, nearly folding the Demon in half. If Doeg had been mortal, it would've been dead on the spot. Moaning, Doeg lay back as its eyes rolled back in its head. It fought for breath as its tail lashed aimlessly. Caden shook his head as he grinned down at Doeg. This was just too easy!

"You should've left me alone on the cliffs!" he hissed. "You know you'll be defeated! There's no place for you now that King Yeshua is here!"

King Yeshua and the Heavenly Hosts. And, honestly, whatever type of soldier Caden was. A BA, warrior of God? He sure felt BA. Armor that literally glowed and weapons that came when summoned! Next thing, he'll discover flight and conquer the heavens! Nothing, Spirit or mortal alike, would oppose him and survive! The terrified, fleeing lad who once bore his name was long dead. He was Caden, the conqueror. Caden, the avenger! Caden the—

Doeg's tail slammed into Caden's wounded shoulder. Pain electrified his neck and side. He stumbled back, screaming through gritted teeth. He'd forgotten about that, and now more blood dripped down his arm. Gasping, Caden faced Doeg and hefted his Morning Star. It wasn't there. Caden frowned and summoned it.

Claws seized his shield and wrenched down. Caden grabbed it with both hands, unable to hold the summoned weapon. Doeg was on its feet. Caden braced himself, unwilling to move. His eyes widened as he stared through the shield. It was like he was watching a dog mad with rabies. Doeg caterwauled, biting and slashing until blood oozed from between fangs and claws. It slammed a shoulder into the shield, sending Caden back a step. Doeg did it again and again, its movements feverish.

Sweat dripped down Caden's brow as all his focus was keeping Doeg behind the shield. But his shoulder felt like a hot blade was lodged into it. His right hand's grip was slick with blood dribbling from the wound. Gritting his teeth, Caden growled and planted his feet, shoving back. Instantly, Doeg moved. Caden flew forward, landing on the shield. *I have armor on my back, you idiot.*

*"How about your throat?"*

Caden's eyes widened. His hair was seized, wrenching his chin up. Caden yelled and twisted, finding Doeg straddling him. Caden made a fist. Doeg drew back a clawed hand. *Please, God!*

The Morning Star materialized. Doeg slashed. Caden swung. He didn't know if he made impact. He only knew he wasn't breathing right. Something was dripping down his airways too. It wasn't like water; he knew that feeling. This was thicker and warm. His mouth filled with blood.

Raking in a gasp, Caden dropped the Morning Star and clasped his throat. Blood seeped between his fingers. Sharp burning shot from his neck across his face. Cold panic swallowed him whole. Doeg stomped on the Shield of Faith, pinning Caden's left arm to one side. Caden kicked, his back arching, but Doeg wasn't done.

Without a word, Doeg jabbed a clawed hand down. Caden's entire body bucked as he felt each individual claw stab into his abdomen. He choked, spitting up blood, and his body shook as Doeg withdrew. His stomach was on fire. It was a dull, distant pain, but it was spreading. Grinning from ear to ear, Doeg stooped lower and hissed in Caden's ear: "Self-worship is you mortals' weakest link."

The Demon stepped back, and Caden rolled onto his side. He didn't notice the Morning Star was gone. So was the Shield of Faith. Caden's halting breaths shook his body as he watched blood pool beneath him. His world narrowed to that one small window of space and time. He couldn't hear the Heavenly Hosts' song. The cries of Demons and freed Zealots were no more. Mount Megiddo wasn't a thing in his life. Even Tarek and Yeshua were distant memories.

Caden only knew he lay, choking on his own blood, as a vengeful Demon stood over him, watching. He felt every pebble and blade of grass beneath him. He even heard Doeg's excited breathing. His limbs became colder and colder as his core heated from the extra blood flow. *Not like this!* his sharply focused mind screamed. *Not after everything I've overcome! This cannot be! My strength goes beyond this! I am immortal by my own power.*

Caden blinked, sputtering again as his throat continued flowing. *No self-worship!* Doeg hissed as Caden's eyes narrowed. *Yahweh! I need You!*

Claws sank into his thighs. Caden screamed as Doeg dragged him backward. The Demon heaved him upright and slammed him against the boulders. Caden wheezed between gasps, blood trickling from both sides of his mouth. Doeg drew back its claws, readying to stab again. *Yeshua!*

Caden slouched, feeling his body splitting open further. Doeg withdrew its claws and stabbed again. All thoughts stopped as Caden slumped into Doeg's chest with a gurgled moan. He grabbed a fistful of white fur in a shaky grasp as his other hand went to his middle. His hand was suddenly very warm. He could feel coiled things like big, slimy worms. Caden slowly looked down and saw his hand had slipped inside his abdomen up to the wrist. Blood was everywhere. Searing pain exploded from his middle, enveloping his entire body.

"You should've leapt from those cliffs as I instructed," Doeg sneered. Caden's eyes fluttered as darkness closed around him. Doeg growled and grabbed his throat, straightening him against the boulders. "Look at me!" Doeg hissed. Caden gasped for air. Doeg slammed his head back again. "Look at me!" Caden's eyes widened, and they locked with Doeg's.

The Demon knelt over him, its face inches away. Caden's mouth kept gaping as he weakly tried to breathe. Doeg licked its jowls and it scooted closer. "Do you see me now, human fool?" Caden's hands fell at his sides. *"Just as*

*I swore to you years ago,"* Doeg said within his mind. *"I am the last thing you will ever see."*

Caden's vision went in and out of focus. He didn't have the strength to sit up. He couldn't move his arms. He suddenly couldn't feel his spilling innards. Through the shadows fogging his mind, Caden formed a thought. He knew it would be his last. It was a prayer and the simplest one he'd made yet. It was one word: *Help.*

Doeg threw back its head and laughed. *"As I always said!"* the Demon yelled inside Caden's mind. *"You are abandoned and forsaken! No God would ever fight for you!"*

Caden's eyes glazed over as his chest heaved for more air. He knew Doeg was speaking, but he couldn't follow it anymore. *Help,* he managed to pray again before every thought stilled. He didn't notice when Doeg released his throat. He didn't feel his head bounce when he slumped over and collapsed. His eyes slid open just enough to stare into nothingness.

His mouth and chest moved to force in air, but it was an automatic motion. He wasn't in control. He was never in control. Only Yahweh had complete control. A tear slid from Caden's eye as he stared. Doeg was watching him, slinking backward with fur bristled. He was readying to pounce again. Caden didn't move. He couldn't. He just—

Doeg spat, its ears turned back as its tail tucked between its legs. Without trying to defend itself, Doeg spun and ran. Caden stared after it and, very slowly, realized a shadow crossed over him. It wasn't a very big one, maybe the size of a man. Mustering every final reserve of strength and focusing all he had on this final act, Caden craned back his head and looked up.

Standing on the boulder over him was a man. A terrifying man of violence. Caden knew he'd be fleeing as quickly as Doeg if he could. The man was an Israeli. He carried no weapon, and a robe wrapped around his shoulders and hung down his back. The robe was wet and dripping. Caden blinked, realizing it was soaked in blood. Actually, every bit of the stranger was. It splattered his face, drenched his hair, and smeared across his body.

He wore an odd hat. It was golden and glittering with gems and spiked irregularly, like several crowns merged into one. Every inch of the man's face and hands were covered in deep, old scars. Caden knew he saw only a fraction of this wild man's wounds. The stranger stared down at Caden, but his eyes weren't visible. Instead, fire licked from the sockets, masking all expression.

He wore armor that surpassed any Caden had seen. It looked like a hurricane and wildfire were trapped inside the plates. White lightning-like brilliance flashed across the breastplate and shield as white-hot fire raged. Caden wanted to fall limp and turn away from this destroyer, but he couldn't. He could only look up and tremble.

The stranger leapt from the boulder and landed close to Caden, his boots creating mini craters. Caden stared at the flashing boots as another tear fell. The stranger held out a hand, and Caden closed his eyes, unable to tense for the blow. None came. He looked up and stared at the hand. It reached out as the man simply waited. Caden strained to stay conscious as his eyes ran along every scar and indent in the stranger's hand. A peculiar scar ran through his wrist, like a rod was shoved right through. No, not that big. It was more like a nail.

Caden's eyes widened as he looked up to the face of raging beauty. *Yeshua?*

*"Rise up."*

The voice struck Caden in the chest. It was a voice that filled his entire being, flooding into his innermost parts, and showing him how small he really was. It was a voice of eternity. A voice to instantly obey.

Sputtering through blood, Caden held his middle to

keep his body intact. Inch by inch, he scooted his legs beneath him. He rose, his head feeling a hundred pounds as blood streamed from his mouth and nose. He tried to raise his head but couldn't. Darkness surrounded him. He couldn't feel anything, but icy cold as sweat drenched him. Gritting his teeth, Caden raised a hand. It felt so far away and heavy, but it moved. He heaved it toward the outstretched hand, bloodied fingers straining. One fingertip latched onto the Man's pinkie. Caden's body trembled; that was all he could do. It was pathetic.

The hand seized his wrist and pulled. Caden's head slumped back as his limp legs unfolded. He fell forward, slamming into his Savior. Without thinking, Caden grabbed the back of Yeshua's neck, smearing blood on His cheek. Caden dragged himself upright, his forehead bumping Yeshua's. Trembling and hanging onto life by a thread, Caden clung to his King.

"Yeshua," he wheezed. His lips parted to plea more, but nothing came. He was done, he could feel it. There was nothing left.

He felt strong arms wrap around him, supporting him. Yeshua leaned forward and breathed into Caden's mouth. The breath filled him just as fully as Yeshua's words. Caden inhaled sharply, like a drowning person bursting from the water. He straightened, his grip on Yeshua strengthening. His legs drew beneath him. His back stiffened.

Caden raked in breath after breath, finding his airways were clear. He blinked and grabbed his abdomen. His hand didn't sink in. He felt whole, restored flesh. As he moved his neck, no pain burned from the wound. His shoulder, too, didn't scream in agony. Caden barked a hoarse laugh. He looked up at Yeshua and found those flaming eyes burning into him. With a hissed curse,

Caden's legs buckled to send him to his knees at the King of King's feet.

Yeshua's grip tightened, and Caden stayed upright. **"The time of kneeling will come,"** He said softly. **"For now, Caden,"** Caden inhaled sharply, **"let us claim our inheritance."** A wide smile split through Caden's fears. King Yeshua drew Caden back and smiled. **"This will help."** Caden felt something press against his chest. Looking down, he found that a shimmering breastplate shielded him. He laughed again, seeing the *Akal Esh* raging inside the Breastplate of Righteousness. **"And this."** Yeshua held out a helmet, reminding Caden of a medieval-styled armor. Caden reached for it, but Yeshua moved first, placing it on Caden's head. The face shield was a solid plate, but Caden could see through it clearly, the *Akal Esh* so refined, Caden hardly felt he wore anything over his eyes. Caden lifted his chin as Yeshua secured the helmet in place and clapped him on the back.

Yeshua stared at him and then nodded approvingly. **"Fits you well."** Caden tried to find words but couldn't. Yeshua didn't seem to mind. **"Come,"** He said, turning. Caden fell in step beside Him, his heart racing as the thrill of Heaven's song rang in his ears. He summoned the Morning Star, and the spiked club materialized instantly. He had never felt as strong or capable in his entire life as he did in that moment, while he literally followed Yeshua.

Caden lifted his chin and faced the chaos of Heavenly Hosts and the New Kingdom colliding. He gaped; he couldn't help it. Zealots fired at will, the bullets completely useless against the Heavenly Hosts. Missiles, grenades, bazookas, and so many earthly weapons were deflected or passed through the Heavenly Hosts, ricocheting into Luca's followers. Already, many bodies littered the ground. Leovirs thrashed, engulfed in flames. Giants staggered as their Demonic spirits were ripped from their bodies. It was chaos. It was justice.

Caden's shoulders bunched as his gaze fell on one man. A Refiner limped over the dead as he held a weighted cane like a bat. Caden's eyes narrowed, and hatred tightened his chest. His fingers flexed along the Morning Star. As though feeling the weight of Caden's stare, Grant turned and froze. All color washed from his face as he stumbled back. *Now this is justice!* Caden thought as he stepped forward.

Yeshua grabbed his arm. **"Conquer the evil Spirits,"** He said softly. **"Leave the mortals to Me."**

For the smallest moment, Caden considered ripping his arm free from Yeshua's grasp. *Don't be stupid!*

*"Yes. Please don't."*

Caden blinked and turned from Grant as he stepped back. He dipped his head. "Yes, my King."

Yeshua nodded as He returned His attention to Grant. The Refiner was visibly shaking. Taking a deep breath, Yeshua walked forward. He spoke. Caden didn't hear His words, but he felt it, even to his joints and marrow. No. It was deeper than that. His *soul* recoiled, as though touched for the very first time. A touch so quick and powerful that it could expose his real, intimate thoughts and intentions without effort. Caden inhaled sharply as Yeshua's words shifted the very air he breathed.

Instantly, something shot from Yeshua's mouth. It shone with white fire as the *Aka' Esh's* blaze moved feverishly. The closer it was to Yeshua, the more translucent, ghost-like it was. The further away, it solidified into a solid, tangible object. *It's both Spiritual and physical,* Caden thought. The thing was nearly fifty feet long and narrowed down to a fine point. Caden blinked, realizing it was a sword.

At the same time, Grant did too. His body tensed as

his mouth opened to scream. None came as the sword swiped through the closest Zealots. Bodies slid in half, arms dropped to the ground, and heads rolled. Caden hissed a curse and flinched back as blood splattered across his helmet. Panting, Caden reached up to wipe it off, but stopped. What was the point? The ground was already muddy from the blood.

Without slackening His pace, King Yeshua calmly walked into the enemy armies. Caden knew He kept speaking, His words touching Caden again and again with fire. But it was a fire Caden knew. The *Akal Esh* was on *his* side; he wasn't going to get burned. Caden stared in blatant shock as anyone of mortal flesh close to Yeshua was slaughtered. Their screams were filled with terror and short-lived. Behind Yeshua, the bodies piled up as blood flowed like little streams through the mud.

Caden stared at the reddened streams, suddenly remembering Noam and Auset's blood. *And their child*, Caden thought, his eyes narrowing. That loose woman had gotten drunk on their blood. Most of them had. These people had watched and cheered as Elijah and Yohanan were ripped limb from limb. They also hunted down Caden's fellow believers, sending them to labor camps or mass graves. They had murdered Trace and Ellie. Caden took in a deep breath, his eyes narrowing as steel entered his gaze.

*Justice*, he thought. *This is Yahweh's justice. And His love.* Rolling a shoulder, Caden turned from Yeshua inflicting Yahweh's vengeance. *Conquer the evil Spirits*, he thought. *Where'd you go, Doeg?*

As he looked, he saw things that looked like Angels, but their armor didn't glow as much. They seemed more concrete than Spiritual. *Those are mortals*, he thought. *And they have Spiritual armor too!* Each believer shone with the

*Akal Esh* as they battled Demons with various, medieval-styled weapons.

Through the flaming warriors attacking Demons and dying mortals between, he saw a white form. It was running away from him like the wind. Caden couldn't hold back a grin as his boots dug into the ground and he took off after Doeg. He was humming again too. It just felt so right! After a few heartbeats, Caden realized his strides were longer than humanly possible. The blood-soaked mud also didn't slow him down. He glanced down, seeing the ground fly by, until something brushed his shoulder. He shrugged it off until seeing a boulder shatter as it scooted away from him, bits of rock exploding to and fro. *Did I just slam into a boulder?*

Someone was laughing beside him. It was a woman's laugh. It was an Angel! No, the armor wasn't as fiery and seemed more concrete than a Spirit. It was human in Spiritual armor. She easily kept pace with him. "Watch where you're going, Sammy!"

Excitement rushed through Caden like a hot wave as his grin widened. "You're alive!"

"Of course, silly! We all are! Asher's over there, charging with Jaden." Caden laughed and continued singing as he leapt over a fallen Giant and around a turned-over Humvee. He could hear Dasha singing too, their rhythms timed perfectly. They were closing in on Doeg. The Shade fled, tail still between its legs and ears pressed back. Caden sucked in a breath and shouted,

"Bring down Your warriors, Yahweh!"[1] Bolts shot from Caden's mouth, clipping Doeg's shoulder. The Demon stumbled, nearly falling headlong into a pile of bodies. It steadied itself and zoomed around the pile. Caden and Dasha didn't slacken their pace and leapt directly over. They almost landed on top of Doeg.

"Let the nations be roused; let them advance into the

Valley of Armageddon!" Dasha cried, singing the next line.

The two inhaled sharply and proclaimed the next verse as one: "For King Yeshua will judge all the nations at every side!"

Doeg yowled, bolts assaulting it twice as strong. The Demon's body slammed to the ground, splattering through the bloody mud and rolling over bodies. Without hesitating, Caden swung the Morning Star. It cracked into Doeg's chest, rocketing the Demon into the air. The two humans skidded to a halt, their boots digging ruts with the force of their speed.

Dasha whistled as Doeg slowly crested the apex and started falling. "It's all yours."

Caden sniffed and shook his head. "I've given this dog too much of my attention."

Dasha shrugged. "Suit yourself." She made a fist and a massive sword answered the summons. She stepped forward, took a stance, and sliced right before the Demon slammed into the ground.

Doeg's body twisted in midair, half falling in one direction as the other half thumped a distance away. Caden glanced down at the struggling body. Doeg rasped as it looked all around, trying to find its other half. Its fur was red and trembled with each breath. Panic filled its pale eyes. Caden shook his head as he stepped closer to Doeg. The Demon whimpered, and it pressed its face in the mud.

"Pathetic," Caden spat as he stepped over it. He didn't look back as Dasha and he left Doeg to struggle in its own blood.

"Where to now?" Dasha asked.

Caden looked across the chaos as bodies piled on one another, Demons writhed in terror and pain, and the streams of blood were now mini rivers. His eyes flickered to Mount Megiddo. Tarek's red, writhing heads looked like a dark shadow against the brilliance of the *Akal Esh*. Columns of water gushed from its mouth at any who drew too close. Beneath the dragon stood two men, protected under its wings. Caden squarely faced the hill and motioned to Dasha.

"Come on!" he cried. "Let's go slay a dragon!"

## TWENTY-FIVE
# HELLFIRE

BY THE TIME Dasha and Caden reached Mount Megiddo, they were covered in blood. Not that they hacked their way through the fray, but there was just so much blood already. There wasn't mud anymore. It had turned into a swamp with bodies for islands. Caden knew the stench alone should've stopped him, but not even that penetrated the Spiritual armor. Caden splashed across the battle, around a burning tank that was cut clean in half, and body piles all around also severed. Fire lashed about on everything not cut in two.

A Wither screamed as it fled, but Dasha flicked it with her blade, sending it against fractured boulders. Two hot sections burned Caden's back, and he turned, knowing a Fiend was close behind. He drew back his Morning Star, but Dasha had already sent her blade up, the point lodging beneath the Demon's jaw. The Fiend screamed as its liquid fire spurted from the wound and ignited its misty form. It writhed through the air as they charged on. Through it all, Caden knew where Yeshua was. The King's very steps sent ripples of power across the battlefield. When He spoke, the authority shook Caden to the core. It had startled him at first, but he was getting comfortable with it.

They rounded a split Giant and found Shades surrounding one mortal in Spiritual armor. The stranger held a long, gleaming spear he whipped back and forth, jabbing at the Demons. Caden hummed through gritted teeth as he motioned for Dasha to cut left. He went right, and they circled their enemies. One Shade straightened, ears upright, and yipped in alarm. It was too late.

"Let Yahweh's faithful people rejoice in the honor of being crowned," Dasha and Caden cried. "And sing for joy!" Bullets of energy blasted from them. The Shades recoiled, screaming, unable to move fast enough to avoid the lethal blows.

"May the praises of Yahweh be in our mouths," Caden screamed in tune, releasing his shield to take the Morning Star with both hands. "And a double-edged sword in our hands!" He swung, sending three flying at a time. "To inflict vengeance on the nations and punishment!" They quickly cut through the ring, and all three knights drew together, back-to-back. Each continued crying the song's lyrics. Caden couldn't understand how he wasn't out of breath. In fact, the more he sang, the more strength he gained.

"We will bind the kings with fetters!" The Shades and Vipers' shrilled cries rose to hysteria as energy blasted from each knight like the cacophony of a machine gun. "And the noble with shackles of iron!" The three moved as one through the survivors, stabbing and bludgeoning. Caden knew the Demons couldn't die, but, man alive, they could be wounded! It felt like they were cutting down pesky weeds in the backyard. It didn't take long to dismantle any who didn't flee.

Panting, covered in sweat and blood, and never feeling more alive, Caden faced his team. He recognized the new knight's voice and he grinned. Asher nodded to him as he clutched his spear, the tip rising several feet overhead. "How's your bad leg?"

Asher's teeth flashed with a smile. "What bad leg?"

Caden smiled back. "We're going to destroy Tarek. Wanna come?" Asher hefted his spear, and Caden chuckled. The three gained upon the hill easily. Zealots fled before them, and Caden had to tell himself to stand down. They weren't his to destroy.

The Zealots' lower half collapsed as their upper slid forward with leftover momentum. Strangled screams filled his ears as bodies splashed in the ever-growing rivers of blood. Caden sucked in a sharp breath and grabbed his middle, realizing Yeshua's blade had passed through them all. He was done for! Spiritual armor couldn't combat Yeshua Himself.

Caden blinked and caught himself from falling as he continued running. *I'm in one piece?*

**"You are one of Mine."**

Caden stiffened, unfamiliar with a good voice entering his thoughts. *Um, thank You, my King.* Yeshua didn't answer, and behind them, Caden heard another wave of screams.

Before they continued, Caden couldn't help noticing one of the Zealots. It looked like Rapham. He writhed in the mud, arms weakly grasping his severed torso as blood and innards spilled. Caden turned away with a sharp hiss, finding Asher staring down at his tormentor. He expected to see satisfaction in his eyes. There was only sorrow. "Let's go," Asher said gravely, and the three started out again.

Picking up the pace, Caden led Dasha and Asher up Mount Megiddo. It felt like they were rising a bunny hill, not a rocky plateau that had withstood wars throughout history. Water streamed off the hill. Caden's jaw set as he made one final leap, splashing into ankle-deep water on the crest. He froze as an idea finally struck him: he was a madman.

Tarek couldn't be conquered by him. Even with Dasha and Asher's help, that was only three of them. Tarek had seven heads! They were sorely outnumbered! Everyone who had tried to face Tarek wasn't doing so well. Around the edge of the hill were knights limping back or even running down the hill. A hard lump formed in Caden's throat as a coldness crept across his feet and hands. *This isn't going to work. This…*

His eyes met with one of the two men beneath Tarek's protective wings. One was Hugh, hunched and hidden in a cloud of Fiends. The other was Luca. He stood just as straight and proud as when Elijah and Yohanan were slaughtered. And that charming, smug smile was still on his face. Caden's nostrils flared as he gritted his teeth. One of Tarek's heads swooped low, regarding him. Its black eyes narrowed, and it gave a sudden growl.

*I can't do this,* Caden thought, more dragon heads facing him. *But Yahweh's Akal Esh can destroy anything!*

Not giving himself another chance to think, Caden charged as Tarek's mouths opened wide. He hoped Dasha and Asher followed as he screamed the chorus: "We carry out the sentence written against Yahweh's enemies!" Other bolts of energy shot up into Tarek from different directions in time with Caden's song. Columns of water gushed from the reptilian mouths.

Caden sucked in a breath and raised his shield, bracing himself while lunging to one side. The flood slammed into the shield and glanced off as he kept moving. Panting, Caden saw movement like racing fire. Other knights had joined and sang along with him, assaulting Tarek at the same time. "This is the glory of all Yahweh's faithful people!" Another volley rocketed into Tarek, breaking the dragon's stance. Hugh held up his hands and cried out as Luca's smile finally slipped.

Caden dropped, rolling under a watery serge that sent a Humvee over the hilltop's edge. He leapt up and focused his attention on one head. It stared back at him, its mouth hanging to one side. *"This is my world!"* Tarek's multi-voice screamed in his mind. *"I fought for it long before your very nation was conceived! This is* my *inheritance!"*

*No,* Caden thought coolly. He released the shield and leaped high into the air. Grabbing the Morning Star with two hands, Caden brought it up over his head. The dragon's head craned up, eyes wide. *It's mine.*

The dragon's mouth opened, water pooling down its throat. With a wild cry, Caden hurled the mace down into the watery depths. The dragon's head lurched back, eyes bulging, as the Morning Star ripped right through. Caden flew down, landing feet first on Tarek's head. He heard a crunch and felt the scaled body give way. He summoned the mace and drew it back but stopped. The head didn't move as the eyes pitifully watched him.

"Drop!"

Caden fell to his knees, hearing water surge overhead. Another knight leapt forward, shouting as he sent arrows from a crossbow into the dragon's throat. The surge stopped suddenly as the head whipped back with screams of agony. The knight landed heavily and held out the crossbow. Arrows materialized along the string, already taunt to shoot again. Caden's eyes narrowed, this guy's armor was different. The armor was detailed with decorative patterns, swirls, and shapes. The *Akal Esh's* inner power was hotter somehow. Brighter. They had the same Consuming Fire, yet the stranger's armor made Caden's look like a campfire.

*You're not an Angel,* Caden thought. *What are you?*

The man stared at his freshly knocked arrows and laughed. Caden's brows rose. "Genius!"

*Noam?* The man started firing again, gouging out both the dragon-head's eyes. Fierce joy filled Caden's chest as he rose. "Noam? Is that…It's you!"

Noam glanced over his shoulder and grinned. His smile fell. "Your six."

Caden pivoted instantly, mace swinging. He felt it stop abruptly against red flesh and bone. The dragon head didn't even have a chance to spew its waters.

"Hey!" a woman cried. "That was mine!"

Caden looked up, seeing another ornately designed knight rushing by him. "Auset?" Auset flashed him a quick smile as she joined Noam.

"Pay attention, Cade!"

All breath rushed from him. A knight, her armor like a work of art, leapt into the air. Her sword slashing straight through a dragon's neck. "El!" She landed, the head thumping behind her.

"Fight, brother!" Caden's ears rang from Ellie's voice. The voice of a living, breathing person. Not a Spirit, but flesh and blood. "Fight!"

Caden summoned his shield and advanced, his fierce joy igniting his body. He ducked beneath Tarek's sweeping wings as his Morning Star solidified in his grasp. Swinging up, he heard the crack of shattering bone. Tarek's wing shot back, turning over a hummer.

Out of the corner of his eye, Caden saw that at least six other knights stood with him. Each fought differently, carried uniquely styled weapons, whose armor design differed. Four of the three glowed brighter than the others, their armor engraved with beauty instead of the others' plain plates. They fought as a team, advancing through on cue, and singing in time with one another. They sent volleys of bolts into Tarek and hacked away at heads and limbs. The dragon writhed and screamed, flooding the hilltop with water. But nothing could extinguish the fire of the *Akal Esh*.

Caden gasped for breath and belted another lyric as Tarek blasted water into him. Caden calmly held up the Shield of Faith, the waters flowing with enough force to break a man in two, not even worth raising his heartbeat. A much-more-glowing knight charged the dragon-head, a scimitar flashing in his hands. His armor was far more detailed than the others as it glowed brighter. The dragon head roared and reared back, desperate to avoid his curved sword. There was no escape from it.

The knight moved with the efficiency of one who knew the *Akal Esh*. It was as though the two moved together with one mind, advancing and lashing with joined will. Caden found himself frozen as he stared at the knight's dance-like steps. He blinked and straightened. *Who is this?*

Tarek's head screamed as the knight leapt, driving the sword deep into the dragon's mouth. The head shivered and fell back, the black eyes rolling back into its head. Rising slowly and casually wiping off his blade, the knight turned and faced Caden. He was tall and lean with a thick beard and an amused, mischievous smile on his face.

Caden's mouth dropped open as he lowered his shield. He couldn't speak for a moment. "Yohanan?"

"Nice armor, bro!" Yohanan said, his smile widening. Caden didn't answer. Yohanan chuckled and snapped his fingers. "Focus! We've got some captives to get!"

"Hum?" Yohanan's eyes flashed, and he jerked his head to the two cowering mortals who hid beneath Tarek's collapsed wing.

Caden stared down at Luca and Hugh. The three Fiends had abandoned them. They were left armed only with an M16. Caden's eyes narrowed as he saw them shaking, drenched in water and sweat as mud caked their clothes. Hugh shivered next to Luca as the Antichrist held the gun, pointed and ready. It was pathetic, like a child defending itself with a stick against seven tanks.

*You are just mortals,* Caden thought. *Mortals King Yeshua will destroy.* He stepped toward them, his heart quickening in his ears. He was going to enjoy watching them die. It was justice. They deserved suffering for what they had done.

Movement. A dark shape. A clawed thing. Tarek's hand crashed into him. Caden was thrown off his feet, slamming into the knocked-over hummer. The windshield shattered instantly as the vehicle lurched a few feet to one side. Caden landed, his head spinning. Someone was screaming. He looked up, seeing the reptilian hand descending toward his head. *It can't squish through the Helmet of Salvation,* Caden thought. *Could it?* He raised his arm and summoned his shield.

A glowing Halbert sliced through the air, easily severing the hand. Tarek's final heads weakly screamed as the red dragon's body shook and slumped to the ground. The stumpy arm recoiled, blood mixing with the water swirling around it. Caden blinked the flashing lights from his eyes and found an outstretched hand. He took it and groaned as he stood.

"Thanks," he muttered.

"Of course, son."

Caden's head snapped up. He stared wide-eyed at the knight, his armor surpassing them all. A wild smile overtook his face as Caden made a fist and slammed it against the man's Breastplate of Righteousness. "Ha!" He cried. "Where's Death's sting? Where's its victory over us? Nowhere!" The man chuckled softly. "Hey, Abba."

Elijah grinned as he hefted the Halbert. "Look at you." He clapped Caden on the shoulder and grunted. "No wonder you always favored bats." Caden laughed as he spun the Morning Star. "I'm proud of you." Caden lifted his chin. "And there is still more to conquer."

"Yeah! Yohanan said we need to take those two bozos captive."

A firecracker started popping. No, wait. Not that. It was something that had been dangerous at one time, but now seemed silly. It was a gun. Luca's M16. The Antichrist was firing on them as Hugh covered his ears and cowered. Luca was screaming at them, too, as though that would add power to the volleys. Each of the seven turned and stared at Luca without moving, the bullets plinking off their armor easily.

Yohanan scoffed as Asher lowered his spear. In moments, Luca's gun started dryfiring, and he stared down at the useless weapon. He looked up at them, his lips drawn back into a teeth-bearing snarl from a crimson face. Hugh cursed and bolted, splashing through the water and blood. Auset stepped in his way, and he fell, cowering before her.

"I am god!" Luca bellowed.

Caden cursed. "No, you're not!"

"That's it!" Asher cried.

"Let's shut this one up," Yohanan grumbled as they advanced.

"They are King Yeshua's," Elijah said, stopping all of them in their tracks. No one stood down as each were ready to inflict Yahweh's vengeance.

*It's not mine to inflict,* Caden thought as he reluctantly stepped back.

Noam muttered something as he motioned to Hugh. "Join him," he ordered, and Hugh quickly scrambled away, falling deeper into the water. He splashed to Luca and knelt, panting. Luca stayed standing and held the gun like a club. It was pathetic. It was *more* than pathetic. He spun in a circle as the seven knights stood around him, their weapons drawn yet at ease.

Caden couldn't deny the hatred that heated his blood as he watched Luca stand in defiance. *He should at least kneel! He's defeated!*

Even as they stood, Caden could hear the screams of the dying mortals all around him. The cries weren't as loud as before and he knew, deep down, most were already dead. The Demons' cries and struggles had quieted too, for most were like Tarek, sliced into weak, near-dead pieces that struggled and gasped. The Heavenly Hosts' song and praise was louder than ever. The ground and air were electric with the *Akal Esh* as its power lit the world, for the sun was still dark.

"My King," Elijah whispered. "The Antichrist and False Prophet are captured." A warm heaviness settled on Caden, and he knew Yeshua was looking at them.

A Narrow Gate appeared in the center of their ring right before Luca and Hugh. The door swung wide, and a warrior walked through, whose names are Faithful and True. King Yeshua's crowns and armor and brilliants made the seven knights look plain and ordinary. Overhead, dark clouds rolled, and thunder flashed as the hilltop trembled with Yeshua's footfalls.

Caden knelt instantly. It was as reflexive as breathing. Everyone else dropped too, the knights out of reverence and Hugh and Luca out of terror. King Yeshua stared down at the Antichrist and False Prophet as Hugh screamed in horror. Luca's white face was buried in his hands. Tarek crawled back, even its severed heads twitching to get away. Through reverberating singing, the final screams of the dying, and the shrieks of Demons, a calm voice cut through:

**"I am the King of kings."**

The water rippled under Yeshua's voice as Luca trembled and Hugh screamed for mercy. Without another word, King Yeshua reached forward and grabbed both men. A lump formed in Caden's throat as his mouth dropped open. Luca and Hugh thrashed and kicked but could do nothing as Yeshua picked them off the ground. Yeshua lifted His chin, and a Narrow Gate opened beneath their feet.

Incinerating heat rushed from the Gate. Water and blood evaporated. Anything natural still left on the hillside instantly burst into flames. Luca and Hugh's bodies ignited and writhed. Caden recoiled and stared breathlessly, their bodies shriveling down to char in seconds. The ashy remains flaked away as two still streaming, still squirming things hung in Yeshua's hands. Caden blinked and stared. It was still Luca and Hugh. They were naked, their bodies pale and faintly transparent.

*Their souls*, Caden thought, his blood turning to ice. The condemned souls' blistered and cracked, their cries turning to shrieks of agony, yet their souls stayed in one piece. Their eyes rolled back in their heads as they screamed pleas of mercy. King Yeshua didn't bother responding as He stepped forward, unfazed by the Gate's intense heat. He released them.

The souls reached up, clawing for anything to grab onto, as they plummeted. In a blink, they were gone. Caden heard their descending screams continue on and on, fading into an echoing oblivion. Stepping back, King Yeshua motioned with His hand, and the Narrow Gate closed, sealing off the scorching heat.

Caden stared where it had been, his eyes stinging from not blinking as he sucked in breath after breath. He didn't need anyone to tell him, but he knew that Gate had led to Hell. Caden fell on his face and started praising Yahweh and Yeshua and the *Akal Esh*. He shook uncontrollably. He couldn't help it. The fear of Yahweh struck him like a blow to the face, and he screamed praises as the sting of Hell's heat still pricked his face.

"I am nothing without You!" he cried. "You are worthy. You who were slain! You have all power and wealth and wisdom and strength and honor and glory and praise!" Caden sucked in a breath through gritted teeth. "You are worthy to sit on the throne! You are worthy! You are my King! My King!"

**"And you are My kingdom."** All breath rushed from Caden as he lay, King Yeshua's words washing over him. **"And priests to serve Yahweh. You will reign on the earth. Arise."**

Caden didn't know how he could stand, for he had no strength, but he fought to obey. He straightened and faced Yeshua. He was drenched in even more blood, His red robe wetly sticking to His armor, for He had conquered. The King was smiling at each of them, His eyes of fire flashing. He lifted His chin, and Caden literally felt the pride and love Yeshua felt for him. Caden's mouth opened as his eyes watered. The fierce goodness of God was overwhelming.

**"Well done, all of you."**

The seven knights bowed again, unable to stay upright. King Yeshua calmly told them to stand again, and He turned to the valley below. The Heavenly Hosts covered the skies. Knights, both mortal men and those raised to life again, filled the land. Not a Demon stood. Not a mortal against Yahweh was left. Caden blinked, realizing the mountains around Megiddo had moved. Many had flattened or shifted to one side. The ground was replaced by blood, making it look like a vast, red lake. The Heavenly Hosts' horses waded through the blood, which rose to their bridle. The blood flowed from Megiddo, and Caden saw it heading south, down the Dead Sea, and spilling into the Red Sea miles away.

As he stared in awe at the total destruction, he noticed someone kneeling at the hill's edge. It was a Refiner. He could hardly drag himself upright as water and sweat drenched him. He pulled his leg awkwardly, and Caden realized his foot was bent unnaturally. *Why are you still alive?* Caden lifted his chin as the man gasped and struggled through overwhelming pain. The man turned, and their eyes met.

Fury rushed through Caden's veins, flushing his body with heat. His eyes flashed with vengeance as a muscle in his jaw flexed. Wounded and struggling to survive, Nathaniel stared up at him. His face had turned a shade paler. Without a word, Caden marched forward and summoned the Morning Star. Nathaniel raised a hand and dipped his head, knowing a fight was futile.

"Murderer!" Caden hissed. "Your blood will join the others!" He heard others shouting but didn't know what they said. It didn't matter. His brother and sister's slayer was ready for justice. It would be Caden's honor to help Yeshua and —

A firm hand grabbed Caden's arm and yanked him back. He stumbled with a curse and spun, ripping his arm free. He turned, coming face to face with Elijah. "He is not yours to kill."

"He has to die!"

"If King Yeshua wills it."

"He does! Do you know who this man is? Do you know what he has done!" Everyone was staring at them.

Nathaniel shivered in pain and cold as blood oozed from his wounded leg. "Mercy," Nathaniel whispered. "I was wrong."

"We begged for mercy!" Caden cried, wheeling around. "But you still executed Trace! And Ellie!"

"Cade!" Ellie called, stepping closer. "This is vengeance! Not God's justice!" Caden didn't answer as he felt the familiar grip of the Morning Star. Just one swing. That's all it would take. He knew how to crack skulls; Luca had given him practice.

A glowing knight stepped between him and Nathaniel and lay a gentle hand on his chest. "Sammy," Dasha whispered. "Ask our King."

"I don't need to ask Him."

"Stop being stupid and ask." Caden blinked through the haze of bloodlust and glanced at Dasha. Her left brow arched sharply as she lifted her chin and planted her feet, making it clear she wasn't moving.

With a hissed curse, Caden turned and glanced at King Yeshua. The scarred, mighty Warrior quietly watched behind them. "My King," Caden called, coming closer. "When can I kill him? You know who he…of course You know, um…This is justice, my King."

Yeshua nodded calmly as He turned from Nathaniel to Caden. **"Yes,"** He said softly. **"To kill Nathaniel would bring justice."** Caden nodded and opened his mouth to speak. **"But where is the mercy?"**

Caden's mouth snapped shut as he stared up into Yeshua's flaming eyes. "But —"

**"Even now, if anyone returns to me with all their heart, I will answer. I am gracious, Caden."** Caden's fury mounted and tightened his chest. He held his tongue, knowing if he spoke his mind, he'd blaspheme his God. **"I am compassionate and slow to anger. I love Nathaniel, just as much as I love you."**[1] Caden's eyes flashed, and he had to turn away. **"He has rend his heart in anguish for his wrongs. He begs for My mercy."**

"But," Caden stammered. "But! He doesn't deserve it!"

King Yeshua's head tilted to one side as blazing eyes studied Caden. **"Do you?"** Caden struggled to speak, but sealed his mouth shut. His fury roared inside, and his fists clenched, longing to break Nathaniel down with his mace. *"Forgive, Caden."* Caden's eyes closed as he dipped his head, hearing Yeshua's voice echoing within his heart. *"Forgive, just as I have forgiven you."*

Caden turned and stared at Nathaniel. The one who haunted Caden for so long hunched in the mud, white as a ghost and covered in his own blood. Helpless. Terrified. Defeated. *I can't do this.*

*"I forgive you fully,"* King Yeshua said within Caden's mind. *"The record is cleared. I remember it no more."* Caden closed his eyes as a muscle in his jaw flexed. *"And I choose to welcome you into My kingdom."*

The hilltop stood quietly as everyone waited for Caden to decide. Opening his eyes, Caden faced Yeshua once more. The One named Faithful and True nodded once, and Caden set his face to stone before marching to Nathaniel again. The Refiner ducked low and raised a hand, muttering something between gasps of pain. As Caden reached him, he released the mace and grabbed Nathaniel under his arms. Thanks to his Spiritual armor, Nathaniel weighed nothing at all, and Caden steadied him, wrapping an arm across his shoulder.

"What-" Nathaniel wheezed, pain twisting his face. Caden glanced down and saw his leg was a mess of shredded flesh as bone poked from the skin. "What are you doing?"

Caden drew Nathaniel closer and set his gaze on Yeshua. The Savior quietly watched, a soft smile on His face. "Obeying my King," Caden said. "Can you walk?" Nathaniel shook his head. Caden grunted and nodded to Dasha. She rushed forward and took Nathaniel's other arm, laying it across her shoulders. They started limping closer to Yeshua.

"I," Nathaniel gasped, "I shouldn't be here."

Yohanan snorted. "Nobody should."

Caden kept looking at Yeshua. *"He will never walk again,"* Yeshua said in his mind.

*You won't heal him like Asher?*

*"His chronic pain will constantly remind him that he should've chosen Me sooner."*

Caden nodded as they stopped before their King. Nathaniel slid to the ground and buried his face in the mud. He praised Yeshua and begged for his life in indistinguishable words. King Yeshua quietly reached down and lay a nail-scarred hand on his head. Instantly, Nathaniel started trembling and sobbing.

Yeshua straightened, grinning ear to ear. He squared his shoulders and looked out across the valley once more. All eyes were on King Yeshua as He stood at the pinnacle of Mount Megiddo. The singing slowly died down as everyone, mortals, resurrected, Spirits, even nature itself held its breath to cling to Yeshua's every word. **"Come,"** He said, His voice calm yet blasting from His lips like the blare of a trumpet. **"Let us claim our inheritance."**

He motioned behind Him, and massive Narrow Gates swung wide like double doors. Beyond, Caden could see it led to the Old City of Jerusalem. A tall building lay before them, its golden pillars catching the Heavenly Host's light. It was the Final Temple. Heart quickening and grinning, Caden obeyed as all of Yahweh's armies drew together and followed King Yeshua through the Narrow Gate.

# TWENTY-SIX

# RAW PEACE

IT WAS JUST like stepping through a door. Caden thought the Narrow Gate would feel differently somehow, maybe a strange pulling as he shot miles and miles away. He stared all around as he walked through, feeling like he stepped from an elevator onto another floor of reality.

Blinking, he identified the Temple Mount, yet it was very different. The Dome of the Rock was gone. The walls that segregated between religions were also gone. The Final Temple was surrounded by a vast courtyard in preparation for the victorious army. A dusk-like light covered the land, but it grew brighter the more Heavenly Hosts walked through. The Temple shone with brilliance, and the blood spilled on its steps mere days before was washed away. It was pure and how Yeshua first intended it.

"Beautiful!" Someone whispered beside him. Caden turned and found Dasha grinning ear to ear. Tears were in her eyes.

*We made it,* Caden thought as he smiled too, emotion tightening his chest.

The two followed King Yeshua to the Temple's steps,

which He ascended, and they stayed below, waiting. Behind them, the sound of millions drew together. Caden glanced back, doubting the space could contain even a fraction of them. He laughed, seeing the Heavenly Hosts had risen into the air and watched from above as all the mortals gathered below. There were still a lot of mortals. They stuffed the courtyard, their armor glowing and making them look like a wildfire. Everyone was covered in blood. The ground quickly turned red with millions of bloody footprints. Each horse was soaked. Everyone wiped it from their helmets and weapons. Yeshua was covered most of all.

*He is our mighty warrior,* Caden thought, turning back to Yeshua. The King stood straight and proud, His hands casually behind His back as He waited for everyone to join. Standing on either side of Him were Cherubim; one was Han. The Angel met eyes with Caden and smiled, his countless eyes glowing with excitement. Caden dipped his head in thanks, knowing he'd be dead long ago if not for Han.

A moaning roar made Caden's hair stand on end, and he whipped around, summoning his Morning Star. From the Narrow Gate came a limp, red mass. It twitched now and then and cried out as Cherubim dragged it through the crowd as the mortals scattered, their voices murmuring louder and louder. Caden set his jaw as his eyes narrowed; it was Tarek. Its pieces, at least.

The Demon Prince's severed heads had to be carried as its broken, twisted body dragged behind its enemies. Each black eye was wide with horror. The tongues flicked restlessly as the clawed hands weakly scraped at the ground. Its tail flopped, trying to sweep under the mortal's legs, but they kicked it away easily. A few of the attached heads' mouths were sealed shut by Cherub's hands, and it weakly tried to wiggle them off. Water dripped from the sealed mouths, and Caden knew it wanted to drown them all. He heard Tarek screaming from inside his soul. Its multi-voices threatened and begged and shrieked, yet it was quiet compared to the song Caden still sang in his heart. They all still sang their battle cry, and many were humming in time together. Tarek's words meant nothing compared to the truth of their victory.

Of *Yeshua's* victory. Caden shook his head, unable to believe Tarek had been such a threat at one time. How could such a terrifying foe become lumps of severed flesh and weak threats? He noticed Yohanan and Elijah staring at it, their chests puffed and eyes flashing. Tarek couldn't meet their gaze, each of the seven heads turning away from their thriving enemies. Caden's smile grew wider as God's fierce justice quickened his heart.

As Caden glanced at Elijah, he noticed a glowing woman standing beside him. She, too, was covered in Spiritual armor, and a bow and quiver of arrows slung over a shoulder. His eyes narrowed as he stepped closer. "Ophir?"

The woman turned and beamed. "Caden! There you are!" Caden laughed as Ophir drew closer and wrapped her arms around him. "You survived?"

"Barely. I'm starting to think I got the shorter end of the bargain."

Ophir laughed as she glanced down at her radiant, glorified body. "No, you receive whatever King Yeshua thinks is right. We need the next generation to reign in the Millennial Kingdom, so some of us must stay in physical bodies. We need you." Ophir nodded to Dasha. "You both."

*That's right,* Caden thought, lifting his chin, remembering Gideon. He smiled, longing for his grandson tightening his chest.

Dasha huffed a quick laugh and nudged Caden, but he

noticed she didn't object. "I'm looking forward to seeing that *thing* dealt with," she said, nodding to the red dragon.

All three turned and watched as Tarek was dragged before King Yeshua. A handful of Leovirs who had chosen to stand with the true King yanked it along. Leading them was a lion whose fur seemed tipped in gold that faintly shone. He turned, clipped ear swiveling. Caden sucked in a breath and waved. "Benaiah!" The Leovir pivoted and stared, his great, maned head dipping. He nudged a Leovirness beside him, and Jael turned, her fur also alight with glory. An onlooker glanced between them and spun, seeing Caden. He straightened with a wave and grinned. Caden smiled back, recognizing Chuk.

Ophir grinned, and Caden and Dasha waved. "I love when the Enemy's creations choose Yahweh." Elijah nodded as the four watched Jael and Benaiah throw Tarek down before King Yeshua. The red dragon lay there, helpless, whining, each eye bulging from its heads in petrified agony.

King Yeshua stared down at Tarek and turned away as though it wasn't worth His time. He lifted His chin and faced His people. Caden's heart quickened as he stepped closer with Dasha, and the mass of victors quieted. **"Well done,"** Yeshua said. His voice boomed across them, moving the air with each word with gentle gusts. Caden felt Yeshua's voice inside his inner being, filling his body and captivating his heart. **"I personally selected you for this time of wrath and judgment. You have survived Our fires and are more than conquerors."**

Caden's chest swelled with pride as he lifted his chin. **"It is time to release One member of the Godhead across the earth once more."** Caden's eyes widened, an excited thrill washing over him. **"For He will send this beast where it belongs."** Tarek's eyes rolled back in its head as several heads moaned in agony. No one listened as every mortal drew closer together, holding their breath as they watched and waited.

"Who's He talking about?" Dasha hissed. Caden shook his head. King Yeshua smiled across His army and looked up to the still-covered sun. Instantly, the sun returned. Its brilliance was so weak and soft compared to the flashing *Akal Esh* all around them.

Caden's eyes narrowed as he realized it had hardly moved across the sky. *How long did that battle take?* It couldn't have been more than an hour.

His thoughts silenced instantly, for something was moving above the Heavenly Hosts. Each flying, fiery warrior bowed their head and cheered, their horses' white-hot hooves stomping and heads bucking with excitement. Then the sky broke.

The clouds above the Final Temple blasted away, as though fleeing across the sky, as a column of fire rocketed to the ground. It landed beside King Yeshua, the ground shaking around it as a shockwave washed over the masses. Caden gasped in the sudden blast; it was filled with heat and power! Dasha grabbed his hand and stepped back, her eyes wide as she too stared breathlessly. King Yeshua didn't move as the flames leapt beside Him.

Caden swallowed the hard lump in his throat, and he stared at the wild blaze without blinking. His eyes filled with tears; he couldn't help it. He was so insignificant, so pathetic before the fire. Unworthy. Why would the fire let him live? He was nothing before its might! Nothing but failure and—

Caden blinked. He'd thought the same thing when the *Akal Esh* fell into Elijah and Yohanan. Inhaling sharply, Caden lifted his chin and fought his urge to fall on his face and beg for mercy. *If Yeshua wanted me dead, I'd already be dead. The Akal Esh doesn't mess around! Oh, it is beautiful!*

As he stared in awe, the flames became longer until

they were as tall as Yeshua. The fire moved differently, too, and was spaced out oddly. The fire was rounded on top but had strange curves and edges. The *Akal Esh* didn't look like fire so much anymore. It looked more like the outline of a man.

Caden's heart leapt into his throat, and a rush of excitement tightened his chest. The fire wasn't in a man's shape, it *was* a Man. The *Akal Esh* stood just as firm and calm as Yeshua, ignited arms held behind His back and flaming feet planted. Caden could make out His eyes, like flashing braziers, as His entire being flickered with orange and white-hot tongues. *Who is that?* Caden's mind shouted.

As the shockwave reached the back of the assembly, everyone fell on to their knees. No one spoke as they knelt, feeling the weight of power and raging beauty of Yahweh's *Akal Esh, thank You for not killing me,* Caden's mind screamed. *I am not worthy even to see You! Please, have mercy on me!* He was shaking. He couldn't help it. Even if he had the strength to stand and hide, he knew he couldn't get away. The *Akal Esh* would find him.

He heard Dasha struggling to breathe beside him as everyone felt the weight of glory. Yet, no one shrunk back as far as Tarek. The red dragon's heads screamed and fought to rise. The broken wings flapped uselessly as weak claws scraped the ground. Water pooled around it, but the dribble was ridiculous before the *Akal Esh's* blaze.

**"Beast,"** King Yeshua said, His voice reverberating through every kneeling mortal. **"You have been vanquished and now will receive your punishment."**

*Oh, God!* Sweat gathered at Caden's brow as his hair stood on end.

"No!" Tarek's multi-voice screamed. "Please, I—"

**"Join the Antichrist and the False Prophet."**

"Banish me somewhere else, Master!"

**"There, you will writhe in agony for a thousand years."**

*What?* Caden's mind yelled. *Just a thousand years? What happens when it gets out?*

Tarek's heads shrieked, the shrilled cry curdling Caden's blood. King Yeshua stepped back and nodded to the *Akal Esh*. The flaming Man stepped forward, and a glowing hand made a fist. *What's It summoning?* Caden thought, suddenly terrified to find out.

Links of a white-hot chain appeared, each link materializing one after the other and encircling Tarek. The red dragon thrashed as the chains appeared around its body, cinching its limbs close together and wings down. The several heads whipped back and forth until chains materialized around them, too, choking the screams and holding them back. The *Akal Esh* held the end of the chain like the leash of a dog. Something else was in His other hand too. It was a ring that held a long metal key.

A panic crept over Caden as he stared at the key; his deep, inner self knew what that key unlocked. He had seen that specific door before, the screams of Luca and Hugh's petrified souls still chilled his blood. *Please don't summon that Gate,* Caden thought, longing to crawl back, but unable to move. *Please.*

The *Akal Esh* turned and inserted the key into an invisible door beside Him. Turning the key, the Gate unlatched, and overwhelming heat instantly swept across the massive army. Caden cursed under his breath and ducked his head, terror of God's wrath striking his chest and tightening his throat. The Gate swung wide, and the heat of Hell poured out with a vengeance. Sweat dripped from Caden's nose, and he summoned his shield, panting as he watched the large Gate swing wide.

Again, the Gate was a wide, black mouth, longing to swallow everything alive and consume them. Again, any organic life around the Gate ignited. Fire caught the ground. The Final Temple lit. He felt the sky itself was melting. Caden moaned painfully, the heat overwhelming him, and he knew without a doubt the only thing keeping him from combusting was his Spiritual armor.

Tarek had no Spiritual armor. The dragon screeched in agony. Its flesh sizzled and peeled back yet didn't flake away. Its eyes rolled back in its head as it tried to beg but could only cry in misery. Without any reserve, the *Akal Esh* stepped back, flames lashing, and pulled. He calmly walked straight through the Gate, into Hell. Tarek dragged behind Him, its screams mounting to hysteria. Its body coiled and twisted, red scales burning, yet not disintegrating.

The *Akal Esh* steadily dragged the beast into Hell. Tarek's screams muffled the more it was dragged in. One head managed to twist back and wrap around the Gate's frame. Its two horns hooked around the edge as it screamed. With a lurch, the horns gave a sickening crack and fell to the ground. The head yanked through the Gate, its scream muffled. Just as calmly as He had entered the Gate of Hell, the *Akal Esh* strolled out without looking back. The Narrow Gate swung closed, sealing off the heat and beast together.

The Heavenly Hosts let out a cry, their voices like thunder that never stopped rolling. Their horses stomped white-hot hooves as each drew their weapons, waving them in the air. The mortals let out a shout, too, as their Spiritual enemy was locked away. The fire that consumed the Final Temple, the ground, and any natural life ebbed away. Instead of destroying all things, the fire had purified it. The Final Temple's gold shone brighter. Caden exhaled loudly as the heat that threatened his very life and soul ebbed away. Sort of. The *Akal Esh* was still there.

Caden stared at the flaming Man, and his stomach

twisted. *Why do You feel kind of like Hell? Are You...are You Hell's fire?* The *Akal Esh* turned His head, and those flashing eyes of raging light locked onto Caden. Caden's mouth was dry as a wave of adrenaline shot through him. He was paralyzed as his heart tried to beat from his body.

King Yeshua lifted His scarred hands and turned to His army, smiling. **"May you receive our free gift and be filled."**

Caden's eyes narrowed as sweat dripped from his face. *What is He—?*

The sky broke. Not just once. Thousands of times.

Caden gasped, energy blasted as fire fell directly above every single mortal. He looked up in time to see flashing and roaring light collide with him. He flinched back, crying out, and fell quiet, realizing someone was standing before him. A Man on fire. Caden panted and curled into a ball, tears filling his eyes. He whispered pleas and waited.

Through his panic, he realized the entire courtyard of mortals, Heavenly Hosts, and Yeshua were silent. He glanced around and noticed everyone else was frozen. No one moved as they all stared up, fire falling onto them too. They weren't even breathing. "What?"

**"We are in your conscious thought, Caden,"** the *Akal Esh* said. His voice was a whisper, soft and calm. It didn't blast from His lips like Han or Yeshua, but rather a still, small voice. **"I wanted to take a moment and speak with you. It will literally take a fraction of a second."**

Caden took in a slow breath as he raised his hands, unsure of what to do. "How, how can I serve You, Master?" The *Akal Esh* smiled and knelt to Caden's level, the fire quietly lashing across His body. He reached out a flickering hand, and Caden drew back but knew it was foolish to run.

**"You don't have to fear, Caden."** The flaming hand lay on his shoulder. Even through Caden's armor, he felt the heat. It was fierce and wild and powerful. And loved him. He didn't know how he knew, but it adored him. A gentle calm settled over Caden, and he slowly stopped shaking. The calm wrapped around him like a warm blanket, expelling all worry and dread. He lifted his chin, his tears spilling over, as he received the strength to face those flashing eyes.

The *Akal Esh's* smile grew. He suddenly didn't seem like an inferno of devastating power. He was something more, something Caden had seen before. *Who are You?* Caden thought, his eyes narrowing. The *Akal Esh's* sudden peace he recognized. He'd only seen bits and pieces, but now was the real thing. Peace unhindered. Peace without end. Peace in its purest form. *Raw Peace.* Caden's eyes widened as the Flaming One gently nodded.

"Hello, Caden."

Caden sucked in a breath as he moved closer. "Who... who are You?"

"I have many names. For a long time, the church called me the Holy Spirit or Holy Ghost. You've called Me Raw Peace, which has been one of My favorite nicknames. You may call me that or Akal Esh if you like."

"If I like? I...I am Your slave! What are You doing anyways? I am not worthy of Your attention!"

"But I like you. I want to ignite your Spirit with My Fire and be one flame together. I want to be a part of your life. I delight in who you are, Caden. You're very special to Us."

Caden laughed breathlessly as he drew closer to Akal Esh. "So, are You...what do you need from me?"

"Your permission." Caden blinked in surprise. "I don't blast My way into people's lives," Akal Esh said. "It may look like it, but I only fill those who want me to. So, Caden," Akal Esh leaned closer, and Caden could feel His fire warming his face. "Do you want me? I want to live in and through you and lead you into all truth. I'm here to help and support you. We can be a team. And friends. May you let me in, Caden?"

Caden's heartbeats were loud in his ears as he grabbed Akal Esh's hand, tears spilling from his eyes. "Yes!" he shouted. "Yes! Please! Do everything You want with me! I am Yours! I want you! I've been wanting You since I first felt You in America!"

Akal Esh chuckled softly. "Do you remember how terrified you were, seeing a Narrow Gate for the first time?" Caden laughed too and sniffed, wiping tears from his eyes. "You freaked out so much, you fell over and just stared." Akal Esh shook His head and stared into Caden's eyes. "Look at you now." Caden dipped his head. "Battling Demons with a Morning Star!" Caden grinned. "I'm proud of you." Caden choked, the peace deepening and making his head swim with joy. "And this is only the beginning." Caden looked up sharply, and Akal Esh laughed. "Don't look so surprised!"

"What are You talking about? Aren't we headed to Heaven?"

"Not yet."

"What!"

"Relax," Akal Esh said, waving a hand. "We'll get there."

"But, but why aren't we going to Heaven *now*?"

"You will, I promise. We're not done with mankind though. The story isn't over." Caden didn't answer as his brows furrowed. Akal Esh chuckled and clapped him on the back with a whoosh of flames. "For now, we celebrate. We won!"

Caden smiled fiercely. "We won."

The Akal Esh dipped His head, His flames flashing brighter. Without another word, He leaned forward. Caden drew back, bracing himself for searing fire. He only felt Peace. Raw Peace. He closed his eyes and relaxed, feeling Akal Esh fill his entire being. The fire warmed him as the heat burned off anything not from God. Caden doubted his mortal flesh could contain such might, but it could. He instantly knew Akal Esh somehow censored His flames, making it compatible with his weak, mortal body. He didn't minimize Himself, yet there was a protective barrier, keeping Caden alive.

He gasped, realizing he wasn't breathing, and felt the fire's flickering within his chest. The tears kept falling. He had sought after Raw Peace this entire time. Now, it wasn't just around him, but lived *inside* him. He carried the literal Spirit of God inside his mortal body. Caden smiled as joy burst from his chest. He stared ahead, seeing Akal Esh still standing beside King Yeshua. *And You're inside me at the same time?*

*"And in everyone else too."*

Caden glanced around as though remembering he was surrounded by fellow believers. They were no longer frozen as every mortal knelt, and the Heavenly Hosts sat on their horses, filling the sky with their brilliance. Everyone basked in the Raw Peace's gentle embrace as King Yeshua contentedly stood watching.

Benaiah, Jael, and other Leovirs who chose King Yeshua roared their praise. Asher knelt beside Caden, head dipped and eyes closed in reverence. Noam and Auset knelt close together, a luminescent little girl grinning on Auset's lap. Yohanan and Ellie sat side by side, one arm raised in worship as the other wrapped around each other. Elijah and Ophir quietly knelt, their heads dipped low and gently touching as their hands clasped.

Caden laughed under his breath, joy mounting in his heart, as he returned his focus on the two Members of the Godhead. He raised his hands in praise but stopped. Someone was holding his hand. He looked down, realizing

Dasha still held him. They turned to one another, and he could see tears glistening in her eyes too. She smiled and moved closer, her hold of his hand tightening.

*We made it,* Caden thought, stunned at all God let him survive. He felt Akal Esh glowing brighter inside him with joy. He sat in awe, his Heavenly family surrounding him and his future wife drawing close. He could do nothing but bask in the glory of King Yeshua and Akal Esh. They had taken a fearful, pathetic human boy and made him a Demon-conquering, mace-wielding warrior for Yahweh. The homesickness that haunted him was gone. He was safe and where he belonged.

*"Welcome home, Caden."*

He laughed and dipped his head, overwhelming gratitude filling him. Caden couldn't stop smiling as he knelt before his King. The *true* King of Kings and Lord of Lords. The One who was, and is, and Who had come. May King Yeshua receive all glory and honor and power and praise forever and ever. Amen!

# SPIRITUAL ARSENAL: BIBLICAL REFERENCES DECLARED DURING THE BATTLE OF ARMAGEDDON

## 23. SING PRAISES TO YAHWEH

1. Revelation 2:26-27

    To the one who is victorious and does my will to the end, I will give authority over the nations—that one "will rule them with an iron scepter and will dash them to pieces like pottery"—just as I have received authority from my Father.

2. Psalm 2:7

    I will proclaim the Lord's decree: He said to me, 'You are my son; today I have become your father.

3. Psalm 2:8

    Ask me, and I will make the nations your inheritance, the ends of the earth your possession.

4. Psalm 46:8, 10-11

    Come and see what the Lord has done, the desolations he has brought on the earth. He says, 'Be still, and know that I am God; I will be exalted among the nations. I will be exalted in the earth.' The Lord Almighty is with us; the God of Jacob is our fortress.

5. Psalm 149:6-7

    May the praise of God be in their mouths and a double-edged sword in their hands, to inflict vengeance on the nations and punishment on the peoples.

6. Revelations 2:27-28

    That one "will rule them with an iron scepter and will dash them to pieces like pottery"—just as I have received authority from my Father. I will also give that one the morning star.

## 24. JUSTICE

1. Joel 3:11b-12.

    Bring down your warriors, Lord! 'Let the nations be roused; let them advance into the Valley of Jehoshaphat, for there I will sit to judge all the nations on every side.

## 25. HELLFIRE

1.  Joel 2:12-13

'Even now,' declares the Lord, 'return to me with all your heart, with fasting and weeping and mourning.' Rend your heart and not your garments. Return to the Lord your God, for he is gracious and compassionate, slow to anger and abounding in love, and he relents from sending calamity.

# IF YOU LIKE THIS, YOU MAY ALSO ENJOY:
## REVELATIONS
### BY TERRY JAMES

Tyce Greyson, a TV journalist and reporter, visits the Wailing
Wall at the Temple Mount in Jerusalem. He is confronted by a
Jewish cleric while he is photographing the area for a story he
will be doing for a magazine. The Rabbi says to him: "Israel is
the sign of the end." A blind writer in the genre of Bible prophecy
is later interviewed for a book in his study by Greyson, who is a
television reporter for a nearby TV station. The writer tells the
story of the interview and the young reporter informs him that
he is now interested in Bible prophecy. Greyson tells the writer
he intends to go to Patmos in the Aegean to visit the cave of the
Apocalypse where John was given the Revelation. Greyson is
given a new job as an anchor for a local station in New York
City. While doing broadcasts, Greyson has episodes, that bring
on visions. While on air, he makes predictions that come true. He
becomes well-known as excerpts of his "prophecies" go
viral. Greyson must fulfill the destiny appointed to him as one
who is of Jewish parents. The blind writer wraps up the story in
a twist that confirms it is all part of human history's
consummation. It is a story that both he and Tyce Greyson know
must be told.

*AVAILABLE NOW*

# ABOUT TERRY JAMES

**Terry James** is an author, general editor, and co-author of more than 40 books on Bible prophecy and geopolitics — hundreds of thousands of which have been sold worldwide. He has also written fiction and nonfiction books on a number of other topics. His most recent releases are *The Disappearing: Future Events That Will Rock the World* and *Lawless: End Times War Against the Spirit of Antichrist,* a compilation by top authors, speakers, and broadcasters on issues facing this generation. His most recently released novel, *Michael: Last Days Lightning,* achieved number one in Christian fiction on Amazon.

Terry is a frequent lecturer on the study of end-time phenomena and interviews often with national and international media on topics involving world issues and events as they might relate to Bible prophecy. He is partner with website founder Todd Strandberg and general editor of www.raptureready.com — rated the number one Bible prophecy website with more than 250,000 unique visitors and 3 million hits per month.

Terry speaks often at prophecy conferences and has appeared on national secular programs such as *The Nostradamus Effect*. He is a member of the Pre-Trib Research Center, founded by Dr. Tim LaHaye. Currently, he lives with his wife Margaret near Little Rock, Arkansas.

# ABOUT HEATHER RENAE

**Heather Renae's** ministry is writing sci-fi and fantasy for Jesus. She's inspired by her walk with the Master and her mountainous home in Eastern Oregon. When she's not writing, she's hiking, enjoying friends and family, and chasing after her two kiddos—lovingly nicknamed her scallywags. To see what she's up to, follow her on Facebook at Heather Renae.

www.ingramcontent.com/pod-product-compliance
Lightning Source LLC
Chambersburg PA
CBHW011344010726
47493CB00011B/2943